Winston Chu

vs. the Whimsies

Winston Chu
vs. the Whimsies

by STACEY LEE

RICK RIORDAN PRESENTS

Disney • HYPERION   LOS ANGELES   NEW YORK

First Edition, February 2023
1 3 5 7 9 10 8 6 4 2
FAC-004510-22357
Printed in the United States of America

This book is set in Minion Pro, Cherily Blussom, CCScoundrel/Fontspring;
Aeonis Pro/Monotype
Illustrations by Amber Ren
Designed by Tyler Nevins

Library of Congress Cataloging-in-Publication Data
Names: Lee, Stacey (Stacey Heather), author.
Title: Winston Chu vs. the whimsies / by Stacey Lee.
Description: First edition. • Los Angeles ; New York : Disney-Hyperion,
2023. • Audience: Ages 8-12. • Audience: Grades 4-6. • Summary: Winston
Chu saves the owner of a curiosities shop from a robbery only to be
gifted a broomstick and a dustpan for his trouble—items that turn out
to be more a curse than a blessing when they sweep away important stuff,
like his baby sister.
Identifiers: LCCN 2022010392 • ISBN 9781368074803 (hardcover) •
ISBN 9781368075060 (trade paperback) • ISBN 9781368074919 (ebk)
Subjects: CYAC: Folklore—China—Fiction. • Magic—Fiction. •
Changelings—Fiction. • Families—Fiction. • San Francisco
(Calif.)—Fiction. • LCGFT: Fiction. • Novels.
Classification: LCC PZ7.1.L43 Wi 2023 • DDC [Fic]—dc23
LC record available at https://lccn.loc.gov/2022010392

Reinforced binding
Follow @ReadRiordan
Visit www.DisneyBooks.com

For Bennett and Avalon.
This book is not about you. (Mostly.)

SO UNFAIR

Life is full of unfairness.

For instance, Winston Chu lost his father to a friendly fire accident in Iraq. Now it's just Winston, his mom, and his two sisters, muddling through life as best they can in their tiny San Francisco apartment. Winston's mom is barely holding it together. His big sister, Philippa, has turned grumpy and withdrawn. His little sister, Coco—well, Coco is awesome, but she's just a toddler. She doesn't even *remember* their dad, which makes Winston incredibly sad.

Also unfair? One day, Winston happens to save a local shopkeeper from getting robbed. Then, as his reward, he gets to choose the first thing he touches in the shop. That doesn't *sound* unfair. After all, Mr. Pang's Whimsies is full of expensive and possibly magical things like "Eggs of Truth," "Far-Seeing Eyeballs," and "Kick-Me Boots." But when Winston unintentionally touches something else instead, he goes home as the proud owner of a grungy old broom and a matching dustpan. Yippee.

It gets worse. The broom and the dustpan seem to hold some kind of curse. Important things start disappearing from Winston's home. Then *people* start disappearing. And Mr. Pang's shop itself vanishes, along with its owner, who may or may not have been dead for fifty years. . . .

Soon, Winston and his friends are plunged into an impossible adventure to figure out the truth about Mr. Pang and his whimsies, and hopefully undo the bad luck that has made Winston's life a flying pizza of disaster.

But the thing I find most unfair of all: Why is Stacey Lee such a good writer? She's got sympathetic, believable characters that instantly feel like your new best friends. Page-turning action and intrigue. Quirky, witty writing that will make you laugh out loud. How does she do all that and make it look so easy? I mean, *come on.* Stop being such a talented storyteller, Lee. You're making the rest of us look bad!

I'm kidding (mostly). But I will confess that as I read *Winston Chu*, I went from thinking *I wonder if I'll be able to offer any helpful advice to Stacey* to *I'm going to start taking notes because Stacey is totally schooling me on great storytelling.*

I love Winston's big heart, his courage, and his loyalty to his friends and family. I love his impulsive, awkward stumbling through middle school. I love Mr. Pang's whimsies and all the beautiful chaos they create in Winston's life. Most of all, I love the way Lee weaves together Chinese folklore and modern San Francisco into a magical book so clever and fun it just demands to be read aloud with the whole family or the whole classroom.

Like I said: Totally unfair. Lee is so good that her book feels like Mr. Pang's shop—chock-full of hidden treasures in every nook and cranny, ripe for exploration, endlessly surprising and rewarding. I am *so* glad Stacey Lee is unfairly talented because it will make many happy readers! Just be careful what you bump into as you explore this shop of whimsies. If you end up going home with a bad-natured broom and dustpan . . . Well, you'll find out soon enough.

Rick Riordan

CHAPTER 1

Dad used to say that qi, like the Force, ran strong in our family. That if we nurtured this life energy, we could heal a broken bone, even change the flow of water. Bet he never thought I would use the Chu family qi to bake the most gooey-licious shoofly pie on the planet.

Balancing on my skateboard, I slid back and forth past the windows of the San Francisco Cooking Academy. On the pastry box containing my still-warm pie, Mav had added IS A WIENER after my name, WINSTON CHU. He was getting back at me for writing IS A MEATHEAD on his box, after MAVERICK MCFEE.

Mav finished tying his shoelace. A bit of flour dusted his thick brown hair, which had a natural wave that looked styled without his having to do anything to it. He scooped up his pie from the sidewalk and got to his feet. Nearby, an elderly woman waiting for the bus shook her fist at a too-fast truck sweeping down the busy boulevard.

"Excuse me, ma'am." Mav held out his box to the senior, one foot on his own skateboard. "Would you like a pie?"

The woman's deeply lined face lost its scowl. "Why, thank you, son."

Good ole Mav. Even if his dad wasn't a millionaire, Mav was the kind of guy who'd swap his designer headphones for your brownie and call it even.

The door to the San Francisco Cooking Academy swung open, blasting us with warm air. Out marched our baking instructor Chef Kim, her lime-colored clogs bearing her toward us like pet crocodiles. For someone who made dessert for a living, you'd think she'd look happier, not like a stocky tyrant with Caesar-short black hair who could rip the wheels off my Volt 500 skateboard with her teeth.

Her niece Dani followed her, a cello slung on her back. In class, I had admired how Dani's sleek black hair draped down one side of her face and the careful way she had dried her mint leaves, as if they actually had feelings. But the only words I'd spoken to her were *Is this your butter?*

Chef Kim glanced up at me and Mav, both of us towering over her barely five-foot frame by a head—Mav because of his grandmother's Senegalese roots, and me because of my skate-board. After four weeks of putting up with us, she was probably celebrating the fact that she would never have to see us again. She frowned at my wheels. "Hold on tight to that box, Mr. Chu. It is bad luck to drop a pie."

"Er, right. Thanks, Chef Kim." She had no need to

worry about me skating home with it—I was an ace boarder. And I needed this pie to commemorate the anniversary of Dad's death—three years tonight. Pie was Dad's favorite dessert.

Chef Kim grunted and continued marching down the sidewalk toward the intersection. Dani glanced at me, but her eyes lingered on Mav. Whatever. Girls were always noticing him with his puppy-dog looks—and the good hair, of course. Girls were not into floppy-haired weaklings who wore size-ten pants even though they were almost thirteen years old.

Dani hurried after her aunt, who was already halfway across the street. I checked to see if Mav was watching Dani. No, he was busy zipping up his hoodie with its embroidered logo of his exclusive school, the Towne School for Boys, where he took classes like Intuitive Trigonometry and prepared for a career in the United Nations.

He jerked his chin at my box. "Sure you want to skate holding that?"

"Why not?" The bottom of the box was already starting to feel sticky, but I wasn't going to abandon it. Unlike his mega rich family with its real-estate-tycoon dad, mine watched our pennies, especially now that Mom had been out of work for two months. Besides, I had a lot riding on this pie. Sometimes it felt like Philippa and Mom avoided talking about Dad, and I needed them to remember. Coco hadn't been born yet when he went on duty, so she was excused.

Mav strapped on his helmet. We always skated with helmets. Not only was it the law, we didn't want to be hit by the hissing squirrels that had been dropping out of trees for the past few months, the latest sign that Mother Nature wasn't happy with us. He shot me with a finger gun. "Boba or bust."

With a primordial grunt, I pushed off away from Dani and toward Chinatown, my Hulkbuster key chain swinging from my belt loop and my big toe poking out of the hole in my sneaker. Mav's skateboard grinded the cement behind me. I stayed in front, just far enough that I wouldn't have to talk to him. I was being petty, but why did everything always come so easily to him? He'd come out of the oven grade A—smart, chill, and ready for any ball life threw him, which is why he was our soccer team's best goalie. Well, I skated better than him, even on my secondhand board while holding a shoofly pie.

The summer-afternoon sun was only for show. Anyone who's been to the foggy city in the summer knows to bundle up. I was wearing two T-shirts under an army sweatshirt.

The streets grew more colorful as we drew closer to my neighborhood, which had seen five generations of Chus. A rainbow of awnings overhung storefronts. Strings of red lanterns were draped across the streets. People darted in and out of shops, plastic bags ringing their wrists.

Mav finally caught up with me on the descent. "Hey, Win, why didn't the toilet paper roll cross the road?"

I sighed. Of course he had no clue I'd been throwing myself a pity party. "Dunno. Why?"

I slowed to avoid crates of lychees, mangoes, and oranges by the curb. Mah-mah, my paternal grandmother, had said we should buy oranges to commemorate the third Dad-iversary, but Mom thought all those rituals to honor the ancestors were nonsense. Still, I thought we should do *something* instead of just sitting around feeling sad, like usual.

"It got stuck in a crack."

I groaned, shaking my head.

The familiar purple awning of Boba Guys with its aard-vark logo appeared a hundred feet ahead. Our teammates and best buds, Bijal and Cassa, were already standing in a long line of mostly teenage customers that snaked out onto the side-walk. Cassa was trying to whip Bijal with her grubby blond braid probably in response to one of his wisecracks—while he defended himself by twisting from side to side. Those two had been bickering ever since we met in soccer class when we were all four.

Two men in bright Hawaiian shirts and sunglasses were peering into the round front window of a brick store next to Boba Guys. Both were linebacker big, but one was shorter, put-ting me in mind of Bert and Ernie from *Sesame Street*. Their noses were covered in zinc sunscreen. They looked out of place—two coconuts on a field of soccer balls.

The next few moments happened in slow motion.

Something solid and wiggly plopped on my helmet, then slid off. The pie box flew out of my hands like a pink meteor. The Volt 500 skidded out from under me, giving me a flash of the ACTIVATE WONDER sticker on the underside.

As a solid, wiggly thing—a cat-size squirrel—scrabbled off with a hiss, my pie box arced toward Bert and Ernie. Bert's long face, directly in the line of fire, stretched even longer. The yellow flamingoes on his Hawaiian shirt pulled in one direc-tion, then the other. Ernie dabbed. Well, he wasn't trying to dab, just trying to dodge the pie that was hurtling toward his friend. The box dropped away from the pie like boosters from the space shuttle. Then *bam!* The impact was gooey. Crumby. Crusty. Buttery.

Many things spun through my head as my body succumbed to gravity.

What made you think you could skate with a pie?

Dingus.

Thank goodness I was wearing my helmet.

This is going to hurt.

Not my pie!

I'd fallen lots of times, but never quite so . . . spectacularly. I braced myself. I didn't witness the pie's impact. I was too busy trying not to break any bones.

So long, goodbye, shoofly pie.

"That bites," I heard one of the teens say from his place in line.

When I looked up, Bert was scraping whipped cream out of his eyes. Bits of molasses stuck to the sparse black hair on top of his head while chunks of crust dropped off his cheek. Ernie rubbed his head, probably relieved he wasn't the victim.

With his vision finally cleared of crumbs, Bert looked like he wanted to grab me off the pavement by my elastic waistband and spin me around like a pinwheel.

I held up my dirty palms, trying to ignore the hoots of the Boba Guys crowd. "Sorry, sir. I—"

Ernie tugged on Bert's sleeve, jerked his stubbly chin down the street, and ran in that direction. Bert bared his teeth at me. But then he shook himself like a wet dog and loped after his buddy.

That was weird. What was their hurry, not that I was complaining? I'd been sure Bert was going to clobber me with a sticky fist.

Then Chef Kim's words flashed in my mind. *It is bad luck to drop a pie.*

Right. Especially in a stranger's face. I hoped I'd never have to face that face again.

CHAPTER 2

Luck is serious business. Mom said she didn't believe in it, but if that were true, why did she serve fish, a symbol of abundance, on the Lunar New Year? She also never cuts noodles because that could cut short someone's life. I felt for Dad's dog tag underneath my shirts, hoping my good-luck charm would cancel out the bad.

Bijal and Cassa crowded around me as I lay on the sidewalk. Cassa pulled me up. The squirrel was gone. All that work on the pie. I kicked at the ground. Now I had nothing for Dad-iversary.

"What the Hello Kitty just happened?" Bijal waved his arms, and his purple windbreaker made swishing noises.

"A hissing squirrel fell on Winston, and then he pied someone." Cassa's voice was constantly husky from all the yelling she did on the field as our soccer team, the San Francisco Stealth's best striker. "Great shot, by the way." She slapped dirt off the sleeve of my sweatshirt. In addition to playing soccer, she also pitched for the school softball team, which meant a bruise was probably forming on my arm.

Mav, who had followed the men to the corner, returned shaking his head. "They got into a car and took off. Didn't even wait for an explanation."

Bijal and Cassa swept pie fragments back into the box with a discarded flyer. "Those two looked shady," said Bijal. "Why'd they run off so fast?"

I glanced at the shop's tinted black windows, the kind that said *none of your business*. A half-dome awning covered a circular door painted grasshopper green. On the door hung a sign with the words MR. PANG'S WHIMSIES in swirly gold letters. In all my years passing this corner, I'd never noticed this shop before.

A gong rang from somewhere close by, and the green door swung open. The most peculiar man I had ever seen emerged. Mr. Pang, maybe?

Most of his five-foot frame was wrapped in a floor-length Chinese jacket that looked spun out of gold. His tortoiseshell eyes drifted like a driver whose mind wasn't on the road. An orange Adidas headband pinned down the wispy threads of his salt-and-pepper hair. He walked right over to me. "Young man, thank you. You must have been sent by the gods." He tapped his fist against his chest and pointed to the sky, like pro soccer players did after scoring.

The gods of mischief maybe. "Thank you for . . . what?"

He snorted. "Those men have been casing my joint for years. This time they almost got in. If it weren't for your pie,

I'd have been at the wrong end of a stickup." Despite the gravity of his statement, Mr. Pang's voice was friendly and warm.

"You think they were *burglars*?" Criminals didn't usually disguise themselves as sunburned tourists. Then again, Bert did have a mean stare. Still, I wouldn't have looked very happy either after being hit in the face with a pie.

"The Peeps have been standing guard, but you know how flighty they can be," the shopkeeper said.

Bijal glanced around him. "Those Peeps?" He pointed at a bright yellow object in the corner of the doorway, where people usually mounted surveillance cameras. When I looked closer, I saw it was shaped like a chick. On the opposite corner, a marshmallow bunny the size of a pink eraser peered down at us. The guy was relying on Easter candy as a security system?

Cassa suppressed a giggle. Mav's eyes slid to me. *This guy is one sandwich short of a picnic*, his look said.

"I have many rare mementos in my shop," said Mr. Pang. "I'll let you choose one, Winston, for your help." He waggled his straggly eyebrows, and his headband shifted.

"H-how do you know my name?"

"It's on your box." We all looked at the nearest trash can, where Cassa had stuffed it.

"It was just an accident," I admitted, wondering if I'd still be qualified to look inside Mr. Pang's shop. Then again, maybe I didn't want to. A person who stationed marshmallow Peeps for surveillance was the type who might also collect scabs in yogurt tubs. I stared hard at the front window, but it seemed to blacken, reflecting my sweaty face and scraped nose.

"Alexander Fleming discovered penicillin by accident," said

Mr. Pang. "Does that mean we should take away his Nobel Prize?"

I scanned my friends' faces for assurance that I wasn't the only one seeing this. Cassa's eyes were wide and bright against her ruddy skin and matched the green rubber bands in her braces. Bijal was holding his elbows, his round face pinched. Mav wore his *figuring it out* expression—eyebrows crouched low, freckles twitching on his skin with its built-in tan.

"First, where are those wipes . . . ?" Mr. Pang rummaged through his silken pockets and pulled out gardening gloves. "Oh, I was looking for these." He stuffed them back in his pocket and drew out a flashlight, a jar of peanut butter, a new pack of shoelaces, a walnut, a walnut cracker, then, at last, a packet of hand wipes. "Here you go. Clean your hands before entering my house." He returned everything else to his jacket.

"How'd you fit all that stuff in there?" asked Bijal, who always thought with his mouth.

"Yeah, how?" Cassa briskly opened the wipes and handed one to each of us. She wasn't a neat freak, but she did like to get things done.

"I like big pockets," said Mr. Pang. "How else would I keep all my secrets?" A grin spread across his face, and he opened his hands. Blue veins striped his smooth palms. I couldn't help noticing that his fingernails were narrower than most and curved at the ends, almost like talons. Maybe the guy had some sort of medical condition, like nail fungus.

"Now are you ready?"

"What if he's a Chester?" Bijal hissed behind me. He was the Stealth's best defender, not because he was braver than the rest of us, but because he was extra sensitive to danger, like a car alarm that went off whenever the wind blew. "Let's forget this and just get boba."

Cassa scoffed. "He doesn't look like a child molester. I could take him."

She probably *could*. She trained harder than all of us put together. Her mom had split long ago, so Cassa was used to looking out for herself. Not to mention Mr. Pang looked like he was a hundred years old and might blow away in a good breeze. I didn't think he was dangerous, just kooky.

Mav glanced back at the shopkeeper, who was watching us with a curious gleam in his tortoiseshell eyes. "I vote we go in. There could be some cool stuff in there."

"I did want to get something for Dad-iversary." My pie was history. Maybe I could find something else Mom would like.

The door made a sucking sound, and Mr. Pang gestured to a dark hallway. Rolling back my shoulders, I stepped inside.

CHAPTER 3

We moved in a clump behind Mr. Pang, who led us down a dark maze of hallways.

Mav sniffed. "Smells like popcorn in here."

"Oh my Allah," hissed Bijal. "He probably uses it to lure children."

We turned right, then left, then right, another right, another left. How many hallways did it take to get to the shop? I lost track. The smell of popcorn intensified with every step. I was reminded of the fun house Mav and I used to explore on Fisherman's Wharf in our younger days. We pretended not to be scared, but when someone jumped out at us, we ran all the way back to our moms.

"My collection can be quite delicate," said Mr. Pang. "Sometimes even . . . temperamental. My rules are as follows: The first item you touch will be the item you choose. There are no givebacks. Also, avoid anything with a red label. And be out by five p.m. I always hunt for dinner at five. Do you understand?"

I licked my lips, which had gone Sahara dry. "First thing I touch. Avoid red labels. Be out by five. Yes, sir."

At last, when Bijal had decided he'd had enough and was trying to drag Cassa in the opposite direction, Mr. Pang pivoted and raised his hands like a preacher. "Welcome to my shop!" Lights turned on overhead.

We all gaped, even Bijal, who was pressing his hands on his thighs like he was trying to get the lay of the field during a game. The shop reminded me of the giant ski lodge where the McFees had taken us one year—wooden log walls, oak floors, and antler chandeliers. Except there were also a dozen high shelves holding hundreds, maybe thousands of oddities. Among them I saw a pair of red cowboy boots, a china doll with unnervingly lifelike eyes, and a fur-covered ukulele.

"This place is unreal," said Mav.

Mr. Pang waved off the comment. "It's nothing. It's not, say, an island. Islands are the best place for hiding magical things. They're like English muffins with all those nooks and crannies."

"Check that out." Bijal pointed at a realistic-looking slice of pizza on a wire stick. "Smells like cheese and everything."

Farther down the aisle, a trio of marble busts, each with arms wrapped around a drum, bore the label ASK-ME-ANYTHING BEETHOVEN BUSTS. In fact, every item in the collection had a hang tag, some white and some red. Not all the labels were facing the right way, but I resisted the urge to turn them, as that would mean touching something. No way was I going to fall for that.

I felt giddy as I thought about all the choices. And those were just the things I could see on the lower shelves. I grinned at my friends. Coming in here hadn't been such a bad decision, after all.

"That is a sweet canoe." Mav was looking at the ceiling, where a birchbark vessel stretched at least fourteen feet between two antler chandeliers. A sign next to it read NOT FOR SALE. DON'T EVEN THINK ABOUT IT. "Looks antique."

Also hanging from the ceiling were a herd of unicorn piña tas with a strange glow about them.

Ah-ooga! Ah-oogah!

A sound like a jalopy horn started blaring. Mr. Pang pulled a smartphone out of his bottomless pocket, displacing the walnut, which he caught just before it hit the floor. "Mr. Pang's Whimsies."

His placid face creased as he listened to his caller. "Hold on a second. Excuse me, kids. I need to take this call in my office. Remember my rules, Winston." He disappeared through a black curtain on the far side of the room. The smell of popcorn was coming from that area. I pictured it all buttery and golden with just the right amount of salt. It made my mouth water even though I hadn't been hungry before.

Bijal walked in a circle with his customary gait, feet slightly turned out like a duck. He clamped his hands on the sides of his head. "This place is bizonkers. How's it so big? We must have walked two blocks to get to this room. They'll never find our bodies."

Mav fiddled with his phone. "That's weird, my phone doesn't seem to work. Even the camera's frozen." He slipped it back into his pack. "We should get cracking. We only have half an hour, and there's a lot of stuff here. What would your mom like, Win?"

I wasn't sure she'd like any of this stuff, but she would pretend like she did.

"What do you remember about your dad?" Cassa prompted.

"He was fun. We were always happy when he was around." During his visits back from Iraq, where he'd worked as an army translator, we'd kept him busy. He'd make the meals, do the chores, then take Mom, my grumpy sister Philippa, and me out on separate "dates." Mine always included skateboarding in Golden Gate Park and watching old superhero movies, like the original *Superman*.

Bijal pulled his sleeves down. "That's not really helpful, man."

"Fine. Let's walk around." Maybe I'd know it when I saw it. I flexed my fingers. This time I would be careful. I would stroll down every aisle easy as pie—well, maybe not pie—and I would not touch anything. The red tag on the pizza read HOVERING PIZZA SWAT. CAUTION: HOT. The cowboy boots were labeled KICK-ME BOOTS. I steered clear of them.

The china doll also featured a red tag: CHANG-AH-LING. I could have sworn its eyes blinked slowly at me, and I backed away, nearly bumping into a shelf behind me. Whoa, that was close.

"Where did Mr. Pang get all this stuff?" I asked no one in particular. It might all be dressed-up junk, like the kind used as accents in those home-and-garden shows Mom watched, but it was still cool in a creepy way.

Mav squinted at a tag. "Beats me. It's probably all gof. Still, those Beethoven Busts are freaking me out. Don't choose them."

"Yeah." I laughed, though the busts looked ferocious, with their eyebrows like bat wings, and eyes that followed you around. Of course all this stuff was gof. In the game *Zombie Infestation*, gof, or *fog* spelled backward, was a deceptive mist that turned everything nonsensical. Up became down, left became right or nowhere at all. The only way to get through it was to hit the Activate Wonder button, which turned the zombies into different things, like butterflies. If only I could inspect the items more closely. Could the pizza swat actually hover? What if the Beethoven Busts could answer anything? Right. Gof. Even so, some of these items would be plain cool to have. I bet I could impress Dani Kim with the furry ukulele, whose label read WARM FUZZIES SAY-LULLA-BYE-TO-YOUR-TROUBLES UKULELE.

I continued down the aisle, heel-toe, heel-toe, giving wide berth to a stuffed grizzly bear that had been posed with its arms stretched over its head, as if on the verge of attack. I didn't even want to read its label. There was no way I was taking that monster home.

Cassa stopped a few steps ahead of me. The number seven on her jersey was peeling on one corner. "No way."

"What?" We clustered around her.

She was staring at a trading card of Luke Skywalker, circa 1977, with his trademark shaggy blond-brown hair and stormtrooper armor. "This card is worth at least a grand. Wish I could read the label." She grabbed her lavender phone with its

Activate Wonder sticker on the backside, and tried to snap a picture. "My phone doesn't work, either."

A thousand dollars. With that much money, I could help with the rent. Suddenly, the hunt took a new urgency.

"You should go for the most valuable item," Cassa said firmly. Her dad, a foreman, let her handle the finances for the two of them. "Money gives you options."

Yeah. I could buy a slew of mementos for Mom, a new pair of sneakers for me, maybe even a phone for Philippa to replace the one I accidentally dropped out a window—a long story I'd prefer to forget. If she had a cool phone, maybe her social life would improve and she wouldn't be so grouchy all the time.

Bijal's hands and mouth started working. It was always a toss-up as to which of those two parts would move faster. "Money can't buy happiness. Didn't you read *Charlie and the Chocolate Factory*? Willy Wonka had a whole mansion of candy but no one to share it with. Only a bunch of Oompa-Loompas. Besides, this stuff looks fake. I doubt there's anything of value in here."

"I say we split up," Mav said in his team captain's voice. "Everyone find your best choice—but just look, don't touch— and meet back here in fifteen." As goalie, he kept an eye on the action from his vantage point at the end of the field, which meant he always had a larger view of the situation.

Fifteen minutes later, Bijal was pulling me toward a black run-a-mile tracksuit, with its formfitting leggings and zippered sweatshirt decorated with gold sequins. "I still think it's all gof, but this looks first class, man."

"Thanks, but I'm not auditioning for a music video."

"All right, all right. But if it could help you run a mile, maybe it could help us win tomorrow's game." It was the last one of the summer, and a win would really boost our morale going into the fall season. Still, if I was out of uniform, I'd be out of the game, even if I could convince myself to wear sequins.

Mav led me to a bunch of marbles bound in a net bag. Each of the marbles resembled an eye. "'Far-Seeing Eyeballs,'" he read. "Maybe I could use these instead of my contact lenses. Though, that wouldn't exactly be helpful. Oh, maybe you could use them to see faraway places, like Nepal. Could be cool."

Cassa joined us, her gaze thoughtful. "Or maybe 'far' means the future, and you can see lottery numbers."

"Or 'far' could mean the past." My mind switched to Dad again. I imagined being able to see what he'd been like before I'd come along. I let out a shaky scoff. "Seeing the past, right. Cassa, what did you find?"

She led us to the row closest to Mr. Pang's office and pointed to a cardboard box containing four eggs. The carton was open, and the eggs were numbered with black ink: 20 minutes, 30 minutes, 20 hours, 30 hours.

Bijal threw up his hands. "I thought you were trying to pick something valuable. Those are just eggs. Probably rotten."

"Shut up, you bot," said Cassa. "Look what it says."

We bent over the tag, which read EGGS OF TRUTH.

"With these, maybe you could tell when adults were lying to you." Cassa yanked her braid.

I couldn't help noticing that she'd said *adults*, not *people*. She wasn't even using her sales-pitch voice. Was she talking about her father? I didn't think so. Mr. Kowalski was so honest, he never even parked crooked.

I scratched an old mosquito bite on my elbow. "I don't know. Those look messy."

"Fine. Then take the Luke Skywalker card," pressed Cassa. "Money in the bank."

Mav shrugged. "I still think the canoe's pretty cool."

"It's not for sale. Besides, Mom would kill me." Some college student rented the garage below us, which meant we didn't have a parking space for the car, let alone a boat.

I narrowed my choices down to the Far-Seeing Eyeballs, which, even if they couldn't see far, could remind us that Dad was always watching over us, and the Luke Skywalker card, which was lucrative. A part of me wanted the Warm Fuzzies Ukulele, too. Coco always seemed to be teething, and maybe the instrument would help her sleep. And if I learned how to play, I could impress Dani, assuming I ever saw her and her cello again.

A loud cawing pierced through the black velvet curtain. The fabric rustled, and a green blur shot through, knocking down an old broom that had been leaning against the wall.

The bird ricocheted through the room like a pinball, colliding into objects. Bijal shrunk back, holding his hands in front of his face. "Is it attacking us?"

Something dark and furry tumbled from its spot on the shelf and landed without a sound. I hoped it wasn't a dead animal. Seconds later, the bird flopped onto the ground beside the dark furry thing and began flapping around, scooting itself under the three-inch space between the shelf and the wood floor.

"It's hurt!" Cassa dropped to her knees and peered under the shelf. "Poor thing. It's just lying there."

The rest of us knelt to take a look. Mav, who had the longest arms, tried reaching for it. "I can't . . . get it."

The bird squawked pathetically. It lay on its back, orange legs sticking up like bendy straws and one burgundy wing fanned out. Its pale green body heaved. I scrambled to my feet and grabbed the fallen broom. Trying my best to be gentle, I pushed the creature out.

The bird righted itself, showing an impressive cape of emerald-green feathers and a black stripe running across its eyes like a mask. That was one slick chick.

Cassa drew in her breath. Bijal blew out his.

Mav ran a hand through his hair. "That's a Javan green magpie. It's not from around here." He didn't like people to know, but he loved birds. He could go the distance in any sport, but give him a pair of hiking boots and binoculars and he was happy.

The bird stretched its wings, and a rather friendly-sounding squawk burst from its red beak. It didn't look injured. The magpie bobbed its head at each of us, staring at us with its red-rimmed eyes. Then it lifted off and sailed back through the curtain.

I shrugged. "Guess it's okay."

Mr. Pang emerged a few moments later, breathing hard. "I'm sorry. My bird escaped while I was on the phone. Hope Maggie didn't scare you."

"Where'd you get her?" asked Mav.

"Oh, she's always been with me." Mr. Pang picked up a fallen silk cushion and set it back on the shelf. It occurred to me that he didn't really answer the question. His eyes widened, noticing me with the broom. The gong sounded, and the antler chandeliers swung, shifting the light around the room. A saintly smile pulled his wrinkles in new directions.

The gong crashed yet again, and I caught a flash of something small and rectangular in Mr. Pang's hand. Was that a . . . remote control? "Oops, already pressed that." With an embarrassed chuckle, he slipped the remote into his pocket. "Congratulations! I hope you and your new broom are very happy together."

CHAPTER 4

"What?!" I pushed the broom back at Mr. Pang. "But . . . I wasn't choosing this!"

"Oh, dear." Mr. Pang shook his head sadly. "I was afraid this would happen. I thought I was clear. No givebacks."

"That's not fair!" said Mav. "Winston didn't want the broom." His forehead bunched up.

"Yeah. What kind of racket is this?" Bijal's usually goofy face was ferocious, like when he was defending on the field. "That's an ugly old broom. Not even regular-looking. Probably jinxed. Carries buckets of water and tries to drown you."

I held up the broom, which did look different from the ones I was used to seeing. Instead of having a plastic handle and a flat end made of straw, this one was a bundle of dark sticks bound with leather cord.

"We agreed you could take the first thing you touched, did we not, Winston?" said Mr. Pang.

I shifted from leg to leg. "Well, yes, but I had to help the bird."

"Did you? You could've called me. There were other solutions at hand."

Good gof, I could've had the Luke Skywalker card. The Far-Seeing Eyeballs. Even the dark, furry object on the floor whose tag read MISCHIEF MUSTACHE. That might have been good for a laugh, at least. I squeezed the broom handle so hard I felt a pain in my palm. I dropped it. Probably full of splinters and spiders.

Cassa gave me a sympathetic poke with her elbow and then began pacing. "Look, Mr. Pang," she said in her bright, sales-pitch voice. As striker, Cassa was our closer, the one always putting the money in the till. Plus, of the four of us, she was the best at talking to adults. "Winston scared off your burglars *and* tried to help your bird. Giving him an old broom as a reward is an insult."

Mr. Pang stuck his hands in his pockets. "That's not exactly what happened, is it, Winston?"

Annoyance crawled around my skin like a rash. Mostly, I was mad at myself. I *had* agreed to play by Mr. Pang's rules. And it wasn't as if he owed me anything. I wasn't a hero, just a kid who'd made a poor choice to skate home holding a pie. The man could have chosen not to step out of his store at all. He could've minded his own business, let his Peeps do the work. No one would've been the wiser. All his stuff was cool to look at, but gof. The gong wasn't real, just a remote. The Far-Seeing

Eyeballs were marbles, and Warm Fuzzies was a regular ukulele with . . . fur.

I forced a smile. "It's okay, guys. This was fun. We should get going."

Bijal's treads made squeaks as he dug them into the floor. Mav knotted his arms, his mouth pursed into a scowl. Cassa stopped pacing and glared at Mr. Pang.

Mr. Pang picked up the fallen broomstick and crossed back toward the curtain. But instead of going through, he scooped up the wooden dustpan propped against the baseboard. I hadn't noticed it before—it might as well have been a piece of the wall. "I am sorry you are disappointed. But for your troubles, I would like to throw in this dustpan as well. Matched set. Very old."

Mr. Pang held out the dustpan and broom, his diamond-shaped face tilted and his orange headband scrunched up. He looked so earnest, like an old man asking for help sweeping leaves.

I took the janitorial duo. "Thanks." Mom said I should say thank you even for things I didn't want, like when our minty-smelling neighbor put a toothbrush in my trick-or-treat bag.

"You're welcome. I will show you out."

$$* \quad * \cdot * \cdot * \quad *$$

My friends and I trudged up Telegraph Hill to my place, the silence as heavy as when we lost a tournament we'd been favored to win. I wasn't even cheered by my favorite boba drink—basic black milk tea with a generous serving of chewy tapioca balls, all served in a clear cup with a friendly aardvark logo. Bijal carried the broom, Cassa carried the dustpan, and Mav and I walked with our skateboards under our arms.

"Squirrel!" yelled Bijal as a dark blur dropped out of the tree onto the sidewalk in front of him. The rodent was as large as a cat. It hissed at us, showing sharp teeth, and we cut a wide path around it.

Some said the squirrels were growing as a result of humans feeding them processed foods, while others believed these were a new invasive species from South America. Whatever they were, I hoped scientists would figure out how to get rid of them before we all developed a fear of walking under trees.

The sky had begun to darken, though according to my sports watch, it was only 5:06. Were we in for a summer storm? A cold breeze swept around us, rattling the leaves. We plodded up a steep flight of cement stairs called the Peter Macchiarini Steps. We had renamed them For Pete's Steps because tourists were always blocking the way, taking pictures of the city view. Election signs littered each side of the staircase, silently barking slogans at each other. As we neared the top, something rumbled, like the sound of commercial-size garbage bins being rolled across pavement, though I didn't see any around.

Bijal pulled a cap from one of his many windbreaker pockets and jammed it onto his head. The rest of us zipped up. "Rain wasn't in the forecast or I would've worn my waterproof sneaks," he said. Both of Bijal's parents worked for the National Weather Service, so he was never caught unaware.

"I love the rain," said Cassa.

Lightning bolts shot across the sky. Thunder bellowed in response. We all looked at each other. Then we began to run.

Raindrops fell as thick as if someone was squirting them from a turkey baster.

I tried to keep a grip on my cup, but with the rain attacking us, it slipped out of my hand, and my whole drink went sliding down the steps. As he watched my boba bounce down For Pete's Steps, Mav threw his own half-finished tea in the nearest trash can and covered his head with his skateboard. I did the same.

"That's some serious H_2O!" he gasped out. "Tsunami level."

"We're almost there." My shoes sucked at the pavement. "Just another block."

By the time we reached the three-story Victorian whose top two floors we rented, our clothes were plastered to our skin, and mini rivers had formed in the gutters. Cassa wrung out her braid, and water splashed thickly onto the front stairs.

"So, you love rain, huh?" Bijal groused. Even his eyelashes were dripping.

The wooden stairs complained loudly as we trooped up to the second-level entry, sloshing and heaving. I reached for my key chain, only to grab empty space. "My Hulkbuster's gone. I must have dropped it. . . ." I thought back. Maybe when I was crawling around on the floor of Mr. Pang's shop.

Mav's eyebrows lifted. He had bought both of us the limited-edition key chain of Iron Man wearing his special Hulk-proof armor during a trip to Monaco.

"Sorry, dude," I told him.

"Don't sweat it. Maybe you can go back tomorrow and see if Mr. Pang found it. "

"Yeah. He better not sell it," I grumbled as I fished out the spare key Mom kept hidden under a cactus plant by the door.

"Hello?"

The place was empty. Philippa was still at her job trimming waffles with scissors. Mom and Coco were probably on their way home from Coco's toddler class at the CuriOdyssey museum. After we kicked off our wet shoes and socks in the foyer, I led everyone upstairs to get towels and dry clothes. Bijal reached out and tapped the tiny crystal that Mah-mah had hung above the stairs. According to her feng shui principles of harmonious living, a stairway facing the entryway, like ours, will cause the energy of our house to rush out the "mouth of qi," or the front door. The crystal lifts the energy from its downward slide.

Cassa headed to Philippa's room. The rest of us threw on my supply of sweats and T-shirts, which were too short on Mav and too tight on Bijal. Mav pushed open my window curtain. "Look, it stopped."

I finished toweling off the broomstick and dustpan and peered outside. Sure enough, the sky was clear again. Bijal joined us at the window. "That felt like a witch's storm. And that Mr. Pang was one Peep short of peepy-creepy."

"Or maybe just one Peep short." Mav pulled a chocolate kitty Peep from the front pocket of his hoodie.

I gaped. "You *stole* it?"

"No! I found it stuck to my sleeve. Want it?" He waved it in front of my face.

"No, thanks." It would just remind me of my epic failure at Mr. Pang's.

"I do." Bijal held out his hand.

"No way. You'd eat it, and it's probably full of bacteria. I'm keeping it." Mav put it in his pocket.

I didn't think the broom and dustpan would make a good Dad-iversary present, even though Mom appreciated practical gifts, like the barbecue gloves for our firepit. It just didn't seem respectful to Dad.

I carried the pair to the walk-in closet I shared with Philippa, glancing around for a spot to store them. A door on the other side led into Philippa's room. She'd kept it locked ever since Mav and I had burst in on her one morning shooting Nerf bullets. I'd have to stash the cleaning tools in a corner where she wouldn't notice. I didn't want her grilling me about them.

I stuffed the objects behind my hanging clothes, including my soccer jersey, sky blue with the number 11 and CHU printed on the back. Then I hung up all the clothes that were on the floor to provide even more cover.

But just when I thought I'd gotten the broom to stand upright, it karate-chopped back through the clothes. The thick and uneven twig bristles that splayed in every direction probably made the thing squirrely. No wonder Maggie the magpie had knocked it over so easily. Under the closet ceiling light, I saw that the broom handle was not splintery like I had thought, but polished, with a silvery sheen. I maneuvered a Macy's shopping bag holding an old hurricane lamp in front of the broom, then closed the door.

When I emerged from the closet, Mav and Cassa were sitting atop my bed with its Iron Man comforter and looking at Cassa's phone. She and Mav had real phones. Bijal carried an emergency one, while I used one of Mom's old calls-only cellular gizmos.

Bijal was peering at my bubble-headed orange-and-white goldfish, Lucky, on my dresser. I figured the fish was male because he had a bit of a mustache. "Could I feed him?"

"One flake only." Overfeeding can kill goldfish, and Lucky was the last present I got from Dad. Also, I'd been counting on Lucky to help Mom find a new job.

Bijal dropped in a flake from my fish food cannister. Lucky zipped out of his turquoise castle and consumed it in one quick jab.

"No way," breathed Mav, still staring at Cassa's phone screen.

Cassa bounced off the bed. "I searched '602 Jackson' with 'Mr. Pang,' and look what I got." She showed me her screen. I saw a photo of a round-cheeked man with white hair like a dollop of whipped cream. He was holding an Elmo puppet. Under the picture it read:

OBITUARY

Ross Pang was born on August 31, 1923, in Oakland, California, and passed away from natural causes on September 4, 1979. The owner of the eclectic toy store known as Dream Castle at 602 Jackson Street in San Francisco for over twenty years, Pang was well loved by his friends and customers. He had no known survivors.

"That's not *our* Mr. Pang." Bijal, beside me, poked a finger at the screen.

"Maybe it's just a weird coincidence that there were two

Mr. Pangs operating similar shops in that same location," said Mav, sounding not at all convinced. He trapped my mini soccer ball between his feet.

Cassa glared at her phone. "Or maybe our Mr. Pang stole this man's identity. Happens all the time."

"I knew we couldn't trust him," said Bijal.

Mav tossed the ball up and caught it again with his foot. "Bijal's right. All that stuff looked cheesy, like what they sell on late-night TV. You're lucky you got a broom and dustpan. They might be boring, but at least they're useful."

"Right," I said, trying not to grimace. I felt for my dog tag under my shirt, silently apologizing to Dad for not finding a gift for Mom. "Let's play *Zombie Infestation*."

CHAPTER 5

After my family came home and the other parents picked up their kids, everyone commenting on the crazy weather, I tried to forget about Mr. Pang by playing with my little sister.

"Come on, Coco! You going to let a mail truck boss you?"

She zoomed her favorite cement mixer truck through the living room, which was just the carpeted end of the dining room, while I raced her with the mail truck. Philippa grumbled in the kitchen. The door to the microwave shut, and the beep of buttons set off a chorus of electronic whirring.

Philippa slouched in through the arched doorway of our kitchen. The way she moved always reminded me of a moray eel emerging from a hidey-hole. Her hair looked like a tangle of black seaweed held in place with a scrunchie on top of her head, and her eyes somehow managed to be ferocious even when they were only halfway open. In her arms, she held—no, *withheld* a casserole dish of spaghetti, grimacing as if to remind me the only reason she had to share food was that I had been born.

She'd never been the doting type, but before Dad died, she'd at least seemed to enjoy hanging out with me. I wished we could go back in time. Now she was a moody bully who would one day be the kind of old lady who hit people with her walking stick.

"So you're a klepto?" She stared at my pockets, which I had stuffed with Coco's toys to see if it was possible to fill them without it being obvious like Mr. Pang did with his gold jacket.

So much for that experiment.

I jutted my chin. "Yeah, I'm a klepto." She could keep her high-school-dropout words to herself.

Rolling her eyes, she set the casserole on a wool trivet on our dining table, where I had arranged chopsticks and plates. The dings on our IKEA table marked different eras in my life— the time of banging blocks; the permanent marker phase; a few climactic events, like the golf club disaster of 2019; and the nail polish remover explosion of 2020, which nearly caused the piece of furniture to go extinct.

Philippa removed the lid to her casserole as if unveiling a new species. The spaghetti looked saucy in the center, but dried noodles were glued to the sides of the dish. That would take me at least fifteen minutes to scrub out. Ever since I'd agreed to wash the dishes for a year to make up for the phone incident, I swear she tried to make the biggest mess possible for me to clean up. "Stop making that face. You're lucky I'm such a good cook."

"You call that cooking, Chef Girlardee?"

She held up one of her oven-mitted hands, in which I knew a rude gesture had formed, then stomped back into the kitchen. In her wake, one of Coco's works of art, hung by a clothespin on a string against the wall, dropped to the floor. Philippa was a study in contrasts—spicy but cold, slithery but stompy.

Coco rolled up clutching Putty, a soft scrap of chenille with ribbon loops on the edges for her fingers to poke through. With all the bacteria riding on it, the chewed-up thing could probably kill a zombie. "Oopsie!" She knelt to retrieve the picture.

"I got you, Coco." I rehung Coco's abstract finger painting, then emptied my pockets.

The door to Mom's bedroom opened, and she emerged smelling of shampoo and wearing her favorite Snoopy T-shirt. It had faded so much that one of the beagle's paws was missing. With wet hair, Mom's asymmetrical bob looked more black than gray, framing eyes that still sparkled despite the shadows under them.

"Muk," Coco told Mom in her cute munchkin's voice, her eyes round. "Want muk. Only warm muk, not cold." She pointed to the kitchen.

"I've got your warm milk right here." Philippa emerged from the kitchen again with Coco's sippy cup.

"Thank you, Pippa!" Coco climbed up into her booster chair.

I dished Philippa's gourmet zombie brains onto plates; then we all dug in. No one had mentioned the Dad-iversary. I *really* wished I hadn't dropped my pie. Now I'd have to think of another way to bring it up.

"Who looks most like Dad—Philippa, Coco, or me?"

Mom gave me a tight smile. She pushed a lock behind her ear, something she frequently did even though the hair always fell back into her face. Coco threw spaghetti on the floor.

I jabbered on. "I mean, Mah-mah said I was a Wood type like him, so I thought it would be me."

Of the five elements that make up the world—Wood, Fire, Earth, Metal, and Water—Wood people are the most steadfast, solid, and determined. They even look similar to one another, with long faces, broad foreheads, and the tendency to stay thin no matter how much we eat.

"But Coco has his big eyes," I added.

Coco was a Water type. She had an iron will and would go wherever she wanted.

Philippa frowned with her vampire-red lips. I don't know why she bothered putting on lipstick. There was no one to make kissy faces at her.

"And Philippa has big ears—"

"Why don't you ever know when to drop it?" she snapped.

"Oh, you mean like you do your classes?"

She glared at me. After passing her GED test, she'd enrolled herself at San Francisco State . . . only to drop all her courses. It was a sore point between her and Mom.

Coco threw down more spaghetti.

"Okay, we're done," Mom sang, somehow talking to each of us at the same time. She helped Coco down from her chair and led her to the sink. I stabbed my garlic bread with my chopsticks. What I wouldn't give to go back three years. Coco wouldn't be born yet, but Dad would be here, and we would be happy again.

There was a knock at the door, and I hurried to answer it. I checked the peephole. It was Mom's old boss, Mr. Gu, holding a pink pastry box. What was he doing here?

I opened the door to the lawyer turned junk dealer. "Hi, Mr. Gu."

"Hello, Winston." Despite his age—as old as my grandfather—he favored colorful shirts, cargo shorts, and hip red-framed glasses. He looked like he'd spent a lot of time on the islands, with a round, tanned face that made his white hair almost glow. He pushed the box at me, and my eye caught on his color-changing analog Swatch-brand watch, which had always fascinated me. Tonight it was glowing red. "Banana cream. Your mom said your dad loved pie."

"Wow, thanks." At least someone had remembered. "Do you want to come in?"

"No, no, just stopping by. Your mother mentioned she had an old lamp to donate."

After retiring early from his job as an environmental lawyer, Mr. Gu now polished up old junk. Then he sold it for ten times its worth at his funky store in the Dogpatch, a nearby artsy industrial neighborhood. He'd taken several of our castoffs, including two bags of Dad's old stuff.

Mom came out of the kitchen. "Oh, Ned! I forgot you were coming. So nice of you to bring dessert. Come in, come in. Winston, go fetch that lamp."

Setting the pie on the table, I ran upstairs. The broom had fallen again, and it blocked my path like a railroad crossing arm. I grabbed the handle, then quickly dropped it. Why was the broomstick on Philippa's side of the closet?

There had to be a reasonable explanation. Maybe she or

Coco or Mom had moved it. But why? The Macy's bag with the hurricane lamp had been pushed aside. I returned the broomstick to its place, moving the hanger holding my bulky Jedi robe to the clothes pinning the broomstick in place and wishing I didn't feel so uneasy.

* ❋ · ❋ · ❋ *

Around three o'clock the next day, I rubbed on sunscreen. My dad's dog tag winked at me in the bathroom mirror. Holding it up, I read the familiar entries: Name: CHU, PHILIP; Department of Defense number; blood type: O POS; and religion: NO PREFERENCE. Philippa wore Dad's second dog tag on a ball chain around her neck. We'd thought they'd been lost, but then, two years ago, they'd shown up in the mail, no return address.

I wondered if my father would recognize me now.

Anger surged in me as I remembered the senseless way he had died. One of his army buddies had shot him by mistake during his tour in Iraq. My face clamped into a scowl.

Then the weirdest thing happened. Out of the corner of my eye, I caught two figures watching me in the mirror—a tall young woman with long black hair and a billowing dress, and a squat man in simple clothes and one of those inverted-cone straw hats they wore in the old days. I whipped around.

No one was there. All I saw was our family picture from my kindergarten graduation hanging on the wall. I spilled into the hall, glancing wildly about. But it was empty, and the only sound was the pounding of my heart.

I must have imagined it. Surely Mom would've mentioned

something if we were having houseguests from medieval China. Maybe all the video game playing had finally messed up the wiring in my brain.

I shook myself free of my stupor and returned to the closet. We had a soccer game to win. I flipped the switch, igniting the single bulb on the ceiling.

My jersey wasn't on its hanger. Behind my clothes, the broom and the dustpan stood like aliens from another world, the silvery streaks in their dark wood giving them an unsettled appearance. The dustpan in particular looked like a shadowy and dark space, not the kind of kind of thing you'd want to stick your hand in.

What was going on? Had Philippa taken my shirt? I could hear her snoring through the thin door to her room, sleeping late on a Sunday. Maybe she had pinched my jersey for some evil purpose, like for stuffing between her toes to keep them separated when she painted her nails, or wiping the car dipstick of oil. If she was mad enough, she probably would do those things. But she wasn't mad at me, was she?

I scratched my head, trying to remember the score between us. I had eaten the last piece of garlic bread at dinner, but that wasn't worth stealing my shirt for, and on game day, too.

Maybe Mom knew where it was.

I ran downstairs. Something dark caught my eye at the base of the bannister. I slowed, looking around. I hoped it wasn't a tarantula. I'd had to use a butter tub to catch the last one, and I swear it had tried to punch through the cardboard box I'd put over the tub. Not seeing any spider this time, I rolled on.

"Ready to go?" Mom asked from the dining table without lifting her eyes from her laptop.

Coco, eating a sandwich, pointed at my bare chest and giggled. "Win's naked."

Mom looked up.

"Have you seen my soccer jersey?" I asked.

"It should be in your closet."

"It's not."

"Did you look in the laundry basket? I'll check my room."

The laundry closet, located in the kitchen, had been designed to fit only a washer and dryer, but it also contained our laundry basket, an ironing board, and the collapsible dolly Mom used for carting groceries. I opened the double doors and upended the basket but found no shirt.

"You didn't borrow it, did you, Coco?" Mom asked, emerging from her bedroom.

"No," Coco said very seriously, her face smeared with grape jelly. She grabbed her blanket scrap, Putty, then stuck her thumb in her mouth, her pinkie sticking straight out like the pin of a grenade.

"Check your room again, Winston. I'll search the living room."

Ducking into my closet again, I riffled through my clothes. The broomstick chopped down on me. When I pushed it back up, I saw a blue thread caught between the bristles. I pulled it loose. Sky blue, the same shade as my soccer jersey. My skin tingled, and I rubbed at the goose bumps on my arms.

With pregame warm-ups beginning in twenty minutes, I didn't have time for itchy tinglings. Probably a thread had come loose and fallen onto the closet floor, where the broom's bristles had picked it up when it was moved. That was how brooms worked, after all, picking up lint and dust bunnies. I shoved the broom back in place, blocking it again with my Jedi robe.

When I emerged from the closet, Mom was right behind me, as if she'd appeared out of nowhere. I screamed; then she screamed. "Winston! Don't scare me like that. Any luck?"

"No." I sighed. First my Hulkbuster, now my jersey. I didn't have that many things to lose, but the ones I did have were important.

"Well, put on something else and let's go."

"Coach won't let me play without a jersey."

"I don't blame him. You only had one jersey to keep track of. Maybe there'll be an extra you can borrow just for today. I hope you find yours, or I'm going to have to order a new one."

I grimaced, remembering how expensive they were. They had to be custom printed with your name and number. I grabbed my soccer bag. Even if I couldn't play in the match, at least I could look forward to a post-game *ZI* tournament at Mav's with Bij and Cassa.

Before leaving, I dropped a few flakes into Lucky's bowl. He zipped out of his turquoise castle, ruffling the surface of the water in his haste to get them. "Eat up, bud. You have an important job to do." Goldfish only brought luck when they were healthy and well fed. "Mom has an important interview tomorrow. Hook her up, okay?"

Lucky circled his bowl a few times. Then, in a cloud of bubbles, he wiggled back into his castle.

I followed Mom and Coco out to our secondhand Volvo station wagon in the driveway.

We headed south toward Franklin Square soccer field. As we passed Jackson, I stared down the street toward Mr. Pang's, though it was too far away to see. "Could we stop by Boba Guys?"

"You don't want to drink boba before a game."

"I think I dropped my Hulkbuster key chain there."

With a sigh, she flicked on her blinker. After a series of right turns, Boba Guys' purple awning with its distinctive aardvark logo appeared on the left.

She stopped beside the row of parked cars. "See any spaces?"

"No. I'll just run in. Be right back."

Knowing she had her eyes glued on me, I waited until traffic cleared, then circled around the car to the sidewalk. I passed Boba Guys, then stopped short.

Gone was the brick facade of the shop with its tinted round window, the half-dome awning, and the grasshopper-green door. Instead, the front now matched the rest of the building—stucco with two rectangular windows and a chipped black front door. Gone also was the MR. PANG'S WHIMSIES sign in gold letters. If any marshmallow Peeps were standing guard, they were invisible.

My mind buzzed as my feet led me up to the black door, scattering a pair of seagulls pecking around the sidewalk. I knocked. No one answered.

"Did you find it?" Mom called from the car, which she had moved closer. "Winston, come back."

"Come back, Win-son," echoed Coco.

I knocked again. In the corner office window on the second floor, there was a sign that said ACUPUNCTURE and showed a diagram of a foot labeled with pressure points. I didn't remember seeing that before.

Still getting no answer, I ran my hand along the stucco exterior and the dusty dark rectangular windows until I reached Boba Guys. My stomach seemed to have detached itself from the rest of me and was swooping around my insides like a UFO. I bypassed the line and stumbled up to the counter, where a hipster with a waxed mustache was ordering a drink from Shaggy, the store manager.

"Sorry," I said to the hipster. "This won't take long." Then I turned to Shaggy. "Hi there. What happened to Mr. Pang's Whimsies next door?"

"Mr. Who?" Shaggy pushed up his purple visor, giving me a better glimpse of his confused expression. He had grown up in the seventies and wore his gray hair in a ponytail.

"The shop with the green door?" I hooked my thumb to the right. "Where'd it go?"

"That space was abandoned before I opened this place. Someone mentioned there was a fire. . . . It happened a long time ago, I think."

"But . . . I was in there yesterday."

"Do you mind?" The hipster shot me a glare.

Mom tooted the horn, but I barely heard it. The words *abandoned* and *fire* spun through my mind. But Mav, Bijal, Cassa, and I—we'd all seen it. I had a broom and a dustpan to prove it. Had it all been a weird hoax? A prank? But why?

Mr. Pang's words echoed through my head, loud as a gong. *I like big pockets. How else would I keep all my secrets?*

CHAPTER 6

Before the game began, I briefed my crew on the missing shop. I probably shouldn't have, because we lost. It wasn't exactly a surprise, with three distracted players and a rookie midfielder subbing for me. (There were no extra jerseys for me to borrow.)

My friends and I couldn't discuss it further until post-game tacos, which Coach had bought us to celebrate the last game of the summer. After our parents gave us hugs and fist bumps, they meandered back to their cars. Mav's mom hadn't been able to make the game, but she was supposed to pick us up and take us back to their place for the *ZI* tournament.

Bijal picked the jalapeños off his taco and stuck them in Cassa's. "Maybe you went to the wrong building."

"There's only one on that side of Boba Guys."

"The wrong door, then."

"No, I'm telling you, it was gone. The door looked like a regular door and was farther to the right."

Cassa chewed thoughtfully. "Let's investigate after this. See if we can look into the windows." She glanced at Mav. "Can your mom drive us?"

Bijal's mouth dropped open, giving us a good look at the contents. "Why would we do that? Mr. Pang was creepy. We're lucky we escaped the first time. I'll be glad if we never see that shop again."

Mav set down his Gatorade. "We're just going to look. But my mom can't take us—she'd ask too many questions. Monroe, on the other hand . . ." Mav's older brother was a stretched-out and grungier version of him. "I'll ask him to come get us and let Mom off the hook." Mav pulled out his phone and began texting.

Soon Monroe drove his electric LEAF into the soccer field parking lot. We collected our gear, then piled in. Mav sat in the front, where he could stretch out his long legs, and Cassa, the shortest and least-offensive-smelling member of our crew, took the hump in the backseat, with me on her left and Bijal on her right. The sounds of Hawaiian music filled Monroe's compact car with its vinyl smell and the troll hanging from his mirror.

"Thanks for driving us," I called up to Monroe.

"Thanks for setting me up with your sister." He waggled his eyebrows at me through his rearview mirror.

I gaped. "What did you say?"

Mav twisted around and met my death stare. "Nothing's free, man."

Monroe gave me a toothy grin. "Sorry, bud. I gave up a gig to drive you kids."

Bijal, who'd been hula dancing in his seat with wavy movements of his arms, slapped Monroe's shoulder . "A ukulele gig? But you're terrible."

"Maybe he's paying *them*," said Cassa. Everyone laughed except me. I was too busy planning my funeral.

Monroe shook out his premium McFee hair, which always hung in a messy shag that touched his shoulders, then backed out of the parking space. "Hey, man, I've gotten better."

"I can't fix you up with the moray," I told him. "She hates me." And anyway, I wasn't even sure Philippa liked boys, mostly because she didn't seem to like *anyone* except for Coco and Mom. She was a Metal type, with an unyielding personality that valued solitude.

Bijal wiggled out of his shoulder strap. If he couldn't move freely, he couldn't talk. He grabbed the backs of the front seats and leaned into the space between them. "You better not kiss her," he told Monroe, "or Winston will have to beat you up."

"Unless she beats you up first," Cassa said. "Philippa's tough. She has a black belt." Her eyes pinched into mirthful triangles.

"Just get me a couple minutes with her," said Monroe. "I just want to say hi. That's all I'm asking."

I glared at a grinning pink-haired troll swinging from the mirror. His request seemed harmless enough, but it was going to cost me. I'd be stuck doing the dishes for life.

Minutes later, we reached the corner of Jackson and Kearny, and Monroe let us out. The familiar smells of cigarettes, garbage, and cooking smells blew in our faces. "I'm going to park and nap," said Monroe. "Text me when you're ready." The LEAF putted away.

I rubbed my eyes, not believing what I was seeing. A string of tiny white Christmas lights outlined Mr. Pang's door, which was circular and grasshopper green once again. It looked even more magical than it did yesterday, with the lights causing the gold lettering to sparkle. The chick and bunny Peeps, stationed at their opposite corners, peered down at us.

"I swear this was all gone a few hours ago!" I insisted, clutching my dog tag.

Beside me, Mav craned his neck in every direction. "Looks to me like it's always been here." His face grew concerned. "What's really going on with you? Is it girls?"

"Shut up, Mav," I said automatically. *Was* there something wrong with me? Was it the brain fogs of puberty?

There was no handle that I could see, but a doorbell sat in the usual place. I pressed it. Crickets began chirping.

"What's that?" asked Bijal. "I don't like nature sounds." He bumped into Cassa, who pushed him away.

"Breathe, you gobsmacker. It's just the doorbell."

When no one answered, I called up to the Peeps, feeling ridiculous. "Er, hello, Mr. Pang? It's Winston. I was hoping I could speak to you about the broom and dustpan. Can you come out?"

Mav banged on the door with his fist. "Mr. Pang! Hello, anyone in there?"

Cassa stared up at the marshmallow bunny. "Bij, give me a boost."

"But you're heavy!" It was true. Despite her petite size, Cassa was dense, like a shot of plutonium. She said it was from her Polish ancestors, who had needed big bones to survive freezing winters. Grimacing, Bijal made a sling with his hands. Cassa stepped into it, holding on to his shoulder for balance. She poked the Peep in the stomach. Its belly dented, then popped back out.

Cassa tried prying the Peeps off the corners, first the bunny, then the chick. "It's like they've been superglued."

"Thanks, Sherlock. Can you get down now?" Bijal wobbled, pulling us all to one side.

"Hellooo, Mr. Pang," Cassa said, her face less than a foot from the chick. "Winston needs to talk to you!"

Mav googled *Mr. Pang's Whimsies* on his phone. "The store's not listed."

Bijal put Cassa down, and I stepped away from the door. Cassa shone her smartphone flashlight into the round window while Mav used his pen-size black light, the kind used to find criminal evidence. Still, the round window remained as mysterious as the moon.

Suddenly, the shop door opened wide. Two large men in Hawaiian shirts burst out.

"Not again!" I cried.

CHAPTER 7

It was Bert and Ernie.

Cassa beamed her flashlight on them. Ernie was clawing at something stuck to his face. "Get it off! Get it off!" he cried.

Golden brown and wedge-shaped, the thing on his face smelled like cheese and tomato.

Bert wrestled the offending object off his buddy and then shook his fingers as if they'd been burned. "Ow, hot!"

Mav was pointing. "P-p-pizza . . . It's alive!"

The Hovering Pizza Swat!

Most of the cheese and pepperoni topping had slid off and landed on Ernie's flip-flops, but the crust was animated, slapping both men's cheeks as if it were Chef Kim's hand beating two lumps of dough. I glanced at my friends in disbelief.

Bert and Ernie managed to throw the slice to the ground, where it thrashed like a landed fish. Then the two men ran off. A triangle-shaped tomato print stamped the back of Ernie's shirt.

Bijal's eyes had popped open, and his mouth gaped, like the time a rat crawled over his shoe. "Did a . . . slice of pizza . . . just attack those men?"

Cassa's big eyes eclipsed the rest of her face. "I think so."

I stepped back from the pizza crust, now a squashed bready lump on the sidewalk. Mav snapped a picture of the exhausted slice.

"Let's not stick around here," said Bijal, pulling Cassa toward Boba Guys. "Who knows what'll come through the door next? Mav, call Monroe."

Retreating did seem like a good idea at this point. The line of Boba Guys customers, none of whom had noticed what had happened, provided the comfort of normalcy even at a distance from where we were standing.

So the magic of Mr. Pang's Whimsies was real. There was no doubt about it now. But if he was inside, why hadn't he let us in? Was he afraid or trying to avoid us? My head buzzed, and all my muscles had seized up. I felt like a pinball right before the launch lever is pulled.

While Mav texted Monroe, Bijal walked in a circle around us, talking fast. "That was weird. No, that wasn't just weird—it was bizarre. Out of this world. Stuff like that can't happen, can it?" He glanced back over his shoulder at the shop, which glowed faintly under the awning. "Bet those creepy Peeps are watching us right now."

Mav's nose scrunched. "Those were the same guys who tried to steal from Mr. Pang before. He must have sicced the

Hovering Pizza Swat on them. I've got to post this." He tapped at his phone.

Cassa tugged at her braid, something she did when she was thinking. "But what were they trying to steal?"

Mav's face had gone slack. "That's odd."

I leaned closer. "What?"

He showed us the photo he had taken of the pizza. It was blurry, though the sidewalk where it had fallen was in focus, down to a wad of gum in one corner. He scrolled to the next picture, which showed the same thing but at a different angle. Again the slice was blurry and everything else was clear.

"Maybe something's wrong with your phone," said Cassa.

Bijal pointed a finger gun at Mav. "Or your shooting."

"This whole place is wrong," I said, scanning the corner lot, with its unusual round door and window.

Before we could continue, Monroe rolled up in the LEAF.

"Should we tell him about the . . . whatever just happened?" asked Cassa.

"Negative." Mav slid his phone back in his pocket. "He'd never believe us. Besides, he has something else on his mind." He made big eyes at me.

Before I could even click in my seat belt, Monroe turned to me. "Okay if we make a quick stop at your place? Time to call in my favor."

* 茶 · 茶 · 茶 *

Mom opened the door before I had chance to insert my key. Coco stood beside her, holding Putty and sucking her thumb.

"Hey, kids, this is a nice surprise. Monroe, it's been a while. Don't you look nice."

It occurred to me that Monroe was more neatly turned out than usual, with ironed slacks and a blue oxford shirt shrugged over a UKES NOT NUKES T-shirt. He carried a silver backpack exactly like Mav's—a sleek all-weather model with compartments for all his devices, and attached gadgets like the pen-size black light and even a mirror flap for checking your teeth.

We all piled into the foyer and de-shoed. Bijal pointed his Vans toward the door, the way he always did to save time in case of emergency. Coco stared up at Monroe as if he were her favorite playground slide.

"I thought you're all going to Mav's," said Mom.

I nodded. "We stopped here to get some snacks."

Her brow wrinkled, maybe wondering what was so special about our food when the McFees had a pantry bigger than our kitchen. "Oh, okay. Help yourselves."

Mav, Bijal, and Cassa headed to our snack cache while Monroe bent down to let Coco touch his hair.

"I'll be right back," I muttered, taking off my shoes.

I climbed the stairs, wondering what this "favor" was going to cost me.

Philippa was rummaging in the closet. She emerged, pulling on a sweatshirt. "It's so cold in this house. What do you want?" She flopped back onto her bed and stuck her nose in her book. The sole of her right sock read IF YOU CAN READ THIS, and the left sock continued YOU'RE TOO CLOSE.

I visualized a peaceful tropical island, hoping it would help me project calm and compassion. "Do you ever feel . . . lonely?"

"No. Go away."

"I was thinking, instead of just reading about romance, maybe you could, you know, date?"

"This is an inappropriate conversation." She flipped onto her stomach.

"Just trying to help. I happen to know an upstanding guy—"

"Not interested."

"Well, I sort of promised he could talk to you for a few minutes. You don't even have to say anything back."

She put the book down. Her usually squinting eyes had opened all the way, cannons ready to fire. "You . . . *what*?"

"It's Mav's bro, Monroe. Remember him? Super nice. He's a musician. Even gets gigs." I rushed out my words before she could shut me down. "Smart, too. He wants to go to Berkeley and study the environment. And did I mention he's hot? I mean, yeah, he's a little hairy, but that you can change."

"Winston. I'm a little confused why you would promise something you couldn't deliver. But I guess that's your problem, not mine."

"Monroe helped me out, and I thought this would be a nice way to thank him."

"By pimping out your sister?!"

The palm trees on my tropical island of calm blew off like rocket launchers. "It's one conversation!"

"What's in it for me?"

"Does there always have to be something in it for you? Why can't you do it because I'm your brother?"

"Nah."

I clenched my hands into fists. "Fine, what do you want?"

She shrugged. "I don't need anything."

"Good evening." Monroe stood in the hallway. Coco was trying to drag him in by the hand.

Slithering from the bed, Philippa crossed to the doorway. Her sweatpants fell at different heights on her legs—one below the knee, the other halfway down her calf. Before Dad died, she had cared about her outfits, even ironed them sometimes. Now she favored baggy clothes that hid all the weight she'd lost. With her hair bun bobbing around like a crow on her head and her vampire-red lipstick, she looked like something out of a Halloween horror flick. "Are you serious?"

Monroe grinned, his teeth so white they made our walls seem dingy. I bet if Philippa said *Are you vomitous foot fungus?* he would still think it was delightful.

"Er, hey, Monroe," I said. "I'll give you two some privacy."

Monroe cleared his throat. "Okay, Win."

"No, you sit, Winston." Philippa's eyes glittered, and she directed me to a spot on the floor. Feeling a bit like a scolded puppy, I plunked myself down. Coco pulled her favorite book off Philippa's shelf—*Tales from the Middle Kingdom*—and settled next to me, flipping through the pages.

I felt sorry for Monroe. Putting him in the ring with Philippa was like siccing a grizzly bear on a puppy. She stood with her hip jutted to one side, arms crossed in front of her. It was her all-purpose *impress me* stance, which she used when buying makeup, accepting UPS packages, and even checking out library books.

"Actually, Philippa," Monroe slid in, "I was just wondering if you still had Babar."

I glanced at her bed. The old ratty plush elephant with its yellow crown and green felt jacket lay against her pillow, as always.

Philippa stepped to one side, as if to block Monroe's view of her bed. Her eyes became slits. "How do you know about Babar?"

"I won it for you."

"What are you talking about? I got it at the Saint Mary's Carnival."

"Yeah, Saint Mary's. I was there with Maverick on the same night. You won the Ping-Pong ball toss, and they gave you Bruce the Moose even though you wanted Babar."

"Okay . . ." Philippa steered her heavy gaze to me, as if I were to blame for her winning the Bruce the Moose.

"I won the Babar and dropped it in your bag when you weren't looking," Monroe said.

"*You* did that?"

"She sleeps with it every night," I dropped.

Philippa speared me a glare, then refocused on Monroe. "How do you know I didn't *want* Bruce the Moose?"

"Er, well, you tossed it in the trash can. But I rescued it if you want to trade back."

A smile slipped from Philippa's mouth, but she bullied it away. "Okay, so now you're looking for a thank-you?"

"No, I wanted to thank *you*. Bruce the Moose has given me the best years of my life."

The smile appeared again. Monroe was *good*.

"Babar!" said Coco. She stood, and the book fell from her lap. It opened to a page with an illustration of a broom.

I read the caption:

> *Chinese custom dictates that brooms only be*
> *used for cleaning, never for games or play.*
> *Brooms are inhabited by spirits who will*
> *cast bad luck upon the house if they are used*
> *incorrectly.*

I sucked in my breath, my eyes drifting to the door to Philippa's side of the closet, which she had left open.

Philippa emitted a foreign sound like a series of coughs. Was that . . . a chuckle? Monroe had pulled a stuffed moose with brown felt antlers from his backpack and was dancing it in front of her.

"It hardly looks loved," she said.

"I guess my heart was always set on someone else." Monroe squeezed the moose. "If I could just hold Babar one last time, I promise I'll leave you alone."

Coco, who had wandered near the closet, bent over something on the ground. "Uh-oh." She straightened, a look of horror on her face. "Babar is gone!"

I glanced at the bed again. The elephant, which I had just seen not moments ago, was missing. I hurried toward Coco, my legs as stiff as plastic straws from sitting on the floor. The broomstick was lying across the threshold with the dustpan beside it. "Did you take those out?" I demanded.

"No." Coco's babyish face pulled into a look of dismay. She picked up the dustpan and waved it like she was flagging down an airplane.

"No, Coco, don't touch it!" I yanked the dustpan out of her hand.

Her stubby arms flopped down, and her mouth began to open wide. Good gof, I'd overdone it. The silent scream was on its way. Once the silent scream started, the not-so-silent scream was sure to follow, like a train speeding out of a dark tunnel. There was no turning back.

The sound poured out with a ferocity that made my whole body vibrate, worse than a burp that followed a whole can of Dr Pepper.

Philippa pushed me out of the way. "What's going on? Where'd that broom come from?" Kneeling, she put an arm around Coco, who was crying hard enough to make her lips quaver.

Monroe let Coco hold the Bruce the Moose, which helped stem the waterworks. Coco rubbed her teary eyes. "Babar is gone," she told Monroe, as if he hadn't already witnessed the whole thing.

"But he was just here." Philippa pulled the pillows off her bed and checked the floor.

"I'll help." Monroe flattened himself on the floor while Philippa shone a flashlight under her bed. Coco got down on her belly, too.

I checked around Philippa's desk and in her dresser, refusing to believe the toy was gone. She slammed shut her underwear drawer, which I had left open. "Do you mind?"

"Babar go bye-bye?" Coco said softly.

Philippa got to her feet and hugged herself. Babar meant a

lot to her. Dad had always used the elephant to tell her bedtime stories, using a goofy voice.

I stood over the *Tales from the Middle Kingdom* book, which was still open to the broom page. *Brooms are inhabited by spirits. . . .*

Those things from Mr. Pang's shop had definitely brought bad luck. And the sooner I got rid of them, the better.

CHAPTER 8

The rain started as soon as we left the house. Mav with the dustpan, me with the broomstick, Bijal and Cassa with snacks, and Monroe, his keys. By the time we got into the LEAF and headed off, the rain was falling heavily, as if someone were bailing out heaven by the bucket.

"Can you stop by Pier 27?" I asked Monroe from the backseat. I didn't know what these creepy objects were up to, but I was going to make sure they couldn't take more of our stuff.

"Right now?"

"Yes, now," Mav growled. "Go, go!" He gestured urgently at the road ahead, as if this were a black ops.

Lightning flashed, and Bijal shrank away from the window. "It's another one of those freak storms!" he said through a mouthful of banana bread. He'd had to stuff it in when I'd raced down the stairs and announced it was time to leave.

Monroe steered us off. Despite the foul weather, he was in a good mood, drumming the wheel to his ukulele music and bobbing his head. I wondered why he was so happy, when he hadn't gotten much face time with Philippa. Maybe, after seeing her freak out over Babar, he was glad to have escaped.

Five minutes later, we arrived at a pier where, during the day, you could take a ferry to Alcatraz Island. We rolled along it until the end. Then Mav and I jumped out of the car.

Wasting no time, we crossed to the side railing, cold rain pummeling us from every direction. The sea was a shiny black mass. I couldn't help thinking about the times Dad had taken me pier fishing, and I wondered what he'd think of me littering the water. At least these objects were biodegradable. Mav nodded at me, and we dropped the broom and dustpan into the ocean at the same time.

The wooden objects floated on the surface. Then the ocean gave them a shove, and they drifted out to sea. Good riddance to bad rubbish.

* ✳ · ✸ · ✳ *

The next morning, a pelting noise like a hundred BB guns on repeat fire woke me before my alarm. Had it been raining all night? Rain on the first day of school was not ideal, since it was also picture day. But I hoped that now that the broom and dustpan were swimming with the fishes, they had taken all the bad luck with them.

I shook the wrinkles out of my Iron Man comforter. The bathroom was unguarded, and the field was clear. Philippa always slept late and only worked afternoon or evening shifts at Waffle Fury. I powered through my grooming routine. Using Philippa's styling gel, I slicked my hair into a wave that I hoped would withstand getting wet. I rubbed my elbows with some of her expensive face cream, even though they were probably not going to be in the picture.

"Morning, Lucky," as I reentered my room to get dressed.

There was no response from my goldfish. He was probably asleep in his castle.

Mom had already left to take Coco to daycare before her big interview. While my breakfast burrito was microwaving, I packed a lunch, then hiked upstairs to get my backpack.

Lucky still hadn't come out of his castle. I tapped the glass bowl with a knuckle. "Lucky? You in there, bud?"

I bent down and peered into the castle door. Nothing. I pushed up the sleeve of my sweatshirt, dipped my hand into the bowl, and lifted the castle.

Lucky was gone.

The castle sank back into the pebbles, landing on its side.

My pulse began to pound in my ears. After setting the bowl back down, I searched all around the dresser, moving aside my bobblehead collection and the tissue box. I'd heard of fish jumping out of their containers, but Lucky was kind of a coward. Aside from the drips I'd made, there were no wet spots anywhere, and no sign of my bubble-headed lucky charm.

It couldn't have been Coco. She was a climber, but if she'd been up here, all my bobbleheads would've been messed up. Had I . . . ? Suddenly sick to my stomach, I lifted my slippers one at a time.

I let out a lungful of air when I didn't see his corpse pasted to the bottom of either sole. But still, maybe I tracked him into the closet. I ripped open my closet door, scanning the carpet, but didn't see a single scale.

The empty space where the broom and dustpan had been caught my attention. Had they nabbed him before I'd taken them for a long walk on a short pier, as the mobsters say? I hadn't paid attention to whether Lucky was in his bowl before. . . .

I pounded on the door of the closet that led to Philippa's room. A missing goldfish definitely qualified as an emergency. "Philippa? Wake up!"

When I heard nothing, I ran out of the closet and circled around to her bedroom door. I knocked, rattling the MERMAIDS ONLY sign against the wood. "Philippa?" Normally I might have waited a few seconds, but since I was freaking out, I helped myself to the doorknob.

Philippa's bed was empty and neatly made, her faded crochet blanket pulled up to her pillow. The canvas purse she kept on a hook was missing. I crossed to her Sherlock wall calendar. On today's date, she had written: 7:45 MEPS.

What was MEPS?

I checked her alarm clock and found that it had been set to 6:15. So she had a meeting with MEPS and left early. I ran back downstairs to our kitchen phone and called her. It went straight to voicemail. The microwave clock read 7:28.

I'd missed the bus. I'd have to walk. In the rain. My slippers made slapping sounds against the linoleum as I paced. I called Mom's cell phone.

"Honey? Is everything okay?"

"No. Lucky is missing. I checked everywhere."

"That's strange."

The sounds of people talking and cars honking in the background meant she was on the bus.

"Do you know where Philippa is? She's missing, too."

"I do know that. She needed the car for an interview of some sort."

"But you needed the car for an interview, too."

"It's fine. Mine's just downtown. I'm glad she's looking at opportunities."

"Would she have taken my goldfish?"

"I can't see why, though you know how secretive she can be. Shouldn't you be headed to school by now?"

"Yeah, I'm on my way."

"I don't know what to tell you about Lucky, only that he lived a good life and has probably swum on to even better things."

"So you think he's dead."

She made squeaky noises, as if she was stalling while she tried to think of something to say.

"But Lucky was from Dad," I pressed.

"I know, kid. And I'm sure he would've been proud of the way you took care of him."

"But I *didn't* take care of him! He's gone!" My voice had become shrill. "I should've put a hairnet on the bowl. Why didn't you make me do that?"

"Winston, I'm sorry about your fish. How 'bout we talk more about this when I get home?"

"Bye," I mumbled.

"Good luck on your first day," she said.

I hung up just before realizing I hadn't wished her luck on her interview. I jammed my feet into my sneakers. Outside on the front steps, I opened my umbrella. Before I shut the door behind me, a breeze snaked past, so cold it almost felt like a burn. The force of it nearly knocked my umbrella from my hands.

Then, abruptly, the rain shut off. I set down the umbrella and waved my hands in the air, as if I could feel out the mystery of the arctic freeze. Like a basketball player practicing without a ball, I went high, low, and all the spaces in between. But the strange wind had vanished.

At least with the halt in rain, I could skateboard to school. Fetching my Volt 500, I pushed uphill toward Coit Tower, nearly colliding with a battalion of newspaper vending machines. A thin drizzle hung in the air. This was how I imagined zombie breath must feel—cold and wet and reeking of garbage. I crested the hill, then coasted the drop, through neighborhoods with houses painted colors that would make Easter eggs weep. I slowed before I reached the school parking lot, not wanting to blow in like a raging moofus (that's an angry zombie cow with no eyes).

I had trouble staying focused in homeroom. It wasn't just the missing fish bobbing around in my mind, stirring up bubbles. And it wasn't the fact that my now messed-up hair made me look like a new species of hedgehog.

Dani Kim was in my class. Dani Kim from the San Francisco Cooking Academy was standing by her desk next to me, reading aloud her "about me" note card.

"I just moved here from Austin, Texas." She glanced around her at the sea of onlookers but avoided my gaze. I couldn't help thinking she looked very patriotic in a navy cardigan over red pants. "I like to bake with my aunt, and I've been playing the cello since I was four. Once, I performed a concerto with the Austin Symphony in front of three thousand people." She didn't sound braggy, just matter-of-fact. She repositioned her hair over one shoulder before sitting back down.

"That's extraordinary, Dani," our homeroom teacher, Mr. Bottoms, trilled, causing his dark mustache to flap. "We hope you'll be very happy here." Then he turned to me. "Winston?" His horn-rimmed glasses magnified his brown eyes to twice their size.

I stood. "I'm Winston Chu. I play soccer." It occurred to me that all the sentences I'd jotted on my note card were the same things I said year after year. I'd known most of these kids since kindergarten. I decided to improvise a little. "I'm also pretty good at . . . ukulele."

The word just slipped out. Good gof, I'd never played ukulele in my life. But now Dani was looking at me curiously. I knew with certainty my lie would come back to bite me, but I couldn't stop now. "I've never played with a group, but I do gigs now and then around the city."

"That's so cool!" said someone.

"What did the cello say to the ukulele?" asked Jude, the class clown who was always dripping—sweaty white-blond hair, runny nose, spilled drink.

"What?" asked someone.

"Uke, I am your father.'"

Kids laughed, and I did, too.

Mr. Bottoms held up his hands for quiet. "*San Francisco's*

Got Talent is coming up in two weeks. Maybe one of you would like to volunteer to be our representative?" His humongous spectacled eyes toggled from Dani to me.

I liked being included in the same sentence as Dani, even if it was just because of our instruments, and even if I didn't actually play mine.

"Dan-ee! Dan-ee!" Jude the clown began to cheer, pumping his fist. Others joined in the chant.

Dani shifted around in her chair, clicking her pen. "Actually, maybe Winston would like to play his ukulele."

"Oh no." All my sprinklers went off. I was even sweating from my earlobes. I tried to laugh off the suggestion casually, but it sounded like I was laying an egg. "I couldn't. You're way more qualified."

Dani shrugged. "How 'bout we do a duet?"

"Not a good idea. I have a lot of work on my plate."

Mr. Bottoms straightened his argyle vest. "It's only the first day of school."

Everyone began talking at once, and soon another chant started up. "Du-et! Du-et!"

Mr. Bottoms clapped a few times. "Settle down, class. I've never heard a cello-ukulele duet before, but I bet you'll be great."

There was no way I could play a duet with Dani, the cello prodigy. Now I would have to fess up, not just to Dani, but the entire class. I would be ridiculed, maybe even shunned like the Hunchback of Notre Dame. I would have to live in a tower and ring bells. Either that or become an outlaw, moving from town to town like the Man with No Name.

I said nothing.

By the time the period ended, the back of my shirt was stuck to my chair. I made Jude look as dry as a saltine. I followed Dani out. She marched through the hall like she knew where she was going. "Hey, Dani . . ." I started.

A kid going the opposite direction pushed another kid, setting off a chain reaction that almost knocked me into her. I hotfooted my way clear. She barely noticed me skittering by her one way and then the other while her white sneakers stayed on a straight path.

"So, Dani . . ."

Finally I got her attention. But a sweet dimple appeared to the east of her mouth, making me forget what I was going to say.

"Do you play any other instruments?" she asked me. Her brown eyes reminded me of the teardrop-shaped jewels on Philippa's purse.

"Nope. Ukulele's my jam. Been playing since I was knee high."

"Oh." Her mouth twisted to one side.

"Why do you ask?"

"Ukulele is usually the instrument they start you on so you can learn basics before moving on to the real instruments."

Oh, great. She probably thinks I'm a dumbo.

"Actually, I've been learning some special techniques"—*stop, you rodeo clown, stop!*—"that take years to master. Makes the sound real smooth." *Kind of like how you sound right now. Real smooth.*

"That's great! Then maybe we could do something advanced like Tchaikovsky or maybe Debussy to show our range."

All my fake swagger drained away. I wished I could vacuum up all my words.

"Or maybe we should do a crowd-pleaser. Something simple that everyone can get behind." She glanced at me, her short eyelashes blinking.

"Yes, that's a better idea."

"Do you like the Muppets?"

"Who doesn't?"

"Do you know 'Rainbow Connection'?"

An image of Kermit sitting on a log with a banjo leaped to mind. *"Why are there so many . . . songs about rainbows?"* I sang in my best Kermit voice. *Why are you doing this? Stop now, while you still have a shred of dignity.*

"And what's on the other side?" she sang back in a sweet soprano that melted my insides like a marshmallow over a flame. "I usually have cello classes after school, but I'm free tomorrow. We can practice at my place. We live near the Exploratorium." She pulled a business card that read *Dani Kim, cellist* and listed an address, phone number, and social media handle. "Our house is the same lime green as my aunt's clogs. It's so bright, you could probably see it from space."

"Great. Works for me."

She ducked into her classroom, and the door closed after her.

I plodded toward math class, my soles squeaking too loudly against the linoleum. What had I done? I could almost feel my back begin to hunch as I loped away, *ding-dong, ding-dong* ringing in my ears.

CHAPTER 9

The sight of Bijal and Cassa waving me over to their collaborative desk square where they had saved a spot cheered me a little. Cassa's blond hair, usually pulled back in a business-like braid, today flowed free under a striped headband. Bijal smelled like deodorant and sported a hoodie so new it looked glossy.

A balloon flower lay on Madame Khoury's desk. Bijal always gave the teachers balloon flowers on the first day of school to set the right tone.

A freckly kid approached from another table and slipped five dollars to Cassa, who smoothly pocketed it. "Two number threes," he told Bijal, code for two packets of Flava-gum.

Bijal coolly nodded, and the kid glided back to his desk. He'd fill the kid's order at recess from a locker he and Cassa leased from another kid. Separating purchase from delivery and using code words ensured that teachers would never catch on to their two-person racket.

"Back in business," he said. "Sure you don't want in?"

I shook my head, and Cassa scowled. I used to be part of their enterprise back when we sold fake vomit for a quarter—we made enough to buy a starter set of Soccer Legend bobbleheads each. But after Dad died, a lot of things had changed.

"This year's going to slice," Bijal continued. "Eighth graders are the Jupiters of the solar system, orbiting the cold space of middle school with class and sass." Bijal leaned back, cradling his head. "What happened to you? You look like trash. It's picture day, dude. That photo's going to be on your ID all year. It has to be tight."

I gripped my silky-soft elbows. "Lucky's gone."

"Oh no." Cassa stopped digging through her pencil case.

Bijal jerked up. "I hope it wasn't that flake I fed him."

"No." I summarized my frantic morning.

Cassa zipped up her case and tossed it into her backpack. "It could've been Coco. That kid was climbing before she was crawling."

"Maybe. Also, I might've agreed to play the ukulele in the talent show."

"You play ukulele?" asked Bijal, scribbling on his notebook to get his pen ink flowing.

"No. I'm supposed to do 'Rainbow Connection' with Dani, the cello prodigy."

"Oh." Cassa suppressed a smile and slid her eyes to Bijal. She grabbed his pen and picked the little plastic ball off the end. "Monroe can teach you."

"Yeah, how hard could it be?" said Bijal. "Even a puppet could play it."

I rested my head in my hands. What was it going to cost me to get another favor from Monroe? A date with Philippa this time?

That reminded me—I needed to look up what MEPS was.

According to my lunchtime computer search, MEPS either meant Military Entrance Processing Station or Malaysian Electronic Payment System. No way would my lazy sister enlist in the military. She made me answer the phone even if she was closer to it. But an electronic processing system—whatever that was—seemed just as unlikely.

The smell of snickerdoodles—Dad's favorite cookie—greeted me when I got home. I perked up. Mom must have felt bad about Lucky and maybe even forgetting Dad-iversary.

At the dining table, she was reading to Coco from *Tales from the Middle Kingdom*, which Dad had read aloud to Philippa and me when we were little. The book was open to Coco's favorite story, "The Cowherd and the Cloud Weaver," which was like "The Little Mermaid" except instead of mermaids, it featured cloud weavers who spun weather. And instead of King Triton, there was Mother Cloud Weaver.

"How was your first day?" Mom caught and hugged me as I headed toward the kitchen.

"Fine."

Coco slid off her chair and followed me. Flour dusted her solemn cheeks and the front of her yellow onesie. "No Lucky." She pointed Putty at our dish-drying rack, where a cleaned-out fishbowl and castle were all that remained of my fish.

"I'm sorry, kiddo," Mom called from her dining chair. "We searched your room. Lucky must have flipped out of the bowl, and, well, who knows."

I poured myself some milk and bit into a cookie. Dad always said snickerdoodles solved many problems.

But these tasted different—less butter-y and more bean-y. "Are these snickerdoodles?"

"Yes. Coco and I are going to a dinner playdate with Mabel in an hour. I made them allergy-free for her."

So she hadn't made them for Dad. Even the cookies here were all wrong. I tossed my half-eaten one down the disposal. I should've asked Mom how her interview went, but I was too annoyed. Anyway, she'd tell me if she got the job.

"Win-son, read." Coco pulled me back to the dining table.

While I glugged my milk, she pointed to an illustration of a young cloud weaver goddess standing in the middle of a lake. A talking ox was convincing a mortal cow herder to hide the cloud weaver's special rainbow dress until she agreed to marry him. That seemed shady, even though it all worked out in the end.

"Win-son, why did the cloud weaber marry the cowherder?"

Coco had never understood why someone who lived among rainbows and clouds and could conjure fog with her breath would want to marry a stinky human being.

"Because some people are just destined to get stuck with raw deals."

Mom sighed and stood up. "Winston, moping never solved anything. Would you be a good brother and finish the story while I take a shower?" She closed her bedroom door behind her.

Coco smacked her palm on a picture of the Milky Way with an arch of magpies flying over it. I summarized the rest of the story in one breath. "Mother Cloud Weaver created a giant river of stars between the heavens and earth to keep her daughter and the cowherd apart, but then she felt bad and ordered her magpies to form a bridge once a year so that the two could meet. The end."

"I build a bridge," Coco said. She hopped down from her chair and headed for the living room, where she had parked all her trucks.

I fetched my phone and called Mav. He answered on the first ring. People were yelling in the background.

"Hey, Mav. Everything okay?"

"Yeah. It's just . . . the TV. Status?"

I told him about Lucky.

"That's rough. Sorry about your fish. I know he meant a lot to you."

"Thanks." My throat began to close up, but I managed to say, "Is Monroe there? I need to ask him for a favor." I left it at that, not wanting to admit how foolish I'd been about Dani.

"Well, be careful," said Mav. "He drives a hard bargain."

"Yeah, I know."

"What's up, my man?" came Monroe's easy voice.

I got right to the point. "How long would it take you to teach me how to play 'The Rainbow Connection' on the ukulele for the talent show?"

"The good news is, there are only five chords. You could do it in a week if you practiced."

"And the bad news?"

"There's never bad news when it comes to ukuleles! She must be pretty special."

"She who?"

"Risking public humiliation by playing a song about rainbows? That has to be about a girl."

The picture of the fair cloud weaver in her rainbow dress caught my eye. "So what's it going to cost me?"

"Just tell me Philippa's favorite song."

I relaxed in my chair, relieved I'd gotten off so cheap. Now I just needed a uke. "It's 'Remember Me' from that movie *Coco*." Philippa was the one who had chosen our sister's name.

Speaking of, I looked around for Coco, but she wasn't in the living room.

"Uh, Monroe, let me call you back."

I hurried up the stairs.

"Coco? Where are you?" She could probably scale Mount Whitney by herself without a problem, but one of us was always supposed to keep an eye on her.

She wasn't in my room. But the door to my closet was open. I poked my head in. "Coco?"

All I saw were clothes and . . . I recoiled so fast, I nearly tripped on my feet. Behind my Jedi robe stood the broom and dustpan like two criminals hiding from the law. How the chickens had they returned?

They were definitely possessed by evil spirits. My mind flashed back to the arctic breeze I'd felt this morning when I opened the front door. Was that when the spirits had slipped inside? Had they needed someone to open the door for them?

Grabbing the broomstick, I throttled it where I figured the neck might be. "Why are you still here, and where's my goldfish, you creepy-sweepy?"

The wood remained cool in my grip, and I felt a little ridiculous. So what were these two hoodlums hoping to take this time?

Or had they already taken something?

My eye caught a beige scrap by the dustpan. Putty.

Feeling sick, I picked it up, sticking my finger into one of its ribbon loops. Coco took her blanky buddy everywhere with her. "Coco?" I called.

The door into Philippa's room opened slowly. Coco stood before me, her yellow fleece a bright spot framed by shadowy darkness. Relief washed over me.

"Hi, Win-ston."

That was strange. She never pronounced the *t* when saying my name. "Hey, Coco. What are you doing up here?"

A devilish grin walked up her rosy cheeks. "Exploring. Is that so wrong?"

The simple response sent tingles down my arms and legs. It wasn't just the grown-up words she'd used, it was the aloof way she'd said them. Even her voice was different—no longer cute and munchkin-like, but clear, like a young girl's.

"Are you feeling okay?"

"I feel fine." Coco's cheeks had lost their dimples. She blinked real slow . . . once, twice.

"You sound different."

She crossed her arms and lifted her chin. I couldn't remember her ever posing like that before. It made her look older. "I sound the same."

I tried to reason with myself. Coco *was* growing up. My seventh-grade health teacher had said the brain develops faster in the first five years than during any other time in life. It expands like a Froot Loop left in milk. Her vocal cords were bound to grow, too.

She glanced at Putty hanging loosely in my hand but didn't ask for it. An older voice was one thing, but not asking for Putty was extreme. She slow-blinked again—once, twice—triggering a memory. The china doll at Mr. Pang's had blinked the exact same way.

A siren began to wail inside my head. I gripped the carpet with my socked feet, feeling in danger of falling. I'd once seen a video of this guy who goes out onto his second-story deck, not realizing it had iced over, and spends at least fifteen seconds slipping and sliding and trying not to fall down the stairs. In that second, I felt like that guy.

The broom and dustpan had taken something all right. They had taken Coco.

CHAPTER 10

Suddenly, Mom was behind Coco. "Hey, kiddo, it's time to get dressed for Mabel's." Her amber eyes scanned the broom and dustpan. "What are those things, Winston?"

"Mr. Kowalski found them on a construction site." The lie neatly came to mind. Cassa's dad was a foreman. "Cassa knows we collect old things for Mr. Gu."

Mom picked up the broom while Coco watched with a disturbingly smug expression. "That was thoughtful of her."

My skin crawled as I watched Mom examine the evil bundle of sticks. What if she disappeared, too? "Don't touch that, Mom. It could be dirty."

She propped the broom against the wall and dusted off her hands. "Well, let's put them in a bag for the time being."

Like a bag could contain their wickedness. "Mom, Coco's acting weird."

"What do you mean?" Mom glanced down at the imposter, whose face had become all babyish smiles once again.

The kid lifted her arms toward me, wiggling her fingers. "Hug?"

A bit of drool was snaking down her chin. She looked like Coco again, but I hung back.

"Winston," Mom chided, "give your sister a hug."

I tentatively held out my arms, and she threw hers around my neck. Her fingers felt cold, almost clammy. "Mom, I think Coco's sick. Feel her skin."

Mom felt Coco's cheeks and forehead and shrugged. "I'll get the thermometer."

While Mom was gone, I squatted before Coco. "Do you feel sick?"

Coco's cheeks lost their dimples. Her eyes became cold again, like pools of dirty rainwater. Or was that my imagination running wild? "No, Winston. Do *you* feel sick?"

I did feel sick, but not the kind of sick that required a doctor. Mom returned with the digital thermometer and stuck it in Coco's ear. Coco held strangely still while we waited for the device to beep.

"Ninety-seven. A little low but still within normal." She watched Coco climb up onto my bed. "And she still has her energy. Come on, Coco, we need to get you dressed. Philippa will be home soon with the car."

While Mom led Coco back downstairs, I shut the doors to the closet and called Mav from my room, daggers of panic slashing at my insides. While the phone rang, I stuffed Putty in my sock drawer. Then I lined up my Soccer Legends bobbleheads on my dresser, which was a mistake, because now they were all shaking their heads at me. Mav answered.

"The broom and dustpan came back," I blurted.

"What?! How could they—"

"I think they took Coco. I can't be sure, but she's acting different, but only when Mom's not looking. It's like she got switched with someone else. Do you remember seeing a china doll about knee-high sitting on one of Mr. Pang's shelves? She had a porcelain face, hands, and feet, and she wore green pajamas."

"Yeah. Her name was Chang-Ah-Ling."

A chill ran over me, like a million baby spiders crawling over my skin. "Right."

"Stay cool. I'll rally the others. Monroe can drive us to your place. I'll tell him Philippa asked for him."

Footfalls and voices sounded from downstairs. Philippa had gotten home just in time to see Coco and Mom on their way out. And soon, to see Monroe.

"Do you have somewhere you can lock up the broom and dustpan so they can't get at any more stuff?" Mav asked. "An empty room or something?"

I snorted. Mav's house featured extra rooms within their rooms. "Gee, I don't know. Let me ask my butler."

"Okay, okay. Just hang tight. We'll be there in a nanosecond."

We hung up. I decided I could transfer the wicked wanderers to our laundry closet. I approached the pair cautiously, then snatched them up before I could change my mind. All I felt was cool wood. I hurried down the stairs.

The house was quiet except for the banging of our metal

spatula against the wok. Philippa was making fried rice, something we did to use up leftovers, even spaghetti. The slouchy sleeves of her sweatshirt waved like a bat ray's wings as she cooked, her hair held back by a black bandanna.

I crossed the kitchen and opened the laundry closet, rattling the full-length mirror on the back of one of the doors. Mah-mah had made Dad move the mirror from the guest room into this closet because it was bouncing away the qi in that room and preventing her from sleeping. After removing the laundry basket and the grocery tote, I stood the broom and dustpan next to the ironing board. As far as I was concerned, they could take that old board, which we never used anyway. "Don't go in there and don't touch those things," I told Philippa. "They're evil. I think they've been taking our stuff, like Babar."

She gave me the kind of look reserved for people who wear Bubble Wrap on their heads. "Why are you so weird?" Grabbing the wok handle, she expertly tossed the rice a few times.

"I'm serious! And that's not all. Coco's not acting like herself. I think she's someone else. She has this crazy look in her eye, and she talks different."

"She sounded the same to me."

"That's because she's trying to trick you into thinking she's Coco. Besides, I can prove it. Guess what she left behind?"

Philippa's eyes bobbed around the room. "I don't know. Why don't you just tell me?"

"Putty. She always takes Putty with her." I pulled the scrap from my pocket. That had to be an ace in the hole.

"Interesting. But maybe she's outgrowing it."

"Putty?! Putty is her buddy. You don't outgrow buddies. Did you outgrow Babar?"

From the fridge she pulled a bottle of chili sauce as wide as my calf and flipped it like a bartender. "Winston, what's going on with you?"

The story poured out. I told her everything, from the pie-ing of Bert to our objects disappearing. "It's not the same Coco, I'm telling you. I mean, she looks the same, but inside she's different."

She clamped the lid on the wok. "Winston, I know things have been hard since Dad passed, but it's time both of us move beyond it."

"What? This has nothing to do with Dad. You think I'm lying?"

"No. I'm saying that instead of accepting reality, you're escaping into fantasy."

My face felt hot. She was always trying to make me doubt myself. Even if I was wrong, could we really take that chance?

"You should talk," I spat back. "You're the one always escaping into your dopey romance novels."

"Maybe you should see Dr. Toy again. You liked her."

"This isn't about my mental health." I had nothing against the family therapist with the really high Minnie Mouse voice. We'd all gone to see her together after Dad's death. But every time we went, Mom had ended up crying, and I'd hated that.

"Maybe you're not the best judge. I'll talk to Mom—"

"You'd better not. Or . . ." The last thing I needed was for Mom to think I was having a breakdown. She had enough to worry about as it was. Plus, we couldn't afford to spend money on a problem whose answer had nothing to do with my sanity.

"Or what?"

"Or I'll have to tell Mom about your visit to the MEPS. Why'd you go there, huh?'

"You don't know what you're talking about."

"Sure I do," I said, banking on a fifty-fifty chance. "Military Entrance Processing Station. Are you going G.I. Jane on us?"

Her mouth became a cavern of stalactites dripping poison. "Have you been spying on me?"

The doorbell rang. I glared at my sister a moment longer before slogging toward the door.

"Hey."

Mav bustled in, his back hunched under the weight of his backpack, followed by Cassa, wearing flannel pajama pants and a sweatshirt, and Bijal in a tracksuit. Bijal lowered the hood of his jacket. "If anyone asks, we're writing pen pal letters to Tanzanian orphans. That's what I told my mom."

"That's strangely specific," said Cassa, watching Bijal line up his Vans. "Why couldn't you just say you're doing homework?"

"Rookie," he scoffed. "Homework assignments can be verified. Plus, this way she can humble-brag about me to her friends. I have to give her material."

A grinning Monroe brought up the rear, bearing two ukuleles. I wasn't sure how the guy managed to look so cool in basic jeans and a wrinkled plaid oxford. Maybe it was the way he'd rolled the sleeves to just below his elbows.

He stepped out of his sneakers. "I brought you your own practice ukulele, plus chord charts." He deposited the ukuleles in our living room, then handed me a sleek presentation folder.

"Wow, thanks."

Before I could even take the folder, Mav pulled it from Monroe's hands and set it on our glass coffee table. "Where are the goods?" he asked me in a low voice.

Philippa stuck her head out of the kitchen. "You didn't tell me we were having guests. It is dinnertime, you know."

"Smells great," said Monroe, making himself at home on our lumpy living room couch, which Mom covered in dark fabric to hide stains. "We'd love dinner."

"You two can go ahead," I told Philippa. "The rest of us aren't hungry yet."

"Winston, can I speak to you?" Philippa asked in a strained voice.

I followed her back to the kitchen, already anticipating her question. "He's here to give me a ukulele lesson," I said.

She drowned the fried rice in chili sauce. Like she needed the extra heat. "I see. And your friends are here for moral support?"

"They're here because the broom and dustpan took Coco." My anger flared like the gills of an iguana. "At least *they* believe me." I lifted my chin. My judgmental sister could go chug her chili sauce. "Guys," I called out to the living room, "in here."

Philippa filled her lungs, probably getting ready to smite me with her anger, but just then Monroe stepped into the kitchen with his easy smile. "Help you with that?"

With a grunt, Philippa doled out her rice, clanging her spatula against the wok like a drummer in the lion dance parade.

When she was finished blowing out our eardrums, Monroe carried two bowls to the dining room. Philippa stomped after him, as if the floor were on fire.

My friends crowded around as I opened the flimsy laundry closet door. My breath flew out of me. The ironing board stood there looking forlorn, the sole occupant of the shadowy space.

With a shiver, Bijal hugged himself. "Where'd they go? And why's it so cold in there?"

"They went invisible again," I said grimly, shivering, too.

Cassa took a step back and peered around as if trying to spot something. "Look!" she gasped, pointing to the mirror on the back of one of the closet doors. Reflected in it was a goddess-like figure in a flowing gown, and a short, plain man with a farmer's hat. They were the same two I'd seen in my bathroom mirror! Abruptly, the image vanished, along with the cold air.

"S-s-spirits?" Bijal grabbed Cassa's arm. "Those were spirits."

"I saw them before," I said. "On the day my soccer jersey went missing." I'd seen them somewhere else, too, though I couldn't remember where.

Cassa shook off Bijal's grip. "They might be just as scared of us as we are of them. How do we pin them down?"

"We can try to smoke them out." Mav set his backpack on the counter, riffled through it, and passed a cigar-size bundle of dried leaves to each of us. "I brought some of my mom's smudge sticks. She uses them in her yoga studio to drive away bad energy. Maybe we can do the same." He pulled out a foot-long gas lighter, like the kind we use to light the firepit. He ignited each bundle and, before I could protest about the fire hazard, blew them out.

A clean smoky smell drifted from the leaves. "Let's split up and search the house," said Mav. "If you feel a cold spot, holler."

Bijal and Cassa stayed downstairs, extinguishing any embers of conversation developing between Philippa and Monroe. Mav and I went up, trailing tendrils of gray smoke that I hoped wouldn't set off the fire alarm. I checked my closet first, then the bathroom, the linen closet, under Philippa's bed and behind her curtains, but didn't see a single bristle or feel any cold spots.

The place was beginning to smell like lasagna. My gaze fell to the book on Philippa's desk—*Tales from the Middle Kingdom*, which I'd last seen in the dining room. It was still open to the story about the cloud weaver and the cowherd. The goddess's long black hair and flowy rainbow dress spilled from the left page to the right, while the cowherd's plain form occupied a modest spot in the bottom right corner. Those were our spirits!

I slowly sank into Philippa's desk chair and yelled, "Gang! Up here!"

My teammates filed into the room.

"We didn't feel any cold spots, unless you count the area around Philippa," said Cassa. "Monroe's trying to warm her up."

As if she'd heard us, Philippa yelled up the stairs, "Winston, enough with the shamanism. You're stinking up the place!"

I showed my friends the book. "This is the couple we saw in the mirror."

Cassa flipped through the pages. "That's them all right. She was even wearing that hairpin." She pointed at a jeweled accessory in the cloud weaver's hair. I hadn't noticed.

Mav's *figuring it out* expression took shape on his face. "So, the cloud weaver and the cowherd are possessing the broom and the dustpan. But how? And why?"

Bijal used the smoke from his smudge stick to write his initials in the air. "And why are they so set on your things? No offense, Win, but it's not like your stuff is Gucci." Bijal rubbed his thumb against his fingers. "They should be stalking Mav instead."

"Very funny," Mav said. "I do have a Gucci wallet some-where, but I don't think that's what they're after."

"We need to talk to the spirits," said Cassa. "Find out what they want, then negotiate. Who knows? They might just want something simple."

Bijal's eyebows lifted, and he slowly nodded. "Yeah, like how Frankenstein's monster just wanted a friend."

"I don't need friends like that," I grumbled, catastrophic thoughts flooding my brain. What if they kept taking from me until there was nothing left? "You guys better go. It's not safe here. If they took Coco, they could take you, too."

Bijal started backing toward the stairs.

Cassa bumped me with her elbow. "We don't know Coco's gone for sure."

Mav collected the smudge sticks. "We'll strategize tomor-row. Don't worry, dude. We've got your back."

I nodded, too upset to speak.

Tomorrow. Tomorrow we'd sweep these spirits out of here and life would return to normal.

Right?

CHAPTER 11

It took both Philippa and Mom to wrestle Coco to bed that night, after a disastrous dinner playdate involving a hamster being set loose and Legos being thrown down the toilet, causing a minor flood. Everyone believed this was normal behavior for a toddler, but I doubted Coco would get an invitation back to Mabel's house.

Later, even though I was still annoyed with Philippa for not believing me, I padded into her room while she was settling into bed. "Can I sleep in here?"

"No." She twisted around, fluffing her many pillows, including the chubby one with the picture of a sloth and the emoji with the expressionless face. Her own face became a frowny emoji as she lifted her covers and looked underneath. Probably still searching for Babar.

"Come on. I'll be on the floor. You won't even notice me,"

I insisted. My eye caught on a MEPS brochure on her desk: *America Needs You.*

"Are you afraid to sleep by yourself?"

Yes, and you should be, too. "No. I just need a change of scenery."

She squinted at me. I wasn't fooling her, but if she pressed me, it might seem like she actually cared. And Coco had already wrung her out.

She set the alarm clock on her dresser, then tested it. Complicated piano music blared before she shut it off. She pulled her scrunchie out of her hair and turned on her side, her back to me. "Fine. But just for tonight."

I ran to get my pillow from my room and the sleeping bag from our hallway closet. Philippa switched off the light before I'd even finished unrolling my bed onto her plushy rug.

"Philippa?"

"Hmm?"

"Do you believe me about Coco now? She's not the same."

"She probably has another ear infection. She's always a brat when she has one of those."

I sighed, knowing I wouldn't be able to convince her right then. I'd have to be patient. Tomorrow I'd prove it to her, and she'd be sorry she ever doubted me. I changed gears. "Why'd you go to MEPS?"

The squeaking of bedsprings and the sound of a pillow being punched followed. After rolling around on her bed for at least a minute, she exhaled heavily. "If I tell you, you won't tell Mom?"

"Cross my heart and swear to eat snail pie."

She turned over, and her clear eyes shone down on me. "I wanted to find more information on Dad's buddy Vic Fisher."

Just hearing the name set my teeth on edge. I much preferred calling that sorry sack Ratface. He had robbed me of the most important guy in my life.

"Why the heck would you do that?" I growled.

"Because I need . . . I don't know. Closure."

Closure. It sounded so formal, and final. Ever since Dad's death, I'd felt as if I were falling down a hole. Sometimes, the hole was suffocating and narrow. Other times, it was wide and empty, but the falling part was always the same. If you closed off the hole, would you just stop being sad? That didn't seem right. I didn't want to forget about what Dad had meant to us.

My sleeping bag made slithery noises as I inched closer to her bed. "How would seeing Ratface make it any better?"

"I'm not sure, Winston. But I don't think it'll make it any worse."

I wanted to tell her that was a terrible reason, but her voice had grown small, like it had gotten tangled up in her hair.

"Does Mom know him?"

"No, and you're not going to say anything." Her tone had iced over, and she kicked up her sheet. "She's barely holding it together, if you hadn't noticed."

"I've noticed," I said defensively, though I hadn't realized it was so bad. Even more reason not to tell Mom the truth about the broom and the dustpan. "So, did you find him?"

"Not yet. But they gave me his address."

"They just *gave* it to you?"

She flopped onto her back again. "I showed them Dad's dog tag and told them why I wanted to find him."

I snorted. "Let me guess. A *guy* waited on you." I didn't get why, but the moray could turn heads when she wanted to.

"Vic was discharged after Dad died, and now he lives in Lodi, near Stockton. I'm paying him a visit on Wednesday."

Stockton? We'd played a soccer tournament there last year. The trip had taken half a day. "Can't you just call him?"

"I tried, but his phone was disconnected."

I didn't know how I felt about Philippa driving out to the middle of nowhere to visit a guy we didn't know. Maybe I *should* tell Mom just to stop Philippa from going. Then again, he'd been Dad's buddy, which meant Dad had trusted him. Also, underneath those messy tresses, Philippa was really a moray at heart. Thanks to the Wushu martial arts classes she'd taken before Dad died, she could move with lightning-like speed and paralyze her prey if needed.

Philippa started snoring. The noise reassured me. I may have had a broom and dustpan trying to ruin my life, but as long as my sister snored beside me, I had half a chance

* 茉 · 茉 · 茉 *

My alarm clock began to beep from where I'd put it next to my pillow, and I shut it off. Philippa's snores reminded me where I was. Slithering out of my bedroll, I glanced around for the broom and dustpan. At least they hadn't killed us in our sleep.

And Philippa was still there, lying under a mountain of pillows.

Unlocking her closet door, I cautiously opened it. Gray light trickled in, falling on the closed door to my bedroom. I felt for the light switch. But before I turned it on, I saw them. The felonious cleaning tools with the sticky fingers. They were lurking behind Philippa's ratty bathrobe! Quickly, quietly, I closed the door. I had caught them!

But now what?

I needed to tell Philippa not to open the door until I could figure out how to stick it to *them*. "Philippa," I whispered urgently, nudging her.

The mountain began to break apart, like a volcano erupting. She opened a baleful eye and stared at me through tangles of hair. "Why, Winston, why?" she uttered, though to my ears it sounded more like *Die, Winston, die.*

"The broom and the dustpan are in the closet," I continued whispering. It had occurred to me that the spirits might be sleeping, and that's why the tools had become visible again.

"Your breath is killing me. Go away."

"This is important! Don't open the closet doors. You have to promise."

"So you want me to go to work wearing pajamas."

"You can wear something from my dresser."

She growled, and the other eye opened. I backed away in case lava started shooting from her red orbs.

"Athletic shorts and *Star Wars* T-shirts aren't exactly my vibe."

"I'm begging you. Please just stay out of the closet for one day, okay?"

She didn't answer me, but there wasn't much I could do. Before leaving for school, I twisted the privacy lock on both sides of the closet. For extra measure, I wedged two of Coco's triangular rubber blocks under each closet door. Sure, the spirits had returned from the ocean, so you'd think getting through doors would be a snap. But nothing about the pair was logical, and I wasn't taking chances.

* ✳ · ✳ · ✳ *

At least it wasn't raining.

By the time I rolled into homeroom, the class was already streaming out.

Dani, packing up her pencils, gave me a little wave. Even though it was August, she was dressed in a Valentine's Day theme—a red sweatshirt with black and white hearts and a red headband.

I brought my late slip to Mr. Bottoms, who nodded at me. "Morning, Winston."

I couldn't stop staring at the man's upper lip. He had shaved off his mustache. But there was no white spot marking the place it had occupied. "Everything okay?" said his mouth.

"Yes, just got off to a late start."

"Winston?"

Behind me, Dani was hugging her backpack, with Yasmine, a popular girl, standing beside her. "Are we still on for practice this afternoon?"

"Actually, I can't. I injured . . . my hand." At least that excuse would hold for a few days.

Her mouth became a red Life Saver. "Sorry to hear that. How?"

"Uh, lifting . . . weights."

She glanced at my skinny arms. Yasmine barked out a laugh, stroking her black braid like a snake. My face began to sizzle like an egg hitting the pan.

"Nothing I can't handle," I grunted, struck with the urge to come off as manly as possible. Yasmine rolled her eyes to the holey ceiling tiles.

"I hope you can rest it." Dani's nose scrunched as she peered at my right hand, which I was using to pull at my face. Her eyes shifted to my left hand, which was grasping my backpack, probably weighing which one was injured.

Before the conversation grew more elbows, I hefted my pack over my shoulder. Surely the spirits' mischief-making couldn't follow me all the way to school? Yet somehow, I was leaving the room with more problems than when I'd entered.

CHAPTER 12

The McFees' Tesla was already waiting in our driveway when the school bus dropped Cassa, Bijal, and me at the stop across from my house. Mav exited his sleek navy ride. He was seriously out of uniform, in a camouflage shirt and bright orange track pants.

But I had more important things on my mind than his clothing violations. Mainly, the violators in my closet. Mav's mom, talking on her cell phone, waved at us distractedly, then glided away.

Once we were inside, Bijal kept on his backpack and shoes and stared nervously up the stairs to my bedroom. Cassa threw her sweatshirt on a wall hook. Mav slung off his silver pack and rubbed his hands together. "We need a game plan."

I clenched my fists. "The game plan is, I grab 'em and you

start to roast them with the lighter until they tell us where Coco went."

"Too many variables. Like, they could turn invisible before you catch them."

"And then knock you on the side of the head," Bijal muttered, finally stepping out of his Vans.

"Or set the house on fire," offered Cassa.

Mav headed into the living room and plopped down on the carpet. We all settled around him. "I say we start with a more peaceful approach. In Conflict Resolution class, we learned that getting what you want starts with understanding what the other party needs. Let's go over what we know about them. Win, you go first."

I pulled at my knees, itching to get a move on. "You all read the story. The cloud weaver spins weather with her sisters and their controlling mother. The cowherd is your everyday simp who she's only allowed to see once a year. I'm not sure why they're down here."

"To be together?" Cassa guessed.

Mav put his finger on the bridge of his nose, an old habit from when he used to wear glasses. "What happens to the team when we're down a man?"

Cassa snorted. "Or down a *woman*. The team tries to compensate, but it's an upstream paddle."

"Exactly. Maybe that's the reason we've been having such bad weather lately. Heaven's out of sync."

Bijal was stretching a floppy purple strip—one of his tying balloons. "Bet Mother Cloud Weaver is having kittens about now."

"*I'm* having kittens right now," I muttered, slapping the

floor. Though being haunted by spirits was creepy, I was more ticked off than anything, and anger was more powerful than fear. As anyone who has watched *Star Wars* knows, anger gets the job done . . . at least until you start losing body parts. "What we need is a way to contain them so I can threaten to dump them off the bridge if they don't give back Coco."

"You tried that already," said Bijal. "I think they can swim. Besides, how do you catch something that's invisible?" He began blowing up his balloon.

"Air is invisible," I said, thinking out loud. "But if you put it in a balloon, it suddenly has a shape."

The balloon slipped from Bijal's fingers and shot away with a loud *thppbt*. "You want to put the broom and dustpan into a balloon?"

"Not exactly . . ."

Cassa slapped her knees. "We could cover them with something!"

I nodded.

"Like a blanket?" said Mav. "That actually might work."

"Then let's get this over with." Jumping to my feet, I led the others up the stairs like a sheriff leading his deputies to confront Bonnie and Clyde.

We huddled next to Philippa's closet door.

Mav knocked on it, two sharp raps. "Hey, Cloud Weaver, Cowherd. We know you're in there, and we know you took Coco."

"And Lucky, and Babar, and my jersey," I growled.

Mav held up a hand, meaning *stay cool*. "Winston thinks we should keep you locked in there till you rot."

Philippa would never let me, but they didn't know that.

"But I told him we should give you a chance. Give back Coco—"

"And Lucky," I added.

"And Lucky, and get the Hello Kitty out of his life, and he might be willing to let bygones be bygones."

"What if they don't speak English?" Cassa whispered.

Mav scratched his head, then spoke a few words in Mandarin. He'd been taking lessons since sixth grade. "I said, 'Give back little sister and good-luck fish, or bad times.'"

We put our ears to the door. Mav's peanut butter breath blew out at me from a few inches away. I could feel my grimace deepening as the seconds ticked by.

At last, we heard a faint female voice. "She is in Mr. Pang's shop," she said in perfect English. "Her spirit is in the changeling's body."

Cassa's green eyes became moons, and Bijal clapped his hand to his mouth. Mav rolled the word *changeling* over his tongue, as if trying it on for size. A confused look spread over his face.

"The last we saw her, she was alive and well," the voice continued, louder now. "It was never our intention for her to pass through."

"*Pass through?* What's that supposed to mean?" It sounded dangerously close to *pass on*, which was how people talked about Dad, as if he'd refused a second helping of noodles or something.

"Maybe she went through some sort of portal," Mav suggested.

"Shh! Don't tell them any more," came a gruff man's voice.

"How do we get her back?" I cried, and when again no answer came, I added, "Where's the portal?" Silence. "What do you want from us?" More silence.

Mav showed us his watch—3:42—then flashed us five fingers. I gave him a thumbs-up. While he stayed in Philippa's room, Bijal, Cassa, and I tiptoed to my room, very gently closing the door behind us. I removed the Iron Man comforter from my bed. Cassa took one end of the cover while Bijal took the other. Creeping over to the closet, I shook out my hands, the way I did before playing *ZI*. Slowly, I untwisted the privacy lock, then removed the wedge from under the door. I wiped my sweating palm on my pants, then carefully wrapped a hand around the doorknob.

My alarm clock read 3:46. One more minute.

At exactly 3:47, we heard Mav rap twice on his side of the closet. Bijal and Cassa, standing behind me, lifted the comforter, looking as determined as a pair of goalies. They weren't going to let anything through their "net."

"Looks like you want to do this the hard way," said Mav, his voice muffled on the other end of the closet. The broom and dustpan would expect us to enter from *his* side, where I had seen them last. At least, I hoped so. "Fine. We're going in on the count of three, and we're done being nice. One . . . two . . . three."

I opened my side of the closet, scanning hard for the troublemakers. As I'd expected, they had turned invisible, but a blast of cold air revealed their presence. "They're coming out!"

Cassa and Bijal unleashed a battle cry, tackling the cold breeze with the comforter.

"We got 'em, we got 'em!" Bijal stretched himself over the duvet, pinning it down with his hands and knees. Cassa did the same on her side. Something jumped underneath, and Cassa dove over it like a baseball player sliding home.

Another cold breeze hit me, and I grabbed at it, but my hands clutched at nothing. "I don't think you got both of them!"

"What's going on in there?" Mav yelled from the other side of the closet.

"We got the dustpan, I think," grunted Cassa. "The broom got away!"

I ran around feeling for cold spots, but the room was overheated now from all our activity. And there was no visual sign of the broom anywhere—not a single splinter. Would the cloud weaver leave the cowherd by himself? If not, she might still be here, lying low.

"I'm coming in." A second later, Mav barreled through the closet, a wild look in his eyes as he assessed us—me waving my arms around, and Cassa and Bijal playing a weird game of Twister on my comforter.

"Now what do we do?" asked Bijal.

I eyed my soccer bag, which I'd thrown on a chair. "Let's put it in there."

I emptied the bag of my ball and shin guards. While I held it open, Cassa and Bijal scooted around and bunched up the comforter until a wooden handle peeked out.

"I can see it now!" cried Cassa.

"Get it!" Bijal screamed.

Feeling oddly like we were helping my comforter give birth to a dustpan baby, I pulled out the squirmy thing, stuffed it into my bag, and tugged the zipper closed. The cursed object thrashed around like a caged animal. Through the mesh flap, I could make out its silvery surface. "Tell me how to get my sister back or I'll feed you to the nearest wood chipper."

The dustpan went still.

Mav punched his palm. "I say we light it up in your firepit. It's closer, and this is an emergency."

I didn't want to leave my room in case Cloud Weaver was lurking nearby. Then again, maybe she would show herself if her husband was in trouble. . . .

Carrying my soccer bag, I led the way downstairs into the kitchen, stopping to get the lighter from our utensils drawer.

"Are you really going to destroy it?" Cassa asked from behind me. "It—he—might have valuable information."

"It's up to the cowherd," I answered in a loud voice. "Cooperate or incinerate."

Mav, Cassa, and Bijal fetched their shoes. I kept a pair of old boots by the door that led from our kitchen to the patio. Mom had surrounded the concrete square with vegetable plants in assorted pots and containers. My friends followed me down the back stairs.

Cassa held my soccer bag while I unzipped it just enough to get my hand in. Taking a firm grip on the dustpan handle, I removed it from the bag and dangled it over the firepit at the center of the patio.

Behind me, Mav clicked the lighter a few times. "Old wood is the best for fires."

"Last chance. Talk now or it's ashes to ashes." Last week, I would've felt like an idiot for threatening a cleaning tool. But now I was ready to toast this dustpan man.

Suddenly, a hot jag of lightning illuminated the sky, striking the street behind our house with a loud *craaack!* With a scream, I dropped the dustpan on the ground and grabbed my ears, bright streaks searing my vision. Thunder answered, as loud as if pumped through a pair of twenty-inch subwoofers right by my ear. Rain came pouring down.

"The sky's attacking us!" screamed Bijal.

The dustpan came alive again. Moving like a giant click beetle, it flipped and clattered its way across the concrete toward an empty barrel-size pot lying on its side.

"Get back inside, everyone! Go, go!" Mav cried.

Lightning flashed again, this time striking the patio. My soccer bag, sitting between the firepit and the pot, instantly caught on fire.

Mav pulled me away by my shirt, and we ran up the back stairs. Cassa yanked open the door, and we all tumbled into the kitchen. But before I could close the door, a cold breeze from inside the house blew past me into the yard.

"Did you feel that?" I asked the others.

"Shut the door!" Bijal screamed.

"But that could've been the cloud weave—" I started.

Another lightning bolt hit the patio. And another. I slammed the door and locked it for good measure. We crowded around the window above the kitchen sink, which gave a full view of the backyard. But the dustpan was too deep inside the pot to see.

The lightning struck on all sides of the container. "It's like it knows the dustpan's in there," Mav murmured.

Bijal nearly knocked over a glass. "Yeah, it's going to fry it."

Even though the dustpan was a thieving miscreant who was losing me health points, I wasn't ready for it to be zapped out of existence. I still needed to know how to get Coco back. And if the cloud weaver had escaped, who else could help us?

"Your mom's going to rage," cried Bijal. "Look at all her plants!"

The backyard, once a cheerful collection of everything from tall cornstalks to purple hydrangeas, now looked like a witch's kitchen full of burning cauldrons.

"And your soccer bag." Cassa pointed to the smoking mess.

"Guys, the dustpan!" Mav craned his neck further.

The wooden tool had begun to scrabble out of its terra-cotta refuge. Another gnarly bolt fell, spearing the cracked pot, and we all grabbed our ears. As thunder roared, the pot split open like two halves of a melon. And when the smoke cleared, the dustpan had vanished.

CHAPTER 13

Bijal walked in a tight circle around our living room. "That dustpan is dust. It's gone. Poof."

After the lightning smoked the dustpan, the storm had shut off abruptly, like someone had turned a spigot, leaving only a drizzle that had doused the plant fires. We'd gone outside to search for the broom but came up empty. We'd have to figure out how to find Coco on our own.

Cassa, on one end of our couch, pulled a Pocky stick from its bright red box and threw the container to Mav on the other end. "We didn't even see it go up in smoke—it just . . . disappeared."

Mav nodded. "You know, every time we've had the broom and dustpan outside, there's been a storm." He joined me by the living room window to look out onto the street. The rain had gotten heavier, but there was no more lightning. He slid a few Pocky from the box, then passed the rest to me.

"It must be the cloud weavers," I said. "They control the weather, after all. But I don't get it. Why would they want to take out the cowherd?"

"There could be lots of reasons," Cassa said from the couch. "Maybe they don't like him. They might think he's not treating their sister the way she deserves. Or maybe they just think she could do better."

"He only gets to see her once a year," said Bijal, still pacing. "Maybe *he* could do better." After nearly tripping on one of Coco's trucks, he parked it under the coffee table.

"When I felt that cold breeze pass by, I think the broom spirit was going out there to save him," I said, rubbing the goose bumps that had suddenly sprung up on my arms. "I think *that's* why the dustpan just disappeared—she turned him invisible."

"Why didn't he just turn invisible himself?" asked Mav.

"She's a goddess, the one with the power," I said. "He's just a boring ole human."

The rest of us boring ole humans stood crunching our Pockys as we considered the possibility.

Mav's nose scrunched. "That night we dumped the broom and dustpan off the pier . . . she didn't make him invisible then."

"We were holding them separately," I said, remembering. "Maybe they have to be touching. You know, like in Harry Potter—you have to be under the invisibility cloak to disappear.

"And speaking of disappearing, we need to get moving if we

want to save Coco." I dropped onto the carpet, and the others planted themselves around me. "The cloud weaver said she's in the changeling's body. I think she meant that doll we saw, Chang-Ah-Ling."

"I don't like the sound of that," said Bijal, gathering his knees to him.

Mav pulled at his sleeves. "We studied changelings in Monsters and Mythology class. Fairies sometimes steal human children in the middle of the night and replace them with fakes. Changelings aren't human, and they don't have real human emotions."

"So that's why this Coco is *not* Coco," I said. "I knew it!"

Bijal's crossed legs began to butterfly up and down until Cassa shoved his knee.

Mav went on. "We watched this movie where a couple received a changeling baby. They started realizing something was wrong when the baby's eyes glowed in the dark. And then it had this ravenous appetite even though they were constantly feeding it." His voice fell to a hush. "One day, they woke up and found it eating their pets."

Mav's phone honked. We all jumped as if a pack of rubber-glove-wearing Zubber Zombies had just descended upon us, the fiercest kind. Their gloves squeak when they tear you limb from limb. He checked his screen.

"So, how do you switch out a changeling?" Cassa asked in a low voice.

"I don't know exactly," Mav whispered back, though I wasn't sure why we were being so quiet. "But I remember they hate eggshells. Anyway, gotta go. My mom's waiting downstairs."

He looked at Cassa and Bijal. "She can drop you at your places, if you want."

My friends gathered their things, their faces somber as funeral lilies.

"But what about Coco?" I asked, my voice rising. "I can't just leave her in Mr. Pang's shop!"

Mav bumped me with his shoulder. "Hang tight. If Coco's there, my dad might be able to get us in tomorrow." Mav's real estate mogul of a father got the McFees access to all sorts of weird stuff, like the underground bootlegging tunnels of San Francisco. "In the meantime, I'm sure she's not feeling any pain."

My teeth clenched as I pictured my little sister as a frozen doll on a shelf full of bizarre knickknacks. What had we done to deserve all this?

No cold breeze tried to enter when I opened the door to let out my friends. That should have been a good thing, but now that Coco was in trouble, I *wanted* the spirits to return. They were the key to rescuing her. The cloud weaver had coughed up some information, and I was sure she had more. I kept the door propped open with a shoe.

After everyone left, the house seemed eerily quiet. I made as much noise as possible cracking eggs into a bowl and setting the shells into the plastic tub Mom used for compost. We'd see if changelings didn't like eggshells. Mom's laptop was on the table, and even though she didn't want me to use it, I opened it and searched for *how to get rid of changelings.*

All sorts of wacky results came up, from bathing them in holy water to putting them in the oven. No way was I going to put Coco's body in an oven, and I didn't know where you got holy water.

Philippa and Mom blew through the front door, arguing.

Mom's eyes skimmed over me guiltily closing her laptop. "But Lodi's two hours away," said Mom. "Winston, why was this door open?"

I joined them in the living room. "It was stuffy in here."

"Weren't you just telling me I need to be more proactive about my life?" Philippa tugged off Coco's shoes and wrestled her out of her jacket. I approached Coco carefully, the way you'd move toward a strange dog.

Mom stepped out of her heels and ran a hand through her hair. "Who exactly are you meeting?"

"A possible job contact. I don't want to jinx it by talking about it. Just relax." Philippa cracked her neck to one side.

I coughed. *Just relax* is exactly the wrong thing to say when you want someone to calm down.

Hearing me walk up behind her, Coco turned around. She was sucking her thumb, the pinkie sticking out like it always did. A puff of doubt fogged my mind, strong as a stinkbug fart. Maybe this had all been a mistake. Maybe she'd had an ear infection like Philippa said and was now back to normal. I waited for her to ask for Putty, which I'd stuffed into my sock drawer.

A thin smile spread across Mom's face. "I'm sorry, Philippa, but you can't use the car," she said lightly. She always kept it classy, even when Philippa or I behaved like a wrestler on WrestleMania, barking threats into a live camera. "The law firm called me back for a second interview tomorrow."

"That's great, Mom!" I said, though anger spiked through me. Lucky should have been here to celebrate this small victory.

"Yeah, congrats," added Philippa. "But . . . can't you take the train?"

"Why should I take the train when I have a perfectly good working automobile?" Mom was cool as a gambler with a royal flush, waiting to play her hand. "One that *I* pay for."

Philippa's lips became a sharp beak, hard enough to crack open walnuts. She stormed upstairs, her elephantine stomps multiplying into what sounded like a herd of elephants.

Mom sighed, focusing on me as if only now realizing I was there. She looked me square in the face, her eyebrows shaped like tiny boomerangs. "Hi, honey. I don't want you using this laptop. I have some important writing samples on it I need to send to the firm."

"Sorry."

"It's okay. How are you?"

I glanced at Coco, still innocently sucking her thumb as she looked at me. For a moment, I was tempted to try to convince Mom that I hadn't been lying about our things being stolen, including—maybe—Coco. But I doubted she was ready to hear the truth. She'd think I was having a mental breakdown and send me back to Dr. Toy.

"I'm fine, but the garden's not. The lightning killed all your plants."

"Lightning? There was *lightning* here?"

She crossed to the kitchen and peered out the window, but our dim outside light only illuminated a thick fog. "I'm glad you weren't out in it." She hugged me. "The weather's been something else lately. You haven't been skateboarding to school, have you?"

"Well . . . I won't tomorrow."

She began setting our empty cups in the dishwasher. "Oh, I wanted to ask you . . ."

I braced myself. Had she noticed that Coco was different? Had something else been stolen?

"Philippa said you're taking ukulele lessons?" she asked.

I sucked in my breath. I'd completely forgotten about my promise to Dani. Mom had stopped loading the dishwasher and was watching me.

I shrugged. "Monroe's teaching me."

"I think that's great. A much better use of your time than that zombie game."

I just nodded. If only she knew that we might be living with a real monster. I side-eyed my little sister. "I'll get Coco her milk."

"Thanks," said Mom. "I need to change." She walked down the hall to her bedroom.

I led Coco to the kitchen and removed the milk from the refrigerator. She watched me with her big eyes. *Please ask me to warm it. Please be Coco.*

She popped her thumb out of her mouth and pointed at the carton. "I want that."

Goose pimples prickled my skin. The addition of the single letter to her usual *want that* was like a heavy book that threatened to upend a crooked shelf. I set the milk on the counter.

"*How* do you want it?" I asked.

"I don't like you, Winston," she said in the too-grown-up voice.

It hadn't been a mistake. This was not Coco.

"I don't like you either, *Chang-Ah-Ling.*" I grabbed the plastic tub with the eggshells and shoved it at her.

Instead of shrinking away, she reached in and pulled out the still-drippy shells. She crunched them in her fist and laughed, which pulled all her dimples into one maniacal expression. Seeing my sister's face so twisted sucker-punched me right in the solar plexus. Poor Coco was somewhere lost and alone, and it was my fault. I'd wished to go back three years ago to when Dad was still alive, even if it meant Coco was out of the picture. I'd wanted it so bad, and now I was paying for that wish. "Tell me what you did with Coco, you fake!"

At the sound of Mom's bedroom door opening, Not-Coco's zombie scythe of a smile evaporated and she began to whine, a sound that quickly morphed into wails. This was definitely not how Coco cried, with no silent-scream buildup.

Mom ducked into the kitchen, eyes widening at the sight of Not-Coco, who had gooey eggshell shards all over her clothes. "What's going on?"

"Winston gave me eggs!" Not-Coco yowled in a shaky voice.

I hastily cleaned the mess on the floor. Mom brought Not-Coco to the sink and threw me a grimace. "What's come over you? I thought you were getting her milk."

"But she . . . But I—"

Mom raised an eyebrow, shutting off my protests. I groaned. Not-Coco was clever, only revealing her true nature to me when no one else was around. Mom wasn't going to believe she was a changeling without some serious proof. Until I figured out how to get it, I needed to play along.

I rattled through my evening routine of dinner and homework, my mind a shaken barrel of plastic monkeys. The biggest monkey was, how was I going to get the real Coco back?

I considered calling the police. But what would I say? *Good evening, Officer. My sister was abducted by a couple of spirits, put into the body of a doll, and replaced by a changeling.* Yeah, that would work. And if they *did* come check our house and Not-Coco started making trouble, they might call Child Protective Services and arrest Mom for child endangerment. There was no way I could get the police involved.

Dad would've known what to do. He was good at problem solving, like using duct tape to open stuck lids, or PVC pipes to organize plastic bags and store knives. If Dad were here, that broom and dustpan wouldn't dare mess with us.

Philippa closed her door loudly, making the walls rattle. She'd barely spoken a word during dinner, obviously still mad at Mom about the car.

I shut off my laptop. Before going up to bed, I joined Mom as she watched the ten o'clock news. The camera cycled through shots of our lightning-zapped neighborhood as well as localized flooding that was afflicting homes and businesses.

"The forecast is sunny and clear through next week," said the meteorologist. She winked one set of her fake eyelashes. "But I would bring an umbrella, just in case."

I hopped onto the couch, making Mom bounce. "Congratulations on your second interview. That must mean they're really interested."

"Thanks, honey. I hope so."

I tried to think of a good segue but couldn't. "So, I think . . . maybe you should let Philippa take the car tomorrow."

She tucked a leg under her and angled herself toward me, her expression bemused as light from the television danced on her pupils. "You do?"

"Yes. She's going through a lot right now, and you need to give her some slack."

I wasn't sure why I was getting involved in this. Maybe it was because I'd already lost one sister. Though I wasn't crazy about Philippa's plan to see Vic, I was glad she'd told me about it, at least. I didn't need another sister going rogue right now.

"What do you mean by 'a lot'?"

"I'm not at liberty to say. But sometimes we just have to trust each other, you know? She is nineteen, after all."

Her expression shifted, as if she suspected the statement might be self-serving, which I guess it was. But it was also true. I sighed, questioning the wisdom of bringing it up at all. I had awakened the paralegal in her, and she'd grill me until I confessed to a crime I hadn't committed. Maybe even serve time, too, by cleaning the oven out with a toothbrush or polishing the chrome surfaces with Vaseline like she makes us do every few months, even though we don't know why.

But instead of going on high alert, her face softened. "You are my light, Winston, helping me see clearly." She ran a finger through my hair. "I'm glad your sister can talk to you. Sometimes I feel like I can't be there for her as much as she needs me to be." She clasped her hands as if holding coins that she didn't want to drop. "I'm sorry. I shouldn't burden you with this."

"It's okay, Mom." Who else could she talk to? For the first time, I realized that Mom was lonely. She had all of us, but she never got to hang out with friends, never went out for boba or played sports. There wasn't time, not with all of us to look after, her temp jobs, and her looking for a real job.

No, I would definitely not be burdening her with the worry that I might be coming unhinged. As the man of the house—or at least the only one with a Y chromosome—I had to figure this out on my own. Mom had enough on her plate. She had a demon toddler to manage, for clam's bake. As for Philippa, moray eels might be dangerous on the outside, but on the inside they were gooey as snails. Nope, my job was to keep any more zombies or bewitched baddies from getting into our place, before everything went completely gof.

I hope you bought a parachute, Mr. Pang, because tomorrow, you're going down.

CHAPTER 14

Mom and Not-Coco were gone by the time I stumbled out of my room the next morning, looking around for signs of mayhem. Everything seemed surprisingly normal, which worried me even more. Not-Coco was definitely going to be hard to catch in the act.

I checked all the closets and found no broom or dustpan, either.

My phone chimed.

Mav: Dad got us meeting w building owner @ 3:30

Me: Cool CU

I couldn't wait to learn what the building owner knew about Mr. Pang's Whimsies. Maybe Mr. Pang himself would be there this time. I just needed to get this school day over with.

When I set out to catch the bus, the sky was swimming-pool blue and as bright as hope. The weather was getting to be as moody as Philippa. At least her stormy episodes were predictable. The cloud weaver and the cowherd must still be invisible, or they'd found a good spot to hide, maybe in someone else's house for a change. Even so, I had a feeling I hadn't seen the last of them.

In homeroom, I slunk into my chair.

Dani glanced over at me quizzically from where Yasmine was reading her palm, and I realized I was wearing my WOOKIEE POWER T-shirt inside out. My face warmed. I wasn't sure why I cared so much about this girl's opinion of me when I had far more important things to worry about. Yet, even in the face of mortal peril, I wished I'd had time to practice my borrowed uke yesterday.

Finally, Dani faced front, her ocean-blue dress falling in waves to the floor. I silently worked out how to say *How are you?* in the coolest way possible. *How's it going?* would do the job. Or a casual *What's up?*, or even a *Hey*.

Feeling me staring at her, she looked over. "How's the hand?"

"Uh . . ." *Great. She must think I have the social skills of a pink eraser.* "It's okay," I said, feigning toughness over my nonexistent injury. "Thanks for asking. What's the holiday?"

"The holiday?"

"Um, your outfit. I've noticed you dress in holiday colors." I wanted to bite my tongue. *If she didn't think I was a creeper before, she definitely thinks so now.*

"Oh, my *theme*. Today, it's 'beach vacation.'"

Mr. Bottoms clapped twice. "Before I read the announcements, I've got exciting news. Our local cable news station has informed us that they will be covering *San Francisco's Got Talent*! Dani and Winston, you two will be famous."

The class erupted in excited chatter. Dani snuck a look at me, her fist shaking triumphantly. Wonderful. Like it wasn't enough for the whole school to witness my epic fail. Now the whole city could be in on the joke, too.

Dani flashed a red carpet smile. "Thanks, Mr. Bottoms. We'll do our best."

"Thanks," I mumbled. Best or worst, it was all going to be about the same.

⁑ ❋ · ❋ · ❋ ⁂

When Cassa and Bijal and I arrived at the corner of Jackson and Kearny, Mav was already there, talking to a bald Indian man in a purple tracksuit holding a FOR RENT sign. Though I'd half expected it, I was still disappointed to find the door next to Boba Guys back to its dusty black and rectangular form.

"Hey, guys, this is Mr. Suresh." Mav introduced us all. "He remembers the fire in this unit when it was Dream Castle, the toy store."

Mr. Suresh nodded. He was a senior with a thick brown mustache that was at odds with his white eyebrows. In fact, the mustache looked eerily familiar. With rolled tips, it was the spitting image of the one my homeroom teacher Mr. Bottoms had shaved off. "Yes, that was in 1979, the year before I bought the building." His lightly accented words came out in a fast clip.

"How did the fire start?" I asked.

"The cause was found to be a random lightning strike."

My friends and I eyed each other. The strikes we'd experienced yesterday had seemed anything but random.

"I got it for a good rate—a fire sale, as they call it. I'd hoped Mr. Pang would continue his store after I renovated it, but the man was ready to retire."

"Is this him?" Cassa showed him the obituary of Mr. Ross Pang on her phone.

"Yes, that's him. I didn't realize he had passed." Mr. Suresh rubbed his scalp. "Such a shame."

The man's mustache had an animated quality to it, like a tiny crow about to launch itself. Maybe it was a stick-on mustache that Mr. Bottoms and Mr. Suresh had bought at the same store. Or maybe . . .

Bijal stopped fidgeting with his umbrella and pulled me aside. "Why do you keep looking at that man's lips?" he hissed in my ear.

I whispered back, "Remember when the magpie knocked stuff off the shelf? There was this mustache—"

"Mischief Mustache?" Bijal's eyes swiveled to Mr. Suresh's upper lip and widened.

Cassa gave us a questioning look. Bijal whispered to her, and her gaze also traveled to Mr. Suresh's facial hair.

Mav elbowed me with a stare that said *Focus, people.* "How long has this space been unoccupied?" he asked the landlord.

"Well, we had a couple tenants—corner lots are always in demand—but they never lasted more than a few months." His eyes shifted right and left before he added, "One claimed the place was haunted. Probably just angling for a discount in rent."

"No shirt it's haunted," Bijal muttered, stepping back from the window.

"Another tenant even tried to sue me for emotional distress. The nerve." Mr. Suresh tsked before he remembered who he was talking to. "Uh, do you think your father might be interested in the space?" he asked Mav.

At that moment, a whip crack of thunder made us all jump. Before Bijal could even get his umbrella open, it was pouring. Were the cloud weaver and cowherd on the lam from the family again? I peered around us suspiciously.

"Let's get inside." Mr. Suresh unlocked the door and pulled it open by its brass handle.

The space looked nothing like Mr. Pang's Whimsies. It was completely empty, measured about forty by sixty feet, and smelled musty, like an old basement. Mr. Suresh flipped a switch and recessed lighting shone off a continuous slab of mottled concrete under our feet. A second door occupied the far corner.

"Do you think the broom and dustpan spirits are somewhere around here?" Mav whispered to me.

"I don't know, but that thunder sounded awful close," I said.

Mr. Suresh crossed to a dent in the wall that had been painted over but not repaired. "See here? A tenant threw a chair. He said he was attacked by a grizzly bear, if you can believe that. I think it's more likely he was wearing beer goggles."

We gathered near the dent.

"There was a stuffed bear in Mr. Pang's shop," I said, remembering.

Mav rubbed his chin. "Yeah, it was called the Were-Bear."

"As in 'werewolf'?" Bijal hugged his umbrella.

I sucked in my breath. "Maybe it comes alive on the full moon."

Mav checked his watch. "That's in five days." He glanced back at Mr. Suresh, who was fitting his FOR RENT sign in the window. "Did any of the other tenants see a grizzly bear?"

"No," said Mr. Suresh.

Cassa took out her phone. "What was the name of the last tenant?"

"Micelli's Cakes. They sure left a bad taste in my mouth."

Mav and I moved around the room, knocking on walls, tapping the floor. The place was solid—no trapdoors or false walls that I could detect. I couldn't help noticing that one of the recessed lightbulbs at the back of the store was missing.

Hauntings, fires, but no Mr. Pang.

"There's a Micelli's Cakes on Fisherman's Wharf." Cassa showed us her screen, which displayed a pink-and-white website.

Crossing to the back corner, Mav placed his hand on the push bar of a heavy-looking door. "Where does this lead?"

"Into a hallway."

"Could I see it, please?" Mav asked. "Then I can report back to my father."

"Allow me." Mr. Suresh gestured for us to go through the door.

A long corridor led to a stairwell at one end, and an exit to Kearny Street on the other. A bucket near the stairs collected water dripping from the ceiling. A Viking of a security guard jogged down the stairs. His blond hair grew unchecked everywhere, including two hornlike tufts on the sides of his head. "Got two more leaks upstairs," he told Mr. Suresh. "The flood specialists are on their way."

The landlord nodded at him. "I'll be up in a second."

"We'd better get out of your mustache—I mean hair . . . er, I mean . . ." I cringed, remembering that Mr. Suresh didn't have any on top. "Thanks for all your help."

"You're welcome. And, Maverick, tell your father that if he's interested, there's an open house on Saturday morning. All leaks will be fixed by then, guaranteed."

"Sure thing, Mr. Suresh."

The building owner followed the Viking upstairs while we made our way toward the Kearny Street exit.

I couldn't believe it. We'd struck out once again. No shop, no Mr. Pang, no whimsies, and no Chang-Ah-Ling. Which meant no Coco. I was the one who needed a parachute now.

The door opened before we reached it, and two men in blue overalls and striped caps entered. They barely fit in the hallway walking side by side. As they got closer, I saw that the shorter one had a wedge-shaped blister stamped across his face, as if he'd been burned by a steam iron.

Or a Hovering Pizza Swat.

CHAPTER 15

"*You're* the flood specialists?" Bijal squeaked from behind me.

Now that they were right in front of us, I could see that Ernie's round face had grown scowl lines, and Bert's hands had become grapefruit-size fists.

"Out of our way," Ernie growled. His blond hair was as dry and spiky as a thatched roof.

"You were here the other night. Why?" I tried to keep my voice from shaking.

Bert crossed his thick arms, which were crisscrossed with raised white scars. "Hey, that's the Chu kid."

I gaped. "How do you know me?"

Ernie's face drew nearer. He snapped his gum, pulling his pizza burn out of shape. "The real question is, why is it we keep running into you?"

Bijal's windbreaker tsked as he tried to tug me back.

I held my ground. "Do you know where my sister is?" I asked the men. "Who has her?"

Bert bared teeth so short they seemed more like gummy ridges. Ernie's teeth were similar. Were they related?

"We don't know anything about your sister," Bert barked. "But if you see Pang, tell that sneaky scrap of penguin jerky to watch his back. We're coming for him. Now scram before we turn you into jam." With one push, he knocked me into my friends. We tumbled like bowling pins onto the tile floor.

We took falls all the time on the soccer field, but this one knocked the wind out of me. Cassa pulled up a frozen Bijal while Mav and I scrambled to our feet. Then we sped to the exit like zombies were breathing down our necks.

The storm had passed, leaving the trees heavy with water. Mav skidded to a stop and pointed at the dripping branches of a ficus tree whose canopy stretched to the second floor. "Look!"

A green bird with orange feet was staring down at us.

Mav whistled. "Unless there are two Javan magpies on this corner of Chinatown, I bet that's Maggie."

Up on the second story, the window of the acupuncture store was cracked open a few inches. Cassa fingered a soccer earring. "If Maggie is here, I bet Mr. Pang is nearby."

And Coco, too? I wondered, even though there was still no sign of his shop.

"Why would he let his bird fly around like that?" asked Mav.

"Maybe he trusts her to return," I offered. "Maybe he even sends her out."

"Like a spy," Bijal breathed. Water dripped on his face, and he wiped it off.

The bird became a greenish blur before my eyes. If the bird could act as a spy, what else could she do? Could she, for example, fake an injury? An injury that would cause some unsuspecting kid—namely me—to try to save her? If so, Mr. Pang had juked me—faked in one direction, hiding his true intent. What was it?

"Squirrel!" cried Bijal, pointing up at the tree and scrambling away down the sidewalk. We hustled after him.

But the giant squirrel didn't drop out of the tree. Instead, it seemed to be in a staring contest with Maggie. The magpie flapped her wings as if it shooing it away, even though Maggie was ten times smaller. With a hiss, the squirrel at last dropped out of the tree and dashed across the street. After it disappeared under a bush, Maggie darted through the open window.

Bijal squinted up at the acupuncture shop. "Maggie told off that squirrel like a boss."

"Do you think Pang's up there?" I asked.

Cassa had already dialed a number and put her phone on speaker.

"Acupuncture," said an airy woman's voice. "This is Judy. How may I help you today?"

"Hello," said Cassa in her confident adult voice. "I'm looking for a man named Mr. Pang. Do you know him?"

"No. Our doctor is Dr. Kay, and she's the only doctor here. Please hold. Do you have an appointment?" The woman's voice had grown fainter, like she was talking to someone else. "Flood specialists?"

We all glanced up at the window.

"Now what were you saying?" asked the woman, returning to us.

Cassa pulled at her soccer earring. "Er, have you seen any birds fly into your window lately?"

"Birds?" The woman's tone had become suspicious. "Is this a prank call?" She hung up.

The window of the acupuncture shop slid up, and suddenly, Bert's and Ernie's faces were peering down at us. Bijal started twisting back and forth, the way he sometimes did when zombie attackers were descending on him. "Let's go. Those guys look like they want to barbecue us."

We rounded the corner and jogged uphill, Mav setting the pace. "What do Bert and Ernie want with Mr. Pang?" he asked, barely winded.

Bijal grimaced, "Maybe they got some cursed cleaning equipment, too, and they want a refund."

Though, as a midfielder, I was supposed to have the most endurance, I could barely keep up with the others. The facts that (1) I still hadn't found Coco and (2) two moving mountains of muscle knew my name weighed me down like two extra sandbags. "Mr. Pang should sic his Were-Bear on them," I muttered.

"I bet Mav's shin guards that Mr. Pang was behind all that weird stuff Mr. Suresh mentioned." Bijal tucked his umbrella under his arm and squinted up at the darkening sky.

I stared up, too. There was not a cloud in sight, and the faint outline of the waxing moon was rising. "Probably. But where is he now?"

"Tomorrow, we find out," said Cassa. "I'm craving some cake from Fisherman's Wharf, aren't you?"

* ✳ · ✳ · ✳ *

Philippa was on the couch knitting a blanket around her when I got home. The dining table had been set with cloth napkins and even the dried flower centerpiece we took out on special occasions.

"Are we having company?"

"Mr. Gu wanted to stop by, and Mom suggested dinner. She's picking up something on her way home."

"Did you take the car to meet Ratface—I mean Vic?"

"Nope." She seemed bored and distracted, the way she looked when Mom and I forced her to play Monopoly. "But I did see his mother. She said he's been living in San Francisco since he got back from Iraq."

"So you went all that way for nothing."

She shrugged. "Got his contact info. I'm meeting him Saturday. Maybe you should come with me."

"I would rather be eaten by a python."

"Fine, but don't blame me if you have mental issues lasting well into adulthood."

"I don't have mental issues!"

I must have really freaked Philippa out yesterday if she was offering to take me somewhere. I'd have to be poisoned and barfing up my brains before she'd drive me to the hospital.

"Turn on the heat. This cold draft blew in, and I still haven't warmed up."

Cold draft?

I ran upstairs.

My closet door was open. The inside was cool but not cold, and I didn't see a broom or dustpan hiding behind my clothes. Still, I knew they were near, the same way you know there's a spider on the ceiling above you without having to look. Maybe the freezing air could only be felt when the spirits were on the move. I waved my hands around the space but didn't hit any invisible objects.

"Cloud Weaver? Cowherd?" I sank to my knees. "I'm begging you. Where's my sister? How do I get her back?"

The silence was chilly. Lifeless.

Then something cold blew on my cheek, making all my nerves jump. The broom and dustpan had the advantage here, being invisible. It was going to be hard to catch them again now that they knew our plays. I hoped that Cowherd wasn't too sore about us threatening to roast him on the firepit. Worse than being haunted by a spirit was being haunted by an angry spirit.

"I'll get you whatever you want. Well, as long as it's not Mom." I pressed my hands together. "Or Philippa," I grudgingly added. "Just help me get Coco back."

Something began to shimmer by the closet doorframe. The broomstick materialized, like in a magic trick. Then a filmy layer, like a Jedi hologram, began to superimpose itself over the wood. The image took shape and became a woman in a billowy, cloudlike dress with a soap-bubble sheen. She was as tall as the closet door. Atop her flawless face her hair had been rolled into a ball and stuck through with a silver pin. She even had a smell, like rain.

While I gaped at the woman who had to be the cloud weaver, the dustpan made a less showy entrance beside her. Soon a ghost man with a straw hat and farmer's clothes scowled at me. He—the cowherd—smelled like soil. The pair looked like they'd stepped off the pages of *Tales from the Middle Kingdom*.

I slowly got to my feet, unable to produce a sound. It was as if my mouth had just become a storage locker for teeth.

The cloud weaver's shimmery form swirled around the broom, her dark brown eyes with flashes of silver watching me closely. "We need Puh-tee. Can you get us Puh-tee? Then we will help you get Coco back."

"Puh-tee? You mean *Putty*? Why do you want *that*?"

The cowherd twirled the dustpan in his hand, his scowl deepening. He had the kind of pinching eyes that noticed every stain on your shirt. "We don't have all day," he said in a grumbly voice.

"Neither does my sister," I snapped.

The cloud weaver placed a ghostly hand on the man's arm, and he stopped spinning his dustpan. "Putty will help Mr. Pang enchant my hairpin so I can draw a bridge across the river of stars." She drew the silver stick from her hair, causing her shiny locks to spill like ink down her back, and mimed the drawing of a line. "Without the bridge, my husband and I cannot be together."

"But I thought your mother made a bridge of magpies."

"It only appears once a year. The bridge we seek to build would be permanent, spanning from the Middle Kingdom to the heavens." The cloud weaver's fingers twitched like she was plaiting something. Maybe it was a habit, the way Cassa made phantom pitching motions when it was softball season. "We need much-loved objects to create this magic. Mr. Pang knew there was powerful qi in your family."

"But . . . I just met him!"

The cowherd shrugged. "He told us the Chu family qi enchanted the most magical item in his shop—the Up, Up, and Away Canoe."

The birchbark canoe hanging from the ceiling came to mind. "How does he do it?"

"We are not sure, but we think the machine that smells of corn is used."

Mr. Pang's shop had reeked of popcorn. "So you thought you'd just help yourselves to our qi?" I asked with annoyance.

The cowherd removed his hat and fluffed an epic man bun. "We thought your soccer jersey would be enough, but Mr. Pang kept wanting more qi."

"The more qi we got him, the more powerful he could make my pin," the cloud weaver explained, "and we need very potent magic to create this bridge." Unlike her grouchy counterpart, she seemed genuinely apologetic. "We observed how much your sister liked her little blanket. She tried to grab the Putty just as I was about to sweep it into the dustpan, and I swept her in—at least her spirit—by mistake. Once she entered Mr. Pang's Whimsies, Chang-Ah-Ling captured her wandering spirit and sent her own into your sister's body."

So the dustpan was a portal to Mr. Pang's shop! He *had* juked me, sticking me with the pair of tools so that they could smuggle for him. Lightning bolts of anger surged through me. I imagined my poor sister's look of confusion, her mouth open and drooling as she wondered who these strangers were and why they were taking her favorite snuggle buddy.

The cowherd had glided into my room and was inspecting my bobblehead collection. When he saw me watching him, he made a great show of drawing back his hands, as if to prove he hadn't taken anything. "Usually we only transport objects. Living things can resist and, like your sister, end up leaving their bodies behind."

"Did Lucky resist?" I asked, my toes gripping the carpet and my hands clenched.

The cowherd snorted. "He's a goldfish."

I really wanted to kick him. The cloud weaver shushed him with a wave of her hand.

"He was *my* goldfish. What did Mr. Pang do with him? Flush him down the toilet? Eat him as a snack?" I was fed up with this pair and their wet smell.

"Oh, no. Mr. Pang prefers grubs," the cloud weaver said, as if that was the important thing. "We are sorry we had to take your things, but you must understand"—she held out her slender hands—"every day my mother's fury grows worse. She could kill my husband and zap me back to heaven with one lightning bolt."

"So she's the one behind the storms."

The cloud weaver nodded. "Each day that the moon grows fuller, my ability to create a water mirror grows weaker."

"A water mirror? Is that what makes you invisible?"

"Yes. I draw water from the air and spin it around us."

No wonder they smelled like damp dishrags.

"Why didn't you create a water mirror when we brought

you to the pier?" Perhaps it wasn't such a great idea for me to bring up how we'd tried to snuff them out, but I really wanted to know.

"If I had done that, you could have gotten caught up in it and frozen forever. You see, Winston, we are not as heartless as you think." The cloud weaver seemed to flicker a little, like a dying flame.

"Give us this Putty, and we will stop bothering you," the cowherd said gruffly, putting a ghostly arm around his wife's shoulders. "Summoning all these water mirrors has weakened my wife. It took all her energy to return us to your house without being seen."

My throat knotted in annoyance. "First tell me how I can get my sister back."

The cloud weaver bowed her head. "Find the doll Chang-Ah Ling, where Coco's spirit resides. A spirit and its body can only be reunited by the light of a full moon."

That was in five days, Mav had said. "What if I don't find her spirit by then?"

"Then it will begin to lose its attachment to the host. It may become lost forever."

Philippa called my name, but I barely heard it. The word *forever* clanged and clattered around my head like a stray penny in the dryer.

I shook myself free of my stupor. "Hide, quick!"

CHAPTER 16

"Winston, what's taking you so long?"

Philippa's voice grew louder and sharper, and suddenly, she was staring down at me. The cloud weaver and the cowherd had disappeared into their objects. "Why are you playing with that old broomstick again?"

I hastily placed them in the closet and shut the door. "I wasn't. Just organizing my stuff."

Her face grew annoyed, like when I borrowed her tweezers. She made a shoving motion toward the hallway. "Let's go. Mr. Gu will be here any minute, and you have to help straighten up."

With her watching me like I was a squirrel that might snatch her sandwich, I slogged downstairs, determined to sneak away at the first chance.

In the dining room, Not-Coco was shrieking, her fists two miniature white cannonballs. The house smelled of curry.

Mom, still in business attire of pantsuit and pearl earrings, was trying to lead Coco to the bathroom. "It's time to wash our hands!"

Philippa fetched Coco's concrete mixer and made flying motions with it toward the bathroom. "Come on, Coco, follow the truck."

"No!" Not-Coco scowled even harder, causing little white frown lines to appear. Abruptly, she ran toward the front door.

Philippa grabbed her and swung her around, which would've made the real Coco laugh. But this kid began screaming, her red eyes full of venom. Philippa carried her like a football to the bathroom.

"Looks like you were right, Winston," said Mom from the dining room table, where she was unwrapping curried lamb and scallion bread. "She *has* changed."

She *believed* me? "Yes, because she's a changeling, and—"

"She's become a threenager."

The doorbell rang.

"Hello, hello!" When I opened the door, a grinning Mr. Gu handed me a pink box containing a Kahlúa pie, according to the sticker. On the street below was his green van, its hue as vibrant as that of a Javan magpie. Its gold logo read: TREASURE: ESOTERIC ODDS AND ENDS.

"Hi, Ned. You're right on time, as always." Mom hung his jacket while he stepped out of his sandals. Cheerful hibiscus flowers engulfed his shirt.

"Thanks to this." He tapped his Swatch watch, whose red glow began to change to purple.

Not-Coco returned from the bathroom strangely subdued.

"Hello, little lady," he greeted her in his rich voice that always seemed on the verge of a chuckle. "What color is my Swatch?"

Her waterlogged eyes studied the timepiece. "Blue," she said in a small voice.

Mr. Gu liked kids, but he wasn't married. He even took Philippa and me to a Warriors game last year. He unstrapped his watch and knelt to Not-Coco's level. "That's very good. Would you like to wear it?"

She nodded. "Swatch."

He buckled it high up on her arm where it would stay put.

You can kiss that watch goodbye, Mr. Gu. If Not-Coco didn't break it first, she'd flush it down the toilet, maybe even swallow it.

As Mom and Mr. Gu exchanged pleasantries, I slid the takeout onto serving platters, keeping a weather eye on Not-Coco. She climbed into her booster seat. The demon possessing her was no longer raging, but I still didn't trust her.

We all sat down, and Mr. Gu proposed a toast. "To you, Willa, who deserves the moon."

Not-Coco fisted her spoon and dug into her bowl of spicy rice. At least physically she was still Coco. Not many three-year-olds had flame-retardant tongues like hers. It was a trait that ran on the female side of our family.

"You're a good big brother," said Mr. Gu, eating in small, precise bites. "Keep watching over your little sister, even when she's too big to need it." His eyes got that faraway look that adults get when adults think about their childhood.

"Did you have a little sister?" Philippa asked.

"No, but I had a younger brother. Odd, sad little kid.

Always looking right when he should've been looking left. He got beat up a lot when I wasn't there to stop it." He set down his chopsticks and shrugged. "Anyway, forgive me. Willa, how was your interview?"

"Good." Mom sipped from her bottle of ginger ale. "The team's great, but they're still interviewing candidates, so I won't know anything till next week."

I couldn't understand why anyone would *not* want to hire Mom. She worked hard, she was fun to be around, and she never complained. Well, except for when I surgically removed the mushrooms from my chicken pot pie or wore shoes in the house.

Mr. Gu, with his ear cocked toward Mom, resumed pecking away at his food. "You'll land on your feet. Your mom's the brightest paralegal I've ever worked with," he told Philippa and me. "I had to steal her away from her last firm, you know."

"I was grateful for the work," Mom said. "We had a good run until you retired."

"I was only sorry they didn't keep you on. You're always welcome to join me at Treasure. I'm looking for an administrator. It's not legal research, but my products are one of a kind and my customers are interesting. Each day brings something new."

"Thanks, Ned. I appreciate it. But I really want to keep my training sharp. I worked hard for my degree. But business must be good if you're looking for help."

"Yes, very good. Plus, well . . . I've decided to throw my hat in the ring for mayor."

"Mayor?" Food fell from Mom's chopsticks. "Isn't it a little late to enter the race?"

"Better late than never." He chuckled, something he did often. It sounded like someone thumping a baby's back to make it burp. His face turned serious. "The city needs good leadership, especially someone who understands environmental law, what with the sky falling and all. Not to mention those hissing squirrels."

"I have always admired your concern for the environment," Mom said. "You'd be a great mayor—smart, not like all the birdbrains currently in office. Philippa can vote for you, too, now that she's old enough." She winked at Philippa, who was chowing down her food like it was in danger of escaping.

"Maybe Philippa could be your administrator," I dropped.

Glaring at me, Philippa helped Not-Coco down from her chair. Mom's face became thoughtful, her gaze sliding to Mr. Gu, who had slowly begun to nod.

"I'm sure Mr. Gu needs someone with more experience," Philippa said carefully.

Mr. Gu tented his fingers. "If you're interested, we could start you at entry level, with lots of room for upward mobility. You're already great with people."

I snorted, and Philippa kicked me under the table.

"Let me think about it," said Philippa, purposely not looking at Mom.

By this time, Not-Coco was sitting on the living room floor neatly stacking her trucks. The real Coco would've been zooming them along the tops of the furniture, and she definitely would've asked for Putty by now. While she wasn't our fun, carefree Coco, she also wasn't being the mischievous hellion who had been terrorizing our household. I hoped this change in her wasn't a bad omen about the condition of my sister's spirit.

Mr. Gu got on the floor and stretched out his back, which made popping sounds. "Dinner was delicious."

"Wish I could take credit," Mom said. "Ready for some Kahlúa pie?"

"No dessert for me, but I'll take a cup of tea if you have it."

"I'll brew some," said Philippa, slipping out of her chair.

As soon as I finished my piece of pie, I would sneak back upstairs. But before I could make a clean getaway, Mom said, "Winston, could you read your sister her bedtime story? Coco, say good night to Mr. Gu." Mom unclasped the watch from Coco's arm.

"Good night, Mr. Gu," said subdued Not-Coco. The real Coco would've just blurted out "Night!" and probably run a lap around the house.

Barely looking at me, Not-Coco headed to her and Mom's room and climbed onto the bigger bed with *Tales from the Middle Kingdom*. I perched on the other side, where Dad used to sleep. On the nightstand stood a picture of Mom dressed as Wonder Woman, wrapping her magic lasso around Dad, who was dressed as Superman. For the millionth time, I wished he were here. *He* would believe me.

Keeping my distance from Not-Coco, I eyed the creature, wondering how long I would be stuck here before I could sneak back to my room. "You and I both know you're a fraud, a phony-baloney. I don't know what your deal is, but your days here are numbered."

She didn't reply. In fact, she barely seemed to have heard

me. She had opened the book to a page headlined *DID YOU KNOW?* that came after the story of the cloud weaver. Watercolor pictures of magpies doing assorted tasks, like pulling chariots or helping ladies put on robes, filled every inch of the page.

> *Magpies are the most important bird in the heavens. They are fast and smart and always travel in pairs. It is believed that two are needed to balance each other, like peace and war, resolve and delay, sorrow and mirth.*

"Sorrow and mirth, sorrow and mirth," Not-Coco sang in an eerie voice.

> *By working together, the pairs can create harmony. If you have a pair of these noble birds in your service, you are lucky, because they are loyal and work hard. But never cross a magpie. The wrath of a magpie is worse than an angry hurricane and will take a hundred lifetimes to outrun.*

A boom of thunder made the windows rattle. Sleet clattered against the glass, as loud as dried beans poured into a coffee can. My mind flew to the broom and the dustpan in my closet upstairs.

Not-Coco finally glanced up, showing me two rows of her pointy teeth. Her creepy self was back. "Run, Winston, run."

CHAPTER 17

I hurried out of Mom's room, the pie I had eaten threatening to claw its way back up. Mr. Gu was gone, and Mom and Philippa were clearing dishes from the table.

"I hope Ned's not going to have trouble getting home," Mom was saying. She glanced at me. "Is Coco down?"

"Not yet," I mumbled, mounting the stairs. "Just have to check something first."

"Oh, by the way, Winston, we gave Ned that old broom and dustpan," I heard Mom say when I was halfway up. "He said he had the perfect spot for them."

I tripped, banging my knee on the step. "Ow!"

"What happened?" Mom rushed to the bottom of the stairs.

I pulled myself up by the bannister. "You *gave* them to him?"

"I thought they were for him?" She glanced back at Philippa, who had slithered up behind her.

Philippa tossed back her hair. "Good riddance to bad rubbish."

My breath wheezed out of me. "*You* did it."

She shrugged. "You were getting a little obsessed with those things."

Mom rubbed at her neck, her gaze toggling between Philippa and me. "I'm sorry, Winston. I didn't realize you had changed your mind. I'm sure Mr. Gu will understand if you want them back."

"Yes, I want them back. Could you text him?"

"Yes, later. I don't want to distract him while he's driving in this storm."

"Fine, but you promise you'll text him tonight, right?"

"Right. Philippa, put Coco to bed. Winston, you have kitchen duty."

After a hasty cleanup involving stuffing containers into the trash instead of rinsing and recyling, I raced upstairs and picked up my phone.

Mav answered the call, his noisy TV show playing in the background again. In fact, it sounded louder than before and included phrases like *I didn't marry a Tesla.*

"Hey, Win." I heard a door close, and the volume level fell.

"Everything okay?" I asked.

"Yeah," he muttered. "Status?"

The story gushed out as fast as the rain still pouring outside. "I was hoping to use the dustpan to portal into Mr. Pang's shop, but how can I if Mother Cloud Weaver zaps it to death first? Mr. Gu doesn't know he has to protect the cowherd."

As if Mother Cloud Weaver had heard me, lightning flashed

outside the windows, followed by the works—a round of thunder, howling gusts, and sleet that flew like darts at the window. She was on a rampage.

"And another thing," I went on once I could hear again, "if she was behind the fire at the corner lot, what if she decides to fry it again? Coco's in there!"

"Sit tight," said Mav. "I was thinking we'd do a four-four-two formation, like when we played the Surfs, remember?"

"What are you talking about? This isn't a soccer match." The Surfs were a trash-talking team who relied on their big mouths to win. Coach had told us to *turn off your ears and turn on our gears*—in other words, outmaneuver them while they were mocking us. But what did that have to do with anything?

"Lightning doesn't strike twice, but a good striker can redirect the ball."

Now I was really confused.

"Gotta go," he said abruptly. "I'll see you tomorrow. Micelli's Cakes on Fisherman's Wharf, like we planned."

We hung up. Mav was certainly acting weird tonight, but I had bigger things to worry about right now. Like whether I should open the window in case the spirits needed a way to get back in. Mom would kill me for flooding the house. I just had to be patient. Tomorrow, I'd get the broom and dustpan back.

* ※ · ※ · ※ ·

After a night of tossing and turning, which made my bed feel like a hammock in a hurricane, I woke to Mom's warm hand on my face. "Good morning, Winston. Mr. Gu wants to talk to you." She held out her smartphone. "He was in a minor fender bender last night, but he's fine."

More bad luck.

"Morning, Winston," he boomed in his hearty voice, clearing the last of the fogginess from my head.

"Sorry to hear about the accident. Was it because of the storm?"

"Yes, all that flooding made it hard to see. Somehow, in all the commotion, I lost the broom and the dustpan. They must have fallen out of the van when I opened the door. I'm not quite sure how."

Fell out or *ran* out?

"I'm very sorry I lost them," he went on. "Your mom said that you needed them back?"

"It's okay," I said, even though it wasn't really. I could only hope that they had escaped and were on their way here. It wouldn't be the first time.

Then again, Mother Cloud Weaver may have zapped them. It wasn't raining now.

Mom made a sympathetic noise when I returned her phone. She was only half-dressed for her temp job, in ratty sweatpants topped by a crisp shirt. "I'm sorry again about your broom and dustpan. You mad?"

"Nah," I mumbled. "You didn't know." I couldn't blame her for being in the dark, and I couldn't turn on the lights just yet.

After she left the room, I opened my window, hoping the spirits could scale walls. They seemed pretty agile to me. Sure, I was risking major water damage if it started to rain again, but that was a risk I had to take. I covered the window with the curtain so my mom wouldn't see.

Before going downstairs, I collected Putty from my sock drawer. The blanket scrap was my ticket through the portal if the pair returned, and after what happened last night, I wasn't going to take any chances.

In the living room, Not-Coco was hunched over a book, scribbling on a piece of paper. At least she wasn't burning down the house. On the television in front of her, the news anchor read the headlines in a mildly alarmed voice. "*The freak storms that have been plaguing Chinatown have now spread out over the city, with lightning even striking the Bay Bridge.*"

The camera panned to show charred lanes spanning a good length of the bridge, delineated by a series of orange traffic cones. What were the broom and dustpan doing on the bridge? Mr. Gu's shop was in the Dogpatch, which meant the pair were going the wrong way if they meant to come back here.

Not-Coco was too involved with her drawing to notice me. Crossing into the kitchen, I opened the freezer and stuffed Putty into the plastic kimchee jar where Mom hid her valuables. It'd be safe there, out of a toddler's reach. To be extra sure, I moved a bag of frozen pot stickers in front of it.

"Delivery for you, Winston."

I jumped. Not-Coco was standing behind me, holding out the mail truck, in which was placed a piece of paper. Cautiously, I slipped out the paper. She had drawn a banana in pencil. Or maybe it was a crescent moon. Many zigzags marked the page, some made so heavily the paper had ripped. It was bizarre—definitely not something real Coco, who favored colorful random scribbles, would've created.

"Who are you, and what have you done with my sister?"

"I *am* your sister." Her creepy smile made all my muscles twitch. I fought the urge to pick up and throw that sly imp out of the house, all two and a half feet of her.

"No, thanks. Keep your freaky demon scribbles to yourself." I pushed the paper back at her and took out a breakfast burrito, as if that was the reason I'd been digging through the freezer.

Mom bustled into the kitchen, fully dressed this time. The mail truck clattered to the floor, and Not-Coco began whimpering.

"What's wrong, honey?" Mom picked up the mail truck.

"Winston doesn't like my picture," Not-Coco said in Coco's munchkin voice.

Mom glanced at me, standing by the still-open freezer.

"That's not Coco!" I shot back, unable to stop myself. "She's been possessed, can't you see? That's not how Coco draws."

"That's enough, Winston." Mom took the frozen burrito out of my hands and closed the freezer door. Even though her hands were full, she lifted my chin with one finger, inspecting my face from ear to ear. "Are you getting enough sleep?"

"No," I said without thinking. *Great, now she'll think I'm hallucinating.* "I mean, we all could use more sleep, but I'm telling you the truth. That's not Coco."

Not-Coco smirked at me, but when Mom looked at her, she switched her expression back to that of a helpless toddler. She waved her picture at me, but I crossed my arms.

"Take the drawing," Mom said through her teeth.

I pinched it between two fingers like it was radioactive. Mom hefted an eyebrow. With a groan, I crossed to where my backpack lay on the dining table and stuffed it roughly inside, intending to throw it out as soon as I got the chance.

"Want me to heat up your burrito?" Mom stood in the kitchen doorway.

"No. I'm late for school. And you know you're never supposed to turn your back on a toddler, right? She should be watched at all times."

"I have raised kids before, you know." Worry lines formed a haystack over her brow, and she fisted her hands on her hips like Wonder Woman assessing a problem. I backed off. I did not need her to throw her magic lasso of concern around me right now.

"I know. Just . . . it pays to be careful."

She roped me with an arm and kissed my cheek. "I'm glad to hear you say that, son."

✷ ✼ ❋ ✼ ✷

In homeroom, Dani was wearing jeans, a yellow sweater patterned with rainbows, and pink rubber boots. A cocktail umbrella bloomed behind her ear.

She gave me a bright smile and glanced at the water bottle I was holding. "How's your hand?"

I set down the bottle clumsily and gently flexed my hand. "Still hurts." I even winced for good measure. "Sure that umbrella's big enough to keep you dry?" I joked, trying to change the subject.

Dani reached behind her ear. Her cocktail umbrella was fancier than most, with a sparkly pink canopy. "This is my anti-rain charm. My aunt sent it to me when I lived in Texas after I got caught in a storm and my cello was ruined."

"Does the charm work?"

She shrugged. "All I know is I never get rained on when I wear it. I haven't worn it for a while, because California needs all the water it can get, but lately there've been all these weird storms, and they're getting dangerous. Plus, I really need the weather to be good this weekend. I'm guest-appearing with the Kronos Quartet at Golden Gate Park."

"Wow." Dad and I had often gone skateboarding at the Music Concourse, an open-air plaza within the park, but I hadn't been back there since he died.

"You can come if you'd like," she said. "It's free."

As much as I wanted to see Dani play professionally, I had to focus on getting Coco back. Especially now, with only four more days until the full moon.

At my non-response, Dani aligned her spine with the back of the chair and shifted her gaze to the front of the room. "It's okay."

"Uh, maybe another time . . ."

I could feel all my chances with Dani evaporating like morning fog. If she ever learned that I had lied to her about playing the ukulele, I would be dead to her. And since I still hadn't practiced even once, that time would be soon.

Dani wouldn't look at me for the rest of the class.

When I ducked into Algebra, Bijal and Cassa were having

an animated discussion. I sank into my chair, and they pulled me into a conspiratorial huddle.

"Bijal saw Mr. Pang's Whimsies last night," Cassa hissed.

My eyes grew wide enough to signal trains.

"Dad made me go to the senior center last night." Bijal grimaced, even though he liked blowing up balloons with the boomers. His windbreaker made extra-loud swishing noises every time he moved his arms. "As we passed Jackson, I saw it. The green door with the lights."

"Did you stop?"

"Of course not! You know I have a strict policy of separation between church and state."

Though he was fierce on the soccer field, Bijal avoided conflict when it came to his parents, which meant he kept a lot of things from them. According to him, the "state" that governed his life did not need to know how the "church" conducted its affairs. If the state ever found out that their only child was conducting an illegal candy operation at school, they would make him spend the summer in India. They'd done it when he bleached his hair for spirit day, before he knew that bleach didn't wash out. None of us ever pointed out to him how much fun he'd had that summer.

"So the shop is still there." I pulled at my cheeks. "But how come whenever we visit it's gone?"

Cassa tapped out a beat with her pencil. "Maybe the Micellis can tell us."

Mav was waiting by the giant ship's wheel that marked the entrance of Fisherman's Wharf, otherwise known as San Francisco's biggest tourist trap. Once he spotted Cassa, Bijal, and me, he hurried to join us, his navy peacoat with the Towne School emblem flapping behind him. Together the four of us wove our way through pedestrian traffic toward the corridor of shops. The scents of clam chowder and freshly baked sourdough bread, which usually made my mouth water, hardly distracted me today.

Mav gripped his backpack straps. "I might've figured out something. Remember that chocolate kitty Peep that got stuck to my shirt? Well, I found it at the bottom of my pack. I must've thrown it in there and forgotten about it."

Bijal's lips pulled back from his teeth. "Even I think that's gross."

"Well, that's the thing. You'd think it'd be all squished up, or maybe melted? It wasn't. And it was staring at me with those black dots. I stuck it in a box and put it under my bed. But then I got to thinking . . . Mr. Pang said the Peeps were standing guard. What if this one is still working for him?"

"You mean, you think it's been watching you?" I exclaimed, eyeing his backpack.

"Well, I don't know how much it could see at the bottom of my pack. But maybe it's been . . . listening. It looked so, I don't know, attentive."

No wonder Mav had been talking in riddles last night. He'd been trying to assure me we'd outmaneuver Mr. Pang without mentioning his name.

"Wait a second . . ." Cassa had slowed down to study a mime

who was spray-painted silver and only moved when someone put a dollar in his hat. Her eyes shifted to me. "Maybe the reason the store vanishes when we visit is because Mr. Pang knows we're coming. Think back—the first time you returned to Mr. Pang's was before the game. The shop wasn't there. Is there any way he could've known?"

My mind rewound. "The day we got the broom, I lost my Hulkbuster. Mav said I should go back and see if Mr. Pang had found it."

"Aha!" Cassa pointed a chewed-up nail. "So the kitty Peep in Mav's backpack overheard and reported to Mr. Pang, who somehow made the shop disappear by the time you got there."

Bijal clamped his hands to his head. "How does a Peep—"

Cassa waved him off. "Never mind *how*. We don't know how any of it works. We just have to accept that it *does* work."

"The next time we visited the shop was after the match," I said, thinking back to our post-game tacos.

"I didn't take my backpack to the game, so the kitty Peep didn't overhear us that time. And the shop was there. Yesterday I was carrying my backpack all day, so the Peep knew we were going to visit Mr. Suresh."

Bijal's hair stood up in tufts. "And last night on my way to the senior center, the shop was there. Oh my squab, you have a psycho marshmallow kitty under your bed! You'd better destroy that puffy angel of death before it kills you in your sleep!" Bijal's words waterfalled from his mouth in one continuous stream.

"No, don't destroy it." Cassa's teeth glinted in the sunlight. "That kitty Peep's going to lead us right to Mr. Pang. Somehow."

CHAPTER 18

Cassa led us down the plank walkway to a shop with a faded pink awning. It was sandwiched between a store with electric toy trains and a saltwater-taffy shop whose windows were hung with piñatas. Inside the cakery, two display cases full of vanilla-scented confections took up most of the narrow space. There was a small round table in the corner with three wrought-iron chairs around it, and a counter where a woman with a name tag that read LUCE was squirting frosting onto cupcakes. She glanced up at us.

"Good afternoon," said Cassa. "Is Mr. Micelli available?" She switched to her business casual tone as easily as Bijal swapped around our lunches.

"If you're talking about my brother," the woman said, "he's at the law offices of Brown and Bronstein."

"So he's not a baker?"

Luce guffawed. "He doesn't even know how to turn on an oven. I'm the one who got the baking gene. Are you looking to order a cake?" She set down her pastry bag and wiped her hands on her pink apron.

"Actually, no. We're trying to track down a Mr. Micelli who used to rent out a space on 602 Jackson Street in 1985."

Luce's brown eyes floated to the ceiling fan. "We've been renting on Fisherman's Wharf for as long as I can remember."

"Is it possible to speak with your . . . father?"

"Sure, but he won't answer. He died last year."

From behind Luce, a skinny arm belonging to a woman with silver hair pushed the bigger woman aside. She was so tiny I hadn't seen her behind Luce. After she wiped her fingers on Luce's apron as well, she held out a gnarled but cool hand for us to shake. "I'm Mrs. Micelli. So you kids want to know about 602 Jackson Street? Let's sit down. I have ten minutes for my break."

"But don't you . . . own the store?" asked Bijal.

"Yes, and time is money." She cut her eyes to Luce, who was back to finishing her cupcakes. "Plus, I don't want the other employees to get resentful."

"You mean your daughter?"

"Exactly."

Luce rolled her eyes.

Mrs. Micelli gestured to the round table, and I let Mav and Cassa take the other two seats. I was too nervous to sit, and Bijal was too hyper.

The old woman settled into her chair like a hen on a nest and looked nervously around the shop, though no other customers were present. She fished a gold cross from under her collar and kissed it. "I'll tell you, but first, why's it so important?" The woman pursed her lips, cinching all her wrinkles. Her rusty-spade eyes dug around each of our faces.

I cleared my throat, trying to decide how much to reveal. Clearly this woman knew something strange was afoot. If we wanted her to tell us the bad things that had happened on Jackson Street, we had to share, too. But maybe not everything. No sense giving her a coronary.

"I purchased some things from a shop at that location, but when I tried to return them, the shop was gone."

Her papery neck stretched taut. "You mean it went out of business?"

I leaned in closer, and so did everyone else. "More like it disappeared."

Mav nodded solemnly. "But sometimes it comes back."

To my relief, the woman didn't sneer at or scold us. She tucked her cross under her shirt and crossed her arms. "Do you think the place is haunted?"

Mav looked at me, then shrugged. "You could put it that way."

Mrs. Micelli adjusted the napkin dispenser on the table, turning it a fraction. My reflection in the chrome side was a fun-house version of myself, distorted and alien.

"There was a time when I would've laughed at you." She stared into space. "Spirits, hauntings, no such thing. But now?" She shook her head, and something sad gripped her thin face. "He didn't like it, my Gio. He didn't like that space. Said the walls didn't feel like real walls, just pretend, and he'd hear things even when no one was around."

"What kinds of things?" I asked.

"People talking. Furniture being moved. It was almost as if we were part of an illusion and something was going on right on top of us that we couldn't see. At first I thought he was being foolish for wanting to break the lease. We'd lose our deposit.

"Then, one night as we were cleaning up, Gio screamed and pointed at nothing. 'B-b-bear!'" The woman crooked a flour-dusted finger now in imitation of him. "He picked up a stool and threw it. Made a big dent in the wall. After that, he refused to go back."

Cassa held her elbows. "So you never saw the bear yourself?"

"No. But I did experience something else. . . ." Mrs. Micelli angled herself so she was facing a tall refrigerated cake display in the opposite corner. "We had that case in the shop on Jackson, and sometimes I'd see more than cakes reflected in the back mirror."

Bijal flapped his arms like a disturbed penguin. "Like what?"

"Bizarre things, like a glowing Statue of Liberty, or a floating matador cape. Then I'd rub my eyes and the things would vanish, like I'd been dreaming. Anyway, after the bear incident, we gave up on our deposit and got out of Dodge. My Gio led a good long life, but the memory of that bear plagued him for the rest of his days. Well, break time's over." Getting to her feet, she leaned toward us, suddenly looking as menacing as a bear herself. "Take my advice and stay away from that place. Don't give yourself nightmares you don't need."

The four of us traded stares. It was too late for that now.

I asked Mrs. Micelli one last question. "Do you know a Mr. Pang?"

"Can't say that I do," she answered. "Now, can I interest you in some cupcakes? Buy three, get one free."

After leaving Micelli's, we regrouped on a bench to eat our treats. In front of us, the watchtower of the former prison on Alcatraz Island stuck up like a middle finger. To the west, a second land mass, Treasure Island, marked the midpoint of the Bay Bridge. If the two islands were brothers, Alcatraz would be the crook, while Treasure Island, an old naval station, would be the dutiful one who had joined the military. A layer of clouds made its way over the pair like a net slowly being cast.

Bijal sat in the middle, with Cassa and Mav on his right and me on his left. Mav licked his fingers and went into captain mode. "Let's go over the facts. Ross Pang leased the corner space for his toy store, Dream Castle, which lasted until freak lightning struck it in 1979. Then, in 1980, Mr. Suresh bought the building, but he couldn't keep a tenant in the space. One left due to a bear haunting."

Cassa lifted a sneaker and stirred the air with her foot. "How has Mr. Pang operated his store for so long without the owner knowing?"

"Or Shaggy." The store manager of Boba Guys had been there as long as I'd been a customer, which was most of my life. Our questions just raised more questions, like popcorn being pushed out by the kernels hatching below them. "Mrs. Micelli said her husband heard and felt things in his store. My guess is that Mr. Pang's store was operating around him. Like, in stealth mode. You can't see the shop from the outside, but it's still there on the inside."

Bijal threw up his hands, tossing cake crumbs everywhere. Pigeons swooped in to clean up the mess. "Maybe it's like those fish aquariums with the ultraviolet lights. When you switch off the light, all the pretty colors disappear."

Mav snapped his fingers. "He switches off the lights when he thinks we're coming." He grinned. "So, if we feed the kitty Peep false intel . . ."

Cassa stamped down her sneaker. "We might be able to catch him with the lights on!"

"But how do we get through the door?" I asked. "Mr. Pang has probably upped his security, especially with Ernie and Bert snooping around. It'll be harder to break in than Alcatraz."

Winston! cried a voice like a foghorn, low and rumbly. It seemed to come from somewhere over the water.

"Who said that?" I asked.

"Who said what?" Mav replied.

"Who just called my name?"

They all shook their heads at me.

Winston!

"There it goes again." I stretched my gaze over the bay, but there was nothing out there but seabirds. "You didn't hear that?"

Mav's eyes slid around in their sockets as he listened. But now there was just the *shush* of the ocean and the low buzz of the tourist crowd. He shrugged. "Sorry."

Maybe I'd gotten water in my ears or something. But the voice had felt so real I could almost feel its vibrations under my feet. I tapped at my head and tried to tune back in to the conversation.

"Mr. Suresh is trying to rent out the place again, right?" Mav was saying.

"So?" said Bijal.

"Real estate agents use lockboxes with keys inside them so other agents can open the properties for showing. All you need is the combination."

"But wouldn't that just get us into the empty corner space?" I asked.

"My guess is, as long as we enter through the green door, we'll get into Mr. Pang's shop. Give me a day or two—I think I'll be able to get the combination." Mav tossed up a ball of buttercream and caught it in his mouth. "Even Alcatraz had its weak points."

CHAPTER 19

That night, Not-Coco graffitied the living room with lightning bolts and tried to bite Mom during bathtime. Yet when I suggested that Mom carry a can of Dog-Off canine repellent with her, she looked at me like I was the crazy one. I missed the real Coco, and after today, we only had four more days to get her back.

There were no signs of the broom or dustpan in my room or anywhere in the house. I hoped Mav would get the lockbox combination soon. I curled up in bed, hearing the seconds tick by even though I had a digital clock and even though another storm was taking swipes at our neighborhood.

I sucked air in through my nose, the way Dad had taught me. According to him, we were born with a certain amount of qi, but food and good air could strengthen qi. Qigong was the practice that combined breathing, meditation, and flowing movements to enhance good-air qi. I hadn't done it since he died. Without Dad, it seemed wrong, like going to the Music Concourse did. But now, when I felt completely out of balance, I wished I'd kept up the practice. I tried inhaling from my belly and pictured myself bobbing along a lazy river on an inflatable doughnut under a cloudless sky. . . .

* ✳ · ✳ · ✳ *

By the time morning rolled around, the storm outside had cleared, but not the one in my head. Before even getting out of bed, I called Mav.

He answered on the first ring. "Hanging in there?"

"No. What do you have for me?"

"The plan is a go." It sounded like he was crunching cereal. "I told Dad's assistant he wanted me to get the lockbox combination from her. Then I fed the Peep false intel. We'll move tonight like we discussed."

"I think we should go now."

"Too risky. If we get caught ditching school, we'll get grounded. Hang tight."

* ✳ · ✳ · ✳ *

At roughly five o'clock, the sound of feet clomping up to our door had me pulling on my darkest jacket and jamming on my sneakers. Cassa had arranged for us to tag along on her father's Friday-night movie date with his girlfriend. We, of course, wouldn't be seeing the same movie as them. In fact, we wouldn't be seeing a movie at all.

The door opened, but it wasn't my friends, only Philippa and Not-Coco coming back from the library. Not-Coco was holding a klunker of a book with a dusty cover and gold-foil lettering. She squawked in protest when I lifted it from her hands. "*Choose Your Poison: A Guide to the World's Most Toxic Compounds.* That's not weird at all, is it, Philippa?"

"She liked the pictures." Philippa stepped out of her ankle boots and yanked something from her purse. "Did you put this in here?" She pushed the canister of Dog-Off at me. A postal worker friend had given Mom several cans after a rottweiler nearly sunk its jaws into Coco.

"Yeah, so? Danger can strike without warning." I eyed Not-Coco.

"It's like carrying a brick. Take it away. And move." Philippa marched past me up the stairs.

Not-Coco and I eyed each other, her lips forming a creepy smile. "Read it to me, Winston."

I clutched the book to me. "No way, you snake." As if she really expected me to teach her how to poison our family.

Mom emerged from her bedroom. "Coco, you're back. Winston, my laptop's not working."

"What?" Not-Coco was reaching for the book, her clammy hands clutching at me. Coco's hands were always hot and sweaty, not cold and rubbery.

"You're the last one who used it." Mom gestured at her open laptop like a waiter hawking a tray of hors d'oeuvres that nobody wants. "I knew this would happen. It's too young to die but too old for the warranty. For crying sakes, I'm supposed to send the firm writing samples, and they're all on here."

Out of the murky drool of Not-Coco's mouth, a smile emerged, the one that gleamed like a zombie scythe.

She had messed with Mom's computer. I knew it! Not only that, but she implicated me in the crime. If she sabotaged Mom's getting a job, I would . . . Well, I wasn't sure what I would do. How do you fight a villain your mom thinks is your baby sister? I couldn't just dump her off the pier like I had the broom and dustpan.

Someone knocked at the door. Still clutching the book and the Dog-Off, I opened it.

Cassa, Bijal, Mav, Mr. Kowalski, and a woman who had to be Mr. Kowalski's new girlfriend greeted us. Like me, my friends had outfitted themselves for a covert mission, even Bijal, who had turned his reversible purple windbreaker inside out so it was now black. Cassa had tucked her hair into a knit cap, and everyone was wearing dark jeans. The only spot of color was the green rubber bands on Cassa's braces.

Setting her broken computer on the dining table, Mom hurried over, fixing her grimace into a smile. Mr. Kowalski extended a hand to Mom, and they shook. Mr. Kowalski reminded me of dad-bod Thor. He always wore a flannel shirt, but today it looked ironed. "Good to see you. Willa, Winston, this is Janelle Summers."

"Hello." Janelle's warm brown eyes took in all of us. She was tall like Mr. Kowalski, and her short chestnut-brown hair perfectly matched her skin tone. Her black leather jacket and orange boots looked fashionable, though I didn't know why people bothered to dress up when they were going to see a movie. She focused her generous smile on me. "I'm glad to finally meet the last member of the Fabulous Four."

Cassa rolled her eyes to no one in particular.

"Thanks," I said. "Nice to meet you, too."

"Do you all want to come in?" Mom gestured distractedly toward the living room.

Mr. Kowalski held up his rough palms. "Thanks, but we won't trouble you. We have a movie to make. I'll be sure to get everyone home right afterward."

"Thank you." Mom ruffled my hair. "This'll be good for Winston. He's seemed so tense lately."

I ducked away from her hand, embarrassed.

"Cassa, too," said Mr. Kowalski, which earned him a huff from his daughter.

Behind us, Not-Coco toddled into view, the mail truck in her hands. Coco never played with that truck. It was like Wile E. Coyote, who always lost to Road Runner, the cement mixer. Cassa, Bijal, and Mav stared at Not-Coco, who was probably the reason they'd all decided to come to the door. She stared back, her chin wet and her eyes innocent, then began motoring her truck across the floor.

"Aw, how cute," said Janelle.

Yeah, cute as the devil's spawn.

"Anyway, thanks for doing this," said Mom. "Especially in such crazy weather."

"Yes, isn't it something? It flooded my project out in the Dogpatch."

Bijal waved a hand in front of Not-Coco, the way Philippa

always did to see if I was paying attention. Giggling, Not-Coco waved back. Bijal frowned.

Though the adults had not yet finished talking, Cassa led the others down the stairs.

I considered giving Mom the Dog-Off but decided that even if Not-Coco went berserk on her, Mom would never spray her. We might end up needing it anyway. Who knew with all the wild things we'd encountered lately.

I slid into the third row of Mr. Kowalski's Ford Explorer beside Mav. In the middle seats, Cassa and Bijal pivoted to face us. "Did you see that?" I hissed.

"Oh, I saw that all right," said Bijal. The interior lights of the Explorer cast a weird yellow glow on his skin. "That fake Coco didn't even try to shake me down for a treat. I brought her favorite, too." He held up a small bag of M&M's.

"And she was playing with the mail truck," added Cassa. "She hates the mail truck."

"Exactly!" I threw up my hands, thanking the moonroof that my friends had witnessed the truth.

"What's with that?" Mav asked, nodding toward the book on my lap.

"That freakazoid checked it out from the library. I don't want her reading it."

"No way." Cassa glanced back at the house. "Can change-lings read?"

Mav's shoulders popped up. "I don't know, but they're smart."

"She busted Mom's laptop." I hoped Mom would be able to retrieve her documents. Now that she was so close to getting a job, that howler monkey better not have thrown a wrench into the gears.

Mav showed me the provisions he had in his silver backpack, including two gas lighters. It took me a moment to remember what they were for. I added the can of Dog-Off to the stash.

Mr. Kowalski helped Janelle to her seat before starting the car. "Ramen okay with you, kids?"

"I thought we were going to the movies!" Cassa cried.

"Sure, but it doesn't start until seven. This was supposed to be just the three of us, remember?" Mr. Kowalski sounded like he was talking through his teeth. "Dinner and a movie."

"Fine, but I wanted pizza," Cassa stated defensively. "You keep promising we'll go, but we never do."

"Janelle doesn't eat dairy."

"Oh, that's okay." Janelle's rich voice carried to the back row without her needing to shout. "Nowadays, a lot of places offer dairy-free options."

In the rearview mirror, Mr. Kowalski's eyes zeroed in on Cassa. Her seat jerked in front of me, the sitting equivalent of stomping a foot. "I know . . . Why don't you drop us off for pizza, and then you and Janelle can go to the ramen place."

Classic Cassa, finding a kernel of opportunity on a corncob of setback.

"Absolutely not. Janelle wants to get to know all of you. We're not a shuttle service."

Cassa groaned. "At this juncture, I'd like to remind you that you promised you'd see a different movie than us. It's not fun to see movies with adults."

Janelle laughed. "I know what that's like. My mom took my

girlfriends and me to see the original *Scream* movie a million years ago and I didn't scream a single time."

"Winston needs to return a library book," Cassa said abruptly.

"Now?" Mr. Kowalski's puzzled eyes found mine.

"Well, actually, I don't—"

Cassa expelled an exasperated huff. "Yes, now. Do you want him to incur an overdue charge?"

Mr. Kowalski sighed. Janelle slipped her hand into his and squeezed. With another grunt, Cassa pushed her face between the middle seats, her eyes rolled back. "I may not make it through dinner without puking," she whispered to us.

* ✻ · ❋ · ✸ *

The pizza place was jammed with people, but since Cassa had been so insistent on going there, we couldn't back out now. We hunkered down on red plastic chairs while Mr. Kowalski and Janelle read a menu several paces away near a glossy statue of Elvis.

I thought about the time we were wasting, and my leg began to jitter. We were going to be late to see *Circus Bezerkus*, which meant we'd have less time to sneak out of the theater, infiltrate Mr. Pang's half a mile away, and get back before the adults' movie ended.

"Sorry, Cassa, I can't miss this chance," I hissed. "Tell them I have a stomachache and my mom's picking me up."

Bijal grimaced, but Mav nodded. "Tell 'em I have a stomachache, too."

Cassa reached for a braid to pull but then remembered she was wearing a knit cap. Her mouth bunched to one side. "Okay. Let me handle this."

We watched her make her way to her dad and then stand before him, her legs apart and hands on her hips, the way she stood before a penalty kick as she assessed how best to get the ball in.

Cassa's easygoing dad was always making us laugh with his stories about growing up on a farm. But as she pitched him, he looked as serious as Mom when she was doing her taxes. Or maybe it was the contrast between him and the smirking Elvis. Mr. Kowalski glanced at Janelle, then at us, then back at Cassa, and a frown dug into his face.

"That doesn't look good," said Bijal.

Janelle tapped her menu. She smiled at Mr. Kowalski, and he smiled back, and I swore I saw a heart outline form around their two heads. Soon, Cassa was making her way to us. "Janelle suggested we order to go."

"Thank you, Janelle," murmured Bijal, clasping his hands. "I like that woman."

Cassa slouched, crossing her arms over her stomach. "Whatever. Dad's being so salty."

To me, Mr. Kowalski's reactions seemed pretty normal for someone who'd had his quiet evening with his girlfriend hijacked by a bunch of unpredictable teens. He even let us eat our slices in the car since they didn't allow outside food in the theater. By the time we arrived, we were ready to roll.

At last, showtime.

CHAPTER 20

Once Mr. Kowalski and Janelle's movie was underway, we filed out of *Circus Bezerkus*. The air was heavy with mist that left our faces wet. The clouds were thick as lint in the laundry trap.

Mav tightened the straps of his backpack. His red-and-gold Hulkbuster key chain swayed from its gear loop as I jogged after him. Maybe I'd find mine tonight. We traveled past fancy hotels and skyscrapers like the Transamerica Pyramid. Compared to the sprints we did on the soccer field, this was a breeze, especially with all the nervous energy we had to burn.

I'm coming, Coco. I pulled off the knit cap from my now-sweaty head. Assuming we could get through the door, we'd still have to get through all the corridors to the showroom. "Why do you think Mr. Pang put in a maze to get to his shop?"

"Theft deterrent," said Cassa. "It gives him time to react in case someone breaks in."

Mav wiped mist from his eyes. "Plus it confuses thieves who are on their way out."

"Does anyone remember the way in?" I asked. "Right, left, then right, then . . . I forget."

Bijal, holding his umbrella under his arm, turned around and jogged backward. "Right, I think."

We turned one block before Jackson, deciding that it would be better to approach Mr. Pang's from the side than head-on, out of the Peeps' line of sight. In front of Boba Guys, the bright beats of pop music mingled with the sound of laughter.

Mav pulled off his backpack. "Give me that," he grunted, yanking away Bijal's umbrella and handing him and then Cassa a gas lighter. Both clicked the trigger on their handles, and a small flame erupted on the end of each metal stick.

I pulled the knit cap back over my head.

Mav strapped his smartphone to his left hand using a special elastic band that mountain climbers use so they don't drop their devices. He had the best gear. "Win and I will find the changeling and trap it." By *trap* he meant like a soccer ball. "Bijal and Cassa, you'll run defense. Look for something we can use against Pang, if necessary, and keep your eyes open. He could be anywhere. Everyone good with the plan?"

"Roger," we all said.

"Three, two, one," Mav counted. Bijal and Cassa led us off, creeping down the wall toward Mr. Pang's.

In the dim street lighting, we saw only stucco walls, rectangular windows, and the black door. A rusty-looking box hung from the black door's handle.

"Retreat!" Mav hissed, and we shrunk back to Boba Guys.

Clearly, feeding the Peep misinformation hadn't worked. The shop was still hidden.

Bijal stamped his feet. "What do we do now?"

"Plan B," said Mav.

"The lockbox?" I asked.

Mav gave a curt nod. "You remember the combo?"

"Five-nine-seven-seven."

"Ew," said Cassa. "That's so gross."

At first I was confused, but then I saw that she was staring inside Boba Guys. A kid about Coco's age was running his tongue all over a glass case holding several desserts.

Like the one in the bakery. "Wait," I said. "Mrs. Micelli told us she saw bizarre things in the mirrors of her display case. Maybe we could use a mirror to see the grasshopper door." My gaze fell to Mav's silver backpack with its compartments and gadgets.

Mav quickly opened the mirror flap. The reflective surface was only the size of a Band-Aid, but it would have to do. We edged again toward the building on the corner, with Mav awkwardly holding out his backpack flap and us clumped behind him. "There!"

Sure enough, the round grasshopper-green door with its tiny white lights appeared in the mirror, in a different spot than the black door. In fact, the black door was not in the reflection at all. "Use the mirror for reference. Ready? Go."

We moved as one unit. Cassa and Bijal flattened themselves on either side of the green door; then they immediately clicked on their gas lighters and held them to the upper corners. The smell of burning marshmallows filled my nose. The bunny and chick Peeps were toasting, and it was making my mouth water.

Then I noticed the green door didn't have a doorknob. I made Mav angle his backpack this way and that, but no luck.

"How do we—" I started to ask.

"Maybe *now* we use the lockbox," said Cassa. "The way into the magic shop is through the green door, and you can only see it in the mirror. But to get in, you have to use the lockbox *on this door.*"

"But I don't see one on this door," I protested, squinting hard at the mirror.

"Feel for it," she insisted.

I stuck out my hands where the doorknob would be and felt around. Something metal and solid bumped my hands. "I found it!" The lockbox had a few lines of buttons. I assumed the upper left button was 1, and the bottom right was 9. I pressed in the four-digit combination.

Nothing happened.

Something warm dripped onto the back of my hand. I tried to get it off, but it was sticky. Really sticky. My hand shook as I wiped it against my sweatshirt in slow motion, wondering if Mr. Pang was already onto us. Would he sic his grizzly *Were-Bear* on us? Something worse?

"Incoming goo!" cried Bijal. "Watch out below!"

I felt more than saw things brush my face—charred marshmallow bits, along with long strings of melted mallow, like sticky cobwebs. I rubbed my cheeks with my arm and tried the lockbox again. Feeling the buttons, I realized there were actually four rows. Mav was clawing at marshmallow strings.

"Let me see the number pad on your phone," I asked him. He showed me.

Of course! The last row was for the asterisk, zero, and pound sign. I took a deep breath and reentered the combination.

The front panel popped out, revealing a key. "Got it!"

I felt below the door handle for the keyhole and fit in the key. After a few jiggles, it turned. I pushed the door open.

Cassa and Bijal tumbled in after me, and Mav shut the door behind us. I braced for a gong crash but heard nothing. I also saw nothing. We were in complete and utter darkness.

I heard mild cursing behind me. "My phone's not working again," said Mav.

"Neither is mine," Cassa added. "Phones don't seem to work here."

"Wait," Mav said, perking up. "Let me try the black light."

We'd learned in science that visible light disappeared under the ultraviolet rays of black light, and anything containing phosphors, like body fluid or neon markers, would glow. Sure enough, once Mav turned on the pen-like device attached to his backpack, little white, green, and purple specks appeared like lint in the area where he was shining his light, meaning something living had left traces. He moved it around, illuminating the whites of Bijal's startled eyes and his top teeth, visible with his mouth hanging open.

Cassa flicked on her lighter. "Let's go," she urged.

After slapping the can of Dog-Off into my hand, Mav took me by the elbow. With the ultraviolet glow of the black light, and Cassa and Bijal flanking us with their lighter flames, I charged forward, a renewed sense of anger and purpose powering my strides. We were finally here and close to our goal. I led us right, then left, then right, then right, then . . . "Was it left?"

"I think it's right," said Bijal.

"Left," came Cassa's voice.

Mav took a step in one direction, then the other. "I smell popcorn this way."

We turned right, following our noses, especially Mav's, who, as the tallest, got the most concentrated whiffs. At last, the corridor opened up, spitting us into the showroom we'd visited a week ago. It was lit by antler chandeliers that cast spooky shadows on the walls. Our faces were streaked with black ash mixed with sweat, and there were sticky spots on our clothes.

Mav put away his black light and pulled the straps of his backpack tight. "Remember, stay calm, and quiet," he whispered. "We learned in Conflict Resolution not to make assumptions. Maybe there's a good explanation for all this."

As far as I was concerned, the time for explanations was over, but I let Mav hold on to his UN ideals. I gripped the Dog-Off canister tighter, feeling as amped as if this were the final minute of the Junior World Cup and we were 0-1.

The shelves looked just like they had before, piled high with bizarre whimsies. Mr. Pang's most magical item, the birch-bark canoe, had been replaced by an inflatable pool chair. The red-and-silver float looked long enough to sit in with my legs extended. It even had two drink holders shaped like golden fists. Two? Everyone knew nature called after one drink. I'd never seen it before, but something about it looked familiar. THE CANOE'S NOT FOR SALE. DON'T EVEN THINK ABOUT IT sign still hung from the rafters next to the glowing unicorn piñatas.

Mav gaped. "It looks like . . . a Hulkbuster."

I shuddered as if someone had dropped an ice chip down my back. Sure enough, the pool chair had a similar muscular profile to the Hulkbuster, down to its mighty gold fists. I'd been hoping to find it, but not like this. "You don't think . . . ?"

"I don't know what to think," said Mav. "Come on, let's move."

We spread out among the rows in pairs, Bijal with Cassa, and Mav with me.

I headed straight for where I'd last seen the china doll with the staring eyes and green pajamas. She'd been between the red Kick-Me Boots and the Ask-Me-Anything Beethoven Busts. But when I got there . . .

Chang-Ah-Ling was gone.

CHAPTER 21

I nearly howled before my lungs closed tight like two fists. Mav and I checked the entire row as well as the two on either side, but there was no sign of the eerie doll.

Coco, where are you? I pleaded silently.

My other two friends joined us at the end of one aisle, and I noticed the kangaroo pocket of Cassa's hoodie was bulging. She held up two palms and shrugged. No sign of Mr. Pang, either, apparently.

Mav tapped Cassa's shoulder and hooked his thumb in one direction, then gestured for Bijal and me to go off in the other. We all nodded in agreement.

I scanned intently for the distinctive jade color of the doll's clothing, all other objects a blur as I hunted. Bijal padded squeakily beside me, his head pivoting back and forth for attackers. Having not found anything, we met up with Mav and Cassa again in the original aisle. They, too, were empty-handed.

Mav cast a dark look at the end of the room. *Let's check the office*, he mouthed.

Our feet made quiet shuffling noises as we approached the doorway with the black velvet curtain, where the smell of popcorn was most intense. Mav directed us with his hands, and we scooted to one side. The curtain rings screeched against the rod as he yanked it back.

A giant popcorn machine stood in the middle of the room, the size of an actual mail truck. Recessed ceiling lights gave its candy-apple-red base a glossy shine. Windows thick enough to be bulletproof enclosed a silver kettle as big as a snare drum. A machine like that could probably pop a whole cornfield in one go. Except that it didn't contain a single kernel.

Mr. Pang, his back to us and wearing a pair of wireless over-ear headphones, was reaching into the popcorn tray. When he saw us reflected in the glass, something yellow dropped from his hand. It bounced on the bottom of the tray and lay still. Stepping closer, I saw that it was a Pikachu figurine, a Pokémon pocket monster with a mouselike yellow body, pointy black-tipped ears, and a tail shaped like a lightning bolt.

Whatever was going on here had nothing to do with popcorn, though the smell was unmistakable.

Time for some conflict resolution.

"Oh, dear, you're back." He pulled off his shiny headphones, nearly displacing his green-yellow-and-gray sweatband. After adjusting the band, he slid closed the glass doors of the popcorn cart. "How did you get in?"

"Forget that. Where's Coco?" I demanded.

Mr. Pang opened one of his pockets and dropped in the headphones, which disappeared without a single bulge in the gold fabric. "Ah, your sister. It's good to have *ohana*, family. Ohana means no one gets left behind. Except sometimes you should leave them behind, especially if they turn out to be jealous, blood-sucking leeches who just want to put you out of business."

This cuckoo bird was flying in circles. Mav jerked his head toward me to spur me on.

"We know about the spirits in the broom and dustpan," I said, "and we know they swept Coco into your shop. So where is she?"

Mr. Pang actually had the nerve to fake surprise. "Er, which broom and dustpan?" He glanced at a fire extinguisher hung on the wall, only it was purple, not red. Whoever heard of a purple fire extinguisher?

I passed Mav a look that asked *now do you believe he's a Looney Tune?*

Mav snorted. "Forget this. Cassa—"

"On it." She pulled her hands out of her hoodie pocket. In one hand, she gripped a round speckled object. An egg? I suddenly remembered the carton of eggs labeled EGGS OF TRUTH that Cassa found that first day in the shop. *With these, maybe you could tell when adults were lying to you,* she had said.

"Wait! Don't throw the twenty-hour egg!" Mr. Pang lifted his hands, putting his taloned nails on full display.

Mav snapped his fingers at Cassa like a boss ordering a hit. She drew back her arm, and Mr. Pang backed away.

"Okay, everyone keep a calm head. How about we play Twenty Questions?"

"How about we play Just Tell Us before we egg you," I snapped, scowling so hard my jaw felt like it might pop open like a cash register drawer. "Where's my sister? Your broom and dustpan swept her in here, so where is she?"

"Which broom and dustpan?"

"The ones you stuck me with so you could steal my things!" I cried. My ears roared as if full of thunder, and I had to stop myself from kicking the man in the shins. "You were 'rewarding' me for driving away those burglars, remember?"

"Oh, them. I would stay away from those pesky gulls." His mouth smashed into a stingy line, his thready eyebrows crouched low. "They'll eat anything—moldy sandwiches, dead slugs." He pinched his nose and whispered, "That's why they have a fishy smell." Then he addressed Bijal. "Young man, please don't touch my things."

Bijal had picked up a plush hedgehog from a worktable covered with junk and a bunch of padded envelopes. "So you *do* take toys," he said with the *aha!* tone of a detective finding a clue. "Steal any stuffed Babars lately? What do you do, hold 'em for ransom?"

Mr. Pang drew up like a marionette pulled on a string. "I'm not a thief. As a matter of fact, I am returning that to her owner. You wouldn't believe how often children lose their favorite cuddle buddies." He removed something from his pocket that looked like gumballs. "Someone lost these delightful expandable water beads, and I have no way of knowing who the owner is. Would you like one? Soak them in water and they expand to the size of the moon! Well, maybe not that big . . ." He glanced up at an inflatable moon hanging in a corner. Just under it a poster of the phases of the moon ran the length of one wall. He was a real lunatic, a moon fanatic.

My stomach roiled. "Cassa," I spat. "Egg him so we can learn the truth."

He slipped the expandable water beads back into his pocket and stuck up his hands again. "No, no! Your sister's quite safe, just a little, er, *misplaced* at the moment. I was actually just going to look for her with my eyeballs."

I growled. How else were you supposed to look for something if not with your eyeballs? "What do you mean by 'misplaced'?"

"You need to know I was just trying to help." Mr. Pang began pacing back and forth like a duck in a shooting gallery, his sky-blue sneakers mewling the way new shoes do. They were Flip and Dunks, the hottest basketball sneaker on the market. The sweatband also looked like it had just come out of its packaging. Something about this new gear was very peculiar, just like with the pool chair. "You think I wanted to be in this mess, when I could be living my best life, crafting my whimsies?" He patted his popcorn machine. "I use real butter, not the fake stuff the competition uses. True artisans never cut corners."

"Is your headband on too tight?" Bijal stopped twisting the Rubik's Cube he had plucked from the table. "Why would you use butter when there's no popcorn?"

I scowled. This conversation was going off the rails again. "Who cares about—"

"This machine does something better than make popcorn,"

Mr. Pang slid in, waggling his eyebrows and making his sweatband ripple. "It takes the magic from one thing and puts it into another."

So that's how the magic was done? Our faces stared back at us through the windows of the machine, which shone under the recessed ceiling lights like the prized car in a dealership.

"It allowed me to put the spirits of Cloud Weaver and Cowherd into their earthly vessels. Sure, that slows them down somewhat, but at least the Mother can't get them if they're inside."

"So you admit you're in league with them." Bijal shook the Rubik's Cube at Mr. Pang as if it were a damning piece of evidence.

I sighed in frustration, tipping my head back and rolling my eyes. "Tell me where my sister is!"

I couldn't help noticing that one of the ceiling lights was missing. It must be the same bulb I noticed missing during our visit with Mr. Suresh. In fact, the casing didn't look like it had ever held a bulb. It was just a dark hole.

Mr. Pang pincered the Rubik's Cube out of Bijal's hands and set it firmly back on the table. He sniffed and looked longingly at Bijal's front pocket. "Is that an Abba-Zaba bar I smell?"

Bijal shrank away from him.

With a smile that showed a mouth of narrow teeth, Mr. Pang gestured to the popcorn machine. "Would you like me to show you how it works?"

Mr. Pang was stalling, but maybe we could learn something that would help me get Coco back.

"Gather round," he said.

We pressed in closer. The front panel featured two large buttons—one green and one red, which seemed self-explanatory. He slid open the front window and then moved aside.

"Now just allow me to get . . ."

Without warning, he zoomed through the curtain, faster than even I could run at full speed.

Bijal, who had been peering into the machine, snapped up, bumping his head on the metal casing. Cassa made it through the curtain first. We all flew after her.

Mr. Pang careened down the middle aisle, as fast as a flame following a gas leak.

Cassa stopped short, and we skidded into her. With the arm that had made her Francisco Middle School's star pitcher three years in a row, she hurled the egg. It flew with purpose. Even a little swagger.

Splat! The egg hit Mr. Pang right on the butt.

Instead of a gooey explosion of yolk, egg white, and shell, the impact released a puff of smoke. Mr. Pang vanished. I rubbed my eyes. Through the haze, I could not spot a single gold thread of the man, only the yellow floorboards where he had just been standing.

Something green and feathery flew out of the mist, so small and high above our heads, I might have missed it.

A magpie.

CHAPTER 22

So Mr. Pang was a magpie. The Egg Of Truth had revealed his true form. That would explain the man's talon-like fingernails. But was he the same magpie I'd attempted to rescue? Mr. Pang had gone into his office to take a phone call. He could have changed into a bird then and flown out to fake an injury.

The bird darted up over the aisle into the next one.

"There!" I cried.

"Follow him!" Mav yelled, setting off.

The magpie perched atop a fringed lampshade. When he spotted us, he flew to the last aisle.

Mav bent over his knees to catch his breath. "Team, can't win this one without a plan."

"Or a net," said Cassa.

"A net's no good if we can't reach it!" Bijal threw his hands at the ceiling. "We need a tranquilizer gun."

Cassa snorted. "Yeah, like we're going to find one here."

"Well, he has everything else!" Bijal crossed his arms. "Okay, Babe Ruth, what's your suggestion?"

She scowled.

A needle of panic jabbed at me. We could be here all night. There was a reason birds were one of the few animals to survive mass extinction. "Why doesn't he fly away? We've seen him outside before."

Bijal glanced toward the exit. "Maybe he can't open the door by himself."

"There's a hole in the ceiling above the popcorn machine," I said, "Maybe that's how he gets in—he flies through the window of the acupuncture shop and then down that chute. But why doesn't he escape that way now?"

Mav tapped a finger to his chin. "Maybe he can only fly downward. A bird flew down our chimney once, and it couldn't make it back up. The ascent was too steep."

"So Mr. Pang can only exit his shop as a human, and he won't be human for the next twenty hours," said Cassa.

"There's gotta be a way to catch it." I glanced around me. "We're in a room full of magic things. Maybe we could try this?" I reached for the first thing I saw—a top hat, as shiny black as sealskin. As soon as I closed my hand around the rim, my feet started moving. Not just moving, but tap-dancing, except that since I was wearing sneakers, there was no tapping, just a lot of squeaking. I was dragged down the aisle, shuffle-kicking, stamping, and stomping. My hands automatically clutched both sides of the hat and raised it up and down over my head, like I was in a chorus line.

Mav ducked out of my way while I pranced over to Bijal.

"Bijal, catch!" Mav had pulled Bijal's umbrella from his backpack.

Bijal snagged it and fired. The canopy opened as fast as ink from a jettisoning squid and knocked the hat from my hands. I stopped dancing so abruptly I nearly fell over, my feet humming and my breathing labored. The hat rolled in a circle before coming to a stop.

After retracting his umbrella, Bijal used it to pick up the hat. Only then did I see the danger-red label dangling from the brim. I really needed to think before grabbing stuff in here.

"'Top Hat Attack,'" Bijal read, then flipped the hat back onto the shelf with his umbrella.

Cassa snickered. "Hey, Win, nice kick ball change."

Mav reshouldered his backpack. "Fred Astaire, why don't you go keep an eye on the bird while we look for a way to capture it."

"Okay," I mumbled sheepishly.

While the others moved about, reading labels to find something that might work, I ran back to the last aisle, searching the shelves. A couple objects grabbed my attention—a racket called Bad-Mitten Finder, and a glossy red fire hydrant called Fire-Weiler with a red label—I'd steer clear of that. Then I saw movement on a potted cactus with an especially large red tag, several paces away. At the top of the cactus sprouted dark strands of what looked like hair, tied into a ponytail.

The magpie was perched on one of the cactus's upturned arms, preening his feathers. I stopped, not wanting to scare off the bird, but at the same time, I wished the pesky thing would impale himself on one of the cactus needles.

Bijal appeared at the end of the row, silkily pulling something out of his pocket. Soon he was dangling a yellow-and-black-checked Abba-Zaba candy bar from his fingers just a couple paces away from the magpie. The bird froze in mid-preen.

"Abba-Zaba, mm-mm," said Bijal. "Rich and chewy taffy, creamy peanut butter center, sweet and savory with a hint of vanilla. I'll share it with you, my feathered friend. It's a magic carpet ride to a bygone era when people spent hours chewing their candy. I'll even unwrap this bad boy for you." The wrapper crinkled enticingly under Bijal's skilled fingers. He pulled the white taffy like Silly Putty until the bar tore in half. He molded one half into what looked like a candle, the twisted end pointed like a flame, and he stuck it to the ground. Then he began eating the other half.

The magpie started to twitch. Then he flew to the opposite aisle, landing on a stuffed trout. The bird's head bobbed up and down a few times before he flapped his wings again and returned to the cactus. Back and forth he went. Mr. Pang really wanted that Abba-Zaba bar. The question was, how much?

The rattle of Mav's backpack and the shuffle of moving feet sounded from somewhere behind me. The magpie watched me make my way to the Abba-Zaba candle. I bent over the taffy sculpture. "Looks like someone dropped their Abba-Zaba. Good candy like this shouldn't go to waste, am I right?"

Bijal, his face contorted into an expression of bliss, just nodded. His teeth were probably stuck together. I plucked the candy off the floor and raised the flame part to my lips, my movements excruciatingly slow like one of those mushy movie kisses you hope never to see when your mom's in the room. I bit off the end.

With an outraged screech, the magpie swooped down again from the cactus and knocked the bar from my hands. The hunk of Abba-Zaba landed with a sticky thud, and the bird dove for it. How about that? Mr. Pang was as impulsive as me.

Mav swooped in and covered the bird with a plastic colander.

Cassa slid a cookie sheet under it. "Got you!"

Neither Bijal nor I could speak with our mouths sealed with Abba-Zaba, but we nodded vigorously and stuck up our thumbs.

Mav carefully flipped over the colander and cookie sheet. Then Cassa took off her beret and, while Mav slowly pulled off the cookie sheet, stretched the hat over the colander. "There. He should be able to breathe through the colander holes. Now we have to get going. The movie's going to end in less than fifteen minutes."

Mav fit the colander in his backpack, creating a bulge at the bottom. He zipped up the pack, and we headed back to the maze corridor.

"But what are we going to do with him?" I asked.

"We're going to wait until he changes back to Mr. Pang so we can continue the interrogation." Mav switched on his black light. "We still have the eggs in case he needs a little more *persuasion*."

He sounded menacing, especially with his teeth all lit up. But the way I saw it, Mr. Pang had it coming.

The magpie was quiet on the way back to the theater,

probably thanks to the Abba-Zaba. Yet, I couldn't help feeling like something was following us. I stopped and glanced behind me. "Did you hear that?"

"Yeah, I heard footsteps," said Cassa, who was bringing up the rear.

Mav fiddled with his phone. "Let's see if it works now." The flashlight function switched on, and he pointed the device behind us. No one was there.

We continued on our way.

"Ow! Why'd you do that, Cassa?" Bijal rubbed his butt.

"I didn't do anything."

"Someone kicked me!"

"Oof! Someone kicked *me*." Cassa looked behind her, but even under the dim streetlights, it was clear we were alone.

"There!" Mav jabbed a finger. "A pair of boots." A flash of red disappeared into a straggly margin of bush. As the boots retreated from us, the bushes shuddered one by one back down the street.

"The Kick-Me Boots." My voice sounded hollow. "They must have escaped when we left. Like the Mischief Mustache." I hadn't seen the mustache since it had planted itself on Mr. Suresh, and I hoped I never would again.

Mav pulled me by the elbow. "Come on. We have bigger worries right now."

He was right, but kicking boots gone rogue could be disastrous in a crowded city like this one.

Once we were inside the brightly lit theater, we pulled out our ticket stubs for reentry. A red-vested ticket taker glanced at Mav's backpack. "Mind opening that for me?""

People were piling up behind us. Mav unhooked his backpack from his shoulder. Surely the magpie had finished chewing and would screech at any second. Mav unzipped slowly.

"Come on! We're going to be late to the show," grumbled a woman.

The ticket taker shone his flashlight into Mav's backpack, illuminating the two gas lighters. "Well, what do we have here?"

"We just got back from camping," I said.

Bijal raked a hand through his hair. "Is this the TSA? Should we take our shoes off, too?"

"Dad!" cried Cassa, waving.

We all stepped to the side and looked toward a set of doors where Mr. Kowalski and Janelle had emerged, her arm looped through his. Mr. Kowalski lifted his half-empty popcorn box in acknowledgment and made tracks toward us. As we all headed for the exit, he said, "We were looking for you in there."

"Bijal got scared, so we left to get some fresh air."

Bijal cut Cassa a salty look but curled a hand over his stomach. "Yeah, it was pretty intense. But I think I just ate too much popcorn."

"Oh, I'm sorry to hear that. Since you're not feeling well, I'll drop you off first."

"Actually, he'd like to go to Mav's house," said Cassa.

"I would?" Bijal glanced at Cassa, who jabbed him with her stare. "I mean I would."

"But I promised to get you all back right after—"

"Mav's mom has a very soothing tea," Cassa cut in smoothly.

I nudged Mav, who was distracted by his backpack. He shined up a smile. "She sure does. It's called, er, Soothing Tea."

Mr. Kowalski rubbed his beard and glanced at Janelle.

She shrugged. "Maybe just a brief stop . . ."

"In fact, *I* would like some of that tea, too, and so would Winston." Cassa lifted a fist of a chin to Janelle.

"I sure would," I replied, though it would take a lot more than tea to soothe my stomach.

"Great, it's settled, then," said Cassa. "Let's go before you throw up." She grabbed Bijal's arm and led us all to the exit.

Soon Mr. Kowalski was steering his Explorer to the parking lot exit.

"How's the cargo?" Cassa whispered through the space between the middle-row seats. As if he'd heard her, the magpie began to emit a series of harsh chattering sounds: *wock, wock, wock-a-wock.*

"What was that?" asked Janelle, her eyes big.

Mr. Kowalski, who had stuck half his head out of the window to feed the parking ticket machine, turned back to Janelle. "What was what?"

"I swear I heard . . . a bird," she replied.

"It's my phone," said Mav. "Sorry. Can't seem to turn it off."

Janelle's nose wrinkled, and she touched one of her hoop earrings. "But it didn't sound like a ringtone. It sounded real."

"Well, it wasn't." Cassa reached between the seats for Mav's backpack. "She's so annoying," she whispered. "Gimme one of those eggs."

While Mav tried to keep the colander steady, I pulled the carton from the front pocket and unhinged the lid. Cassa plucked out the one with 20 MINUTES inked on its shell. "I think the time means how long the victim will be forced to tell the truth. Let's test it. Time?"

I glanced at Mav's wristwatch. "Nine-oh-seven. What are you going to do?"

"Wait and see," she muttered, her gaze scorching Janelle, who sat diagonally in front of her.

I wanted to see what the Egg of Truth did as much as the next kid, but maybe not this way. . . .

"I don't think that's a good idea," whispered Bijal, waving a hand in front of Cassa's face. "You can use the egg on me. Just don't ask me anything embarrassing."

We pulled into the street, and darkness shrouded the car. Janelle was smiling at something Mr. Kowalski had said about their movie. Cassa clutched the egg to her chest, still glaring at Janelle. With the seat blocking most of Janelle's body, Cassa would have to lob the egg so that it landed in the woman's lap. Easy enough for a pitcher.

But as Cassa tossed up her missile, Bijal blocked her hand. The egg bounced back.

Right onto Cassa.

CHAPTER 23

A puff of smoke mushroomed in Cassa's lap.

Bijal grabbed his face. "Oops."

"One ran away with my sandwich the other day," Janelle was telling Mr. Kowalski, oblivious to what was going on in the backseat. "I wasn't going to argue with it."

Luckily, the smoke evaporated quickly, and it didn't have any smell. Cassa's head was pressed back against her seat, and she was clutching the top of her seat belt as if bracing for an impact.

Janelle twisted around and smiled at her. "I bet you're not afraid of those hissing squirrels."

Cassa glanced around her as if dazed. "Me? No, I'm not afraid of hissing squirrels. I am afraid of abandonment, though. My mom left, and it still hurts, right here." She bumped her chest with her fist. "My dad's all I have. Now that he has you, he doesn't need me. You seem like a nice lady, but what if he leaves me because of you? And what if I like you too much and you leave me, too?"

The whites of Bijal's eyes showed over his seat. "Egg of Too-Much Truth!" he whispered to Mav and me.

Janelle's face had opened with concern, and she reached behind and patted Cassa's knee. "I'm so sorry you're feeling that way. I like you, too, very much."

"Cassa, honey," Mr. Kowalski shot behind him, "let's drop off your friends and then we can talk about this."

The magpie started chattering again. Mr. Kowalski braked, his startled eyes appearing in the rearview mirror. Mav tried to shush the bird, but that only made it cry louder.

"Would you mind turning down your phone, Mav?" asked Janelle.

"That's no phone," said Mr. Kowalski. "Do you have a bird back there?"

I leaned forward to shush Cassa before she spilled the yolk on tonight's adventures, but my seat belt locked and all I got was a fabric burn on my neck. Bijal, however, clamped a hand over Cassa's mouth.

"No, Mr. Kowalski, there's no bird," Mav said loudly. "Cassa might have told you, but I'm a bird enthusiast. If you saw my room, you'd know. I downloaded a bunch of birdcalls on my phone, and I can't seem to shut it off now. Sorry about that!"

Cassa pushed away Bijal's hand. "Stop being so sneaky, Bijal. These aren't *your* parents. You don't have to lie to them."

"You think Bijal's sneaky?" I asked, sensing an opportunity to keep her distracted.

"He's never straight up with his parents," Cassa huffed. "You know how hard it is to keep all his lies straight?"

"I only lie to protect their innocence," Bijal protested. "You don't understand me at all." He leaned away from Cassa.

"That Egg of Truth is rotten," I muttered to Mav.

"Your parents would be proud of you even if you didn't send letters to Tanzanian orphans," Cassa went on. "You're a great guy. You tie balloon animals for boomers and you make people laugh. Plus, you're the best defender I know, and not just on the field. I still remember when you told those jerks who called me a sweat sock to smell your butt." She crossed her arms hard over her chest.

"Cassa, what's going on with you?" asked Mr. Kowalski.

"Probably just the movie we saw," I chimed up. "It was one of those tearjerkers where this kid starts scalping people with a letter opener because he never got a visit from Santa Claus."

Janelle scratched her cheek. "That's what *Circus Bezerkus* is about?"

"Er, indirectly."

Cassa threw me a disbelieving stare. "That's *not* what it's about. And you. You barely make time for Bijal and me outside of soccer anymore. I know your dad died and it was hard, but we're still here. If Coco hadn't been kidnapped, we might not see you at all."

I coughed. I hadn't wanted to spend time with them because I thought I'd bring the party down, with Dad always on my mind.

"What are you talking about?" Mr. Kowalski exclaimed. "Coco's not kidnapped."

She sailed on. "Then we'll graduate and you'll probably go to Mav's school because we all know how much you want to."

I started making squeaking and huffing sounds. Who said I wanted to go to Mav's school? As if we could afford it. Mav knocked my knee with his and glared at me. I stopped huffing. "I'm not going to Mav's school," I mumbled.

Mr. Kowalski kept tapping the brakes, as if undecided if he should go or stop.

It occurred to me that Cassa's truths said more about her than us. Before she could plunge any more stakes into our hearts, we finally reached the McFees' ultra-modern house. Since he was a real estate tycoon, Mav's dad had nabbed the nicest spot in the Marina District with a full view of San Francisco Bay.

Mr. Kowalski parked the car in the short driveway. "Okay, Cassa. What do you think about calling it a night? We can make cocoa and—"

"I think I would rather chew on Mav's cleats," she declared as the rest of us piled out. "If Mav just cleaned his stinky cleats once in a while, we could solve global warm—"

Before she could finish, we pulled the oracle out of the car.

"She'll be fine, Mr. K!" Bijal called over his shoulder.

Mav jammed his house key into the lock and threw open the front door. Monroe, in sweats and a tee, watched with curiosity as we tried to rush Cassa past him.

But Cassa had glued her feet to the tile. "Hi, Monroe. You might not know this, but one day, you and I will get married. With your beauty and my brains, we'll be unstoppable."

A short laugh escaped Monroe's lips, the kind that asked if this was some kind of joke.

I pulled Cassa away by the arm, wondering how much longer it would be until the egg's magic had expended itself. She grunted in annoyance but allowed me to lead her up the glass staircase to Mav's room, bypassing Mrs. McFee, who was on her way down. The woman had the posture of an equestrian rider, and she wore heels even with her tracksuit.

"Hello, kids! What's going on?" Bijal and Mav had already disappeared into his room, leaving me to handle this.

"Hi, Mrs. McFee. Cassa's dad and his girlfriend are downstairs and would like some soothing tea."

"They're here? How nice. Well, I have a lovely selection."

Before Cassa could dispense any bits of unsolicited truth, I yanked her the last few yards. Mrs. McFee's heels made tiny clicks as she continued down the stairs.

Mav's spacious bedroom had been designed to resemble the interior of an old ship. You knew someone was rich when they could pay someone to make their stuff look used. Three walls were covered in distressed wood paneling. The fourth had a floor-to-ceiling window with a brass telescope for sighting whales. There was even an old ship steering wheel that actually rotated.

Mav hauled an old aquarium out of his closet. A duct-taped package that looked like a gray rock had been wedged into the container. He held up the package. "Our informant."

"Our . . . The Peep?" I asked.

He nodded. "I taped insulation around it so it wouldn't overhear anything, though a lot of good that did. I'll dump it later."

He chucked the package like a football into the upper reaches of his closet. Then he carried the aquarium to the far corner of the room, where Bijal was sitting on the map-of-the-world rug, holding the beret down on the colander. The magpie was jumping around inside, its beak occasionally poking out of the knit.

Cassa was rubbernecking Mav's room, as if she hadn't visited a thousand times before. "Ditch this." She waved a hand at his navy-blue comforter. "You can afford an upgrade. I recommend eight-hundred-thread-count Egyptian cotton."

Bijal looked at his watch. "Five more minutes of truth."

Instead of quickly removing the knit cap and dumping the colander over the aquarium, like I would've done, Mav carefully pushed down on the fabric and scooped up the bird with it. Then he put the whole bundle, hat and all, into the aquarium, while I slid the screen cover into place.

The magpie shrugged off the cap and shuddered, as if trying to shake all its plumage back into place. It looked put out, if such a thing was possible. Its head feathers were ruffled like a bad haircut, and one eye was cocked, the other half-shut.

Mrs. McFee appeared in the doorway. "Bijal, I heard your stomach is bothering you."

He held up his hands, as if he'd been caught committing a crime. "It's much better now."

"Good." She drew closer, her bracelets jangling. "Is that a bird?"

Mav rolled onto his butt. "Um, yes."

"Why is it in there? And why is it jumping like that on the black thing? Is that a hat?"

We all glanced at Cassa, who glanced up from Mav's wall shelf, where she'd been rearranging Mav's books. "Actually, Mrs. McFee—"

"Cassa has a really funny joke," I said.

Cassa put her hands on her hips. "No, I don't!"

"Yes, you do. The one about how to make tissue dance?"

Cassa's nostrils flared. "I don't know that one."

Mav rolled his hand, as if trying to get her to play along. "Put a little . . ." She didn't respond. He pretended to pick his nose, which only made her scowl in disgust.

"Boogie in it," he finished.

Bijal laughed extra hard. He even slapped his knees. "Good one, Cassa! Ha, ha, ha!"

She gave an exasperated cough. "But I didn't tell it!"

Mrs. McFee smiled, the tolerant kind adults use when they don't know what's going on and don't want to find out. "Cassa, were you saying something?"

"Yes, I was going to say that's my cap in there. I put it in because . . ."

Bijal covered his face with his hands, though his eyes showed through his fingers.

"Because the bird looked cold," Cassa finished.

Bijal let go of his face and looked at his watch. He grinned and gave us a thumbs-up from under his arm. She was officially over the truth spell.

"Oh." Mrs. McFee drew back her head, not even attempting to cover her confusion with a smile now. "Well, that's one puzzle solved."

Her footsteps faded. Mav put his face closer to the aquarium and drummed his fingers along the top. "Too bad it's not the one that needs solving."

CHAPTER 24

Cassa sat on the floor beside us and pulled her legs crisscross. "It was like going down a waterslide—once I got going, I couldn't stop. I'm sorry for vomiting all my feelings. It's so embarrassing." She clapped her hands over her face.

"It's cool, Cassa," I said. "If you want, we can tell you some truths to make it even."

She peeked through her fingers. "If *you* want."

Mav put his face near the aquarium. "I'll tell you all about how your cleats stink later. But right now we need to figure out a plan."

The magpie began to chitter again and pecked his beak against the glass.

Bijal tapped a finger on the opposite side. "This magpie's as shifty as sand, first playing the victim, then ditching us. He's hiding something. You can see it in the eyes."

"Did anyone else think it was strange when Mr. Pang said he was going to search for Coco 'with his eyeballs'?" I asked. "It's like saying, 'I'm going to smell with my nose,' or 'I'm going to burp with my mouth.'"

Bijal's shoulders popped up. "Some people burp with their butts."

Cassa slapped the carpet. "Maybe he meant 'Eyeballs' with a capital *E*. Like they were one of his whimsies."

"The Far-Seeing Eyeballs . . ." said Mav in a hushed voice. He folded his long legs with ease. "We'll return to the shop tomorrow and get them. That way, when he changes back to Mr. Pang, we can make him show us how to find Coco. If he doesn't, we'll hit him with the ten-minute egg, and if that doesn't work, the thirty-hour one."

I polished my knees. "Maybe we should save one for Not-Coco."

My sister's sweet face with the red bandanna bib tied under her chin appeared in my mind. Guilt washed over me again, sticky as sunscreen, and I dug my fingernails into my elbows.

Mav stared up at the constellations painted on his ceiling. "Not a good idea. What if Chang-Ah-Ling appeared and Coco's body disappeared?"

"Good point," said Cassa. "We don't know how an Egg of Truth works on a body that's been separated from its spirit. Could be risky."

"Half a Coco is better than no Coco." Bijal handed me a packet of Flava-gum.

As much as I wanted to use one of the eggs on Not-Coco, especially in front of my mom and Philippa, my friends were right. I fisted the packet. It was the juiciest gum around, but I had no appetite.

"'Brain Strainer. Seep stress away,'" Cassa read from the label stuck to the colander. She carefully lowered it onto my head.

Bijal made a face. "I hope you checked it for droppings first."

My shoulders relaxed, and I remembered to breathe. "Whoa. This feels strangely cooling." I started tipping backward but caught myself.

At the distant rumble of thunder, we all lifted our heads toward the window.

Mother Cloud Weaver must be searching for the pair again, which meant she hadn't zapped them quite yet. The sound of voices and clicking heels drew near. Cassa's parents were coming to collect us. Mav went into captain mode. "Everyone clear your Saturday afternoon. We have eighteen hours left on the egg. Operation Eyeballs begins tomorrow." He held out a dead zombie arm, and we added ours to the pile. "Zubber time."

❋ · ❋ · ❋

When I got home, the sound of Mom's snoring drifted from her bedroom. I slowly turned her doorknob, bracing myself in case Not-Coco was waiting on the other side, staring with glowing eyes like in Mav's changeling movie.

But Not-Coco was balled up on Coco's toddler bed. That was another sign she was a fake—my little sister always slept like a starfish, not a ball. Not-Coco's breathing sounded even, and her body twitched now and then. I guess changelings required sleep just like the rest of us. Or maybe it was Coco's three-year-old body that needed a rest. I was tempted to put a leash on her, but I figured Mom wouldn't allow it. Plus, I didn't have a leash.

Tiptoeing around, I checked all the potential hiding spots for the broom and dustpan in case they had returned. Nothing.

A thin line of light underscored Philippa's door, so I put the eggs down on my nightstand and decided to risk life and limb.

I knocked.

No response.

I opened the door a crack to see Philippa sitting on her bed, wearing headphones. It looked like she had three buns growing from her head. She slid a pink highlighter across the page of the book on her lap—*Beginning Arabic.*

I plunked down at the foot of her bed. "Any problems?"

She looked up and pulled the headphones off one ear. "With what?"

"The Not-Coco."

She blinked. "Yeah, her mouth started foaming and then her head spun around like a tornado."

"Very funny."

She chuckled and pushed her socked foot into my leg. "Coco's fine. Well, except she doesn't call me Pippa anymore." She chucked her book and highlighter onto a nearby chair and adjusted the sloth pillow behind her back. "But, Win, you're acting sus, too. I mean, you bring a dirty broom and dustpan into our closet and then tell me they kidnapped Coco? Mom chatted with Dr. Toy this evening."

"I don't need to see a shrink!"

"You might not be the best judge of that."

"You have to tell Mom to back off."

She tucked a leg under her, and her gaze sharpened. "Okay, Winston. Come with me to see Vic tomorrow morning at Golden Gate Park, and I'll tell Mom to leave you alone. No promises if you start to act even weirder, though."

With eighteen, closer to seventeen hours now left on the Egg of Truth, I didn't have much time to spare. But I remembered Mr. Suresh was holding an open house tomorrow morning at the store site, so we wouldn't be able to investigate until after noon anyway. "Fine. Better than you seeing that guy alone. Why are you learning Arabic?"

Dad spoke Arabic as an army translator, but why would Philippa want to learn it? My eye caught on the MEPS brochure she was using as a bookmark. *America Needs You.*

Philippa closed her book. "Mind your own beeswax."

The idea that she might want to enlist made me a little sick. Bad enough we'd lost Dad. But I couldn't think about that now. I had another sister on my mind.

Back in my own room, I pulled my Iron Man comforter over my head, feeling guilty that I could sleep in my own bed, unlike poor Coco. Closing my eyes, I visualized my sister's face. I reminded myself that she was a Water type, able to go with the flow. Also, like water flowing through a valley, she was strong-willed and able to carve her own path.

Hold on, Coco. Your brother's coming for you. I just need a little more time.

CHAPTER 25

Philippa knocked on my door. "Open up. Why is your door stuck?"

It was almost ten-thirty. A panicked hammering began in my chest. Only three nights until the full moon. Three more days to find Coco.

"Hold on." Dragging myself out of bed, I pulled out the wedge I'd used to secure the door, in case Not-Coco was planning a little mischief.

I dropped back onto my mattress, dizzy from getting up too quickly.

"We're supposed to see Vic at eleven, remember?" Philippa looked less like her usual bridge troll self and more like a teenager in jeans and a normal-size sweater, though her hair was still up in lopsided buns.

"Where's Mom?"

"She and Coco are carpooling with Mabel and Mrs. Rogers to CuriOdyssey."

"*Not*-Coco, you mean." I sat up, shocked that Mrs. Rogers was allowing her near Mabel again. "That freak messed up Mom's laptop, you know."

Philippa frowned and plucked an Egg of Truth from its bed of straw on my nightstand. "Why are you keeping eggs in here? They're probably rotten by now."

"They're Eggs of Truth. Be careful with them."

She fumbled the egg, and I shrieked.

But then she caught it. "Just kidding."

"Very funny," I grumbled.

Philippa set it back in the box, fingering the tag that Cassa had tucked inside. "Where'd you get these?"

"Mr. Pang's Whimsies. They're very important to finding Coco, so keep your mitts off them." I closed the carton.

Philippa's face became hard to read—her eyes hard and lips squished into a bundle like a wad of chewing gum. With a shrug, she slithered back out the door. "You have five minutes."

I got dressed and then opened my backpack, intending to take the eggs with me so Not-Coco couldn't mess with them. At the bottom of my pack lay the Brain Strainer. Cassa had made me take it, saying I should use it to manage my stress. I sat on my bed and fit it over my head.

Immediately, I felt cooler, like I was floating in an ocean that was exactly the right temperature. My temples stopped throbbing, and my eyes relaxed. This was how I had felt when I did qigong. Calm. Peaceful. Restored.

Why had I been so worried? I had a good team, and the

field—Mr. Pang's shop—was unguarded. Our plan was solid. I knew exactly where Pang kept the Far-Seeing Eyeballs. And maybe we'd find something else in his house of horrors that would lead us to Coco.

The door opened again, and Philippa slid in, holding a pair of tweezers. "Stop borrowing my eyebrow—" Seeing me with the Brain Strainer on my head, she sighed. "Never mind."

It was drizzling when we descended the front steps to our used Volvo. Philippa gunned the engine in the hard way she did everything and turned on the heat full blast. "This weather really bites. Shouldn't have told him to meet me in the Concourse."

I frowned. "Why are we meeting there?"

"He's working a construction gig in the park, and he'll be on his break then. Plus, there's always concerts on the weekends, so there'll be people around to protect us in case he's a nutjob."

Concerts on the weekends . . . I winced, remembering how I'd turned down Dani's invitation to watch her perform. Monroe's extra practice ukulele was collecting dust in my room. I couldn't wait until this was all over and I could have a life again, even a life built on lies.

I looked at Philippa, wondering if I should try again to convince her of the truth. Usually she drove shrunk down in her seat, one hand holding the wheel, the other hanging out the window. But with the windows up, she was like a caged animal, shifting uncomfortably. She turned on a news channel, probably to discourage me from talking.

An impressive thunder-and-lightning show began as we

approached the Panhandle, a strip of green that led into the "pan" of the thousand-acre Golden Gate Park. Was Mother Cloud Weaver growing more desperate? Traffic slowed to a crawl. The windshield wipers, now going at full speed, were honking like geese. The wall of rain before us looked like a giant mass of dryer lint sparking with static electricity.

All the stress that had melted away with the Brain Strainer returned in full force. "This is a doomed operation!" I yelled over the noise. "We should be building an ark, not going to the park on a lark."

Philippa ignored my ingenious rhyme. Instead, she cursed and looked around. We were closed in with the Panhandle on our left and two lanes of cars with grumpy-looking people on our right. It wasn't going to be easy to turn the ship. The eucalyptus trees and pine trees seemed to be swaying and bending in unison, like the passengers on a cable car when it turned a corner.

My ears perked up at the news report.

"*. . . a rash of assaults where victims are kicked in the behind. So far, no arrests have been made, because no one has actually seen the perpetrator. Victims report hearing footsteps, but when they turn around, no one is there.*"

I cringed. Seemed the Kick-Me Boots were on an attacking streak. But for how long?

"*Local businessman and mayoral candidate Ned Gu had this to say. . . .*"

I turned up the volume. "It's Mr. Gu."

"First it's freak storms, now punting punks? More than ever, this city needs strong leadership. Vote for me and I'll make sure San Franciscans don't get kicked around any longer."

Philippa turned down the radio and craned her neck forward, squinting up at the sky. "Look."

The clouds seemed to be dissolving, revealing something golden on the other side. The rain eased, morphing from strings of water to drips and then vanishing altogether. The traffic loosened. By the time we entered Golden Gate Park, the sky was clear as a bottle of Windex. Sunshine poured over us, making the sidewalks sparkle. The ground didn't even look damp. I wasn't sure how far the storm had extended this time, but I could only guess that the broom and dustpan were nowhere near Golden Gate Park. Either that, or . . .

My eyes caught a banner: MUSIC IN THE CONCOURSE: KRONOS QUARTET. I lurched in my seat, my skull bumping the headrest. Dani! The pink cocktail umbrella behind her ear appeared in my mind. *All I know is I never get rained on when I wear it.* Good gof. Was that the reason Golden Gate Park was dry?

While Philippa stalked a pedestrian for his parking space, I twisted a loose thread on my track pants. Dani's aunt, Chef Kim, had given the cocktail umbrella to her. But where had she gotten it? Mr. Pang's Whimsies?

The tip of my finger purpled, and I let go of the thread.

Philippa shifted the car into reverse and hooked an arm over my seat. "One shot to glory."

Dad had always said that. He never needed more than one reverse to parallel park. And just like him, Philippa glided into the parking space like a moray slips into a crack between two rocks.

She shrugged into her puffy coat and jammed an umbrella into a pocket. I zipped one of Dad's old fleece jackets over my sweatshirt, then slung my backpack over one shoulder. Though my fingers felt cold, the rest of me was itchy and hot, like a fire-cracker ready to burst.

After a ten-minute hike, we reached an oval green space between an aquarium and an art museum. The acoustic shell of the Music Concourse sat at the far end of the green space, though I didn't hear any music coming from it yet. As we trekked through one of the pathways that crisscrossed the oval, memories of Dad flooded in. He'd yell Superman's slogan, *Up, up, and away!* and we'd take off, our arms outstretched like we were flying. After wearing ourselves out, we'd get ice cream from a cart.

Why did he have to go off to war? If he'd just had a normal job, like video game repairman or teacher, instead of trying to be a superhero, I would still have a dad.

I accidentally stepped on Philippa's foot. With a scowl, she grabbed me by a claw and pushed me away from her. "One more flat tire and you can walk home," she snapped, though her words lacked bite.

She was probably thinking about Dad, too, but I hoped not about forgiving Ratface. Part of me wanted her to get this "closure" so she could be a nice human being again. But another part didn't want closure if it meant forgetting about Dad. I wrapped his fleece closer around me, as if to keep all the tangled feelings inside me from escaping like the filling from an overstuffed burrito.

Music started up from the stage, two hundred feet away. I looked for Dani and finally spotted her, mostly hidden by her cello. When I squinted, I thought I saw a bright pink spot on the side of her hair.

We approached a bench where a lanky man in a neon vest and yellow construction hat was sitting. He got to his feet and gave us an awkward little wave. His skin had the weathered texture of someone who didn't wear sunscreen, and his stained jeans looked like he never took them off. Philippa said he sanded floors for a living.

He extended one of his rough hands, and Philippa shook it. "Thanks for meeting us," she said stiffly.

"How 'bout this weather, huh?" When neither of us answered, he said, "You look nothin' like the pictures your dad showed me."

Well, he looked exactly like the picture we'd seen of *him*—a pointy rat's face with close-set brown eyes and a military buzz cut. He offered me a hand as well, but I crossed my arms, resisting the urge to hit him.

The crow's feet around his eyes etched in deeper. "Wanna sit?" He gestured with his long arms, then planted his bony seat at one end of the bench. Philippa sat in the middle, and I took the other end.

"Look, kids, I'm real sorry about what happened. I should've visited you and your mom earlier. I mean, I tried to, except . . ." He opened his hands in a weak apology. Nicks and scars covered his palms.

"Mr. Fisher—" Philippa began.

"Vic, please."

"Mr. Fisher, I want to know exactly how it happened. How'd you kill our dad?"

I steered a shocked gaze to Philippa, not expecting that zinger right off the bat. It was a question that should never have to be asked, and like a beached whale, it sat there waiting for the buzzards to pick the bones clean.

He put his head in his hands. "I loved your dad. He was my best friend. I never wanted to hurt him." He opened his mouth to speak, then shook his head and clammed up.

Philippa threw him an easier one. "How'd you two meet?"

Vic watched a man toss a Frisbee to a dog. "He beat me in a sprint in high school. I hated him at first. He had good parents, had his act together. But weirdly, he was the only one who cared about me, even if it was just to outrun me. Long story short, when he decided to join the military, I decided I wanted to go, too. He discouraged me, knew I hated discipline. He thought I should start my own woodworking business." He picked at a callus, lost in his head for a moment.

"So you joined the military . . ." Philippa prompted.

Nodding, he made a move as if to reach into an inside pocket but then dropped his hand.

Philippa hugged herself. "What happened that night?"

"We had a situation. A couple of hostiles decided to take over a school, and we were supposed to eject them. Your dad starts translating the orders to their leader, this angry dude in a camo vest. The guy starts yelling back, and I got real scared for your dad, but he told me to trust him. Phil goes into Yoda mode, like just before Yoda Force-lifts an aircraft, with the breathing and everything?" He took off his construction hat and lifted it demonstrating what a Force-lift was.

Philippa nodded. "Qigong meditation."

"Right." He blew out a breath. "So the angry guy stops yelling, and he and your dad start talking. But then the guy reaches into his vest." Vic blew out a breath. "I freak out and open fire, and before I know it, everyone's firing." He hung his head, and I could see the ridges of his neck. "You know what was in his vest?"

Neither Philippa nor I answered.

"A picture of his children."

Philippa sniffed, the only sign of emotion on her face. She had been grabbing her hands so hard, I could see nail marks on her skin.

So that's how it happened. Ratface's itchy fingers had gotten Dad killed.

As much as I still hated Vic, a part of me knew he'd had a tough call. He'd been trying to protect Dad. And I wouldn't exactly win prizes in the *thinking before acting* category myself.

My phone buzzed—it was Mav. I wanted to ignore it, but he and Monroe were coming to pick me up so Philippa could go straight to work.

"Sorry, gotta take this," I told Philippa, moving a few paces away.

"We have eyes on you," Mav said.

I glanced around. A couple hundred feet toward the aquarium, Monroe was watching the performance, his own ukulele strapped around him. Mav stood next to him, his phone to his ear. "Hey." I held up a hand.

He waved back. "Bijal and Cassa breached Mr. Pang's thirty minutes ago. The Eyeballs are secure. Repeat: Eyeballs are secure. We're going to rendezvous there. Take your time. But don't take too long." He hung up.

Vic's eyeballs weren't secure. He was swiping the corners

with his thumbs. Again he reached for something in his pocket that apparently wasn't there. "I can never forgive myself, but every day I get up and try to be a good man because that's what your father would've wanted. Haven't smoked for eight months now. Started my own business, like your dad suggested." He glanced up at the still-perfect sky. "I wish he knew."

His floor-sanding hands didn't know where to go, and he finally sat on them. He was one sorry sack of excuse juice. But though I tried to hold on to my anger, I felt some of it slip away, like when you pour too much tea into the cup and some of it sloshes out.

Philippa's gaze had become thoughtful. "You said you tried to visit us. When?"

"A few months after the accident. See, I had your dad's dog tags." His eyes drifted to Philippa's neck, then mine, and he blinked. "Those aren't . . . ?"

We both fished our dog tags from our shirts.

"Well, I'll be. How'd you get those?"

"Someone mailed them to us," said Philippa. "There was no return address."

"I was going to bring them to you, but they fell out of a hole in my pocket. I figured it was a sign I should leave you alone, so I went home. I'm not sure how they found their way to you." Vic rubbed at his buzz cut, making scratchy sounds. With his bloodshot eyes and runny nose, he looked as pathetic as those allergy sufferers in television ads.

The Kronos Quartet and Dani had started up a strange number that included boingy sounds and drumbeats, even though they were all playing string instruments. That song was how I felt, a mishmash of emotions that didn't belong together, all happening at once.

"Well, we won't take up any more of your time. Thanks, Mr. Fisher. Good luck with your business." Grabbing my arm, Philippa marched us away, which was fine with me. I'd seen enough of Vic Fisher to last me a lifetime.

CHAPTER 26

Mav and Monroe met us halfway across the green space. Monroe removed his aviator sunglasses and hooked them onto the high neck of his sweater, somehow not getting them tangled in his ukulele strap. "Hey, Philippa. Winston, you been practicing?"

"No."

"Great." He was grinning at Philippa and probably wouldn't have noticed if a rottweiler was chewing on his leg.

Philippa had already set off in the direction of our Volvo, and Monroe hurried to catch up with her. "Hey, Philippa, we'll walk you to your car."

"You really don't need to do that."

"I insist," he said gallantly.

"Plus, our car's parked behind yours," added Mav.

"Actually," Monroe continued brightly, "I want to play you

a song I've been working on." The chords of "Remember Me," from Philippa's favorite movie, poured from his uke.

Monroe's voice sounded good, even though he was forced into a faster pace than he usually walked. Philippa kept marching, oblivious to Monroe orbiting around her like a mariachi singer. She had a flame-retardant heart to go with her tongue.

"Did you find it strange that it's not raining here in the park?" I asked Mav.

"Yeah, it cut off as we were entering, like we'd gone into another room."

I told him about Dani's cocktail umbrella.

Mav looked pensive. "That could be really helpful. . . . What's the radius of that thing, do you think?"

I shrugged.

Monroe had finished his song, and he was trying to engage Philippa in conversation. While Mav muttered to himself and worked the calculator app on his phone, I eavesdropped on the two of them.

"It's nothing personal," said Philippa. "I hardly know you. But the way I see it, we both have a conflict of interest. Mav and Winston are best friends. If anything happened between them, I'd have to take Winston's side, and you'd have to take Mav's."

My general annoyance at her softened a bit. But did she really feel that way, or was she looking for a convenient excuse to let Monroe down gently?

"But it's just a Parcheesi match."

"But next week it'll be a game of Life, and the week after next, Monopoly, and then we'll both be Sorry!" Philippa strode the last few paces to our Volvo, her heavy footsteps a pitying sort of applause.

Monroe watched her go with a pained look, reminding me of one of those exotic birds that spends hours doing elaborate dances for his chosen mate only to have her fly off. The guy had everything—nice family, musical skills, a healthy bank account, and good hair. But certain things were just out of our control.

Despite the rejection, Monroe seemed to be in an upbeat mood as he drove us away, cranking up the tunes and singing along. He was like a rubber egg you could never crack.

Eggs. As soon as the Egg of Truth wore off on Mr. Pang, we'd get him to tell us where Coco was. Hopefully the Far-Seeing Eyeballs would help us find her. Maybe Cassa and Bijal had already figured out how to use them.

Soon we were back in the middle of the storm. Mav tapped more numbers into his watch. "By my calculations, that cocktail umbrella has a one-mile radius of effectiveness. The golden mile."

"So, if the broom and dustpan stay within that golden mile, the mother can't zap them."

"Yep. Basically, it's Dani's house they should be trying to get into."

I checked my backpack to make sure the eggs were okay. A piece of paper rustled at the bottom of my pack—Not-Coco's drawing of the weird banana. I pulled it out to show to Mav. "Look how she nearly ripped the paper making all that lightning."

Mav tugged the drawing from me. "Is that a moon?" He

held the paper vertically, then opened the moon phase app on his phone. "Crescent moon won't happen for about two weeks, though."

I noticed he'd avoided mentioning the full moon on Monday night. Once the full moon came and went, anything that happened during the crescent moon wouldn't matter. I rotated the picture. "She was drawing it this way," I insisted. Then I crumpled the picture into a ball, wishing I could throw it out the window. "I hope Coco's not cold, or hungry, wherever she is."

Mav took the wad from me and stuffed it into his own backpack. "It's the physical body that needs to sleep and eat, and it's fine—Not-Coco is in it. Spirits don't have human needs."

"There could be hundreds of kinds of spirits. Maybe this spirit gets hungry." I refused to comfort myself with thoughts that Coco wasn't suffering, stuck in the body of that creepy doll. His Monsters and Mythology class wasn't science. There was no scientific proof that changelings even existed, much less any studies about how hungry they got.

Monroe dropped us off in front of Boba Guys.

"Thanks, Monroe. Sorry about Philippa," I told him before following Mav out. "I guess she's just not into you."

"It's okay, man. It was an honor to be able to sing for her."

After Monroe putted off, Mav and I approached Mr. Pang's shop, shielding our eyes from the rain. From his backpack he pulled out a hand mirror big enough to reflect my whole face, which we used to find the grasshopper-green door.

The bunny and chick Peeps were back in the top corners, staring down at us with their glittery eyes. "You think those're the same Peeps?"

"I don't know," Mav said doubtfully. "There was a lot of goo before. . . ."

"Maybe they regenerated."

He nodded. "Like zombies."

In *ZI*, zombies were always regenerating after their rotten parts fell off.

Getting through Mr. Pang's door and the maze was easier this time around, especially since Cassa and Bijal had left the entrance unlocked.

In the main aisle of the showroom, the Hulkbuster pool chair still hung from the rafters. The unicorn piñatas with their crinkly tissue-paper ribbons shimmered in the antler lighting, giving them the appearance of movement.

Cassa and Bijal were chattering excitedly behind the partially drawn curtains of Mr. Pang's office. When they saw us through the opening, they gestured for us to join them.

"The Peeps were talking!" Bijal pointed to a black speaker mounted in the upper-left corner of the room. "Through that. Just before you came in, they said"—he covered his mouth with his hand like he was speaking into a walkie-talkie—"'Intruder alert. Two males, thirteen years old. We've seen these turkeys before. Threat level: cloudy with a chance of meatballs.'"

"What's that mean?" I asked.

"No idea. Last night we must have roasted them before they could report us to Mr. Pang."

The glass doors of the popcorn machine were open, but I didn't smell anything coming from it.

"We've been trying to figure out what this machine does, and look." Cassa unhooked the kettle and lifted the metal lid.

A charm bracelet lay inside—a silver chain like a fishing net stuck with shells and a pearl. Bronzy patches showed through the silver, but its blemished state meant someone had worn it a long time.

Cassa shook the kettle, and the bracelet rattled. "Check out what's written on it."

I lifted the bracelet. A silver tag hung by the clasp, engraved with the name ANNA ARDITII.

"So he steals stuff and sticks it in this kettle," said Cassa.

Bijal put a hand under his chin and stared up at the inflatable moon hanging in the corner. "Don't magpies like collecting shiny things?"

"That's a myth based on cultural generalization," said Mav, our resident bird expert, who was inspecting the popcorn machine from all angles. "Corvids—crows, ravens, and magpies—are big-brained birds. They can solve puzzles, make tools, and remember faces. Don't mess with them."

I dropped the bracelet back into the kettle. "Unless they mess with you first."

Cassa rehooked the kettle and shut the glass doors. She lifted a chin toward the worktable. "But why does he put them in the popcorn tray?"

"Maybe it's how he creates all the magic items in his store," guessed Mav. He ran his hand along the underside of the machine. "There's no plug, or sign of where this thing was manufactured."

The Pikachu figurine lay in the tray where Mr. Pang had left it. It was so new, it still had its price and maker tags.

"Why is Pikachu there, while the bracelet's in the kettle?" I asked.

"Only one way to find out." Cassa nodded at me.

I put my finger on a green button.

"Wait!" said Bijal. "We don't know what—"

I pushed it. The button lit up. With a gentle whirring sound, the kettle started spinning. A salty, buttery scent began to fill the room.

After several seconds, the kettle stopped spinning. The green light turned off. Pikachu began to . . . *move*.

"Aaah!" Bijal screamed.

Cassa slapped his arm. "Shh!"

Pikachu rolled so that it lay on its stomach. I was staring so hard, I could have left eyeball prints on the glass. The figurine pushed itself up so that it was standing. Its yellow color, which was already bright with the oiled sheen of a new item, seemed to grow brighter, as if a lightbulb had been placed inside it. The two red dots on its cheeks glowed, and its bat-wing ears flexed. Even its lightning-bolt tail took on sharper pleats.

"It's alive!" cried Bijal, pulling his hair.

The Pikachu extended its arms as if asking for a hug and then froze in that position.

I looked at Mav, who looked at Cassa, who looked at Bijal. He was walking in tight circles.

"Now what?" I asked no one in particular. Something magical had happened, but what, exactly? The kettle lit up and words appeared on the glass: OBJECT SAFE TO REMOVE.

Cassa slid open the doors and reached for the kettle, tipping it out and catching the bracelet. "This looks different. Duller or something." She turned it in her palm.

I began to reach for Pikachu but then stopped, remembering what had happened with the top hat. And the broom, for gof's sake.

A sign lit up outside the glass doors, next to a pair of silicon tongs. A metal plate beside the tongs read: USE TONGS FOR CHURROS AND ENCHANTED ITEMS. Cassa handed the utensil to me.

Gingerly, as if I were picking up a live butterfly with tweezers, I lifted Pikachu and brought it to the desk. Though it no longer moved, its bright colors remained. "How does Mr. Pang figure out what his whimsies do?"

Mav brought his face closer to the figurine. "Maybe we have to touch it."

"*I'm* not touching it!" Bijal's hands disappeared into his sleeves.

Cassa put her hands on her hips. "He must have a safeguard. What if something goes rogue? Like that Hovering Pizza Swat."

Mav, who was surveying the room, snapped his fingers. "The fire extinguisher!"

He crossed to the wall and unhooked the purple canister. Like all fire extinguishers, this one featured a locking pin in the handle and a short hose with a nozzle at the end. "Maybe it's a magic extinguisher in case of emergency."

That seemed like a good guess.

"I'll touch it," said Cassa, the bravest among us.

"No," I said. "Coco's my sister. I'll do it." If I could understand how the magic worked, maybe I'd be one step closer to
knowing why the broom and dustpan took Coco, and more
important, how to get her back.

Mav pulled the pin on the extinguisher and held the hose
ready. I flexed the fingers of both hands like I was about to take
the wheel in the Indy 500. I took a deep breath. The smell of
popcorn still lingered.

"Just a touch," said Cassa. "Use your pinkie. It's the least
useful digit in case you lose it."

"Gee, thanks," I mumbled. I stuck out my pinkie and
grazed Pikachu's ear.

Feeling nothing but hard plastic, I picked up the figurine.
Bijal gasped in horror.

This time, my hand tingled. It was like whenever I had
held the broom—a minor buzz that escalated in pain depend-
ing on how tightly I gripped it. Maybe all the whimsies came
with this self-defense mechanism. At least the nonperishable
ones. Neither the Eggs of Truth nor the Hovering Pizza Swat
had regenerated.

Cassa gripped her braid as tightly as if she were climbing
it. "So?"

"Feels tingly. That's it."

"Maybe you have to throw it at something, like the Eggs of
Truth," said Bijal, who was now nervously stirring the padded
envelopes on the desk.

Mav carefully set down the extinguisher. "I don't think so.
That doesn't seem . . . intuitive. Eggs are asking to be thrown.
Pikachu is a pocket monster."

"Check this out." Bijal pulled an envelope from a pile on the desk. "It's addressed to Anna Ardith, the owner of that bracelet. She lives near here—maybe she goes to our school."

"Could you please focus?" said Mav. "We need all the feet in the game. . . ." His sentence tapered off when he saw what Bijal was holding up now.

A mailing box. This one was addressed to someone else.

WINSTON & PHILIPPA CHU.

All my thoughts scattered like a deck of cards being shuffled by a toddler. Mr. Pang knew my address?

Bijal opened it shook out the contents. A gray elephant with a green jacket and a yellow crown fell out, followed by a sky-blue soccer jersey with the number eleven on the back.

CHAPTER 27

A voice broke through the speaker like a police dispatcher. *"Intruder alert. Two males, forty-something, large as linebackers with a hint of burned cheese. Threat level: run, don't walk—or better yet, fly—to your nearest avian flu recovery center."*

I didn't understand the last part—Peeps sure had a weird sense of humor—but I had a guess as to who the intruders might be. "Ernie and Bert."

Bijal flapped his arms. "What do we do?"

"There was another exit to the main building, remember?" I said, recalling the door to the hallway from our visit with Mr. Suresh.

Mav had begun to bounce on his toes the way he did before a game. "Since this is Pang's office, I bet it's somewhere around here."

Cassa checked the wall behind the popcorn machine,

while Bijal and I searched the one behind the worktable. On the opposite wall, Mav was trying to pull open one of the little drawers of the herb cabinet but having no luck. He tried yanking a few others.

"Linebackers have breached entry. ETA three minutes," squeaked the Peep.

"These drawers are fake!" yelled Mav. "This must be the door. Help me."

I ran my hands over the polished wood of the cabinet. On one edge, I felt a curved indentation that suggested a handle. I pulled it, and the phony cabinet swung open on hidden hinges. The scent of pine floor cleaner wafted in.

"Go!" cried Mav.

Bijal scrambled through the teakwood doorway.

"You guys go," I said. "I'll hide here."

Cassa, who was halfway out, grabbed my arm. "We searched the place and didn't see Chang-Ah-Ling. Don't be a moofus. Ernie and Bert could grind you into meat sauce."

"I might never get another chance!"

"We'll come back." Her eyes flashed. "They have to leave sometime."

"But how will we—"

Mav gave us both a shove and closed the secret door behind him.

We tumbled into a tiled corridor that ran the length of the building. A security guard was standing there. It was the Viking we'd met with Mr. Suresh.

"Hello, Mr. . . . ." I began, forgetting his name.

"Vlad," said Cassa, straightening her sweatshirt.

Vlad scratched his beard. "What are you kids doing here?"

Behind us, the cabinet exit had vanished and been replaced by a standard metal door. "Say, aren't you the ones I saw here last week with Mr. Suresh?"

"Yes, sir," said Mav. "We're checking out the premises for my dad, who might buy the building."

Bijal beckoned to us from the exit that led to Kearny Street, his feet shuffling like a pigeon ready to take flight. I couldn't blame him. Who knew when Bert and Ernie might burst into the hallway?

Mav ticked his head toward the door. "Actually, Mr. Vlad, we saw a couple of suspicious-looking characters hanging around. You might want to check it out."

Frowning, Vlad removed a key ring from his belt and used it to open the door. He stepped through, and we cautiously peeked after him. Mr. Pang's shop was back to looking like an empty space with fluorescent ceiling lights and unpainted walls.

Vlad put his fists on his hips and glared at the concrete floor. "If by 'suspicious characters,' you mean a couple of seagulls, I guess you're right. You left the front door open, and the gulls got in. Boba Guys' customers are always feeding them. Cripes, they left a mess."

Ernie and Bert must have split. For big guys, they sure moved quick.

"Wish Mr. Suresh would tell me when to expect visitors," said Vlad. "I hate surprises." He pulled out his phone. "Larry, send over the cleanup crew. There's some broken glass—get the window guy."

Broken windows? Bert and Ernie were getting more desperate.

We exited through the door to Kearny, its heavy hydraulic hinge shutting fast behind us.

I grabbed at my head. At least it was no longer raining. With Mav leading the charge, we ran a few blocks up the street, then caught our breath at the base of For Pete's Steps. A bunch of scruffy-looking travelers with dirty sandals had gathered in front of a hostel.

I peered down the hill toward Jackson. "I think we should go back. Those goons aren't after us. They're after Mr. Pang."

Mav's nose scrunched. "We can't with Vlad's crew there. Besides, the magpie's going to change into Mr. Pang soon. We can't be late for that."

"At least we have this." Cassa removed a bundle from her pocket—the gauzy bag of Far-Seeing Eyeballs, which she spilled onto her palm. The glassy marbles glowed faintly, and when I rolled one between my thumb and finger, metallic specks dispersed colorful dots on the sidewalk. I put one to my eye but couldn't see anything but a distorted blur.

I returned the marble to Cassa and pulled out Pikachu. "I took this, too." I hadn't meant to, but everything had happened so fast after the intruder alert.

Mav dug out something from his backpack. "And I took this." The charm bracelet swung between his fingers. "I thought we should return it to its owner. She lives on Green Street, a block up."

Bijal held up Babar and my jersey. "All I got was Winston's stuff."

"Thanks, dude!" I said, taking them from him.

My shirt looked worn and tired, as though it had been through several tournaments without a wash. Babar had faded, too, the plush flatter and nearly bald in some places. I stuffed the items into my backpack. A poster on the wall of the hostel caught my eye. *NED GU IS GOOD FOR YOU. Gu for Mayor!* Someone had stuck a bunch of thumbs-up stickers on the poster. Looks like his campaign was off to a good start.

Cassa herded us up the stairs toward Green Street. We walked in single file, squeezing between a tight line of parked cars and short driveways, until we reached a gray building that was split into two residences by a wrought-iron gate. A panel on the gate offered two buttons: A and B.

Without knowing which house was Anna's, I decided to go alphabetically. I pressed A. But when no one answered, Mav shrugged at me and pressed B.

Static crackled. "We don't want any, go away." The voice was female, and a smoker, judging by the rasp.

"We're looking for Anna Ardith," Cassa said into the speaker. "We found something that belongs to her."

"Go away." The static abruptly shut off.

"Maybe we can drop it in her mailbox." Mav looked dubiously at the narrow mail slot.

Bijal, who was looking up at the windows, started waving. "Someone's up there!"

We all backed up a few paces. A little girl of about six or seven was staring down at us through the rain-dotted glass.

Cassa took the bracelet from Mav and dangled it above her head. She pointed at the girl. "Yours?"

The girl pressed her forehead to the glass, and her round face lit up. She disappeared.

Soon the gate opened and the girl came bouncing out, followed by an old lady in a kimono. The woman had wet hair and the tired expression of one who was sick of climbing stairs.

"Are you Anna?" I asked the little girl.

"Yes." She took the bracelet from Cassa and examined it closely. Her expression deflated, reminding me of the cream puffs we had made in baking class after they came out of the oven.

"What's wrong, nena?" the woman asked in her raspy voice.

"It looks dead."

The woman's wrinkled mouth blew out a sigh. "Her brother gave it to her before he left for college," she told us in the too-loud voice of someone who was hard of hearing.

I felt a twinge of guilt for zapping her special bracelet for my experiment, but I couldn't exactly apologize—how could I explain?

The lady smoothed the girl's hair. "At least you got it back. Well, say goodbye to the nice people. My shows are coming on soon." She put her arm around the girl and ushered her through the gate.

We started hiking the two blocks to my place, where Mav's mom would meet us to drive us to the McFees' mansion. Cassa held her braid, looking up at the still-clear sky. "So it wasn't my imagination. The bracelet did look different after we put it through the machine. Duller—"

"Like my shirt, and Babar. And maybe Lucky?" I gulped, feeling a little sick. I'd seen no sign of my goldfish in the shop.

Poor guy. If he hadn't survived his abduction, I hoped the end had been quick.

"—while the object in the tray became animated," Cassa finished.

Pikachu felt heavy in my pocket. "Enchanted."

"Come to think of it, Mr. Pang's new Flip and Dunks were the same color as my jersey."

Bijal rubbed his peach fuzz. "And his freaky striped headband had Babar-colored stripes."

"And his new pool chair looked like your Hulkbuster," Mav added grimly.

Cassa stabbed her braid in the air like a finger. "I think he uses the machine to transfer the properties of one thing to another. That's how he makes his cool junk."

Behind me, Mav kicked a tree pod through my feet. "So he creates magic with the—I don't know—*energy* of the things he finds?"

Bijal nodded gravely. "Yeah, he takes their mojo."

"But why does he want *my* things?"

Cassa dribbled the tree pod with her feet. "What do your jersey, goldfish, and Babar have in common?"

"Besides being at my house? I don't know. We like them?"

"They're *cherished*, like Anna's bracelet." Cassa finally kicked the tree pod. "Mr. Pang puts cherished energy into new objects and creates whimsies. Like the Hovering Pizza Swat. No one cherishes a slice of pizza by itself."

"I do," Bijal piped up from behind me. "With lots of cheese."

I caught up to the tree pod and kicked it another twenty feet. Mr. Pang better not have put Coco in that machine. The thought of him even trying that flushed my veins with venom. If he hurt her, I would tear him to bits like a mob of Zubber Zombies.

When we reached my place, Mav's phone rang. He answered it, and his eyes grew horrified. We gathered around him, trying to listen. "No, no, no!" He extended one hand to the sky as if asking God to pull him up.

But then he sank to his ankles as if his knees had given out. We squatted around him like we were playing duck, duck, goose and he was in the mush pot. With a sickly goodbye, he hung up.

He glanced around at us, his eyes bloodshot. "Bad news, guys. The magpie escaped."

CHAPTER 28

Mav slowly got to his feet. "Mom heard him squawking up a storm. She went to check and said he was caught in the hat. So she took off the lid to help him, and he flew out one of the bathroom windows. She's really sorry. Said she'd buy me another one."

I hardly heard him. The words were having a hard time getting in, like someone trying to throw paper airplanes into a mail slot.

Bijal flailed an arm, the veins on his neck popping. "Dude, that Mr. Pang faked an injury! He's a flopper."

Cassa hissed. We all hated floppers, what we called soccer players who acted like they were hurt so their opponent would get a penalty.

How would we ever find Mr. Pang now? We needed him to help us use the eyeballs to find Coco. And how would I ever get

Mom to believe me about that other fraud, the changeling? A hot ball of anger, and maybe grief, collected in my throat, and I cradled my head in my hands.

"Dude, I'm so sorry," said Mav, patting me awkwardly on the shoulder.

I couldn't talk, so I just shook my head. His white sneakers started punching the sidewalk.

"You going to let a bird boss you?" Cassa hooked an arm through mine and pulled me forward. "Let's go to Coit Tower. It's not raining, and we still have some time before Mav's mom picks us up. We can figure out how those eyeballs work by ourselves."

I forced my feet to move, aided by Cassa yanking me along.

People considered the Golden Gate Bridge San Francisco's best attraction, but I thought Coit Tower left the bridge in the dust. It was peaceful. Plus, it was only a five-minute walk from my house, poking out the top of Telegraph Hill like the horn on a unicorn's head.

By the time we had climbed to the entrance, the ache in my throat had subsided. My leg muscles burned. But a sense of resolve had settled over my shoulders. Cassa was right to bring us here. I wouldn't let a bird get the best of me.

Cars filled the driveway that encircled a statue of Christopher Columbus. The famous parrots that lived here had pooped all over him. Who could blame them? At the entrance of the white tower, a park ranger was chatting with a woman in a visor. I'd never seen a ranger here before—very official-looking, with a beige uniform and gold badge.

"They're targeting the tourist spots, so we're being extra careful," he was saying. "Wouldn't want to give people another reason to stay away from San Francisco. Watch your back. People are getting kicked for no reason."

The woman hugged her purse. "You mean *picked*?"

"Nope. *Kicked*. Since last night, there have been attacks at Ghirardelli, Fisherman's Wharf, and Union Square. We can't be too careful. But the guy's quick. He's evaded all cameras."

We hurried past the murals of California history and waited until we reached the sanctity of an elevator to speak. Bijal rubbed his backside as if remembering. "Those boots are on a kicking spree. Wonder if they come with a kill switch."

Mav grimly watched the floor counter rise on its way to level twelve. "First you'd have to catch them."

We climbed the last two levels to the roofless observation deck, which was still damp. At least we had the place to ourselves. Cutouts in the round walls provided dizzying 360-degree views of the city. It looked like it had been miniaturized.

My dad had proposed to Mom here. He'd pulled the ring out of his pocket, then pretended to drop it out one of the arched windows. Mom hadn't fallen for it.

Taking a spot by a set of three windows, Cassa spilled the four marbles into her cupped palm. We each took one of the glowing orbs.

Telegraph Hill was where, in the olden days, telegraphers used to interpret semaphore flags on incoming ships. If you wanted to see anything in San Francisco, this was the place to do it.

I put a marble to my eye. Again, all I could see was a glassy blur. Starting with the Golden Gate Bridge, I slowly scanned the horizon—the piers, past a cruise ship, and over to the steely

Bay Bridge. If the bridges were brothers, the Golden Gate was the artist, while the Bay Bridge was the one who went to business school. I studied the skyscrapers of the financial district, holding the marble far and then close again. It remained glassy and unremarkable.

"Maybe you have to close one eye." Bijal squeezed his eye shut, causing his mouth to go ajar.

Cassa stared up at a cloud. "I *was* closing an eye."

"Maybe use the other eye."

Mav twisted his marble in front of him. "Maybe shut up so I can concentrate."

I went the other direction, from Treasure Island to its brother Alcatraz Island, and my eyes started to cross. A marble was an unwieldy choice for seeing distances, especially with my fingers starting to sweat.

"I think I pulled an eyeball muscle." Bijal sank down and rubbed his eyes. "Take mine." He handed me his marble. "Maybe you're supposed to use two of them at a time."

Mav dug around in his backpack, handing Cassa the now-crumpled drawing Not-Coco had made, then pulling out his water bottle. While we hydrated, Cassa smoothed out the picture. "It can't be a crescent moon or a banana. This side is too flat."

Bijal wiped his mouth on his arm. "Maybe it's a Pringle."

Cassa gently pushed me aside and took up my position by the window. "You said she 'delivered' it on the mail truck. Which means she was trying to send you a message. Do you think Not-Coco was trying to be helpful?"

I snorted. "She could be more helpful by giving my sister's body back. And if she's so helpful, why would she wipe Mom's computer? She's just trying to mess with my head." My limbs tightened like barbed wire.

Mav returned to his spot at the next window, rolling his marble in his palm. "Changelings are by nature mischievous. And since they're not human, we can't expect them to have human emotions."

"You're not actually defending Not-Coco, are you?" I was getting a little sick of him slinging around his expertise as if it were fact. He'd been wrong about the eggshells. And I was the one living with the monster. "Just because you take fancy classes and you have a perfect life doesn't mean you know everything."

Mav put up his hands. "Dude, I'm trying to help."

"Yeah, like you helped with the magpie?" My head buzzed, as if it had suddenly become a swarm of angry wasps.

Mav's face went red. I knew I wasn't being fair, but as I looked at him, all I could see was a kid with cool gear who didn't have a missing baby sister. A kid who had a dad who could help him when things spiraled out of control. A kid who could go back to his ocean view and jumbo-size bed with no guilty conscience. My reflection in his eyes made my anger burn hotter. I almost wanted him to come at me, because at least that was a fight I could take on.

Cassa fanned me with Not-Coco's drawing. "Breathe, you gobsmacker."

I knew I had turned into a raging moofus, but I didn't care. Coco was gone because of me, and I was doing a terrible job of finding her. With a huff, I broke away from Mav's surprised and pitying gaze and stretched over the concrete ledge. I put the two marbles to my eyes.

I hardly noticed the sound of stomping behind me, until Mav cried out. "What the— Ow!"

Before I could turn around, someone kicked me right in the behind, and I fell onto the window ledge. The marbles slipped from my fingers, disappearing like drops of water into the steep thicket of trees below. "Nooo!"

My friends started yelling. As I whipped around, my butt still smarting, the others seemed to be doing battle with a red blur. Two red blurs. The Kick-Me Boots. Mav swung his backpack at one of the boots. Bijal was hacking at another with his umbrella.

"Move, Bijal! I got this one!" screamed Cassa, winding up, then kicking Bijal's boot attacker sky-high.

The other boot, somehow knowing that its mate had flown the coop, took off after it.

"That's right, you better run!" cried Bijal. "No one kicks us around!"

Mav rubbed at his thigh. "That was nuts. Didn't see that coming. You still have the eyeballs?"

"I dropped them out the window." I panted. There was no way we'd be able find them without a bulldozer and several weeks' time. I fell to my knees, slapping my head. What if you needed all four for the magic to work? My friends watched me like I was a Zumbie, a brainless zombie who ate his own limbs.

I needed to go. I was failing Coco and failing hard. Our only advantage—Mr. Pang—had flown the coop. We'd never find him or Coco in time to kick the changeling out of her body.

"Just leave me alone." Grabbing my backpack, I headed for home, where at least no one would have to watch me fall apart.

CHAPTER 29

No one was home. More out of habit than anything else, I padded through the house, checking hiding places and feeling for cold spots. Still no sign of the broom or dustpan. The collapsible dolly Mom used for groceries was missing from the laundry closet. She must have gone food shopping with Not-Coco.

I plodded up to my room. Mom answered on the first ring. "Thought you were going to Mav's for dinner."

"Plans changed. How's Coco?" I bit back my anger, knowing full well that the creature she was with was Not-Coco.

"Fine," she said, her voice dipping mid-word, as if to ask why I wanted to know.

I had to make one last effort to get Mom to believe me. She might book me with Dr. Toy from now until Christmas, but at this point, I had to take that risk. "Mom? Remember how I told you that I think Coco is possessed?"

"Winston . . ." Her voice was a warning.

"Listen to me." I began pacing the carpet. "That's *not* Coco you're with! I bet she hasn't asked for her Putty once. Yesterday she was playing with the mail truck. She *hates* the mail truck. And she has the crazy smile. You don't see it because she hides it from you, but whenever she looks at me—" My eyes caught on my bobbleheads. Something was wrong. US Women's midfielder Meg Rapinoe with her white-blond hair had switched places with Brazilian forward Neymar. But no, that was Meg's red-and-blue-striped uniform That mischievous prankster had put their heads on the others' bodies! Messi, Ronaldo, Pelé, Lee, Zidane, they were all wrong, too. My skin itched, and I glanced around, wondering what else that child demon had touched. Neymar's head bounced around on Meg's body, his usually confident smile begging me to make the world right again. "She messed up my bobbles!"

"Philippa told me about Vic," Mom broke in. "I've been doing some research, and I think you might be suffering from delusional trauma brought on by incomplete mourning. It sounds worse than it is."

"What? No. My mornings are complete. Vic has nothing to do with this."

Not-Coco whined in the background and Mom's voice faded. "Coco, don't play with that." She sighed and returned to me. "It wasn't easy for me to accept the truth, either. On the other hand, I was glad to know that your dad died trying to help someone. I hope you don't blame him."

"Vic?"

"No, honey. Your dad."

I couldn't afford to be derailed at an important moment like this. But as every soccer player will tell you, even when his mind's not on the game play, when a ball comes sailing toward him, he'll trap it. I wasn't mad at Dad, was I? I was mad at everyone else for moving on without him. Well, maybe I blamed him just a little. He should've known that, unlike superheroes, people can die if they go off to war. I sucked in my breath, trying to shake off my sadness and get back to the crisis at hand. My bobbleheads were all wiggling, maybe writhing in pain.

Mom was speaking again. "We can talk more about this tonight. Don't worry, honey. We're all going to be okay."

I bit back my frustration, feeling that I'd just made everything worse.

I zipped Babar and my soccer shirt into plastic bags and stuck them next to the kimchee jar in the freezer.

Then I showered. I was combing my hair, looking at my steamed-up reflection, when something glinted in the mirror. Dad's dog tag hanging around my neck.

I fingered the engraved letters, as familiar as the feel of my own face. Vic had said that the dog tags had fallen out of a hole in his pocket. But somehow they'd gotten mailed to us. Of course, any kind stranger could've looked us up and done it. But what if . . . ?

I pulled the chain off my neck and hefted the ID tag in my hand. This was just the kind of thing Mr. Pang would have wanted for his machine. They would've easily fit in the kettle. Had Mr. Pang "found" them? I imagined the shiny objects catching the eye of a magpie. Maybe he'd changed into his human form and collected them in his bottomless pocket. Then, once he'd drained them of their magic, he'd sent them back to us. I'd worn mine every day, just as Philippa had hers.

I slipped the chain back over my neck and pulled on pajamas. My bed gave a sigh when I sat down on it and planted my elbows on my knees. My dog tags theory would explain how Mr. Pang knew about me.

My pajama tag scratched my neck, so I ripped it off. The label read 50% COTTON 50% RAYON. WARNING: FLAMMABLE. Someone should invent nonflammable pajamas. Catching on fire seemed the last thing you wanted to worry about when you were going to sleep.

Pikachu beckoned to me from my nightstand, its arms held out in a frozen hug. What was the figurine's hidden talent? The character was known for delivering electric shocks, but this one hadn't zapped me yet. Whatever was placed in the kettle transferred some of its properties to the item in the hopper. Perhaps my Stealths soccer jersey had made Mr. Pang's sneakers extra fast. He had split pretty quick before Cassa egged him. What qualities had Babar given to his headband? And the Hulkbuster?

Mom's voice and Not-Coco's crying sounded from downstairs.

I met them in the foyer. Mom's hair had developed a curl, the way it always did in wet weather. Her eyes looked especially squinty, and she was clenching her jaw. "Honey, do me a favor and put these away." The dolly held several damp bags of groceries. "I need to get Coco to bed."

Not-Coco's eyes were bloodshot, and she was swaying like a

drunkard. "Winston," she said in that voice that was too measured to be Coco's. She hissed and even spit at me as Mom led her to the bedroom.

"I think we'll skip the bath tonight," Mom said to her.

Why couldn't Mom see that this was not Coco? My sister never acted like a mean drunk when she was tired. She usually just fell asleep wherever she was—problem solved. I couldn't help wondering if Chang-Ah-Ling wanted to stay awake and get into more mischief but Coco's body had another opinion on the matter. If so, I was proud of Coco's body for standing up for herself by lying down.

I portered the bags into the kitchen, then put the cold stuff in the fridge and the thawing stuff in the freezer. Then I wiped the dirt off the dolly wheels and mopped up the hallway, which was spotted with mud and leaves. By the time I was done, I heard Mom snoring in her room again. With a changeling masquerading as her daughter, I suppose it had been a long day for her, too.

As for me, I was too amped to sleep. My mind had become a maze of alleyways full of zombies ready to jump me. I slipped the Brain Strainer over my head and lay on my pillow. It was uncomfortable at first, but soon I felt calm pulling at me like a napkin through a ring.

CHAPTER 30

In the morning, I awoke feeling calm, even though it was raining again, and even though tomorrow was the full moon.

First things first.

I picked up my phone and dialed May's number. Thunder roared and lightning lit up the windows, reflecting off Pikachu's glossy surface.

"Hey, Win."

"Sorry, Mav. I was a royal PITA." Pain in the armpit.

"Forget it. Ancient history. But, Win?"

"Yeah?"

"I don't have a perfect life. My parents don't even notice me sometimes. Like that day I went to school out of uniform, they didn't even say anything. They're too busy fighting."

I winced, like the Kick-Me Boots had just landed a good

one in my solar plexus. "Sorry to hear that. What do they fight about?"

He let out a heavy sigh. "It's easier to list what they *don't* fight about. But lots of times their arguments don't have words. It's just . . . silence."

I knew how silent fights felt, having had enough of them with Philippa. But it would be a hundred times worse to have parents who fought. I'd always be worrying about what would happen if they didn't make up. I sank lower in my bed, knowing that if I were a good friend, I would've noticed Mav's unhappiness. "It's not your fault, Mav. You know that, right?"

"Sure," he breathed, though he didn't sound convinced. "So, what's the status?"

I told him my theory about Mr. Pang and the dog tags. "I still need to find him. I'm going to see if Chef Kim knows him, since she's the one who gave Dani that cocktail umbrella."

"Roger that. I'm waiting for my Monsters and Mythology teacher to call me back. I want to show him that picture of the crescent moon and get his opinion."

We hung up, and I called Cassa. "Hey. I wanted to apologize for being a PITA yesterday."

"That's okay, Win." Voices in the background and the sound of something being hammered made it hard to hear her. "Bijal says, 'Don't worry. We know you fal-a-fel.'"

"Ha-ha, yeah, I feel-aw-ful. What's he doing there?"

"I'm at *his* place. Dad and I are helping them patch up some storm damage. And hey, I'm starting to get the hang of the eyeballs. Get this, I might've seen a ladybug—on the Golden Gate Bridge! The trick is to use two marbles and relax your eyes."

"Wow, that's incredible."

"We'll keep practicing and looking for Coco. "

A wave of gratitude washed over me. Even after I had stink-bombed them, and ignored them, according to Cassa's truth bomb, my friends had still been trying to help me. I would definitely try to be a better friend in the future.

"What're you going to do?" Cassa asked.

"Gotta call Dani—I mean her aunt. I need to ask her something."

"Whether you can date her niece?" Cassa teased. "That's so old-fashioned."

"It's nothing like that!" I blurted.

"Uh-huh, sure. Better start practicing your uke so you can make beautiful music together."

"Ha-ha," I muttered, "you really hit a chord."

After hanging up, I called the number on Dani's business card, but it went to voicemail. Then I tried the Cooking Academy and got another automated message. Chances were that Chef Kim was there, though. She always prepped dough on Sunday mornings.

Another round of thunder rattled the windows. Mom wouldn't let me skateboard to the Cooking Academy in this storm. Not that I *would*. I needed someone to drive me.

Philippa was snoring so loud, I swore she was making the MERMAIDS ONLY sign on her door vibrate. No way would I poke that sleeping dragon.

I found Mom in the dining room. Her back was to me as she zipped her laptop into its case. Not-Coco was squatting in the living room, probably plotting something evil.

"I was just going to check on you," said Mom.

She turned around, and I screamed.

Mom grabbed her heart. "Winston, you scared me!"

There, on her upper lip, the Mischief Mustache was poised like a peregrine about to dive-bomb a vole. "Mom, don't move."

Of course, that was exactly the wrong thing to say. She ran to her bathroom, clawing at her face. I rushed after her.

"What is it? Is it there something on my face? A spider?"

"No. I thought—you don't see that?" The mustache was so thick I worried it would clog up her nostrils. "I'll get it off. Hold still!" That freewheeling face rodent could spread germs.

I reached out, but she zoomed her face close enough to her bathroom mirror to see her pores. "See what?" Her eyes switched to me in the reflection.

"That musta—" The mustache popped off and shot out of the bathroom quicker than a spider wearing sneakers. "Er, that *musta* been a shadow. Sorry."

I ran back into the dining room, casing our place for the furry intruder. I couldn't help thinking about the tarantula-like thing I'd seen the day my jersey went missing. If that had been the Mischief Mustache, it had been hanging around me this whole time. How long was I going to be stuck with the creepy face-squatter?

The loud bang of a book hitting the floor made me lift my head from where I was peering under the furniture. Not-Coco had dropped *Tales from the Middle Kingdom* at Mom's feet. "Read."

"Okay, honey, just a minute." Mom picked up the book and returned it to the dining table. "Winston, what are you doing?"

I gave up my search. Mom hadn't believed me about Not-Coco, and I guessed I couldn't blame her. But if I wanted her to drive me to the Cooking Academy in the pouring rain, I had to start acting responsibly. Not-Coco's eyes were flinty and cold, even calculating as she watched me plod over to Mom. "I was just looking for my eraser. Oh well."

Mom held my cheeks between her hands. "I was so tired last night. How are you feeling?"

"Fine."

Her eyes narrowed. "Really? Because you've had me a little worried."

"You're right, Mom. I've had some incomplete mornings. But I had a lot of sleep last night, and I feel much better." The Brain Strainer hadn't hurt, either.

"You know, Dr. Toy is always available if you need to chat," Mom continued.

"Great. I'll let you know when I think that would be an appropriate choice for me."

Her eyebrows lifted. "An appropriate choice . . . Well, good, then."

Not-Coco had toddled to the kitchen.

"Can you give me a ride to the Cooking Academy? I need to speak to Chef Kim about a school project." Spikes of heat began radiating from my head. I hated lying to her, but if she had believed me, I wouldn't have to.

"What's this project for?"

"English. We have to interview someone. In person. Face-to-face."

She blinked. "Is Chef Kim expecting you?"

"Yes. And soon."

Mom looked at her watch. "I suppose we have time before my laptop appointment. Get changed and wake Philippa so she can keep an eye on Coco."

Guess I'd have to poke the sleeping dragon, after all.

The banging of a cupboard drew both our gazes toward the kitchen. "Coco, are you getting a snack?"

In the kitchen, Not-Coco was rummaging through the cleaning solutions we kept under the sink. "No, Coco, these are poison!" Mom pried a jug of bleach out of the demon's hands and passed it to me. "She's figured out the baby locks."

"That's because she's no baby."

With her hands held out, Not-Coco rocked from foot to foot, like a cute snowflake in a Christmas pageant, but I saw through her act. The demon was getting bolder. She was showing me she could poison us if she wanted to, even without that library book. Mom pulled the bucket from under the sink and loaded it with tile cleaner, Windex, and an all-purpose disinfectant. "Take these to your bathroom and let's keep the door locked until I can get a better proofing system."

Not-Coco watched me with her crazed drooling expression as I carted the items back upstairs. Instead of storing them, I poured all the solutions into the toilet. Sure, she had other means of destroying our lives, but we were not going to be poisoned on my watch. After disposing of the containers in our outside bins, I returned to my room, dressing in the first clean clothes I found. I put Pikachu in my backpack, along with the Eggs of Truth. A movement on the windowsill caught my eye. The Mischief Mustache.

"Stop, you!"

The mustache startled, then fell to the floor.

I crouched over it, glaring. "Just what do you think you're doing, following me around?"

The mustache backed up against the wall on the two points of its "legs," quavering.

"You think you're funny? How 'bout you get a life and leave mine alone?" I knew I was taking out my anger toward Mr. Pang on this pathetic scrap of hair, which probably didn't have much of a life to speak of, but I couldn't help it.

Then something occurred to me. If I caught it, I could show Mom the magic. I pounced.

But the squirrelly thing was faster than me, dodging right, then left.

"Oh, so now *you're* juking me? You don't know who you're messing with. I'm the best juker on my team. I'm gonna break your ankles." I matched its fake-out movements, game mode on.

"Winston?"

I jerked up. The mustache seemed to vanish into thin air.

Philippa was standing at the doorway. "Who were you talking to?"

I groaned. "Myself, okay?" She wouldn't have believed anything else. "Mom needs you to watch the hellion while we run errands."

"Fine. I'm up now anyway."

"Also, the cretin wants to poison us. Don't turn your back on her. And the extra Dog-Off's in Mom's tool shed."

She lingered long enough for me to hear the full length of her sigh, then slithered away.

I checked high and low, but the mustache had vanished. "Yeah, you'd better run, you hairball," I muttered.

* ❋ · ❊ · ❋ *

Rain fell hard across our windshield. Even with the wipers going full speed, it looked like we were passing under a waterfall. The car crawled down the street as Mom swerved to avoid a plastic chair, a bicycle, a Tide bottle, and other storm debris. Broken fences lay in heaps. Trees had been stripped of their leaves or downed completely. The whole neighborhood seemed to be crying.

"If you can overlook the weather, things are looking up for the Chu family. The firm recruiter texted me that if things check out with my writing sample, I'm their top candidate. Philippa is going to give notice at Waffle Fury—she's decided to go work for Mr. Gu. She might enroll in a few classes, too."

I looked out my window, hiding my face. Things were definitely *not* looking up for the Chu family. Only two more nights to find Coco, or our family would be cut down to three.

She patted my leg. "And you haven't lost a single thing lately."

Except my sister.

"Winston, I want you to know how much I've appreciated you"—her cheek twitched—"these past few years." She didn't have to say anything about Dad, but I knew he was in this conversation. She gave me a tight smile. "And if I've been distracted, I'm sorry about that. I wanted to ask you, how would you like to do a little day-cation with just me?"

"What do you mean?"

"We could go to Monterey for the day and see the sea otters, or Philippa suggested riding bikes in Sonoma."

"*Philippa* suggested a day-cation?"

"Yes."

"Did she say anything else?" She was supposed to get Mom off my case, not put yellow flags around it.

"About what?"

"Nothing," I said quickly, feeling her studying me, even with her eyes on the road.

Thankfully, the school was in sight. She pulled to the curb right in front of the main entrance.

"You don't have to come in," I said. "Maybe you could pick me up after you drop off the laptop?"

"I want to make sure you're settled first. And I've never been inside this place. I'd like to see it."

Hiding my dismay, I grabbed my backpack and shouldered into the rain. If Chef Kim was here, how would I explain my surprise visit when Mom thought I had planned this out?

Inside the Cooking Academy, yeasty bread-baking aromas bombarded us from all sides. Despite looking like an old bank on the outside, the interior featured modern glass walls and steel signs engraved with things like TEACHING KITCHEN 1 and KNIVERY. A few students were milling around.

"Something smells delicious." Mom started down the short hallway that led to a longer one. With her black turtleneck sweater, dark jeans, and fashionable haircut, she looked like she could go to school here. "Where are you meeting her?"

"In her classroom. You can wait here." I gestured to a bench outside the administrative offices, which were empty. "I can find her myself."

"No, I want to come with. Lead the way."

I trudged like a prisoner down the hallway to the classroom where Chef Kim taught, hoping she was there, and at the same time racking my brain for what to say in front of my mom.

The small window in the door of her classroom was dark. Mom tried the handle, but the door was locked. "What's her phone number?" She took her cell phone out of her purse.

"I don't know. We scheduled through email."

"Ah. Well, let's see if we can find anyone else."

Before I could stop her, Mom had pulled open the door to the neighboring classroom. Students in toques were gathered around a steel counter, where a man in a white chef's uniform was speaking what sounded like Russian.

"Excuse me, but we're looking for Chef Kim," Mom asked. "Do you know where she might be?"

The Russian chef lifted his red nose at us. "We are in the middle of a soufflé, if you do not mind."

"Sorry." Mom closed the door after her and rolled her eyes. Continuing down the hall, we checked the rest of the classrooms, but there was no Chef Kim.

We returned to the administrative offices, and Mom perched on the bench. "I think I know what's happening here."

My heart bounced. Somehow Mom had figured it out. She'd caught the stink of my deceit, stronger than the odor of baking bread.

"It's the rain. I'm sure it's delayed her, though it looks like it stopped."

I let out a shaky laugh. "Right." Through the glass doors, golden sunlight was making the wet sidewalks sparkle. "How about you take your laptop to the shop, and I'll wait here for her," I tried.

"No, I'll wait with you." She patted the spot beside her.

I sank onto the bench, wondering when I should call it quits. If Chef Kim wasn't here already, then she wasn't prepping dough today. I'd just have to keep trying Dani's number.

I stood. "She's a no-show. Let's get outta here."

Mom made a sympathetic noise and got to her feet. I started toward the exit.

"Winston?"

"Yeah, Mom?"

"Isn't that girl from your baking class?"

A familiar figure gracefully made her way down the long hall.

For once, lightning had struck just when I needed it.

CHAPTER 31

"Dani!" I called.

Startled, she turned around. She was a sight for sore eyes, even while wearing a somber outfit of storm-gray pants and shirt. A thin scarf like a jag of golden lightning was wound around her neck. In her hair bloomed the pink cocktail umbrella.

"Winston?" She was holding a glass jar containing multicolored beans in one hand and a set of keys in the other.

"Er, Mom, this is Dani, Chef Kim's niece."

"Oh, hello," said Mom. "I'm Mrs. Chu. Great timing—we were just about to leave."

"Oh?" Dani's teardrop-shaped eyes refocused on me. "And what are you doing here, Winston?"

"I have that meeting with your aunt, remember?" I jabbed her with a *play along* look. Before she could respond, or Chef

Kim could appear, I turned back to Mom. "I'm good now. You can go."

Mom's eyes narrowed, shifting between Dani and me. Had she seen Dani's confusion? Read my desperation?

At last, she slung her purse over her shoulder. "All right, kids. Nice to meet you, Dani. Winston, I shouldn't be more than thirty minutes."

We watched her exit and give us a last wave through the glass.

"So . . . *is* your aunt here?" I tried not to sound too anxious.

"She's waiting in the parking lot. She sent me in to get her lucky pie-baking beans for tomorrow's Bake-Off. Every time she uses the blue ones, she wins first prize."

In baking class, we had used dried beans to weigh down a pie crust while it baked. But there was only a handful of beans in the jar Dani was holding, and usually you needed more than that.

I had bigger mysteries to solve, though. "Dani, do you happen to know where your aunt got your cocktail umbrella?"

Dani touched it. "I'll tell you, but first you have to be honest with me."

I gulped. It was a small price to pay, and I'd been wanting to come clean anyway.

She glanced at my hand. "Did you really injure yourself?"

I shrunk a few feet. "No."

"And do you really play the ukulele?"

"No." I couldn't bear to look at her. I'd sunk so low, I bet my sneakers were melting with the heat of Earth's core. "I'm sorry. I guess I wanted to, er, impress you." I could feel my face turning red from the neck up, like a pitcher being filled with fruit punch.

A smile tweaked her lips. "So why do you want to know about my cocktail umbrella?"

"I think it's magic. See, I actually *did* get a chance to see you play yesterday."

Her eyes lit up. "You did? What did you think?"

"It was . . . different."

"You mean weird. Don't worry, that's a compliment. Kronos is very *moderne*."

"Um, yeah. Anyway, about your umbrella . . ."

"So you noticed what happened with the weather?"

"It was like a dome of sunshine had covered the park."

She nodded vigorously. "Right. I'd always thought the umbrella was just a good-luck charm. But it really *does* seem to protect me from all these weird storms. I haven't felt a single drop of rain all morning. My plan is to only take it off at night when I sleep."

"Great." I exhaled. "So do you know where your aunt got it?"

"No."

My chest deflated like a popped beach ball. Served me right, after I'd lied to Dani.

"But we can ask her now." She looked over my shoulder.

I turned to see Chef Kim coming toward us with powerful strides of her short legs, which were wearing flowing floral pants and her trademark green clogs. Her sleeveless T-shirt read NOT ENOUGH SALT.

She didn't appear surprised to see me. Then again, she never expressed much emotion beyond disapproval, sort of like a bullfrog. She took the jar from Dani. "Good, you found them. It was taking you a while. Hello, Winston. Remembering to preheat your oven?"

"Yes, Chef."

"Very good. Come along, Dani. I'm behind schedule as it is."

"Wait. Winston wants to know where you got my lucky umbrella."

"I want to get one for my mom," I added.

Chef Kim's eyes grew smaller. "I don't remember. But you won't be able to find another like it. I got it from a one-of-a-kind store. The owner claimed the umbrella would 'make every day sunny,' and I thought that sounded like Dani. It was just a sales gimmick."

That sounded nice, but there had to be more to the story. If she thought it was just a gimmick, why was she wearing such summery clothes?

"Does 'Mr. Pang's Whimsies' ring a bell?"

Her face didn't move a muscle. "No. Should it?"

"Do you remember seeing any strange birds following you, say, a Javan green magpie?"

Chef Kim pulled her head back, giving herself a double chin. It was exactly how she looked when somebody turned on the mixer at full speed and sprayed flour everywhere. "No, but that sounds like an interesting name for a dessert. Who is this Mr. Pang?"

"A sneaky, lying PITA. If you're in the market for another whimsy, don't trust him."

"Since he's not the man who sold me Dani's umbrella, I guess I don't have to worry."

"So . . . the person who sold you Dani's umbrella was a man?"

Chef Kim blinked. Her pie beans rattled as she shifted the jar from one hand to another. "Yes, didn't I say that?"

Dani crossed her arms. "No, Auntie, you didn't."

"What did he look like?" I pressed.

Chef Kim drew herself up to her full height of five feet. "I wouldn't remember. Now, Dani, we must be off. I need to hit the bull's-eye with this pie." She pivoted on one heel of her clogs, and marched to the exit with her niece in tow.

* ❊ · ❊ · ❊ *

Once Mom and I were back in our neighborhood, we discovered the entire block had gone dark and the traffic signals were blinking. A power outage, no doubt due to the intense rainstorm earlier.

At home, Philippa was lighting candles on the dining table. Not-Coco cowered in a corner of the living room with her hands to her face.

"Hi, girls. Coco, what's wrong?" Mom quickly shed her shoes and hurried over to the changeling.

Not-Coco pushed herself farther back against the wall. "Turn off the fire! I don't like fire!"

"You mean the candles? If we don't light the candles, we won't be able to see," Mom said reasonably. "It's too dark."

"Turn off the fire!"

So . . . the changeling had a weakness. But why fire? Unlike the broom and dustpan, she wasn't made of wood. Her porcelain face appeared in my mind, with her soft body enrobed in green pajamas. Flammable green pajamas.

Mom sighed. "Kids, take the candles to the kitchen."

Philippa and I gathered the votives.

"I keep telling you," I said in a low voice so only Philippa could hear, "that's not Coco."

She shook her head. It was hard to tell if she had simply given up arguing with me, or if she was beginning to see the light.

After moving the candles, I took a position at the dining table, waiting for an opportunity to catch Not-Coco alone. She had stopped cowering and was now ripping paper into shreds while Philippa knit by flashlight. I would have to create a diversion, one that would get both Mom and Philippa as far from this part of the house as possible, like the upstairs bathroom.

My phone buzzed. It was Mav. I grabbed a candle and made my way upstairs. "Status?"

"About to interrogate the enemy," I whispered. "I think she's afraid of fire."

"Interesting. Get this—my Monsters and Mythology teacher doesn't think she drew a banana *or* a crescent moon. He thinks it represents something she fears."

"Like fire, except that picture didn't look like fire."

"Keep your eyes open. We're closing in. Stay in the game, remember?"

"Right." *Stay in the game* meant play to win even when we were losing.

I rummaged in my backpack for the Flava-gum Bijal had given me. Each pack came with six individually wrapped cubes in flavors like Burst Out of This World Berry and Punchtastic Peach. I shoved two into my mouth at once. The sweet, tangy flavors set off all my saliva sprinklers and brought tears to my eyes. I stuffed in another square and worked my jaw.

Silently, I crept downstairs, the dark working in my favor. Philippa had her back to me, and Not-Coco was focused on her paper ripping. Mom was in the kitchen running water.

It was now or never.

Pushing out my tongue, I started blowing a bubble. With my nerves jangling, I blew too fast, and the gum tore. Steady now. I gathered the gum together in my mouth, not rushing the process. As the bubble took shape, I crept closer to Philippa, relying on the mental map of where I'd last seen toys on the floor so I wouldn't step on them. She was going to go raging moofus on me, but I couldn't worry about that now.

When I was two feet away, she asked without turning around, "Why are you trying to sneak up on me?"

Pop! went my bubble. On my last step, I pretended to trip and ejected the gum. It floated through the air like a rainbow parachute.

Philippa screamed. Not-Coco's head snapped up. Her eyes seemed to glow as they watched me, one mischief-maker appreciating another.

"Sorry, sorry! My bad."

Inappropriate words tumbled from Philippa's mouth as she reached for her hair.

Mom hurried out of the kitchen, carrying a candle. "What is going on?"

"Winston popped his gum on MY HAIR!" She clawed at her locks, which only made the gum get stuck-er. "Agh!"

Mom sighed. The light from her flame highlighted the disappointment on her face. "I'll get the peanut butter."

Philippa stomped upstairs. The last time I'd gotten gum in her hair, Mom had to painstakingly remove it using a combination of peanut butter and Philippa's hair products, a process that had taken almost an hour.

"Keep an eye on Coco," said Mom before following her up the stairs.

Oh, I will.

When I no longer heard their footsteps, I grabbed our plastic lighter from the kitchen. Holding it behind me, I approached Not-Coco. The stingy light from the window outlined her yellow fleecy pajamas. Her creepy smile flatlined when I extended the lighter toward her and flicked it on a few times. "Okay, Chang-Ah-Ling, you're going to tell me what happened to Coco. Where is she, you freak?" I pointed the lighter at Not-Coco's nose. I had no intention of actually burning her. That was my sister's body, after all. But the changeling didn't have to know that.

She scooted back against the wall again, and her eyes filled with terror. "No fire, Winston. Coco went up, up, and away."

Like Superman? What was that supposed to mean?

But then Not-Coco began to tremble, and I was reminded of the time the rottweiler nearly attacked my little sister. She hadn't stopped shaking for a good thirty minutes afterward.

My wand wavered.

Not-Coco grabbed at the lighter and, with one stiff yank, wrenched it from my grasp. She turned it around and flicked the switch. "How do *you* like fire, Winston?"

The lights turned back on. The alarm clock in Mom's room began blaring. I squinted in the too-bright glare.

"Now, aren't we all feeling a bit lighter?" Mom's voice sounded from the stairs. She came down with something black, long, and sticky in her hands. A big hunk of hair. Philippa followed, newly shorn, holding the peanut butter and a grudge toward me.

Seeing Not-Coco waving the lighter around, Mom froze. Then her face tightened, and she hurried over.

"Coco, give that to me."

Not-Coco dropped the lighter into Mom's palm. Finally, Mom sees. At last, she knows the kind of devil she's dealing with. Behind Mom, a grim Philippa, looking slightly ridiculous with her chopped-up hair, hung back.

Mom's gaze corralled mine. "Winston, how could you give that to her?"

"But I didn't! *She* took it and threatened *me* with it."

Not-Coco had begun a sniveling kind of cry. The real Coco never cried so quickly. The real Coco's cry was a silent scream, followed by an explosion.

Mom's shoulders sagged. Holding a plastic blowtorch and part of someone's scalp, she looked like she had stepped off some B-movie horror set. "Young man, please go to your room."

My guts boiled with a silent scream that had nowhere to go. I shouldered past Philippa and trekked up the stairs.

I flopped onto my bed, feeling like I had swallowed my

goldfish. Outwitted again. And every second that ticked by brought us closer to the full moon.

I grabbed Pikachu, turning the figurine over in my palm. I was tempted to throw it against the wall, but I still hadn't learned what it could do.

In the cartoon, the pocket monster could project electricity stored in its red cheek pouches. I wrapped my hand around the figure like it was a joystick, the lightning bolt tail protruding between my fourth and fifth fingers. The red spots on its cheek lit up like buttons on an electronic device. I didn't have a magic fire extinguisher handy, but these were desperate times. Tentatively, I pressed the right cheek with my thumb.

Nothing happened.

I tried the left cheek. Again, nothing.

Then I kept my thumb down a moment longer, the way you do to open an app.

The lights in my bedroom shut off.

Was it another blackout, or . . . ? Without the buzz of electricity in the room, I could hear blood whooshing through my body. I moved my thumb to the right cheek and held it steady.

The lights turned back on.

Left again. The lights shut off.

Right, on. Left, off.

So this Pikachu controlled electricity. I wasn't sure how it would help me find Coco, but I couldn't help feeling that it was going to light the way.

CHAPTER 32

That night, I paced my room, feeling jittery and off-balance. How would Coco's spirit detach? Would she simply float away, like a balloon? Or would she try to hang on, like those people who get caught in a tornado and cling to telephone poles?

The Brain Strainer beckoned to me from where I'd hung it on my bedpost. But I resisted its pull. I couldn't keep using it every time I needed to calm down, especially not in public. Instead I decided to try Dad's qigong techniques, which, after so many years of practice, had become like a superpower to him.

Sitting cross-legged on the floor, I breathed with my belly and envisioned myself bobbing down a lazy river in an inflatable doughnut.

My limbs relaxed, my head cleared.

After floating for miles and miles down that lazy river, I

opened my eyes. Within my open backpack under the window, the Eggs of Truth carton was partially visible.

The eggs revealed the true form of things.

What if I threw one at Mr. Pang's shop? Mom would have to believe me then. I'd ask her to drive me to school, and we'd take a little detour. I'd egg the place, and then the truth would be revealed before her eyes.

I zipped closed my backpack. Finally, I had a solid plan. Thank you, qigong.

* 米 · 米 · 米 *

My alarm jarred me awake earlier than usual. I slid out of bed, feeling as juiced as if I'd drunk a liter of Mountain Dew. Today we'd get Coco back. Today the nightmare would end.

My backpack was open.

I lunged for it, my stomach shriveling like a grape in the sun on time-lapse video. The Eggs of Truth were missing. A chill spider-legged over me. Had the maniacal muppet stolen them?

Then I saw the note on my desk. It read: *Took eggs. Philippa.*

I glanced at my closet, the only way she could've entered with the wedge securing my door. The closet was ajar.

What was she doing up at this hour? She hadn't started her new job yet. More important, what was she planning to do with the eggs?

I called her phone, and she answered on the first ring. "Hey."

"Where are you, and why'd you take my eggs? Bring them back. I need them."

"Sorry, you'll have to be a well-adjusted kid for one day."

"Is this about your hair? I said I was sorry. Can you just come home?"

"No can do. I'm meeting the registrar at San Francisco State."

It sounded important, but so was this. "Philippa, please," I begged. I could feel tears coming. "I'll cook and do the dishes. I'll even clean the gross stuff between your toes."

"Gotta go. Catch you later. Bye."

I called her again, but she didn't pick up.

I yanked open my drawers, then slammed them in frustration, making my wrong-headed bobbles quiver. My hydra of a sister better not drop those eggs before I could get some answers.

"Winston?" Mom appeared in the doorframe. "I have some good news." She tucked her hair behind her ear, revealing a smile in profile. "Last night the firm called, and I got the job."

"Way to go, Mom!"

She beamed. "I start this morning. The firm even has a daycare center for Coco."

I sucked in my breath, wondering how long Mom would keep this job once they found out she had an imp for a daughter.

＊ ·＊·＊·＊·

Mr. Bottoms clapped as he always did to start class. While he read the announcements, it took all my concentration just to stay seated. Suddenly, his eyes zoomed in on me. "Winston, Dani, how's the duet coming along?"

I swallowed hard. I'd intended to talk with him after class. But if I lied now to avoid public humiliation, Dani—wearing head-to-toe pink, including her cocktail umbrella—would think I was a weasel, assuming she didn't already.

"It's going fine, Mr. Bottoms," Dani said before I had a chance to make up my mind.

I stood. I wasn't sure why, but now that I was up, I couldn't exactly sit down. My feet started doing some sort of weird side-by-side movement, step-tap, step-tap, as if I was on the verge of another Top Hat Attack. "Actually, I'm not going to be able to do the performance, after all. I don't play the ukulele. Sorry." I'd probably get razzed for the rest of my days here at Francisco, but on the bright side, at least I was already in eighth grade.

Jude's thin mouth cranked open like a marionette's. "You lied?"

Yasmine coughed disapprovingly.

"What a turkey," said someone else.

"This is a surprise." Mr. Bottoms pushed up his glasses. "Well, thank you for being honest, Winston."

The bell rang, moving us all along.

Dani shone a sympathetic smile at me. "That was admirable. And by the way, if you ever do take an interest in the ukulele, I'd be happy to help you out."

﹡ ✳ · ✳ · ✳ ﹡

In Math 8, Cassa nearly bounced out of her seat when she saw me. "This morning, we used the eyeballs and saw something floating in the sky." Bijal was turned around in his chair, using the remaining two marbles to look out the window. "It was a long dark shadow, but then we lost focus. The trick is, they only work when you don't try too hard. You have to relax your eyes"—Cassa's face zoomed toward me—"and let the spheres combine." Her green eyes crossed, and her Cheerios-scented breath filled my nose.

"Okay, but Philippa took the eggs."

After I relayed the events of this morning, Bijal blew out a breath. "Don't worry, man, Philippa will have to come home at some point."

Cassa pushed her marbles at me. "Until then, we keep on with these. Try it."

I held them close enough to touch my eyelashes, then relaxed my eyes. A few times, the marbles merged. But I didn't see anything but blurry glass.

I slowly scanned the room, waiting for something to happen. I didn't know how to relax my eyes. But I could make out a dark figure, growing closer.

"Table four, we started class five minutes ago." Madame Khoury was glaring down at us. Her voice sounded phlegmy, like she was nursing a cold. "Give me those." She extended a hand. Her fingernails were long enough to balance a marble in each.

I closed my hand around my pair. "We'll put them away."

"We're sorry," Cassa hastily added.

Bijal bowed his head. "Really sorry."

Madame Khoury's forehead bunched under a too-tightly-wrapped turban as she studied my closed fist. "Did you just tell me no?"

That seemed like a trick question. Technically, I hadn't said no, but answering either way could land me in the vice principal's office. But how could I tell her these were magic marbles and we needed them to find my missing sister?

The longer I took to reply, the more defiant I looked. Madame Khoury coughed into her fist, then extended her hand again.

I passed her the pair, which were now warm and slightly wet.

"When can we get them back?" I tried to avoid sounding desperate. I needed to keep my cool or I would lose more than my marbles.

"See me at the end of school today." She stuck them in her desk drawer and locked it.

*   ※ · ※ · ※   *

Somehow I made it to lunchtime. With Dani's cocktail umbrella providing balmy weather over the playground, Cassa, Bijal, and I trekked to the outer reaches of the asphalt to call Mav with an update. Vice Principal Baton zipped around on his electric scooter—the kind that featured a skateboard-like platform for standing and a set of handlebars to steer with. He was known as Batman because of the way his blue coat flew out like a cape behind when he revved his scooter to five miles an hour. He stopped to shoo a group of kids off a pile of risers, then braked twenty feet away from us, his face as stern as a police officer's. He gave us a curt nod, hopped off his scooter, and picked up an empty plastic bag.

We sat at a sun-bleached table. Cassa passed her spaghetti to Bijal. "What did the changeling mean when she said Coco had gone 'up, up, and away'?"

"There's a picture of Mom and Dad as Wonder Woman and Superman on the nightstand. I think she was making fun of us," I said darkly.

Bijal set his potato curry in front of me, but my stomach was a wad of chewed-up gum. Two seagulls wandered over, eyeing the food. Bijal waved his arm, and the birds jumped a few feet back but didn't fly away. "Is it my imagination, or are the seagulls getting bigger?"

Cassa took out her phone and called Mav.

A couple of girls emerged from the building and approached us. You could tell they were in sixth grade because their green-and-yellow PE uniforms still had a shiny look about them. One elbowed the other, and the other nudged back. "You're Bijal, right?" asked the shorter one. "We heard we could buy candy from you. Do you have any?"

Bijal wiped sauce off his cheek with his thumb and crossed his arms. "Whoever told you that should've told you the rules. Candy time's at recess. I like to keep my lunches free."

Cassa waved a dismissive hand at Bijal. "Just give them the candy. We've got one Snickers and one Mars bar, but there's a lunchtime premium. Five bucks each."

The girls made big eyes at each other but coughed up the funds. Bijal tossed them the bars.

Cassa put her phone on the table and let it ring with the speaker on.

Mav answered. "Status?"

"Don't ask," I said. My own phone began to ring. "Hold on." I pulled it from my backpack.

It was Philippa. "So Monroe and I went to check out your Mr. Pang's Whimsies, and, well, we found something."

"You and Monroe went to Mr. Pang's? Together?" A strange warm emotion for my prickly sister flooded through me.

"I don't need an echo," she replied curtly.

"Okay, sorry. I'm going to put you on speaker so everyone can hear."

Philippa grunted disapprovingly but continued. "So at first, we only saw an empty space with a black door. But then a couple of big guys in Hawaiian shirts just appeared, like they'd walked through the walls. I figured they were the burglars you mentioned. I told them they should pick on someone their own size."

Cassa's mouth went slack.

"Well, they didn't seem to like that, because the next thing I know, Monroe's telling them to back off, and blah, blah, blah, I threw the ten-minute Egg of Truth at them."

Bijal grabbed his head. "You threw an Egg of Truth?!"

Philippa coughed in annoyance. "Still hear an echo. Well, I missed. The egg hit the window of the shop, and the stucco turned into brick, and a green door appeared with a sign."

The Egg of Truth had lifted the magic veil that kept the shop hidden, just like I thought it would!

"Then Monroe throws the thirty-hour egg at them, and get this—it must have hit both men, because they turned into seagulls. Seagulls, people!"

I sucked in my breath.

"Guess it's no weirder than Mr. Pang being a magpie," said Mav.

Cassa stabbed the air excitedly with her finger. "Mr. Vlad saw seagulls in the shop, remember?"

"We have a couple of fat seagulls watching us right now." Bijal glared at the two birds that had been eyeing his chips. They were standing about twenty feet away and did seem large for gulls—more like the size of geese, with gray bodies and black-tipped wings.

They had to be Ernie and Bert.

Bijal waved his arms at them. "Shoo, you thuggy kid-shovers!"

The birds at last took flight with harsh squawking. Had they been following us all this time? Who did they work for? And how did they know me?

"So," Philippa went on, "we rang the doorbell but heard only crickets. And then—you might not believe this—a fire hydrant appeared, growling like crazy."

An image of the candy-red fire hydrant flared in my mind. "The Fire-Weiler," I murmured. "It must be part rottweiler."

"Maybe, because it bit us both, me on the arm, and then Monroe when he was trying to get the thing off."

"Are you okay?" My heart seized up at the idea of that thing taking a bite out of Philippa.

"Yeah. Monroe took us for rabies shots."

Bijal grimaced. "At least it didn't pee on you, because that would've been a gusher."

"Where is Monroe now?" asked Mav, sounding worried. We all looked back to Cassa's lavender phone, still lying on the lunch table.

"The doctor wanted him to stay longer for observation,"

Philippa replied. "He got the brunt of the biting, but he said he'd be okay as long as he kept hydrated."

I could hear the smile in her voice. Monroe was sure smooth, joking through the pain.

"So what do we do about the spooky broom and dustpan in the closet?" she asked.

"What?" we all said at once.

"Yeah, they just appeared."

"Way to bury the lede," said Bijal.

"Could you pick me up?" I asked. In the event of sickness, the school let kids go home with approved caregivers, which for me included Philippa.

"What about us?" said Bijal.

Cassa clutched at her neon shoelaces. "I can't get a sick pickup. Janelle decided not to move in with us, after all, so Dad's helping her take back some boxes. He's busy all afternoon."

I couldn't help wondering if Cassa's dramatic truth-telling had influenced Janelle's decision. But Cassa didn't seem too concerned. "You can't go, either," she told Bijal. "If your parents think you're sick, they won't let you go to Winston's later."

"Also, someone needs to get the eyeballs back from Madame Khoury," I added.

"I don't want to know what that means," said Philippa.

"I'll play sick, too," said Mav. "Game on, Mr. Pang. Game on."

CHAPTER 33

We hurried toward the school. If the Fire-Weiler had been deployed as a countermeasure, there was a good chance Mr. Pang was back in his shop. The broom and the dustpan could get us in, and then we'd force him to show us how to use the eyeballs to find Coco. I didn't know how, exactly, but maybe the cloud weaver and the cowherd could tell us. After all, they knew him better than we did. Hope surged through me, like when we made a goal that evened the score. Now that Philippa and Monroe had seen the truth, the odds had shifted in our favor.

On the blacktop, near an area painted with four-square lines, Batman was talking to a couple of girls in PE uniforms—the same ones who had bought the candy from Bijal and Cassa. Batman's head swiveled toward us. He motored his scooter over. "Bijal, Cassa, I would like to speak to you."

Uh-oh.

Bijal didn't seem to know what to do with his arms, so he jammed his hands deep into the pockets of his sweatpants. Cassa put on a smile, though she was strangling her water bottle. "Yes, Mr. Baton?"

"There's a rumor you've been running an illegal candy op here. Today I find the suspicions are well founded." From an inner pocket of his navy jacket, he pulled out the Snickers and Mars bars, now misshapen after having passed through several hands. "The money, please."

From the pocket of her backpack, Cassa fished out the two five-dollar bills she had received from the sixth graders. She gave them to Mr. Baton, who then returned them to . . . his wallet?

"That's not yours—" I began, before realizing what was going on. It had been a setup.

"This is entrapment!" said Bijal.

"It's not entrapment. You haven't committed a crime. But you *did* break school rules, which means, I'm afraid, I'm going to have to call your parents."

"Please don't do that!" Bijal shook praying hands at the man. "I'll do laps. I'll serve time in the slammer shelving books or whatever. Just don't tell them."

Batman's forehead furrowed like a wet magazine. "Library duty is not the slammer. But we take infractions like this seriously. It's a slippery slope. Today, it's candy. Tomorrow, you're overcharging tourists for a little sugar, water, and food dye and calling it shave ice."

"Doesn't sound so bad," Bijal muttered.

Cassa elbowed him. "What Bijal means is, we're sorry and

we won't do it again." Her voice brightened as she switched into salesperson mode. "You can call my dad, but if you call Bijal's, you might have another problem on your hands. His mom is very sensitive. She'll take it hard."

Cassa meant she'd make life hard for Bijal, maybe ground him for the rest of his life.

Bijal nodded vigorously. "When she found out I once ate a slice of pepperoni pizza, she didn't speak to me for a month. We're vegetarians."

Two gray shadows landed on the rain gutters atop the closest building. Seagulls.

Cassa's eyebrows slanted up. "Something like this could really affect your bottom line, if his mom were to press charges for your setting us up."

"My mom knows some great lawyers in case you need them," I added.

Batman turned his stare on me. "Don't tell me you're part of this operation, too?"

"Er, no. I was headed to the nurse's office." I coughed a few times.

Batman rolled his scooter back a foot. "Go on, then."

Cassa made a tiny sweeping motion with her hand, meaning *go, we'll handle this*. I hated leaving, but Coco came first. Plus, if anyone could talk their way out of detention, it was Cassa.

Philippa was already sitting in one of the mold-colored chairs in the office lobby, the gauze wrapping her right arm peeking out through her striped sweater sleeve. Today, her choppy do had a weirdly cool look about it. But there were shadows under her eyes, and her cheek was twitching. As she led me to where she had set our skateboards near the bike racks, I noticed she'd put on her sweater inside out, with the tag showing in the back.

With her left hand, she set down her board. Soon we were rolling the short distance to our house, avoiding recent potholes. She was a good boarder, using her momentum to power her forward so she didn't have to push off as much as I did.

A siren wailed in the distance. Now that the rain puddles had dried, the streets looked beat-up. Workers in orange vests were putting safety cones around a pothole the size of an elephant.

"Sorry I didn't believe you before," she said, riding a few paces behind me.

"When did you finally figure it out?" I said, trying to temper the bitterness in my voice.

"Yesterday, when I saw her give you that scary smile. It was like . . ."

"A zombie scythe."

"Yeah."

I let her catch up. "I think this deserves a reprieve on the dish washing," I said.

"Fine." She bit her lip, already on to her next thought. "How am I going to convince Mom?"

"I don't know. She might think you're suffering from incomplete mornings, too."

Philippa's face buckled, as if she was holding back a laugh. "*Mourning* with a *u*, not *morning*." She glanced at me, her face serious again. "So, what are our assets? What are we working with here?"

"Well, now that you used up the eggs, we have a Pikachu that turns electricity on and off, plus some Far-Seeing Eyeballs." I didn't bother mentioning the pair I had lost. "Oh, and a cocktail umbrella that brings clear skies for a one-mile radius, but it doesn't belong to us."

Philippa fell back to let a pedestrian pass, then shot up to me again. "How do we get into that shop without being torn to pieces by that—what did you call it? *Fire-Weiler?*"

"I don't know, but maybe the broom and dustpan do."

When we reached our place, she tipped up her board to grab it but grimaced as she reached for it with her injured arm. Instead, grabbing it with her left hand, she hiked up the stairs with me tailing her. A harsh squawking halted my step. Circling above our house were two fat seagulls.

"Inside, before they bomb us!" Philippa fumbled with the keys, and I grabbed them from her. Unlocking the door, I threw it open, and we scrambled inside.

We'd scarcely removed our shoes and jackets when the pound of footsteps signaled Mav's arrival. He hustled in, his thick hair leaning to one side, like he'd given up combing it. The birds were perched on the roof of the house across the street, their downturned beaks looking extra tweaky. They turned their heads sideways the way birds do to get a bead on you. One squawked, and then both were squawking.

Mav glanced back at them. "What do those things want?"

"All I know is Mr. Pang didn't like them."

"We learned in Five-Point Diplomacy that the enemy of your enemy is your friend."

From behind us, Philippa snorted. "Five-Point Diplomacy? Whatever happened to the five-paragraph essay?"

We all trekked up to the closet. The broom and dustpan were nestled in their customary spot behind my Jedi robe. I was so happy to see them, I fell to my knees and almost hugged them. Mav took a position on my side of the closet, Philippa and me on hers.

"Cloud Weaver, Cowherd, we don't have any time to lose."

Mav's jaw went ajar as the cloud weaver's figure swirled into view, as pretty as one of those goddesses you see painted on expensive vases in the museum. Her dimples were like tiny stars, on a face as mysterious as the galaxy. The cowherd filled in the space with his typical reluctance. He was missing his hat, as well as his luxurious man bun. His hair stood up like boar bristles.

Philippa tossed back her hair and shoved a hand at me. "Get on with it." It took a lot to impress her.

I scowled at her. "Hello again," I told the pair. "I'm glad you weren't, er, fried."

"Put-tee, we need Put-tee," said Cloud Weaver.

"We gave you the information you wanted," Cowherd grumbled. "You owe us."

"But she wasn't in the store. Chang-Ah-Ling was gone."

The cloud weaver glanced at the cowherd, her face alarmed. "What about the canoe?"

"That wasn't there, either," I said, my voice getting louder. "What's going on?"

The cowherd crossed his arms tight against his broad chest. "Mr. Pang uses Chang-Ah-Ling to pilot his Up, Up, and Away Canoe."

Mav and I stared at each other. Not-Coco had said Coco had gone *up, up, and away.*

The banana Not-Coco had drawn suddenly made sense, as did the long, dark shadow Cassa and Bijal had glimpsed floating over San Francisco through the eyeballs. Eyeballs Mr. Pang had said he was planning to use to look for her.

All the moisture in my mouth wicked away, and I croaked, "Coco's flying around in the sky."

CHAPTER 34

Philippa shifted from foot to foot, her socked feet looking like two pink jelly beans. "Let me get this straight. Not only is our sister trapped inside a creepy doll, but she's also piloting a flying canoe?"

"I'm afraid so," said Cloud Weaver softly.

"How do we get her to land?" Philippa cried, loud enough for me to feel her hot breath.

The shorter spirit dusted off his shirt. "How do I know? I herd cows for a living."

"I believe only your sister can land the Up, Up, and Away Canoe." The cloud weaver's hands made wavy motions toward the ceiling.

Philippa's jellybean feet gripped the carpet. "But she's only three years old! She can barely walk in a straight line."

The cowherd sat down grumpily, hands on the knees of his

worn trousers. "I wouldn't worry too much. Chang-Ah-Ling's body is virtually indestructible."

Philippa wheeled on him. "I wouldn't have to worry at all if someone hadn't swept a perfectly innocent toddler into some Chucky doll nightmare!"

The cowherd tsked, reminding me of those beetles that clicked when they were annoyed.

A knock came at the front door.

"I'll get it," said Mav.

"No, I will." The closet felt hot and stuffy, and I needed out before I hurt someone.

As I hurried downstairs, the knocking grew more insistent. I heard the distinct voices of Cassa and Bijal yelling.

I quickly opened the door.

"Watch out!" yelled Cassa, using her body to block one of the giant seagulls, who looked like it was gunning for the door. Bijal was doing some sort of jumping jack, trying to edge the second gull off the landing.

"Get in, get in!" I cried, holding the door just wide enough for Bijal and Cassa to squeeze through. I was glad those birds wouldn't be human again for at least a day.

I slammed the door shut after them. Both looked out of breath, as if they'd run all the way from school. I looked through the peephole and came eyeball to eyeball with a seagull. I jerked back. "It's staring at me."

"The gulls are getting bold," panted Cassa.

"You need to learn some boundaries!" Bijal barked through the door.

"So you weren't busted?"

Bijal stepped out of his Vans. "I think it was because of the balloon I gave Batman on the first day of school." He punched a fist in the air. "I told you balloon flowers have power. He let us go with a warning."

"That's the good news." Cassa hung her backpack. "The bad news is that Madame Khoury went home sick. We couldn't get the eyeballs back."

I gripped the sides of my head. Without any eyeballs, how would we find Coco now?

The party moved to my room. Philippa sat in an angry ball on my bed, and Mav was standing by the window. The cowherd and the cloud weaver's otherworldly forms floated around my small space, their tools moving along with them.

"S-s-s— S-s-s—" Bijal tried, pointing.

The only part of Cassa that moved was her eyelids, blinking rapidly, as if she was trying to refresh her vision like a misloaded web page.

"S-s-spirits," Bijal finally got out. His arms started flailing. "So many questions. How do you fit in there? How do you move around?" He lowered his voice. "How do you go to the bathroom?"

"Stop, kid," snapped Philippa. She unrolled herself like a hedgehog and, cradling her arm, stood nose to nose with the cowherd. "What do you have on this Mr. Pang? From what I can tell, he's not helping you out of the goodness of his heart."

The cowherd rubbed a hand through his bristly hair and said grumpily, "He owes me a favor." Scowling, he crossed to the window.

Cloud Weaver watched her husband peer out the curtains.

"If a favor is not repaid, a magpie loses face, and reputation is everything to such a bird. You see, before Mr. Pang was Mr. Pang, he was a magpie named Sorrow. He and his brother, Mirth, were heaven's most esteemed birds. They pulled my mother's chariot."

The story Mom had read to Not-Coco floated into my mind. Magpies worked in pairs. But the thought of Mr. Pang being an esteemed anything beyond a trickster was hard to believe.

Cloud Weaver wove her hair into plaits with nimble fingers. "Many years ago, Sorrow grew tired of flying in Mirth's shadow. He offered my husband a favor in exchange for one of his teardrops. A single tear was enough to transform the magpie into an earthly creature."

Cowherd glanced up to see all of us looking at him. "I said no, of course. I didn't want anything besides an eternal life with my spouse, and I didn't think a bird would be capable of giving me that." His eyes dimmed like he was reliving a memory. "But that night, when I was tending my cows, I heard an eerie lullaby blowing through the reeds. I found myself so moved that I . . ." He cleared his throat in a manly way. "Well, I shed a few tears."

We all leaned in, even Bijal, who had latched his arm around Cassa's.

"Something soft, like wings, brushed my face." The cowherd touched his cheek, then shook his head sadly. "I knew I had been tricked."

"Mother was very angry." Cloud Weaver picked up the tale. "When she spotted Sorrow in that ficus, she threw down a lightning bolt to draw him back up to heaven. But now that he was of the earth, she could not make him return. 'Twas a pity about that toy store."

Toy store?

Cassa dislodged her arm from Bijal's. "The lightning strike that caused the fire in the Dream Castle. That must have been when Sorrow became Mr. Pang and started his own store."

Bijal poked his fingers into the smoky illusion of Cloud Weaver's dress, which moved like its own weather system around her. "But that lightning strike happened ages ago."

Cloud Weaver nodded. "Time moves differently here. In your Earth time, we are three thousand years old, but in heaven, I have just celebrated my twenty-first birthday."

"But I thought you were, like, human." Bijal passed his hand through the cowherd's midsection.

The male spirit stiffened. "If your story continues to be told, you achieve a certain immortality."

I fidgeted with my dog tag. Somehow their explanation had just raised more questions.

"So, if Mr. Pang owes you a favor, go back to the shop and lean on him." Philippa pointed her nose toward the dustpan.

Cowherd opened his hands. His fingers were stubby but looked strong enough to wrestle a bull. "My wife and I cannot use the portal to return to the shop, as it requires both a sweeper and a receptacle to pass through. Neither can we use his front door, even if we could get someone to open it for us. Mother Cloud Weaver is always watching his shop, poised with her lightning bolt."

"So you can't open doors by yourself," I said.

"Energy cannot flow through a blocked doorway."

Mah-mah's feng shui principles of harmonious living returned to me. The front door was the mouth of qi. No wonder the spirits needed help getting in.

"If you give us Puh-tee, Mr. Pang will have enough qi to energize my wife's hairpin. Then she can build our bridge and return to the heavens and help you search for your sister. The view of Earth is much better from up there."

A blue vein in Philippa's forehead bulged. "Nope. This is all *your* fault. First find a way to get Coco; then we *might* give you Putty."

"But we can't risk anything more going wrong," the cloud weaver exclaimed. "Every day, the storms grow worse. My mother is closing in on us. A few nights ago, she singed my husband's hat off his head."

The cowherd put a protective arm around Cloud Weaver as Mav edged his way to Cassa, Bijal, and me, his face grim.

"Something's wrong with this picture," Mav whispered to us as Philippa kept ranting at the spirits. We closed ranks around him. "Mr. Pang already put Win's stuff through the machine."

"Yeah. He even stuck them in a box to mail back to you," Bijal added.

I nodded. "Except Lucky." It bothered me that I'd never found out what had become of Dad's last gift to me.

"I think this calls for a little five-point diplomacy," said Mav.

I nodded. The enemies of my enemies were my friends.

My bobbleheads jiggled their heads at us, led by Meg Rapinoe, still on Neymar's body. I hadn't had time to switch them back yet. We had to work as a team—sure, a mismatched one—to get Coco back. "So we turn the spirits against Mr. Pang," I said in a low voice. "Show them that, yet again, he hasn't been honest. Then maybe they'll help us get what we want." I whispered instructions to Cassa and Bijal, who took off downstairs.

Philippa was flattening the carpet with her heavy pacing.

"Have you seen Mr. Pang's new Flip and Dunks?" I asked the spirits.

The cowherd stared down his nose at me. "We have not seen Mr. Pang since we came to your house."

"Mr. Pang hasn't been completely honest with you. You see, he already used the qi in my shirt and Philippa's Babar toy. In fact, he was going to send them back to me, but we found them first."

"I don't believe you." Cowherd crossed his arms and turned his head away.

Bijal and Cassa returned, holding two frost-covered Ziploc bags.

"Guys, show him."

Cassa held out the plastic bag containing my shirt, waving it like a flag to a bull. Bijal, his face arranged in his most intense defender's stare, displayed the bag of Babar, moving it in a clockwise motion like it was a prize in a game show. With a gasp, Philippa took the bag, then pulled out her faded and now-chilly buddy.

"He used the objects you stole from us to enchant his own basketball sneakers and sweatband," I explained.

Cassa wiggled her shoulders, as if warming up for a kick. "I think it's pretty clear that Mr. Pang was milking you, which leaves all of us with a problem. How can we trust Mr. Pang? He's deceived both of you, and he clearly has no interest in returning Coco to her body."

The cloud weaver and the cowherd exchanged a glance, one that put more worry dimples in her cheeks and scowl lines on his forehead.

"Magpies are tricky," grunted Cowherd. "We never should have trusted him."

"Mother trusted him."

"Yes, and he betrayed her by leaving her service. And he was her favorite, too."

Cloud Weaver's eyes brimmed with tears, and she brushed one from her cheek. "Just as I am betraying her. But she has given me no choice, sending those horrible mercenaries after us."

My bagged shirt made crackling sounds in Bijal's hands. "Ernie and Bert?"

"The seagulls," said Cassa.

The cowherd grunted. "Yes, seagulls."

So Mother Cloud Weaver had sent Ernie and Bert to find her daughter. No wonder they'd been trying to break into Mr. Pang's. But that still didn't explain how they knew me.

Cassa lined up for the strike, palms pressed to her thighs, eyes focused. With the gentleness of a mom explaining the importance of a tetanus shot, she suggested, "If we work together, we can both get what we want." Sometimes the ball only needed a light touch to score.

The cowherd looked up. "How?"

"You help us get to Mr. Pang. You've seen his store. You

know how he operates, what his weaknesses are. In turn, *we'll* help you enchant the hairpin with the popcorn machine."

The cloud weaver gasped. "You know how to use the machine that smells of corn?"

Cassa nodded solemnly "Yes, we do."

The cowherd took his wife's hand. "We will have to think about it."

The pair began to fade, until they were translucent as jellyfish.

"What's there to think about? He deceived you!" I cried.

The spirits disappeared, and the broom and the dustpan dropped to the floor.

CHAPTER 35

"That's it?" Philippa gripped her Babar, glancing down at the lifeless objects. "They're gone?"

Mav put his face alongside the broom. "I think so."

"I bet they're still listening, though," said Cassa.

Philippa bent down. "Well, hear this, you heartless splinters. If you don't come back here right now, I'll feed your ashes to those seagulls."

I knew what I had to do. The stairs protested as I descended two at a time. I opened the freezer, and frosty air puffed on my hot face. Behind the bag of pot stickers lay Mom's kimchee jar. I twisted off the lid.

Putty was frozen into a fist-size wad. I massaged it back to life, smoothing it out until it was a damp furry square, basically back to normal.

When I returned to my room, Philippa was sitting on my

bed, rubbing her hand. "How dare you shock me!" she seethed, glaring at the broom.

"Let me try." I dropped to my knees between the broom and the dustpan. "Guys, we don't have time for you to 'think about it.' You said yourself Coco could only return to her body by the light of the full moon, and that's tonight. Here's Putty." I waved the blanket scrap. "You can take it and try to make the goal on your own. Or you can pass the ball and trust your teammates to get it up the field for you. The first way is a lot riskier."

Cassa, Bijal, and Mav were nodding. Philippa was still glowering at the broomstick. "These pieces of trash don't know soccer, Winston. I'm getting the lighter."

"Wait," I said.

The broomstick had begun to flicker. It lifted into the air, along with Cloud Weaver's shimmering form. The cowherd soon materialized beside her, his scowl firmly in place.

"We have decided to trust our teammates," said the cloud weaver with solemnity. "What is your plan?"

* ❋ · ❋ · ❋ *

While everyone else went into a huddle downstairs, I looked through my drawers for my best possession. Our plan was to soften up Mr. Pang with the help of the Warm Fuzzies ukulele, which—the cowherd and the cloud weaver had witnessed firsthand—put people in a good mood. Then we'd bribe him with something of high qi value from my personal collection to help us recover Coco. Surely the man/bird had other ways of tracking his Up, Up, and Away Canoe than the Eyeballs. We'd be doing him a favor, taking a fussy toddler off his hands.

I ran my fingers over my bobbleheads, making each of them nod, as if, yes, they would answer the call of duty. But though I liked them all, none of them would suffice. I rifled through the closet, not seeing much of interest. My nightstand drawer offered only some old comics, a few coins, and a mirror from a bubble gum machine. I held the mirror in front of me. My face looked chewed up, my eyes cranked open too wide.

Dad's dog tag winked in my reflection. I grasped the silver ID, the metal warm and familiar in my hand. This was my best memento of Dad. I knew it because the thought of giving it up was like a fist in the gut. But if Mr. Pang had already used its qi, it had no value. Unless . . .

Qigong helped you restore life energy. Was it possible that the energy in objects could also be recharged, just through the act of cherishing? I never took off the dog tag. If there was any object of value in my life, it was this piece.

Something moved across the carpet. Dark brown, hairy, and matted. The Mischief Mustache was inching toward me.

"Wha—"

It stopped moving and collapsed, its furry mass heaving. I moved closer, wondering why it looked so beat. Under the mustache there were two small round objects, like marbles.

Slowly reaching out a finger, I poked them. A goldish gleam shone through their muddy surfaces.

"Guys, guys!" I cried.

Footsteps pounded up the stairs. The mustache seemed to seize; then it tore under my bed.

Mav, Cassa, and Bijal herded into the room.

"The Mischief Mustache was here! It was muddy and looked really tired, and it brought these." I held out the marbles.

Mav held one to the light. "Far-Seeing Eyeballs."

"These must be the pair you dropped at Coit Tower!" said Cassa.

"But how did the mustache know . . . ?"

"Maybe it was with you when it happened," said Mav.

The idea of a mustache hitching a ride without me knowing was unsettling, but the thing had done me a solid. In fact, I wished it hadn't left so fast. The little guy had grown on me.

Bijal folded his arms and nodded. "That is one helpful critter. From now on, we should call it the Helping Handlebar. Too bad it split."

We rejoined the cloud weaver and the cowherd at the dining table as they studied a diagram of Mr. Pang's shop. Philippa, who'd been rattling around in the kitchen, brought paper plates and chopsticks to the table. "So, what did you find to bribe Pang with?"

Cassa held up the marbles. "Far-Seeing Eyeballs."

"Don't those already belong to him?" asked Philippa.

Cassa folded her hands in front of her and shone a smile that invited trust, the kind that could sell beachfront property. "Possession is nine-tenths of the law. If we're holding them, they're ours."

Bijal tapped his chin. "But, technically, Mr. Pang needs the eyeballs to find Coco."

Cassa's beachfront smile faded. "Whose side are you on?"

"We have something else to trade in case we need it." I pulled Dad's dog tag out from under my shirt.

Philippa frowned. "I thought he already used that."

"He did, but it must have recharged, because it's the only thing I can't stand to give him." Before it cooled too much, I put it back against my chest.

Mav's face grew thoughtful, and he nodded. "That makes a lot of sense. We'll make sure it's worth the sacrifice."

"But if all else fails, what's the fallback plan?" I asked.

"What else does Mr. Pang want?" asked Cassa, tapping her pencil against the diagram, where she had listed the whereabouts of known threats, such as Were-Bear, in neat capital letters.

Cloud Weaver glanced toward the window. "The moon. He looks at it every night with the Far-Seeing Eyeballs."

I thought back to the inflatable moon hanging in Mr. Pang's office, and his moon-phase chart. Even his grasshopper-green door and window had been round like the moon.

"We can't get him that, but if he likes looking at it, maybe he'll be more willing to trade back for the eyeballs." Mav looked at his watch. "Let's move on to threats. What can you tell us about that Were-Bear?"

The cowherd waved a dismissive hand. "It's harmless."

"Unless the moon is full," added the cloud weaver, her eyes wide.

"Like tonight." Bijal's knees started bouncing.

"So it *is* like a werewolf . . ." I murmured.

"Except twice as big." The cowherd looked up at the ceiling as if imagining the animal.

I swallowed hard. We wouldn't be able to help Coco if we were mauled by a vicious bear first.

"What do we do about it?" asked Bijal.

The cowherd shrugged. "It used to be a circus bear. Do any of you know how to juggle?"

We all looked at each other. Cassa stopped writing notes and glanced at Bijal. "How about juggling balloons?"

Bijal scowled. "I don't juggle balloons. I *tie* balloons. Big difference."

"I wouldn't worry too much about the Were-Bear," said the cloud weaver in a soothing tone. We all relaxed a notch. "The Break-Free Cactus is much worse."

Bijal nearly ejected from his seat. "We saw that cactus!"

I nodded. It was the one Mr. Pang had flown to after we hit him with the twenty-hour egg.

"You will be fine," grunted the cowherd. "Just don't say the magic words."

"What are those?" asked Mav.

Cowherd scratched his head, his mouth twisting to one side.

"Hocus pocus?" Cassa asked, pencil poised.

"Abracadabra?" guessed Bijal.

"No, no, it was a name." The cloud weaver pressed a slender finger against her rosebud lips. "Ariana something."

"Grande?" I exclaimed.

"Yes, that's it," the cowherd rumbled. "If you say 'Ariana

Grande,' it will start dancing toward you. Its needles are very sharp. Poisonous, too."

Mav threw me a furtive look that asked, *Seriously?* "Okay . . . How do you get it to stop?"

"We don't know," said the cloud weaver. "We've seen it dance the entire night away."

I helped Philippa bring a big bowl of noodles to the table. With her left hand, she shook sesame seeds onto the heap as vigorously as if she were salting a garden full of snails. "I don't like this strategy. Too many variables and no escape plan." She set down the shaker and sighed. "But it is what it is, I suppose. Winston, when Mom gets home, tell her I'm at work or hanging with friends. Make something up."

"Wait. *You* can't go. Waffle Fury is closed on Mondays, and you don't have any friends. Besides, you have to vouch that we're all at Mav's doing homework. You know how bad I am at lying. Plus, Not-Coco doesn't know you're onto her. You can keep an eye on her without her doing something spiteful. You need to be here for Mom; plus, you're injured."

"But you don't think before you act." She gestured with her right arm, then winced. Sweat licked the sides of her hair. She was in more pain than she let on.

"That's not always a bad thing, you know." A moment's hesitation on the field could mean the difference between a win or a loss. And I was here to win.

We traded scowls. She clocked her head toward the kitchen, and I followed her there, even though everyone could still hear us. "You tried to skateboard home with a pie."

"It was for Dad-iversary, but no one seemed to care about that."

She looked away, but without her hair running defense for her face, I could see her nose crinkle and her mouth pinch. "I cared." She swiped at her eyes with the sleeve of her striped sweater, which was still inside out. "Sometimes, it's just easier to be mad."

"Who are you mad at?" I asked cautiously.

"The world. Vic. But mostly at Dad for leaving us."

My nose and eyes grew warm, and I could only grunt in response. It was such a relief to hear that Philippa felt the same way I did.

She slipped her hands into her oven mitts, their hidey-holes. "But I've been feeling better since we talked to Vic. I realized that looking for someone to blame was just making it harder for me to move on. I won't ever stop missing Dad. But I think I can start living my life again, the way he would want me to."

For a minute or so, the only sound was the hum of the refrigerator. Then I managed, "Now *that* sounds like a plan."

And if a crotchety moray eel could get over being mad, maybe I could, too.

"Come here," she said gruffly, pulling me by her mitts into a hug. "You'll be careful, right?"

"Coco's our sister. I won't let us down."

CHAPTER 36

I remembered Mr. Pang saying *I always hunt for dinner at five,* so that's when we decided to strike.

Mav pulled the hood of his Towne sweatshirt over his head, cinching his face into a smaller circle. In his silver backpack, we'd stashed the cloud weaver's hairpin secured in a zippered pocket, a jar of peanut butter in the side mesh pocket within easy draw in case the Fire-Weiler showed up, and my canister of Dog-Off. "Remember," he told the rest of us, "there could be other threats, or Pang might've installed extra security. Stay sharp."

Cassa pulled away from the cloud weaver, whom she had reluctantly let braid her hair. Now Cassa looked like an annoyed pastry. Bijal kept checking his pockets to make sure everything was there, including his Abba-Zaba bars and his tying balloons.

I zipped up my own fleece hoodie. In my pockets, I carried

Pikachu and Putty. "See you on the other side, Zubbers." We piled on the dead zombie arms.

Philippa was holding her elbows, hip jutted in her *impress me* stance, but I knew she was just worried.

"Put some candles around the doors so Not-Coco can't leave and cause mischief," I told her.

Philippa's ferocious eyes dug at mine. "I'll handle the faker. You bring our sister home."

"Deal."

The cowherd held his dustpan flush against the floor. I stepped up to the receptacle, suddenly feeling unsure. How was I supposed to get into the narrow opening of the receptacle at the back? Should I stand or kneel? Stick in a hand?

The cloud weaver approached with the broom, her dress billowing like fog. "Good luck, Winston." She drew back her sweeper, and with one quick motion, she sent me sailing into the dustpan.

It felt like I'd been knocked off my skateboard. I held out my hands, bracing for the fall, but instead, I slid onto the oak floor of Mr. Pang's shop. I got to my feet in time to avoid a collision with Mav, who tumbled out after me. Cassa followed, then Bijal. As he collected himself, Bijal's windbreaker made swishing sounds. Mav put his finger to his lips. Bijal held up his hands in apology, which made more rustling sounds.

I listened for growling but heard none. Hopefully the Fire-Weiler was guarding the front door, maybe even napping. As quietly as possible, we spread out. While the others scanned the twelve rows for Mr. Pang, I headed to row six, with its direct line of sight into his office, through the partially open black curtain. Overhead, the space first occupied by the Up, Up, and Away Canoe and then the Hulkbuster Pool Chair was empty once again.

Had someone bought the pool chair? An itchy tingling broke out on my skin. The ukulele had better be . . .

Fortunately, Warm Fuzzies, with its chocolate-brown plush surface, hadn't moved from its spot on the shelf. It made me think briefly of Dani, but I shut her out. I could not afford a distraction right then.

I closed my hand around the uke's fretboard, dampening any wayward sounds. I had to be ready to play at the first sign of Mr. Pang, but if I plucked it too early, I might wake a sleeping bear, and we didn't know if Warm Fuzzies would work on animals, especially enchanted ones. Would I need to play a chord, or would I simply strum his pain with my fingers, killing him softly with my song, as the words of one of my mom's favorite ballads went? I would have to play it by ear.

I pulled the ukulele's attached shoulder strap tight around my chest. Moments later, the others were tiptoeing back to me.

"All clear," Mav whispered. Together we proceeded to Mr. Pang's office. The Ask-Me-Anything Beethoven Busts watched us pass with their moving eyeballs, throwing a shiver over me.

Bijal slipped a thin piece of orange rubber out of his pocket and began stretching it. He bent his neck from side to side, producing a series of cracking sounds. Cassa cast him a look as wide as a Beethoven Bust's. I guess Bijal didn't come with a stealth mode.

Beyond the black curtain, I caught a glimpse of the gleaming popcorn machine, but I didn't detect any movement, and there was no smell coming from it now. That was a good sign. We had counted on Mr. Pang being in bird form, searching out grubs for his dinner.

But what if he was at his desk, sitting just out of sight? My heart raised a few inches in my chest, and I gripped the ukulele harder. Overhead, the glowing unicorn piñatas and the antler chandeliers were swinging ever so slightly, maybe feeling us pass underneath.

We stopped at the end of the row to stay hidden from the Were-Bear, which stood at the end of aisle four. Mav and I carefully peeked around the shelf. The bear was facing the wall, but if it turned its head to the right, it would see us for sure.

Glancing back at us, Mav swept his hand. *Go.*

With the ukulele strapped like a baby to my front, I led the pack, walking casually but quickly across the aisle to the office. We made it safely, and Mav closed the curtain tight behind us. There was no sign of either magpie or man. Mav and I quickly stepped up to the popcorn machine while Cassa and Bijal combed the room, in case the magpie was hiding somewhere.

Mav removed Cloud Weaver's silver hairpin from his backpack and placed it in the tray, while I tucked Putty in the kettle. We closed the glass doors and pressed the green button. The kettle spun, then stopped. With the tongs, Mav removed Putty. It had always looked as chewed and sucked on as a dog toy, but now it had gone so tissue thin, I could nearly see through it. By contrast, the hairpin's silver gleamed bright, as if just polished. Its jade stones seemed to catch the light from the ceiling bulbs and scatter it like stained glass. We stuffed both items into Mav's backpack.

"Cowherd said it takes about fifteen minutes for Mr. Pang to do his hunting, which means he's due any minute." Mav checked his watch.

Five minutes passed. Bijal wanted to try out the popcorn machine on his windbreaker, but Cassa stopped him. We couldn't be caught unprepared. Ten minutes. Then eleven.

The missing Hulkbuster Pool Chair still bothered me, and not just because I'd never gotten my key chain back. "Something's wrong," I whispered.

"I agree," Mav whispered back. "But what?"

"Wish there was someone we could ask." Bijal flapped his arms, then sheepishly returned them to his sides. "You know, like Wikipedia, or Reddit, or Siri . . ."

"Or . . . the Ask-Me-Anything Beethoven Busts," I said slowly.

CHAPTER 37

Mav was already on his way back to row six. The rest of us caught up to him, and the three Beethoven Busts glared at us with their ferocious expressions as they huddled over their drums. I didn't remember Beethoven playing a drum, but since when did anything make sense here? Cassa bumped into me, making me step closer to them than I wanted to. I noticed that the middle bust's drum was an hourglass.

"Er, hello," I whispered. "Do you—any of you—happen to know where Mr. Pang went?"

Silence followed. The hourglass slowly turned upside down, and white sand began to pour in a thin stream. The figures raised their right arms, then slammed them onto their drums. As a frantic pounding started up, I stepped back, looking around wildly.

The drumming stopped abruptly.

"He knows," said Bust One, his eyeballs shifting to the right.

"I don't," replied Bust Two. "But he does." His eyeballs also shifted right.

Bust Three opened his mouth. "I don't. He does." His eyeballs slid left.

"Yes, I do," said Bust One. "He went to find the Up, Up, and Away Canoe." His eyeballs bobbed up.

Bijal cupped his mouth and whispered loudly, "Maybe Mr. Pang decided to do the right thing, like the Mischief Mustache."

"Doubt it," I said darkly. "Pang has an ulterior motive. The question is, what does he use the canoe for?"

My statement set off more drumming.

I gritted my teeth. This time, Bust Two started the routine. "He knows." His eyes slid right.

Bust Three said, "No, he knows." Eyes to the left.

Bust One, who seemed to be the only one who actually knew anything, said, "Yes, I know. He needs the Up, Up, and Away Canoe to fetch moon qi."

Cassa gripped my arm. "The cloud weaver did say he wanted the moon."

"But what's moon qi?"

Drumming started up again. The top of the hourglass had emptied by a third.

My jaw began to clench, and I tried to relax it. A necklace of sweat was forming around my collar. The sand shimmered like champagne as it fell, and it finally occurred to me that the hourglass indicated the time remaining for inquiries. If they didn't do so much drumming, I could get in a lot more questions.

"He knows," said Bust Three.

"I'm going to hurt someone," Cassa muttered from my left.

It was torturous, but after another round with the Ask-Me-Anything Beethoven Busts, Bust One finally said, "Moon qi is the powerful energy of the moon."

"Where would he find that?"

The drums went off.

In the meantime, Mav gathered us in a huddle. "What do you think he wants with moon qi?"

"Something big," I guessed. "The moon must hold a lot of power. I mean, we all depend on it."

"Yeah. It makes the grunion run," Mav said.

Cassa snorted. "That's the first thing you think of? Fish?"

Mav ignored her. "Gravitational pull is serious business. Without it, the Earth would spin a lot faster. You think the weather's bad now. Without a moon, every day could bring a different climate."

"And with no moon, how would romance bloom?" asked Bijal. Something caught his eye, and he meandered down the row.

Life without a moon would mean the end of the world as we knew it. But why would Mr. Pang want that? He's the one who wanted to be an earthly creature. Something didn't make sense.

The drums stopped, and Bust One spoke. "Moon qi can be harvested in the San Francisco Bay when the full moon sits highest in the sky."

Mav glanced up at the unicorn piñatas, still swaying in some unfelt breeze. "If Mr. Pang needed the canoe to harvest moon qi, then Coco taking it must have thrown a wrench in his plans."

Bijal started making throat-clearing noises. "Guys?"

Mav elbowed me. "Try this question. How do we catch Mr. Pang?"

The drums started pounding. This was madness. But it was a great question. It occurred to me that we could've started there and saved ourselves a boatload of time. All that United Nations training at the Towne School was paying off. I tried to be patient, focusing on the falling sand, more than half of which had already emptied. But that was as soothing as watching a time bomb tick.

Over the noise, Bijal's voice came again, this time high and squeaky. "Er, guys?"

A snarl made us snap up our heads. Bijal stood fifty feet down the aisle. A hundred feet beyond him, the *Were-Bear* was rounding the end of row six, stretching his massive claws to the ceiling.

Cassa drew in a sharp breath. Zings of panic shot through me like firework rockets aimed in every direction. I fought the urge to run. We were almost out of time, and the Beethoven Busts were the only ones who seemed to know how to find Mr. Pang.

"Steady, Bij!" From Mav's backpack, Cassa dug out our pre-blown balloons, each about four inches in diameter. She turned toward Bijal but froze when we heard it.

A sharp bark like the twisting of metal on the other end of the row, where a hallway led into the maze to the front entrance.

The Fire-Weiler!

"I've got this." Mav pulled out his peanut butter. "Stay here and wait for the bust's answer."

Bijal's elbows jerked about, the way they did when he was stretching a balloon before blowing it up. "Nice bear. Hey . . . I heard you used to work for the circus. Want to see some balloon crying—I mean t-t-tying?" The bear took a step forward, and Bijal took a step back.

The Fire-Weiler had appeared in the hallway, snarling through its hose connector, its thick red body pacing from side to side.

The drumming stopped.

"He knows," Bust One started. By the time he passed the buck again, I had sweated off half my water weight. "Enchant the unicorns!"

I gaped at the unicorn piñatas hovering above. It was hard to stay focused with Mav on one end, trying to unscrew the jar of peanut butter before the Fire-Weiler pounced, and the Circus Bezerkus going on with the Were-Bear on the other. How could a bunch of piñatas help us?

The Were-Bear had stopped roaring and was sizing up Bijal with its bloodshot eyes. Cassa tried juggling her balloon trio, but they all floated off in different directions. Bijal was struggling to inflate another balloon, maybe because he'd lost his breath. The tip of his balloon finally swelled, but then it slipped out of his mouth and, with a loud farting sound, rocketed away.

There were still a few grains remaining in the hourglass, maybe enough for one more question. But I had no idea what to ask. *Come on, think!* "You got any other tips?" I tried, cringing at how brainless that sounded.

The drums picked up.

The bear looked around for Bijal's jettisoned balloon and,

not finding it, refocused its sights on the two clowns in front of him.

Finally remembering the Warm Fuzzies I was cradling, I began madly strumming. Maybe the sound would soothe both creatures. Mav bowled his jar toward the Fire-Weiler, which glanced at it rolling by but made no move to recover it. I strummed louder, making scribbling motions over the strings like I'd seen Monroe do.

The bear roared. The Fire-Weiler unleashed a string of barking that revved my pulse. Neither seemed to be responding to my Warm Fuzzies. Not only that, my friends weren't reacting, either. Was I playing it wrong? Well, obviously yes, but how good did you have to be for it to work?

Mav, standing a few feet away, jerked back as the Fire-Weiler charged.

"Yes, I know," Bust One was saying. "Do not say 'Ariana Grande.'"

My mind jumped back to the question I had asked: *You got any other tips?*

The last grain of sand fell, and the Beethoven Busts froze in place. The room fell quiet for an eerie second. But the name *Ariana Grande* seemed to linger in the air like smoke.

Music started up from several aisles down. It wasn't ukulele music, but a fast-moving techno drumbeat. The kind of beat that would cause strobe lights to start flashing.

The worst threat of all, the Break-Free Cactus, had been activated.

CHAPTER 38

A familiar breathy pop voice swooped in, giving us whiplash with its vocal acrobatics and punctuated by background voices singing *ooh* and *aah*. The bear tore its eyes from Cassa and Bijal, swinging its head from side to side. It didn't seem to care for my island sounds. Maybe pop was more its jam.

"Run!" cried Mav. But with the four of us caught between the Were-Bear and the Fire-Weiler, there was nowhere to go. The Fire-Weiler closed in, growling and snarling. Mav threw me the can of Dog-Off. The cactus's music swelled, drum and bass guitar slapping their four-count beats at our heads.

But then the Were-Bear roared so loud, the piñatas and the antler chandeliers shook from the rafters. Cassa and Bijal grabbed each other.

Suddenly, the bear's massive head whipped around.

Dropping to all fours, it tore off toward Mr. Pang's office, then disappeared into thin air.

On our other side, the Fire-Weiler leaped at us. I depressed the repellent's button. But instead of swooping down, the hydrant meteored overhead. It followed the Were-Bear out of sight.

"We broke free, man!" cried Bijal. "We broke free!"

Mav's eyes were cranked wide open. "They sure were in a hurry."

Then we saw it. Like a lone cowboy at showdown, the cactus appeared at the end of the aisle, blocking the way to the front escape. Two pink blooms resembled eyes. An arm ending with nodes like fingers pointed to the ceiling while the other arm pointed to the floor. Its hips—or where hips would be—pulsed to a beat that came from somewhere inside it. Thousands of spines ran in vertical rows over its waxy green husk, each as long and wicked as flu shot needles, each dripping with poison.

I tore after my friends, already halfway to Mr. Pang's office. Past the curtain, Cassa and Bijal pulled at the false cabinet door. It was stuck.

"What now?" I panted.

Mav caught his breath. "Maybe other whimsies could help!"

While Cassa and Bijal worked at the door, Mav and I reentered the showroom. The Were-Bear had returned to its spot at the end of row four and was back in hibernation. The Break-Free Cactus gyrated toward us, taking its time, stopping every few moments to pose.

Remembering Philippa's complaint about how I didn't think before I acted, I read labels before trying things out. HOT-SPOT STETHOSCOPE . . . JUSTICE MIRROR—FAIREST OF ALL . . .

A pair of teeth connected to a short fishing pole read NEVER-LET-GO TEETH. I hefted it. I knew how to cast a line, thanks to fishing off the bay with Dad.

But why would I want to reel in a cactus? Bad plan.

Dropping it, I scrounged around for something else. Mav threw a gold Frisbee that stopped halfway through its flight toward the cactus and burst into butterflies. I sent something called a Trick Bowling Ball down the aisle, hoping to knock out the Cactus, but it braked hard mid-aisle and came back, nearly knocking down Mav.

"Sorry!" I called as he skittered out of the way.

I'm stronger than I've been before! Lyrics belted from the cactus's mouth. With its long ponytail swishing like a lasso, it wiped the sweat off its brow and flung it to the ground in a shower of needles. Closer it stepped, hips gyrating. It pointed at us, as if saying, *I'm coming for you.*

"Door's still stuck!" cried Cassa from inside the office.

The sound of thumping and kicking followed like they were trying to break it down.

"Ow!" cried Bijal. "What's this made of, cement?"

The cactus bounced off one shelf and used its momentum to flip in the air. More needles went flying. Its head slid back and forth as it appraised us. It pointed at us again.

Why did it keep pointing? Was that an Ariana Grande move, or something more? "Maybe . . . it wants us to dance with it?"

I might as well have told Mav to streak in front of a troop of Girl Scouts. "I can't dance!"

I gritted my teeth. "You think *I* can?" I had as much rhythm as a brick wall. But for Coco, I would do it. Remembering how the cactus had moved, I jutted out my hip. I stuck my finger in the air like I was up to bat and predicting where I'd hit my homer. Mav did it, too, copying me as I moved back and forth, step-touch, step-touch. The cactus stopped in mid-shuffle. Its flower blossom eyes zoomed in on us, the left-foot brigade.

"It's noticing!"

We stepped up our stepping, doing whatever came to us in the moment. I popped and locked like they do on music videos, freezing my limbs in one position before moving again. Mav put one arm straight out and his other behind his head and started twitching his straight arm like a garden sprinkler. He even turned slowly in a circle.

Slick. My competitive spirit roared to life. I held up an imaginary lasso. Yes, I went there. This was for Coco. I rode that horse and giddyapped until the cows came home.

The cactus stopped dancing and stared at us.

When the chorus came around again, Mav and I both froze and threw it back to the cactus, which started moonwalking. It got within needle-spitting distance, and I couldn't scoot away fast enough. But then it turned around. Back it moonwalked down the aisle. It rolled its arms and threw it to us again.

This time, Mav and I really cut up the floor. I pretended to drive a bus with a very high steering wheel, bobbing my knees in and out. Mav grabbed his right foot and pumped his elbow to his knee like a chicken wing. I always knew we could move our feet, but this was next level.

The music began to fade. The cactus put its hands together and bowed. We bowed, too. And when we came up, the cactus was gone.

"So, party people, you going to teach us those epic moves?" Bijal cracked. In his arms was the purple magic extinguisher.

I let out a shaky laugh, wondering why we hadn't thought of that earlier.

Mav, still pumped from our dance-off, puffed out his chest. "When were you planning to use that, you wall huggers?" He pulled off the hood of his sweatshirt and shook his sweaty hair at them.

Cassa waved him away. "It didn't look like you needed our help."

Breathing hard, I squinted up at the tissue-wrapped unicorns with their gold horns and luminescence. The coast was clear for now, but we needed to get a move on before the next disaster hit. "The Beethoven Busts said we had to enchant the piñatas." I spotted a pole with a hook at the top at the end of row six.

As Cassa held the pole, I steered the business end toward a piñata and snagged it by its looped string.

Bijal glanced around nervously. "Where do you think that Fire-Weiler went?"

Mav grabbed the piñata from the hook. "I think it and the Were-Bear hightailed it when a bigger fish swam in. Back to their safe zones, maybe."

Finally, we managed to bring down four of the piñatas, which hovered a few feet off the ground like day-old balloons.

Bijal read the tag. "'Space Piñatas. Caution: Do Not Get Wet.' But they're already enchanted. They float and glow."

"They must be capable of more than that," I guessed. "The Beethoven Busts said to enchant them."

We brought the piñatas to the popcorn machine and fit

all four into the tray even though each one was at least two foot long.

"What are we going to enchant them with?" asked Cassa. She scanned the desk. "I don't see any new objects around here. . . ."

I took a deep breath before saying, "I have something."

I pulled Dad's dog tag from under my shirt and lifted the chain from around my neck.

Mav went pale. "No, dude, you can't use—"

"It's okay," I said, hefting the warm metal in my hand. "I was planning to use it to get Coco back, and I think this is the way to do it."

Solemnly, I dropped it into the kettle and closed the door. I pressed the green button. The kettle began to spin.

This time we didn't need tongs to remove the piñatas, because the unicorns hopped out on their own. Cassa gasped. Bijal grabbed his head. Mav and I just stared. Before our very eyes, each piñata began to grow until it was the size of a miniature pony. Before we were all crowded out of the office, I grabbed my dog tag from the popcorn machine and slipped it back over my head. *Thanks, Dad.*

I joined the others in the showroom.

A pink unicorn stamped its hooves before me. Its tissue-paper mane was as thick as a cheerleader's pom-pom, its twisted gold horn as shiny as a new trumpet. "Hey, buddy."

Mav eyed a blue one warily. "So your dog tag, like, supersized them." The unicorn jammed its nose into Mav's backpack.

A lilac unicorn leaped into the air, its tail a silver streamer. It circled the shop, then landed beside Cassa. She gasped. "It more than supersized them. Now they can fly."

Bijal's orange unicorn threaded itself between his legs, lifting him onto its crinkly back. "Whoa!" Bijal said. "Stop jumping around like that! I get seasick easy."

An all-too-familiar roar rolled over us. The Were-Bear was back.

"Mount up!" yelled Mav. "We gotta split."

I grabbed the Warm Fuzzies ukulele and threw a leg over my unicorn. Buddy made crunchy sounds as I eased onto its back, hoping the papier-mâché body would support me. It felt solid enough when I put my full weight on it.

"How do we hold on?" With the magic extinguisher under one arm, Bijal flailed with his other arm to keep balanced as his piñata careened unevenly down the aisle.

"Grab the rope!" I yelled. The unicorns' tags had grown along with their bodies, with the strings now the size of thick, pliable cord.

The Were-Bear roared again.

"Let's go, Buddy!" I cried, feeling my unicorn leap forward.

Bijal twisted around. "Cassa, what are you doing?"

She hadn't mounted her unicorn yet. Instead, she was reading the instructions on the Never-Let-Go Teeth.

The Were-Bear tumbled into view, slashing at the air with his massive claws.

"Cassa!" Bijal screamed, trying to control his steed. He couldn't wield the magic extinguisher—he was too busy just holding on to his bumpy ride.

She jammed the fishing pole end into her waistband, then finally jumped onto her lilac bronco.

Hooves clopped as we dashed through the maze of hallways.

I leaned as far as I could over Buddy's neck with the Warm Fuzzies on my back. In the darkness, our unicorns glowed even brighter, Mav in the lead, then Bijal, me, and Cassa.

Something lunged at me and grabbed my foot. I screamed.

Fire-Weiler unleashed a metallic growl as it tried to pull me off by my sneaker. I wrapped my arms around Buddy's neck and kicked hard. Sure, I could kick a ball a hundred yards on the soccer field, but the Fire-Weiler had to weigh a good fifty pounds, and I was straddling a unicorn. I began to slip, my weight pulling Buddy off-kilter.

The sound of a fishing line being cast whizzed behind me, followed by the snap of large jaws. With a loud squeal, the Fire-Weiler released my foot. Cassa had sicced the Never-Let-Go Teeth on it! Scrambling back up, I managed to resaddle myself *and* keep my shoe on my foot, despite feeling so panicked I could've spit up all my vertebrae. The line retracted with a whizzing noise, and metal clattered against wood. With a wail, the Fire-Weiler scuttled off.

"Thanks, Cassa!"

"No problem!"

We rounded the last turn. Bijal shrieked as his surging unicorn busted right through the front door.

No one seemed to care that four kids on overgrown piñatas had arrived on the sidewalk. Maybe we looked no weirder than your average San Francisco resident. Or was it possible that, as with Mr. Pang's shop, the magic was designed not to be seen?

A little girl holding a boba drink pointed at us. "Daddy! Look at the pretty horses!"

Her father opened the car door for her, barely glancing at us. "Get in, muffin."

The sun had set, and the sky was streaked with orange. I patted my unicorn's neck. "To the San Francisco Bay, Buddy!" We might not know where Coco was at this very moment, but we knew where Mr. Pang was headed.

With a rustle of paper and the tinkle of strange bells, we shot upward. We were flying!

Mav whooped, and the rest of us whooped back.

"What kind of candy do you think is in these piñatas?" asked Bijal.

Steering was simply a matter of leaning the direction you wanted to go, like skateboarding. To climb, you leaned back. Cars appeared as small as beetles, and people were pencil dots. Treasure Island looked like a clump of mud.

I drew in a deep breath. Somehow we'd escaped that shop of horrors, and I knew Dad had something to do with it. He'd always be part of our lives, even if he wasn't here. I couldn't help thinking about how I'd nearly bowled Mav over with that Trick Bowling Ball, though I was trying to help. Vic had made a split-second decision, too, out of good intent, but his bowling ball had hit. Maybe Vic could never forgive himself, but I was beginning to think I could forgive him.

The blue ceiling of sky began to darken like oil spilling into the ocean.

Lightning shot through the sky. Thunder growled. As I braced myself for rain, my eyes fell to the tag around Buddy's neck: CAUTION: DO NOT GET WET.

CHAPTER 39

"We gotta land before it rains!" Bijal yelled.

"We need Dani's umbrella!" I shouted back. If only I'd memorized her phone number. Or had a phone.

I sat up straighter, remembering something she'd said. She lived by the Exploratorium. *Our house is the same lime green as my aunt's clogs. It's so bright, you could probably see it from space.*

"Follow me!" I called to my friends.

The jutting piers of the Embarcadero looked like the teeth of a broken comb, with the Exploratorium in mid-comb. There were no houses on the pier—Dani's place had to be across the way.

"What are we looking for?" yelled Cassa.

"A lime-green house."

Parking lots and industrial buildings in boring colors

dotted the landscape. We circled the area like hawks—all except Bijal, whose unicorn was the most uneven, sometimes sprinting, other times lagging behind. At least he'd passed the magic extinguisher to Mav, who had tucked it into his backpack. Now Mav was looking through my pair of Far-Seeing Eyeballs, which he'd secured in a sheer netting and tied around his wrist.

Another slap of thunder rattled my head, and a drop of water fell on my cheek. More were sure to follow.

Mav pointed below. "There!"

The lime exterior of a two-story dwelling peeked through the leaves of an oak tree. I sped Buddy down, the chilly air blowing the sweat from my face and making my teeth zing. As we approached, the soft sounds of a cello floated through a second-story window.

Dani was practicing in her bedroom, eyes closed, head swaying. She was wearing a navy-blue hoodie and beige sweatpants with a sheet music pattern.

I rapped at the window. Her eyes popped open and stared.

"Put on your umbrella!" we all yelled, pecking at our temples with our fingers.

She set down her instrument and hurried away, disappearing into what I guessed was a bathroom. More raindrops fell, but a moment later, the storm clouds vanished. The sky was blue again, though darker as evening began to fall. I wished she'd hurry. We needed to find Coco before the full moon set.

Dani returned with the cocktail umbrella nestled behind her ear. Her hair was wet, as if she'd just washed it. She lifted the window. "Are those . . . flying piñatas?" Dani reached out a tentative hand and patted Buddy on its crinkly neck. I wondered why the magic was visible to her and not others.

"We're trying to rescue my little sister . . ." I started to explain.

"It's a long story, and we don't have much time," Cassa finished.

Mav maneuvered his unicorn next to Buddy. "We might be going farther than a mile tonight. If our mounts get wet, they might fall apart. Could we borrow your umbrella?"

Dani touched the canopy. "I think it only works when it's on my head."

"Looks like we need to take Dani along," said Bijal, whose flighty unicorn was getting tangled in the branches of the oak tree.

My stomach turned a loop. "We couldn't ask—"

"Are you kidding? I'll get my jacket."

Soon Dani was climbing onto Buddy behind me. She'd pulled on a thick knitted cap, securing the cocktail umbrella, and tucked her sweatpants into her boots. "I left a note for my aunt that I went to Yasmine's for a project. She lives down the street."

I grinned. Dani was as sneaky as the rest of us.

"I see you do *have* a ukulele, at least," she said.

"Oh, that," I said, my face flushing. I switched Warm Fuzzies to my front to make more room for her. "It's part of the long story."

"You'll have to tell it to me once this is all over."

Mav led us toward San Francisco Bay. The moon was easy to spot, rising in the eastern sky beyond the Bay Bridge. I felt a little queasy, and I wasn't sure if it was because I was flying on a piñata in search of my lost little sister, or because Dani was hugging me from behind.

"I must be dreaming." She pinched me on the arm.

"Ow! You're supposed to pinch yourself."

"Why pinch myself when you're sitting right here?" She laughed, and I laughed, too, and my stomach settled a little. I briefed her on our predicament, grateful she wasn't one of those people who lied and told you everything was going to be okay when they really didn't know.

We passed over the spire of the Transamerica Pyramid, which pointed up at us like Neymar's finger when he made a goal. Ahead, the Bay Bridge, lit with white lights along the top and down the sides, no longer looked so businesslike, but more like a tiara on dark velvet.

As we crested the bridge, a van in a distinctive shade of green caught my vision. It looked like Mr. Gu's car—I'd never seen any other van that color. It reached the midpoint, then exited onto a curved ramp, where it disappeared behind a screen of trees. Did Mr. Gu live on Treasure Island? That would explain the name of his shop.

"So, what kind of uke is that?" came Dani's voice in my ear.

"Its official name is the Warm Fuzzies Say-Lulla-bye-to-Your-Troubles Ukulele. But we just call it the Warm Fuzzies. We were going to use it to soften up Mr. Pang, but I'm not sure it actually works."

"Maybe you didn't play it long enough," said Cassa, coming up on our left. "Things happened so fast."

Bijal streaked by. "Or maybe your playing was just trash. Sorry, Win. Stick to soccer."

Dani's fingers gripped my fleece tighter. "How about I try?"

"You? But you're a cellist." Then I remembered what she had said about ukes being a starter instrument. "Never mind." The girl could probably play anything.

"You said it's called the Warm Fuzzies Say-Lulla-bye-to-Your-Troubles Ukulele," Dani said. "Maybe it requires a lullabye. I know lots of those. There's the Brahms, the Berceuse . . . Bartók has several, though my aunt thinks they sound like nightmares."

"Dani's onto something," said Mav, flying just ahead of us. "Maybe the Warm Fuzzies only works when someone knows how—and what—to play."

"Fine by me." One less thing to worry about. I took off the strap and passed the ukulele to Dani. As soon as she settled it around her, she began tuning it.

"Winston!" The foghorn voice was back! "Winston!"

"Did you hear that?" I asked.

Mav wore a crazed smile as the city grew even smaller below us. "What?"

"Someone was calling my name again. Like that time at Fisherman's Wharf."

"I didn't hear anything," said Dani.

"Hey, everyone!" cried Bijal. "These unicorns come with seat warmers!" His unicorn had begun to create a translucent orange bubble around him. Mav's unicorn now glowed within a clear blue sphere, Cassa's had activated a purple shield, and Buddy was wrapping a protective flamingo-pink skin around Dani and me.

The voice didn't call again, and the others were too busy

flying their Space Piñatas to pay me any attention. I wished I could enjoy the ride more, but my stomach had tied itself into knots. I couldn't have fun while Coco was in danger. She didn't have a glow to protect her. Was Chang-Ah-Ling's porcelain skin cold-resistant? I hoped so.

Once the city was far behind us, Mav picked up the Far-Seeing Eyeballs again and aimed them at the water below.

San Francisco Bay is a mermaid-shaped estuary five times as long as it is wide. It is surrounded by land except where the mermaid's thin arms reach under the Golden Gate Bridge into the Pacific Ocean. As we traveled south through her tail, the skyline of Oakland, shorter and more compact than San Francisco, stood out against a dark backdrop of hills.

Mav craned his neck, the marbles still screwed close to his eye sockets. "I think I saw something flying ahead. A crab?"

"Remember to relax your eyes," said Cassa, floating beside him.

On the Peninsula, a strip of land hemming the Bay on the west, cars sped past the bright lights of San Francisco International Airport. Beyond that, the bay was mostly a dark mass. Incoming planes formed a linear constellation.

Mav carefully passed the Far-Seeing Eyeballs to Cassa. "You'd better do it."

"So what's the play, Captain?" Bijal said, surging by. His unicorn veered too close to Mav's, then overcorrected, nearly bumping me off course.

"Soon as we find our magpie, Dani hits the Warm Fuzzies," said Mav. "Win gets him to see reason. The rest of us will form a perimeter, but don't spook the bird."

Cassa was concentrating on something below us. "I think I've got the hang of this. The detail's crazy. I can see the bird poop on the side of that building. I can even see fish. Wait, that's not a fish, but a really large outline of something like a whale?"

I hoped it wasn't a killer whale. Killer whales sometimes get stuck in the Bay, and I couldn't remember if they ate people.

"Hold the ferries, what's that?"

"What?" We all strained to see where she was looking. Past the airport, the shoreline jutted out to Coyote Point, where Coco's favorite museum, CuriOdyssey, was located.

"It's some sort of pool chair. Mr. Pang is flying it . . . and he's towing the canoe!"

"He's flying in a pool chair?" cried Bijal. "Oh, this I gotta see. Giddyap!"

"Is the doll in the canoe?" I asked.

"I can't tell. He's moving fast . . . heading east. Now he's slowing. He's coming about. He's landing!"

"Landing where?" I asked.

"Follow me."

With Cassa in the lead, we leaned into our crinkling steeds, and they floated down, purple, blue, pink, then orange.

"I think that's him!" Mav pointed. "He's right there."

I combed the smooth dark surface of the water but didn't see anything. Then I saw some churning white foam about a thousand feet away. "There! Come on, Buddy. Get us closer."

"Look at the moonlight in the water." Dani pointed to a shimmering white stripe painting the Bay down the center.

Moon qi.

Two long objects bobbed on the surface—the simple sleek canoe, connected by a rope to the tricked-out Hulkbuster Pool Chair. Mr. Pang's legs poked out of it like straws. He was no longer wearing the Flip and Dunks but some sort of . . . I gaped. "He's wearing the Kick-Me Boots!"

The pool chair slowed, and through forces I could not see, Mr. Pang guided the Hulkbuster to turn about so it lay side by side with the canoe. My chest expanded at the sight of a small figure standing as straight as a post in the bow. The person was just tall enough to see over the hull.

We'd found Coco at last.

CHAPTER 40

Despite her soft body, Chang-Ah-Ling's knees were locked in position, hands gripping the gunwale. I only hoped my sister wasn't too tired inside there, because it was way past her bedtime.

In a flash of gold robes, Mr. Pang rolled himself from the pool chair into the canoe. He cast off the Hulkbuster, which bobbed away, its golden fist cupholders shaking from side to side. The darkness swallowed it with a gurgle.

"Talk to him just like we rehearsed," Mav coached me. "'Let my sister go. It's the right thing to do.' And stay clear of those boots."

"Got it." The others held back, and Dani and I pressed forward on Buddy. Gently pressing it with my thighs, I urged the unicorn close enough that its glow lit the canoe with a pinkish light. Mr. Pang's jaw dropped, showing a pointy tongue.

"Now, Dani," I whispered. "Just keep playing until I tell you to stop."

She began strumming. The sweet strains of "Over the Rainbow" floated from behind. Unlike my haphazard chicken scratching, this was a lullaby, the kind of song that made you want to curl up on the sofa for a nap.

A smile hoisted up Mr. Pang's face. He even did a tap-shuffle with his boots and gave a parade wave to the others circling above us. "Winston. I was wondering when I'd be seeing you. You've enhanced the Space Piñatas. How?"

"My dad's dog tags. Remember them?"

"Sure. I found them on the sidewalk after that fool dropped them. They were what made this canoe fly, you know. And obviously they recharged since. My, my. The Chu clan has the most powerful qi, since it's been tested by tragedy. Only the most powerful magic can enable objects to fly."

A vision tumbled through my head, of Dad zooming through space wearing blue tights and a red cape, with Superman's red *S* emblazoned on his chest. I could feel my cheeks lifting. Dad *had* been a superhero, just like I always knew. And now I needed to be one, too.

"Let my sister go." My words came out slow and loopy, like when I'd stayed up past my bedtime. The music was getting to me. And instead of *It's the right thing to do*, I said, "That's a cool canoe."

"It's my best work. It can fly anywhere in the world, even *out* of this world. It just needs a pilot." His thready eyebrows pumped a few times, moving his Babar-colored headband. "That was supposed to be Chang-Ah-Ling's job. Maybe that's why she left."

A memory tugged at me. Mav's Monsters and Mythology professor had said that Not-Coco had drawn something she feared. Mr. Pang? He was odd, and self-serving, but not evil, surely. It was hard for me to make sense of anything in my current state.

"Why do you need a doll to steer your canoe?"

"I can send Chang-Ah-Ling to places a flesh-and-blood creature couldn't survive. Anyway, turns out your sister is even a better pilot than Chang-Ah-Ling. Not such a sourpuss. She's been joyriding to all her favorite places, like CuriOdyssey."

"Coco?" I called out.

There was no response. The doll's eyes were closed like she was asleep at the helm. The rosy blush of her porcelain cheeks set off her green pajamas, and her short bangs blew back in the breeze.

Sure, she could zoom a truck through the living room with the best of them, but this was gof. Or was it? But did it matter? All I wanted to do was slump over Buddy's neck and snooze. Mav, Cassa, and Bijal were drifting lazily in the sky, probably feeling warm and fuzzy, too. The music didn't seem to be affecting Dani—maybe because she was the one playing it.

"Your sister's in good hands," Mr. Pang said soothingly, stepping out of his boots. They stood beside him like a matched pair of Doberman pinschers. "You all go on home now. I have moon qi to harvest. This is the only night it's strong enough to do anything."

"How do you"—I yawned—"harvest that?"

The shopkeeper had no hesitation in sharing his secrets. "I

had planned to use the Pikachu Harvester. You don't happen to have it, do you?"

Mr. Pang's drifty eyes sure were funny, like two loose cannonballs on the deck of a ship in a hurricane. I giggled.

Behind me, Dani cleared her throat. "I don't think it's working," she whispered in my ear without letting up on her playing. "He's trying to trick you."

Trick me? Not this nice man stretching his headband over the oar paddle.

"What are you doing?" I asked him.

"I've had to improvise. My Babar Band can store an elephantine amount of magic. Once all the moon's qi soaks into it, I'll have enough power to stop him."

Dani nudged me with her knee. "Do something!"

I tried to retrace the conversation. "Er, who are you stopping?"

A shadow edged along Mr. Pang's face. "My brother, that's who. Mirth." He spat out the name like it was a rancid pistachio. Was he . . . upset?

A story poked through the dreamy haze—the one Cloud Weaver had told about Sorrow and Mirth, the magpies who pulled the Queen Mother's chariot. Buddy's tissue-paper mane was surprisingly soft when I planted my face in it.

"Winston!" Dani hissed from behind me. "Winston, are you paying attention?"

I tried to sit up straight again. Cassa, Bijal, and Mav fluttered nearby like fireflies.

Mr. Pang was still talking. "Mirth was hiding in the shadows that night I made the cowherd cry with my song. Yes, I stole a tear, but he stole another one after that. He's codependent—can't leave me alone. I'm just a simple man trying to live my best life. But no, he has to follow me all the way down here. Step on *my* dreams. Fly in *my* no-fly zone. Then he sent those goons to spy on me, steal my trade secrets. Thank goodness seagulls are not known for their bright minds. I just want to live in the world and make my whimsies. He wants to use whimsies to *rule* it."

Dani's strumming had fallen off. With the ukulele sounds fading, my mind began to clear. So Mother Cloud Weaver hadn't sent the seagulls? Was Mr. Pang's bizarre story the ramblings of a lunatic?

"The Warm Fuzzies doesn't work on him!" Dani cried.

"She's right. The ukulele only works on me when I am all human." Mr. Pang's drifty eyes grew sharp for a moment and focused on Dani behind me. Moonlight glinted off his black-and-white hair, which looked more like feathers now.

The marrow began to leach from my bones.

"That's quite an interesting cocktail umbrella your friend is wearing."

Dani gasped, and I felt her shrink back.

"Where did you get it, my dear? Not from me. That's the work of my brother, Mirth. I know he sold it to your aunt, just like that Bull's-Eye Bean that bewitched Winston's shoofly to hit me when I answered the door. We blackbirds can never be too careful when it comes to pies, you know, and we definitely never amass in groups of four and twenty."

I need to hit the bull's-eye with this pie, Chef Kim had said.

Was the Bull's-Eye Bean part of her lucky multicolored pie weights? Dani had said when Chef Kim used the blue ones, she'd get first prize. Did baking with the other colors do more dastardly things? Which ones had we used for the crust of *my* pie? My head reeled in confusion . . . and also a little relief that I hadn't been such a klutz, after all. "But . . . the pie didn't hit you."

Mr. Pang's face turned gleeful. "Because his goons can't even do a ding-dong ditch right."

Ernie and Bert were *Mirth's* goons?

"I took the opportunity to give you the broom and the dust-pan for a good cause," Mr. Pang said. "But Mirth is ruthless. Sure, he fools people into thinking he's a harmless, happy fellow with his loud floral shirts, those ridiculous red glasses, and his annoying chuckle. But you should see the stockpile of magical munitions he has amassed on his island. Without the power of the moon, I will be helpless to stop him from taking over the world!"

Floral shirts. Red glasses. Pie. Island. "Your brother is . . . Mr. *Gu*?"

He flinched at the name, confirming my guess. "Obviously I got the lion's share of good looks, but yes, he is Mirth."

Pieces began to fit together, like the notes of a ukulele chord when you finally get your fingers on the right strings. *I had a younger brother. Odd, sad little kid. Always looking right when he should've been looking left. He got beat up a lot when I wasn't there to stop it.* Mr. Gu had been taking Dad's stuff for his shop. Treasure sold whimsies of a sort. Had Mr. Pang learned of the Chu family qi through his brother? No. Mr. Pang had found our dog tags when Vic dropped them. Mr. Gu had most likely learned of us from Mr. Pang.

"But Mr. Gu's cool. He's Mom's friend. He wants to rid the city of the hissing squirrels."

Mr. Pang cackled. "Who do you think created those silly squirrels? They're perfectly harmless, just part of his plan to make San Franciscans afraid so he can swoop in and 'save' them. All dictators work by first sowing chaos, then offering a solution. When Mother Cloud Weaver started throwing her bolts, that made his day. Then you, foolish boy, went and gave him the goodies."

Mav, who had positioned his unicorn in the sky behind Mr. Pang, was frantically signaling me. I shook myself free of my thoughts. My friend pointed at me, then Pang. Mav needed me to play defense while the rest of them moved the ball—Coco—to safety. She stood resolutely at the bow, within arm's reach of Mr. Pang. *Keep him talking*, Mav signed.

"Er, how will the moon qi help you stop Mr. Gu?"

"It's the only thing with enough power to turn him back into a magpie for good. Then Coco will chauffeur him back to the heavens, where he belongs."

Mr. Pang placed an oar in the water and began to stir it like a spoon in a cauldron.

"Wait! Don't do that. There must be another way to, er, mediate your beef with your bro." What were those five principles of conflict resolution, again?

His eyes floated up to me. But then he shrugged and returned to stirring. "Nope."

Mav moved into place behind and to the left of Mr. Pang,

with Cassa behind him. Bijal positioned himself far to the right. I recognized the Stealth's three-item combo. Mav was setting up to make a diagonal run at Coco, and through a series of unexpected passes, we'd make our run for the goal.

"Come on, Mr. Pang," I coaxed. "You have a good thing going here in San Francisco. Lots of cool stuff. Nice . . . pets." At least I hoped the Were-Bear and Fire-Weiler were nice to him.

The orange unicorn made a sudden loop-de-loop and Bijal cried out sharply. Glancing behind him, Mr. Pang caught sight of Mav hovering a few feet away.

"Kick 'em!" Mr. Pang yelled.

The boots sprang to life, climbing the air toward Mav and taking a swipe at him. He swung to one side, and the kick punched into his piñata's side. With a yank, the boot retracted, leaving a hole. Out poured multicolored wrapped candies—saltwater taffy.

Fortunately, the blue unicorn kept flying straight—just higher, because it had lost some ballast.

The boots lined up for another kick. But then an orange ball of light flew in like a cannonball, knocking them asunder. "Whoa! Whoa! Where are the brakes on this thing?" Bijal cried.

Not wasting another moment, I dove for Coco. Mr. Pang swung his oar, whacking me on the shoulder.

Dani and I both screamed as Buddy nearly toppled into the water.

Mr. Pang snatched the doll to his chest. "Don't try that again, unless you want me to release Coco's spirit."

Buddy righted itself, and Dani clung to me with a death grip. Coco's eyes had opened, and they were shining with light as if there were a lightbulb in her head. "What's that mean?" I spat.

"Her eyes are the windows to her soul, and as you can see, the moonlight opens them. All I have to do is poke her belly button and say her name. And without her own body nearby to reenter, her spirit will fly away." Mr. Pang wiggled his taloned hand like a butterfly sailing into the breeze. "Forever."

CHAPTER 41

"NO!" I stared in horror, my limbs going numb. "Give me back my sister, you animal cracker!"

Mr. Pang swatted at us again. Buddy reared, dodging Mr. Pang's oar like a moth in front of an angry hand. We rocked to and fro, me clinging to Buddy's neck, Dani clinging to me. High above us, Cassa and Bijal were slashing the sky with purple and orange stripes, trying to keep the boots apart. Seemed the boots needed each other in order to kick. Mav freed the magic extinguisher from his backpack, and after pulling the pin, he sprayed the closest boot, producing a veil of mist. But the boot climbed high, avoiding it. Mav went high, too—so high that I couldn't see him, especially with Buddy tossing us around.

But then something fell from the sky. A boot. I charged Buddy toward it, and with a shake of its head, it impaled the thing on its horn like a chunk of meat on a shish kebab. Those unicorn horns had bite. Buddy flung its head again, throwing off the boot. It sailed through the air, and I swore I heard it shriek as it plunged into the water.

But the shriek was actually coming from Mr. Pang. A second *plop* sounded from somewhere nearby. "My boots!" Mr. Pang wailed. "I had to chase them all around town after you let them escape."

The water surged, and the canoe swayed. It was as if something had passed under it. Cassa said she had seen something large like a whale. Mr. Pang lost his balance. Acting more on instinct than anything else, I leaned forward and, as Buddy sped ahead, grabbed the doll from Mr. Pang's hands.

"W-w-win-sonnn!" Coco blinked, and the light from her eyes flickered.

I'd never hugged a doll before, but I held this one close enough to feel a tiny heartbeat against my chest. She really was inside there. My nose tingled, and my eyes suddenly felt warm. "It's okay, Coco. Your bro's got you."

"Winston, watch out!" cried Dani.

The canoe had lifted out of the water. With quick strokes of the oar, Mr. Pang rowed it through the air toward us. "Give me back my dolly!"

A purple orb sped toward me. "Winston, pass it here!" Cassa stretched out her arms.

People think soccer's all legwork, but it's not. A good throw-in can make all the difference in the outcome of a game. I tossed Coco like a hot ball with only seconds left on the clock, hoping Chang-Ah-Ling's body was really durable.

Cassa caught Coco neatly. But Mr. Pang turned his canoe about and charged her. An orange orb appeared by her side. Cassa faked a pass to me, but as Bijal flew by, she handed the doll off to him and dodged Mr. Pang by climbing higher.

"Zubbers!" Bijal cried.

Mav dove in, aiming his extinguisher at Mr. Pang. He squeezed the lever.

But instead of spewing mist, the nozzle just coughed air. Mav grimaced. He tried pumping the lever with both hands, but the canister was empty.

Mr. Pang grinned. "I'd been meaning to top that up. Too bad for you I didn't." The moonlight created dark shadows on his face, carving pits under his eyes. His hair, no longer hemmed in by a sweatband, flew around his head like the broken feathers of an old shuttlecock. He rerouted the boat toward Bijal, who had tucked Coco under his arm. Bijal turned an upside-down loop, avoiding the speeding canoe.

"Guys, no more goals!" Mav made frantic cutting motions with his hands. It was a tactic we used to drive a tied game into overtime. All we needed to do was keep the ball away from the opponent until we figured out our next strategy.

Mr. Pang let out a sharp squawk that raised the hairs on my neck. With quick movements of his head, his uncanny birdlike eyes assessed us buzzing around him. His canoe was faster than the piñatas, but it wouldn't be easy for him to get his doll back, not with four against one. We were at a stalemate. Bijal tossed Coco to me, and I braced myself, trying to anticipate which way Mr. Pang would come at me.

Without warning, the canoe dropped back into the water with a splash. Mr. Pang dipped his oar and began stirring.

The moon, shining patiently overhead, seemed to flicker, the way a lightbulb does before it's about to go out. As Mr. Pang's swirling quickened, the moon's smooth and gleaming reflection grew agitated, emitting silvery-white threads like noodles being wrapped around chopsticks. The whole oar began to glow as if it were electrified.

He was harvesting the moon's qi!

Buddy's pink glow faded as energy from the moon heated the air around us. I'd always thought moonlight was cold, like Mom's feet, but as Mr. Pang's Babar Band soaked in more qi, the heat forced us back.

Something pointy was digging into my thigh. Pikachu! Mr. Pang had planned to use it to harvest moonlight. Maybe the Pikachu Harvester could grab the moon's qi from him!

Bijal was the closest, his unicorn bucking slightly under him.

"Bijal, take Coco and get her home, stat!" I tossed the doll, and Bijal trapped and held her. I heaved a sigh of relief. At least she'd be safe.

Wasting no time, I dug out the small figurine. High and to my left, Cassa watched me, the muted purple glow of her piñata glinting off her braces.

Think before you act, Philippa's voice warned me.

If I used the Pikachu wrong, it could spell the end of me. But if I didn't use it to save the moon, the world as we knew it would come to an end, including me.

Left cheek sucked in energy; right spit it back.

Buddy, Dani, and I hung in the air ten feet from Mr. Pang.

Moonlight, as fickle as firelight, licked at his robes, highlighting a face twisted in madness. Bits of featherlike fluff flew off him as he stirred the water. "Every day the threat grows, but you are all too blind to see."

I aimed the Pikachu Harvester's tail at the river of moonlight that was flowing into Pang's headband. The red spots on Pikachu's cheeks had begun to glow. I pressed the left one.

The zigzag tail lit up. A warm buzz traveled up my arm as the pocket monster sucked up energy.

The moonlight shifted. Instead of flowing into the headband, it became a white sheet blowing in the wind. Mr. Pang squawked. He stirred faster. Like a dog called by two different masters, the moonlight didn't seem to know which way to go. The Pikachu Harvester and the Babar-band pulled at it from either side. The light began to fray like a poorly knit blanket, the holes creating sparks that popped over the water's surface.

"Winston, look!" cried Dani.

Thin trails of smoke were lifting from our unicorn's crinkly mane. Its tissue-paper skin had begun to singe and flake off in patches. "Buddy!"

Dani fanned the piñata with the ukulele to cool it. I nearly dropped Pikachu as I tried to keep my balance. There was no doubt about it—we were sinking.

Buddy's neck lowered until it was as hunched as Eeyore's. My poor unicorn was falling apart, its once-bright-pink exterior now an ashy, colorless mess. While we drooped and bobbled, Mr. Pang's hold on the moonlight strengthened, uniting the strands once again into an opaque strip that flowed in his direction.

Cassa maneuvered her piñata closer. I noticed an object jutting from the back of her waistband. The Never-Let-Go Teeth.

I caught her gaze and tried to gesture to them with my eyes. She threw up her hands, not understanding me.

"Well, Mr. Pang, I guess you've got us by the *teeth*," I said loudly.

"I guess I do, Winston. But I have to give you *squawk!* for trying."

Cassa grabbed at her head, still trying to make sense of the situation.

I tried again. "You're *never going to let this go*, are you?"

Cassa's eyes got big, and she felt for the fishing pole behind her. At last!

"I'm afraid when I sink my hooks into something—*squawk!*—I simply must have it." Once stringy and sparse, his hair had thickened into a glossy black helmet, beaded with water.

Cassa slipped the pole free and wound up. The movement caught Pang's eye.

"Mr. Pang," I said quickly. "How do you make a tissue dance?"

His head snapped back to me, and his oar paused. "I know that one, Winston. Put a little boogie—"

Before he could finish, Cassa unleashed the teeth. They went sailing with a *hiss*, then sank deep into the oar. Cassa pulled up, and the oar slipped from the shopkeeper's hands.

"Nooo!" Mr. Pang jumped to his feet, trying to snatch it back.

The canoe began to pitch. The bird/man flailed like the

Break-Free Cactus under a disco ball of a moon. With the canoe rocking under his feet, he could not keep his balance. He spread his arms and his face sharpened into a gawking beak. Just before tumbling into the sea, he disappeared in a puff of smoke and the beating of wings.

CHAPTER 42

I quickly lifted my thumb from Pikachu's cheek. Suddenly released from the tug-of-war, the moonlight recoiled like a snapping cable, and the water began to churn. Waves grabbed at our feet as if whipped into a frenzy.

"Up, Buddy, up!" I leaned way back in my seat, and Dani did the same, trying to help the poor fraying beast. We couldn't get trapped out here, so far from shore. I could barely see the canoe, which the currents were quickly towing away. The tiny points of freeway lights tracing the peninsula were at least a mile away, a distance farther than Olympic triathletes had to swim. And everyone knew that swimming was the hardest leg of the race. To the east, I couldn't see any lights at all.

Dani tossed the ukulele overboard. But even with that weight gone, Buddy was struggling to lift off. Seared in front and splashed from the back, its paper hide now hung off in wet strips. The saltwater felt sticky on my skin.

The warning label was right between my hands. CAUTION: DO NOT GET WET.

Three balls of dimly glowing light descended, yelling words that blended together. Then Bijal and Mav were floating on either side of me, hands extended. Cassa, hovering in front of us, was now holding Coco.

"Whaaa?" I asked Bijal. "I thought I told you to—"

"Sorry, dude," Bijal said. "I didn't think I could make it that far, especially without Dani's umbrella protecting me."

"We're running out of time!" I snarled. "You have to save Coco before . . ."

My sister's face could only blink, but her hands were making tiny doll-like motions. As Buddy slipped under the water, I saw the Never Let-Go Teeth fishing rod and the oar floating nearby.

"Stop yapping and take my hand, dude. Do it!" cried Bijal, reaching for me.

Mav reached for Dani. "Come on, Dani, grab on!"

The freezing water was now at our waists. I caught Bijal's hands, but another wave hit from behind, splashing us all. Even Cassa, floating several feet above, got doused.

Bijal released me, screaming as his orange piñata tumbled into the water. Another wave surged, pulling down Mav and his unicorn. Behind me, Dani was flailing as Buddy collapsed under our legs. Only the tip of its golden horn was visible now. Bits of paper floated around us. The ukulele had stayed on the surface, too, though I didn't know how, with all its water-logged fur.

Bijal and Mav tried to hold on to their piñatas, but they were dissolving into pulpy carcasses. Only Cassa remained aloft.

I swallowed hard. "Go, Cassa, take Coco and get help!"

But her unicorn had begun to drop, too. I watched in horror as she began a slow descent into the ocean, like a setting sun.

"Sorry, Coco," she gasped, teeth chattering. She held the doll high as her piñata melted away from under her. Coco's eyes blinked furiously, like she was sending Morse code.

"Grab the uke!" I told Dani, who was flapping around like a drowning bee. I didn't know if she knew how to swim, but at least the floating instrument might keep her alive for a few seconds longer. The rest of us had taken swimming lessons, though Mav was the only one who was any good at it. I swam the other direction, toward Cassa, as sluggishly as if I were wearing chain mail.

I took Coco from Cassa. The doll seemed to be whimpering, but it came out as a strange kind of humming. Maybe, with no actual lungs, that was the best Coco could do.

Cassa slipped under the water, then resurfaced, spitting, her braided bun now a soggy pancake on her head. I could tread water, but with no body fat, I was a pair of scissors in Jell-O.

"I'm coming, Cassa!" Bijal dog-paddled over to us. "Relax, remember? Move your arms like this." He swished his arms back and forth in the water.

Mav had fallen the farthest from us and was closer to the canoe. He was hugging his backpack like it was a flotation device. Maybe it was. As he kicked toward us, he grabbed at something on the surface.

Cassa was trying to take deep breaths, but her teeth were chattering. "I shouldn't have pushed Janelle away," she wailed. "If Dad loses me, he'll be all alone. Plus, I kind of liked her."

Bijal shook water out of his hair. "Don't cry, Cassa. At least you were always straight up with your dad. My folks will never know I wasn't the social justice warrior they thought I was. I'm a hardened candy criminal."

"Best balloon tie-er"—Cassa's gasped—"I know."

Dani had snagged the ukulele and was hunched over it, motionless. Surely the sodden thing would sink soon. Her wool hat was missing, and the cocktail umbrella lay flat like a dead pink starfish on her head.

"I'm so sorry, everybody." Tears had begun to paint hot stripes down my cheeks. "I let you down even though you're the best friends I could've asked for." Mom's loving but tired face came to mind. *Philippa, now you'll have to be the light for her.*

"The canoe!" Mav croaked out, pointing. "Look, it's sinking!"

A sliver of white in the darkness, the boat had drifted about forty feet away. But right before our eyes, one end tipped into the water like the *Titanic*. Then the whole thing slid in like a knife. One moment there, the next, gone.

"What just happened?" Bijal whipped his head from side to side, flinging more water. "It's like something sucked it down."

"Uh, team . . ." Mav stopped moving his arms. "I think something's down there."

I went still. A series of bubbles bloomed on the water's

surface where the canoe had just been, like something very large had exhaled. I suddenly remembered the surge that had knocked Mr. Pang off balance, the one I'd attributed to a killer whale. A sick feeling rose in me. It was as if my insides were crawling like a nest of snakes.

"Something like . . . what?" Bijal's voice trembled. "I don't know of any fish that eats canoes. What's down there? Oh my gof, we never should've gone into that nutter-butter's lair. Why doesn't anyone ever listen to me?" Bijal slapped at the water, and one of the gold unicorn horns floated by.

Mav grabbed it. "I've got them all. If something tries to bite you, stab it." He gave one each to Cassa and Bijal, then held one to me, but my hands were full with Coco.

"I'll take it." Dani appeared beside us, the ukulele nowhere in sight.

"You know how to swim?" I panted out.

"Yes. I started to panic, so I had to pray, like I do before I perform." Moonlight glinted off her unicorn horn, putting me in mind of a shark's tooth. "Don't worry, Winston," she wheezed. "We won't let anything get Coco."

"Zubbers don't fear death," Mav said through his clenched teeth.

Would the monster slurp us up one by one, like five and a half oysters? Or would we go all at once, sucked into one tasty mouthful? Either way, I hoped it wouldn't hurt.

The floor moved. I mean, there was no floor, but some sort of platform began to rise under our feet.

"The monster!" screamed someone, probably me.

Mav's horn flashed. "Get your weapons ready. We're not going down without a fight."

Everyone held their twisty golden horn like a dagger. They weren't actually gold—otherwise they would've sunk—but they were made of something hard, slick, and hollow, like an actual horn. Up we went, lifted by the platform, which was more curvy than flat. A series of boulderlike protrusions, too tall to see over, covered one end. Was it an erupting island? Higher it rose, water sloshing off the sides. We braced ourselves, Dani and Cassa facedown and hugging the floor while Mav, Bijal, and I clung to the boulders. My boulder felt rubbery and was covered with round tiles that gleamed. This was the strangest island I'd ever seen, if it was one.

The thing rocked beneath us.

"Win-ston!" a voice like a foghorn rumbled.

That voice . . . The one I'd been hearing but no one else did. It was coming from the thing we were standing on.

I gulped. "Lucky?"

CHAPTER 43

"Your goldfish?!" Bijal gaped at the boulder he was hugging.

The white hump of its spine had emerged along with the translucent sail of its dorsal fin. It was definitely my bubble-headed goldfish, but how had it gotten so big?

Bijal sat down heavily. "It's like it ate Miracle-Gro or something."

"Or Mr. Pang put it in his machine," I said darkly.

Cassa, breathing hard, got to her knees and helped Dani scoot toward the boulders. "He must have put it in the tray."

Mav unzipped his backpack and poured water from it. "But what did he put in the kettle with it to make it grow?"

I thought back to the day we had caught Mr. Pang in his office. He had taken what looked like gumballs from his pocket. *Someone lost these delightful expandable water beads. . . . Soak them in water and they expand to the size of the moon!*

So he had used one on Lucky. And when the fish had started growing, Pang must have thrown him into the Bay. An island of anger begun to erupt in me, but I pushed it back down. This could be our exit strategy. "Lucky, can you take us home?"

My fish began wriggling with strong undulating motions, making us feel like we were on a giant waterbed.

"Hold on, everyone!" Clutching Coco tight, I plunked myself down and huddled with the others, our backs against the rubbery bubbles of Lucky's forehead.

My golden pet powered us away like a speedboat. "That's it, Lucky! You've got this!" I cried. With Mav and Dani on one side, and Cassa and Bijal on the other, I began to feel my limbs again.

"Don't trouble the bubble!" Bijal whooped, setting off the rest of us until we sounded like a bunch of coyotes back from the hunt. The victory lap home felt good, with Coco secure and my friends all around me. It beat wiping all twelve levels of *Zombie Infestation*, or even winning the Bay Area Cup Regionals . . . or at least how I imagined those things would feel.

"How'd your goldfish know where you were?" asked Dani.

"I think he's been following me. I've been hearing him call my name over the last few days. Maybe he wanted to let me know he was okay." I felt another surge of gratitude for the little guy . . . who was not so little anymore.

Mav brought his knees to his chest. "Maybe he was trying to get his revenge on Mr. Pang and that's why he was looking for you."

I sat up straighter. I'd never considered Lucky to be a

vengeful fish, mostly because goldfish aren't known for having much of a memory.

Bijal nervously patted the scales under him. "Nice, Lucky. We're friends, right?"

I sighed. "I just hope that canoe he swallowed doesn't give him indigestion."

"I don't think you'll have to worry about overfeeding him anymore." Cassa squeezed out her sweater. "I wonder if he ate the oar and the teeth, too."

"And the ukulele," Dani added.

"And those terrible boots," said Bijal. "He's the magic-eating garbage truck of the seas!"

The squawk of seagulls reached my ears. It was too dark to see if it was Ernie and Bert, but I wouldn't be surprised if Mirth's goons had been keeping tabs on us. "I wonder where Mr. Pang flew off to."

"Back to his lair, I bet," Mav said darkly. "I don't think we've seen the last of our feathered foe."

Cassa shivered. "What was he ranting about? He didn't look human anymore."

"Yeah, he looked like a human-size cuckoo bird." Bijal flapped his elbows. "Do you think his bro is really plotting to take over the world?"

"After tonight, I'd say anything's possible." I hugged the doll closer. "I just hope time hasn't run out for Coco."

"It's still a full moon," said Mav, checking his watch, which must have been waterproof. "Looks like you'll have another hour and forty minutes."

"And I've never been so happy to see it," said Bijal, gazing serenely overhead. "You saved it, Cassa." He patted the scales again. "And you, too, Lucky."

"It *is* beautiful," said Dani. "No wonder it inspired so many composers. Debussy's 'Clair de Lune' is one of my favorite pieces to play."

No one knew what to say to that.

It occurred to me that as much as I wanted to hate Mr. Pang for what he'd done to Coco, there were certain things about him that didn't make sense. Like, if he was a villain to the core, why had he mailed back all those "found" objects? He could've just dumped them in the ocean, like he did with Lucky. Then again, maybe he just wanted them to be re-cherished and recharged.

Mav pulled out his phone, which, naturally, was also water-proof. It was 9:22 p.m. "I'll see if Monroe can pick us up so we can get you and Coco home as soon as possible."

Mav reached his brother and gave him an update. The sky-line of San Francisco grew bright, the city lights a dazzling cluster of twinkling stars.

As we passed under the Bay Bridge, my mind zoomed back to Mr. Gu's van traveling toward Treasure Island.

Islands are the best place for hiding magical things, Mr. Pang had once said. *They're like English muffins with all those nooks and crannies.* So what was Mr. Gu hiding?

Lucky brought us right up to Pier 27, where we had tried to dump the broom and dustpan. With the ferry landing closed hours ago, no one saw the five of us—six, with Coco—step off the back of a whale-size bubble-head goldfish. I hugged one of his protrusions. "Thanks, Lucky. See you around."

"Winston!" he rumbled in that voice only I could hear.

In two splashes that caused waves to lap over the pier, Lucky disappeared. I hoped he'd find a good life in the ocean, maybe even a pod of bubble-headed buddies to keep him company.

Monroe pulled up in the LEAF and gingerly unfolded himself from his seat. A stack of beach towels and a pile of dry clothes were waiting on the backseat. "The story is, we went out for hot boba." Both of his arms were bandaged, but he lifted a bag from the front seat with a cheerful aardvark logo: Boba Guys.

Mav gave him a love punch on the arm. "You rock, bro!"

"You're the Mon!" I cried.

We all added our love punches, even Dani.

Monroe laughed. "Easy, guys. I might not have rabies, but I'm delicate." He started up the car and blasted the heater. A ukulele version of "On Top of Old Smokey" strummed through the speakers, and Dani and I shared knowing looks and grins. Monroe broke out in song, the spaghetti version, and we all joined in, replacing "Smokey" with "Lucky." Even Coco the doll looked more animated, like she was singing on the inside, eyes bright as beacons. I couldn't remember the last time I'd felt so happy and optimistic about the future. And we didn't even need the Warm Fuzzies for that.

CHAPTER 44

Monroe dropped off Cassa and Bijal first, because they lived closest. Then the brothers waited in the car while Dani and I snuck into her aunt's backyard. She had wrapped Monroe's towel tightly around her.

"What are you going to say to your aunt?" I asked.

"Um, Yasmine has a hot tub?" Dani said. "But Auntie has some explaining to do, too. I just don't understand why she enchanted your pie, or how. She uses her lucky beans to win contests, not hurt people. She's a good person. And I've never heard her mention a Mr. Gu."

I still couldn't believe Mr. Gu was Mr. Pang's brother, much less that he was trying take over the world. I'd considered the man solid. He'd given Mom a job after Dad died. He was running for mayor.

Was that the start of a plan for world domination?

"Forget about it. Maybe it was all a misunderstanding." I doubted it, but I'd put Dani through enough worry for one day.

We reached the oak tree. Her cocktail umbrella still clung to her head, keeping the storms at bay. I had a feeling we wouldn't need it for much longer.

"I think I'm going to like living here." She gave me a shy smile . . . and then a quick kiss on the cheek. "See you at school."

Even though my clothes were damp and my shoes were leaking, I felt warm as a breakfast burrito as I watched her shinny up the tree.

The seagulls were gone when we returned, but they'd sure left a mess of guano to clean up. Philippa gave me a one-armed hug when I got home; she even hugged Mav, both of us still wrapped in beach towels. But she left Monroe in the high and dry. Either Monroe hadn't earned a hug yet or Philippa had used up her quota for the year. I passed Philippa the doll, which was bundled in one of Mav's spare sweatshirts along with Putty.

"Could you . . . uh, put this in my closet with the . . . other things?" I said to her, since Mom was right there. Philippa took the bundle and scurried away upstairs.

Mom grabbed me next, wearing the look she gets when she's annoyed but can't express it in the presence of company. Even the Snoopy on her T-shirt seemed grumpy, hiding in the shadows of her cardigan sweater. Behind her on a portable dinner tray, several vanilla-scented bath candles were burning. "Winston, really. It's a school night. And why are your clothes all wet?"

Monroe tossed out one of his dashing smiles. "Sorry, Mrs.

Chu. It's my fault. I felt like getting some boba, and then we got caught in one of those freak downpours."

"But you're . . . dry." Mom stared at him wide-eyed, waiting for someone to clear up her confusion.

No one offered an explanation.

After a moment of awkward silence, she shrugged. "It's okay, Monroe. Thanks for taking them out." Mom gave his shoulder a pat that also pushed him out the door. "Good night, boys. Oh, don't be disappointed, Mav. You see him more than I do, and there's always tomorrow. Goodbye."

Mav forced a smile for her and mouthed *Call me* in my direction.

After Monroe and Mav left, Mom appraised me, from my salty hair to to my wet sneakers. The cloud weaver's hairpin, Pikachu, and Buddy's horn were hidden under my jacket.

"I will draw my own conclusions," she said.

"How was your first day of work?" I asked innocently, to get her mind off me.

"I'm beat. I already have a full caseload—that is, if they don't kick us out. Coco drew zigzags all over the walls of the daycare center. I'm hoping it was just first-day jitters."

"Yeah, I'm sure she just needs to get used to the place." I tried to sound casual while I planned my next move. I'd have to wait until Mom went to sleep to sneak Not-Coco out of their bedroom.

"I hope you're right." Mom kissed me on the forehead. "Go take a hot shower, and please let tomorrow be a normal day for a change."

Philippa was sitting on the floor of her room stroking the

doll's hair with her left hand. The closet door was open, and the broom and the dustpan were lying side by side on the floor. There was no sign of the two spirits. "Where'd they go?"

"Sleeping. They said to wake them whenever you returned."

The doll's eyes, still bright with moonlight, blinked open for a second, then shut again. It looked like Coco was having trouble staying awake. Philippa sniffed. "I can't imagine what she's seen."

"All her favorite places," I guessed, thinking of CuriOdyssey. "She's pretty tough."

Philippa raised her eyes to me, and her lips budged up, suggesting a smile. "Yeah. Must run in the family."

* ✳ · ✳ · ✳ *

To pass the time while we waited for Mom to fall alseep, I showered. Once I'd worked the chill from my bones and changed into pajamas, I returned to Philippa's room to find her still holding the doll. She set it on her bed, tucking Putty into the tiny china hand.

"I'll get Not-Coco," I said, eyeing Philippa's injured arm.

"No. You stay here and talk to the creepy things."

She headed downstairs, and I stepped into the closet. "Cloud Weaver? Cowherd?"

The pair rose from the broom and the dustpan, filling the small space with the scent of lilies and soil. Their ever-shifting forms spilled into Philippa's room like smoke.

I held out the gleaming silver-and-jade piece. Cloud Weaver picked it up carefully with both hands. "Thank you." She swept up her hair and tucked in the hairpin. Then she patted my cheek. "Mr. Pang chose your family because of your dad's powerful magic, magic he passed on to you. You tell the story of his love each time you try to do the right thing for your family. In that way, your father's story has been immortalized."

The cowherd added, "And the best stories are the ones told again and again."

For once the guy wasn't grumbling.

My smile faded as thoughts of magpies swooped in. "Mr. Pang said he was trying to save the world from his brother, Mirth—or Mr. Gu, as we know him. Why didn't you go invisible that night he came for dinner so my sister couldn't give you away?"

Cloud Weaver's eyes fluttered to the corner. "We both fell into a strange sleep when he arrived. The next thing we knew, we were in his carriage and he was yelling, 'My Swatch!' over and over. His Swatch, whatever that is, had broken in the—what did he call it?"

"Fender bender," said Cowherd.

"Fender bender. We escaped, and that's when Mother singed my husband's hat." The cloud weaver pressed a hand to her heart like it was still beating too fast from that scare.

My mind raced back. Mr. Gu had let Not-Coco wear his color-changing Swatch that night, and she had seemed so subdued. Maybe his watch worked like Dani's cocktail umbrella, except instead of canceling bad weather, it neutralized magical beings, like Chang-Ah-Ling and the cloud weaver and cowherd. But *Mr. Pang* was the one who had deceived us. He was the one who'd nearly cost me my sister. Which brother was good, and which was bad? Or was it more complicated than that?

Philippa returned with a sleeping Not-Coco, dressed in only a diaper, slung over her left shoulder. Not-Coco's skin was so white it almost glowed. I helped her set the changeling down on the carpet. Not-Coco's eyes rolled under her eyelids. She grunted a few times, then fell limp again. On the bed, the doll flinched in her sleep, as though Coco's spirit was prodding it from the inside.

"How do we switch them back?" Philippa knelt beside Not-Coco, holding our sister's hand, though she didn't take her eyes off the doll.

The cloud weaver glided to the bed. With a slender finger, she poked the doll in the belly button. "Coco."

The doll didn't move. But something stirred in the air around it, like heat waves on a hot highway. The right arm twitched. Her eyelids pulled back. Then a swirl of sparkly light poured from her eye sockets, and became a tiny body made of dust motes and air. Coco's spirit rubbed her eyes, her form as flickering and shimmery as Cloud Weaver's and Cowherd's. The goddess began to lead her toward Not-Coco, but the little spirit darted back to the doll and grabbed Putty.

Philippa's face had gone slack with shock. I could actually see the green flecks in her irises, which were usually hidden by a scowl. Cloud Weaver guided Coco to her own body. When she saw it, the little spirit grinned.

Now what? Would we have to perform some complicated ritual to reunite spirit with body? What if it didn't work and she . . . ?

But there was no need to worry. As if splashing in a puddle, Coco's spirit jumped right in through her own eye sockets, vanishing into her true form.

At the same moment, a trail of black smoke exited Coco's eyes and darted toward Chang-Ah-Ling, disappearing into the doll's now-blank eyes in two thin streams. The cowherd picked up the changeling, holding it away from him like a cat that might scratch.

Coco's complexion took on a healthy pink flush. Philippa's face crumpled, and she squeezed our sister to her. I wrapped my arms around the both of them. The pieces that had been missing since Dad had died were slowing fitting back into place.

Cowherd set Chang-Ah-Ling on the dustpan. "Well, it has been fun, Winston," she said in her chilly voice.

"If you say so." I couldn't wait to be rid of her, but I also couldn't help feeling a little sorry for the doll, forced to be Mr. Pang's pilot. Maybe with the canoe gone now, she could enjoy a cushy life on the shelf.

Cloud Weaver drew back her broom and, with one quick brush, swept Chang-Ah-Ling through the portal into Mr. Pang's. Then the cloud weaver and the cowherd set down their earthly tools and swirled around us. The goddess lowered her lovely face to mine, and something as cold as snow brushed my cheek. "Thank you, Winston. We will not forget what you did for us."

"I don't think I will, either," I said. "Good luck out there."

"You too, kid," grunted Cowherd.

Philippa unlatched her window and pushed it open. Cloud Weaver gave her husband a boost up to the sill and together the pair stepped out into the fog.

CHAPTER 45

The next Saturday, Mom, Coco, Philippa, and I took the elevator to the top of Coit Tower. Through one of the cutout windows, we watched the sun sink low, leaving a sky as colorful as a herd of unicorn piñatas streaking across it. Out there lay a world bigger and more complicated than I'd ever imagined.

Mom touched the smooth white walls. "Your dad is like this tower. Always watching over us." She put a warm hand on my back. "You once asked me which of you resembles your father the most. You remind me of him, because of your thoughtfulness."

Philippa's face tightened, but she tried to hide it as she zipped up Coco's jacket. Mom noticed, though. She stroked the back of Philippa's hair. "You remind me of him, too, because of your fierce loyalty. I don't know what I'd do without my big girl looking out for us."

Coco pulled her thumb from her mouth. "What 'bout me?"

Mom pinched Coco's wet digit. "Yes, Coco. You have Daddy's long thumbs."

Coco giggled and then stared with wonder at her hands.

From my backpack, I slid out a present for Mom. "Happy Dad-iversary."

"Wow, what is it?"

"A unicorn horn."

She took the twisty gold object and examined it carefully. Then she pulled me close.

"It's perfect," said Mom. "Your dad was a unicorn. Rare and wonderful. Happy Dad-iversary."

Philippa and Coco joined the hug. I didn't mind the staring tourists, as long as they didn't start clapping.

Dad, don't worry. Wherever you are, your story will live on.